# PRAISE FOR
# LYNN AUSTIN

"Lynn Austin, one of my favorite authors, skillfully weaves together the stories and secrets of three generations of women in this Gilded Age novel filled with forgiveness, love, and the enduring value of legacy."

**JULIE KLASSEN**, bestselling author of *The Sisters of Sea View*

"*All My Secrets* is an enchanting story about the power and complexities of family. In this historical saga, Lynn Austin masterfully weaves together romance, turmoil, beautiful prose, and some lovely surprises. I enjoyed stepping into New York's gilded society with her and slowly peeling back the golden veneer."

**MELANIE DOBSON**, award-winning author of *The Wings of Poppy Pendleton*

"A transformative novel about the complexities of family, the intrigue of long-held secrets, the great love it takes to confess and to offer and receive forgiveness. Lynn Austin has woven *All My Secrets* with mystery, hope, and the overwhelming wonder of God's grace in creating a path to liberty when all doors seem closed. A compassionate story, beautifully told."

**CATHY GOHLKE**, Christy Hall of Fame author of *Ladies of the Lake*

"A glittering tale of choices, consequences, and new beginnings. Every chapter drew me in further to a world of extravagant wealth and unspeakable poverty, and into a society that brims with both waste and purpose. The dichotomies of Gilded Age New York City are laid bare by three generations of women, each shaped by their culture and seeking to shape their culture in turn. *All My Secrets* is a sumptuous novel, rich in character and spiritual depth. I heartily enjoyed every page."

**JOCELYN GREEN**, Christy Award–winning author of *The Metropolitan Affair*

"This is vintage Lynn Austin. The true master of inspirational fiction returns to a narrative device she owns: the multi-generational saga. Deftly intertwining legacies of faith, doubt, and love, Austin advocates for women's voices within their numerous unique callings in a way far more powerful than any other living writer I know. Austin is one of our great character-driven storytellers."

**RACHEL McMILLAN**, author of *Operation Scarlet*

"A masterful, heartwarming, and heartbreaking historical novel, *Long Way Home* contains reminders of human beings' ability to do great evil—and their duty to do great good."

**FOREWORD REVIEWS**

"[A] lovely stand-alone Christmas tale. . . . While fans of *If I Were You* will be eager to read the next chapter of Audrey's and Eve's lives, this charming book will also be a delight for inspirational readers looking for a feel-good Christmas story."

**PUBLISHERS WEEKLY**, starred review of *The Wish Book Christmas*

"Austin's latest novel has endearing characters with flaws that allow growth. . . . There's no putting down this nostalgic, appealing read."

**LIBRARY JOURNAL** on *The Wish Book Christmas*

"Austin shines in this excellent tale of three women who struggle to survive WWII in the Netherlands. . . . As the three women work to evade and break the Nazi grip on the Netherlands, Austin skillfully portrays the dangers they face as they struggle to survive. This is a must-read for fans of WWII inspirationals."

**PUBLISHERS WEEKLY** on *Chasing Shadows*

"Austin has written a powerful tale of domestic heroism and faith, with all three women questioning and then turning to God for strength."

**BOOKLIST** on *Chasing Shadows*

"As always, Austin has penned a moving, intricate, and lovely work of Christian fiction that is excellently researched with an underlying message of hope. Highly recommended."

**HISTORICAL NOVEL SOCIETY** on *Chasing Shadows*

"If you enjoy historical novels set during World War II, you will not want to miss the very moving portrayal of this time period, *Chasing Shadows* by Lynn Austin. This novel gives a vivid look into the lives of those who endured German occupation of the Netherlands. . . . It shows the importance of faith during difficult times. It also emphasizes the importance of doing the right things, even when those things are not easy to do."

**FRESH FICTION**

"Austin transports readers into the lives of her characters, plunking them in the middle of a brutal war and giving them a unique take on the traditional World War II tale. Readers won't be able to turn the pages fast enough to find out how Eve and Audrey met and what could have gone so terribly wrong."

**LIBRARY JOURNAL**, starred review of *If I Were You*

"[A] tantalizing domestic drama. . . . Its message familiar and its world nostalgic and fragile, *If I Were You* looks for answers in changing identities and finds that it's priceless to remain true to oneself."

**FOREWORD REVIEWS**

"Lynn is a masterful storyteller. The characters become people you feel like you know and you truly care about. The plot has unexpected turns and keeps you riveted."

**ECLA LIBRARIES** on *If I Were You*

"Lynn Austin is a master at exploring the depths of human relationships. Set against the backdrop of war and its aftermath, *If I Were You* is a beautifully woven page-turner."

**SUSAN MEISSNER**, bestselling author of *Secrets of a Charmed Life* and *The Last Year of the War*

"I have long enjoyed Lynn Austin's novels, but *If I Were You* resonates above all others. Austin weaves the plot and characters together with sheer perfection, and the ending—oh, pure delight to a reader's heart!"

**TAMERA ALEXANDER**, bestselling author of *With This Pledge* and *A Note Yet Unsung*

"*If I Were You* is a page-turning, nail-biting, heart-stopping gem of a story. Once again, Lynn Austin has done her homework. Each detail rings true, pulling us into Audrey's and Eve's differing worlds of privilege and poverty, while we watch their friendship and their faith in God struggle to survive. I loved traveling along on their journey, with all its unexpected twists and turns, and sighed with satisfaction when I reached the final page. *So* good."

**LIZ CURTIS HIGGS**, *New York Times* bestselling author of *Mine Is the Night*

"Lynn Austin has long been one of my favorite authors. With an intriguing premise and excellent writing, *If I Were You* is sure to garner accolades and appeal to fans of novels like *The Alice Network* and *The Nightingale*."

**JULIE KLASSEN**, author of *The Bridge to Belle Island*

"With her signature attention to detail and unvarnished portrayal of the human heart, Lynn Austin weaves a tale of redemption that bears witness to Christ's power to make all things new."

**SHARON GARLOUGH BROWN**, author of the Sensible Shoes series and *Shades of Light*, on *If I Were You*

*All My Secrets*

# ALSO BY
# LYNN AUSTIN

# ALL MY
# SECRETS

## LYNN
## AUSTIN

Tyndale House Publishers
Carol Stream, Illinois

Visit Tyndale online at tyndale.com.

Visit Lynn Austin's website at lynnaustin.org.

*Tyndale* and Tyndale's quill logo are registered trademarks of Tyndale House Ministries.

*All My Secrets*

Cover designed by Sarah Susan Richardson

Edited by Kathryn S. Olson

Published in association with the literary agency of Natasha Kern Literary Agency, Inc., P.O. Box 1069, White Salmon, WA 98672.

All Scripture quotations are taken from the *Holy Bible*, King James Version.

*All My Secrets* is a work of fiction. Where real people, events, establishments, organizations, or locales appear, they are used fictitiously. All other elements of the novel are drawn from the author's imagination.

For information about special discounts for bulk purchases, please contact Tyndale House Publishers at csresponse@tyndale.com, or call 1-855-277-9400.

**Library of Congress Cataloging-in-Publication Data**

A catalog record for this book is available from the Library of Congress.

ISBN 978-1-4964-3744-0 (HC)

ISBN 978-1-4964-3745-7 (SC)

Printed in the United States of America

| 30 | 29 | 28 | 27 | 26 | 25 | 24 |
|----|----|----|----|----|----|----|
| 7  | 6  | 5  | 4  | 3  | 2  | 1  |

*For Peggy Hach*
*my sister and friend*

# 1

~⁂~

~⁂ *Adelaide* ⁂~

Adelaide Stanhope sat at her father's graveside, as still and upright as the surrounding tombstones. The enormous Stanhope obelisk loomed over the family cemetery plot where her great-grandfather, grandfather, and now her father had been laid to rest. Grandmother Junietta Stanhope's hand, gloved in black lace, lay limp and fragile in her own as the service droned on. Adelaide grasped so few of the clergyman's words that they might well have been in another language—*eternity . . . dust . . . life . . . rest.*

Father was dead.

He was dead, and everything in Adelaide's tightly scripted, well-mannered world had been upended, tossed about, and left to flounder like a luxurious steamship, helpless in the grip of a storm.

The scent of roses and lilies, piled on her father's coffin and heaped all around it, drifted to her on the breeze. The heady fragrance seemed misplaced. It usually accompanied one of Mother's grand dinner parties

1

or balls, filling their New York City mansion or summer home in Newport with their perfume. Adelaide closed her eyes, picturing Father in his tuxedo and starched white shirtfront, Mother reigning beside him in a dazzling gown and ropes of pearls as they greeted guests in their vast flower-filled foyer. It was a picture she had always taken for granted, imagining that nothing in her life would ever change. What would life be like now, without Father?

She opened her eyes again and glanced at her grandmother's face, clouded by a veil of black netting. She sat stoically unbowed as if carved from wax, like the figures Adelaide had seen in Madame Tussaud's museum in London last year. For a parent to lose a child at any age was a tragedy, but Father was Grandmother Junietta's only child, her only son. For as far back as Adelaide could remember, her grandmother had seemed tireless, ageless, committed to the charitable foundation she presided over— a man's job, really, but Grandmother seldom played by society's rules. Adelaide had been close to her as a child, before growing into a young woman and taking her place in the privileged society life she now enjoyed.

Adelaide's own eyes were dry as well, not only because a proper lady never mourned in public, but because her father, Arthur Benton Stanhope III, was a distant figure to her, a towering statue on a pedestal, a giant in New York's business world who had spent most of Adelaide's life in offices and business meetings before his unexpected death. As his third and final child, she knew she had been a disappointment to him from the day of her birth. A third daughter. Not the son he had hoped for. Now he was gone, suddenly and unexpectedly, having died alone in their New York mansion while she and Mother summered at their home in Newport, Rhode Island. Adelaide still felt numb from the shock of his death and the hurried train journey home. Nothing seemed real except the feathery weight of her grandmother's hand in hers and the blistering sun above their heads. The scant shade of the funeral canopy offered little relief from it.

The minister closed his book with an "amen." A sigh escaped before Adelaide could capture it, and she glanced around discreetly, hoping no one had heard. They hadn't. She'd grown accustomed to being ignored while her two older sisters had lived at home, but with Ernestine and Cordelia successfully married, nineteen-year-old Adelaide would be the focus of Mother's attention and matchmaking ambitions next. Adelaide had dreamed of a Cinderella wedding, but now Father wouldn't be there to escort her down the aisle.

She stood when her mother and sister did. Cordelia and her husband had arrived from their home in Boston last evening. There hadn't been enough time for Ernestine, married to a British earl, to travel from her home in London. Adelaide helped her grandmother to her feet with the others. "Are you all right, Mimi Junie?" she whispered, using the affectionate name from her girlhood.

"Yes, child." Grandmother gripped Adelaide's arm with one hand and her intricately carved cane in the other. The cane seemed part of her, an extra limb, and she was seldom without it. She rarely used it as a walking stick though, brandishing it like a weapon to make a point or flourishing it like a maestro waving a baton. But today she leaned upon it as she and Adelaide shuffled forward to drop more roses onto the smothered coffin. Before moving on, Grandmother paused to stare at a floral arrangement with a ribboned banner that read *Beloved Son*. "My son . . ." she murmured. "My son." It would have been a blessing if she hadn't comprehended her loss, but Grandmother's mind was still sharp.

"Yes, Mimi Junie," Adelaide replied. "You've lost your son and I've lost my father. I'm so very sorry. Come, our carriage is waiting."

Grandmother didn't move. She looked up from the flowers and scanned the crowd of black-cloaked mourners as if searching for someone. "I wish my other son could be here," she murmured.

Adelaide's skin prickled. "Who do you mean, Mimi?"

"My other son . . ." Her hand fluttered as if trying to stir a pot of dusty memories and draw out a name. "You know . . ."

Adelaide swallowed. "You don't have another son, Mimi. Only my father. He was your only child." Grandmother stared at Adelaide for a long moment, then shook her head.

"No, he wasn't." She shielded her eyes from the sun and gazed into the distance for another long moment as if searching for him before finally allowing Adelaide to lead her to the waiting carriage. Grandmother was obviously confused. She didn't really have a secret son—did she?

Adelaide shook her head, quickly discarding the outrageous idea, not only because it was an affront to Grandmother's character, but because such a scandal never would have remained hidden in their tightly knit social world. Fear of family disgrace kept Adelaide, her sisters, and all their peers virtuous.

The carriage swayed as Mimi's driver, Henry, closed the door and climbed onto his seat. They rode in dignified silence. Yet Mimi Junie's puzzling words left Adelaide shaken. Had she lost a son through miscarriage or stillbirth or an early death? Wouldn't there be a marker in the family cemetery plot if she had? And she surely would have mentioned such a tragedy before today, wouldn't she? The questions nibbled into Adelaide's thoughts as she stood with Grandmother, Mother, and Cordelia in their mansion's enormous dining room for the funeral luncheon, accepting condolences from streams of people. After a long, wearying hour, Grandmother turned to her.

"I've had enough, Adelaide. Would you kindly help me to my room?" Dark clouds were erasing the brilliant summer sky, and thunder rumbled in the distance as Adelaide helped Mimi Junie to her bedroom suite and to her chair by the window.

But before leaving, Adelaide crouched in front of her. She needed to know. "Mimi Junie, at the funeral you mentioned another son."

"Did I?" She stared into her lap, idly pulling off her lace gloves.

"Yes. And it was the first time I've ever heard of him. Can you tell me more about him?"

Grandmother dropped the gloves and gathered Adelaide's hands in hers, holding them with surprising strength. She met Adelaide's gaze, her faded eyes bright and brimming with love. "You're named after me, Adelaide Junietta Stanhope."

"Yes, I—"

"What plans are they making for you?"

"What do you mean?"

"Have they chosen a husband for you? Decided your future?"

The change in topics confused her, but she answered dutifully. "Mother thought there were several promising gentlemen in Newport, but with Father gone so suddenly, we'll have to observe a period of mourning before—"

"It's your life, not your mother's. Do you have the courage it takes to break free from the mold that society will try to cast for you? You don't have to do things their way, you know."

"I-I don't understand."

"Your father's death means that everything is going to change for you and your mother. And for me too, undoubtedly. As we start all over again, we'll have a chance to make a new life for ourselves and decide how we want to live from now on. Change can be difficult, but it can also be very good for us."

Adelaide's heart picked up speed. "I don't want anything to change. I want to live the way I always have."

"Nevertheless, change is coming, you can be sure of that. But that means you're free to make new choices. To love a man of your own choosing and discover the joy of being loved in return. But it will require courage."

Adelaide couldn't reply. Might Mimi's questions have something to do with her mysterious lost son after all? But no, her beloved Mimi Junie, the upright, formidable grande dame of New York society, would never live a secret, scandalous life, much less urge her granddaughter to live one.

Would she?

There was a soft knock on the door, and a maid entered with a tea tray. The silver teapot was small, and the tray held only one cup and saucer. "Your mother would like you to return to your guests downstairs, Miss Adelaide," the maid said. There would be no more questions or revelations today.

Grandmother squeezed Adelaide's hands tightly before releasing them. "Give me a kiss before you go, Addy dear," she said.

Adelaide did as she was told. She always did as she was told.

## ⟿ *Junietta* ⟿

She would have liked for Adelaide to stay a bit longer. The girl had always been Junietta's favorite among her three granddaughters. That is, if grandmothers were allowed to admit such a thing. She had spent more time with Addy as a child than with Cordelia and Ernestine, who often ran off and left their little sister behind. She'd been a shy girl, sensitive and serious, who'd loved to listen to Junietta tell stories. Bible stories had been her favorites. There was one particular Bible story that had been on Junietta's mind all day—the one where Jesus happened upon a funeral in which a widow was burying her only son. The Lord had taken pity on the grieving woman and raised her son back to life. What Junietta wouldn't give to have her son alive again.

It wasn't supposed to happen this way. Children were supposed to bury their parents, not the other way around. Junietta stared at the silver tray and teapot, her arms too heavy with sorrow to lift the pot and pour tea into the fragile cup. Grief, weighty and suffocating, immobilized her body while her mind refused to stop shuffling through a lifetime of memories and regrets and what-ifs.

Her son was dead. Where had the time gone? His life had passed so swiftly, the days piling up into months and multiplying into years. She could picture A.B. at age nine or ten, curly-haired and bright-eyed and endlessly curious. He'd loved to take things apart to see how they worked, then he would beg her to help him reassemble them again. A music box. The cook's coffee mill. A pair of binoculars. And one time, his grandfather's magic lantern. But when A.B. turned sixteen, she had lost him to his father's and grandfather's influence. Now she'd lost him forever.

Junietta finally lifted the teapot, but her hand shook as she tried to pour, splashing tea everywhere but in the cup. This wasn't the first time in her life she'd experienced this debilitating shock and loss. Back then, she had found the strength, somehow, to go on with her life until time finally sanded off grief's painful edges. She would have to move forward this time, too. Her charitable foundation was much too important to leave to chance. In fact, it was the last thing she had spoken to A.B. about before he died.

He'd surprised her by returning home to New York early from their summer home in Newport. "There's something important at work that I need to attend to," he'd told Junietta. She'd taken the opportunity of their time alone together at breakfast one morning to tell him about the symptoms she'd been experiencing: the racing heart, the fatigue so deep that hours of sleep couldn't erase it, ankles that swelled grotesquely and made wearing shoes impossible, her shortness of breath, her lightheadedness.

He'd been instantly alarmed. "I'll send for the doctor!"

"I've already seen the doctor, dear. Several, in fact. They all say the same thing. There's no cure for an aging heart that's wearing itself out."

"Then you must rest. Get out of this stifling city and spend some time by the sea. Why not come to Newport with me when I go back, and let the fresh salt air revive you?"

"Newport is the last place I would go to get rest! I get dizzy just thinking about the endless rounds of social events that spin like a carousel that's out of control. And the bland drivel that masquerades as conversation would bore me to death long before my heart was ready to give out. No, I want nothing to do with Newport."

She saw his love and concern in his worried expression. "Listen, Mother—"

"No, Son, please listen to me. I didn't tell you about my heart so you would fuss over me and try to mollycoddle me. It's the charitable foundation that I'm worried about." She had founded it nearly fifty years ago and had run it ever since, raising and distributing millions of dollars to help the poor. She'd dedicated her life to her work. But she knew she couldn't run it on her own anymore. "You know how much it means to me, A.B., but I need to step back from it now. Will you help me find someone I can train as my replacement? Someone who'll care about it as much as I do?"

"Isn't there someone on your current staff who could take over?"

"I've given it a lot of thought, and while they're all good at what they do, there's no one who seems just right for the position."

"I see. Yes, of course I'll help. I promise I'll find someone. But in the meantime, you must promise me that you'll follow the doctors' orders and do exactly what they say. That means following directions for once in your life." He'd smiled when he'd said it and kissed her goodbye. Junietta hadn't promised him any such thing, of course.

It was the last time she'd seen her son alive. A day later, he had returned home from work in the early afternoon, complaining of a fierce headache. By the next morning he was dead. She had never imagined that he would be leaving this world before she did.

She thought again of Adelaide. With A.B. gone, Addy was all that Junietta had left. She had never been close to her daughter-in-law, Sylvia, whose interests rarely coincided with her own. And Junietta had been unable to have any influence on her older granddaughters, Cordelia and Ernestine, who'd been married off to a Boston Brahmin and an English nobleman. God alone knew what their marriages were like, how inane and purposeless their lives had become. But she still might have a chance to rescue Adelaide. If she could find the strength. If her aging body granted her enough time. She had to convince her beloved granddaughter not to settle for a life of mindless conformity, squandering the few swift years God might give to her.

Junietta took off her shoes and propped her feet on the hassock as the doctors had instructed. Then she reached for her Bible and opened it to her favorite psalm, though she knew the words by heart. They would be her prayer, for Adelaide and for the foundation. *"Teach us to number our days, that we may apply our hearts unto wisdom . . . establish thou the work of our hands upon us; yea, the work of our hands, establish thou it."*

## Sylvia

The relief Sylvia felt when the last guest departed was enormous. The servants would attend to the remains of the funeral luncheon, and Sylvia could finally be alone. As she left the cavernous dining room to go upstairs, her daughters Cordelia and Adelaide clung to her, offering to go up with her, to stay with her. "That isn't necessary," she assured them. "I'm fine." It occurred to her as she gently freed herself from them that they might need comfort and consolation from her, rather than her needing theirs, but she had neither to give. She couldn't keep up the calm pretense of courage any longer, nor could she allow her daughters to see her break down. She assured them she would be fine and closed her door.

Sylvia's bedroom felt warmer than the downstairs rooms, dim and womb-like with the shades drawn against the summer sun. Her lady's maid helped her change out of her funeral clothes, then asked if she needed anything else. "Nothing, thank you. I'll ring if I do." She stood in the center of her room after the girl left and looked around. Everything was in its place, every surface dusted and polished, the bed linens and rugs immaculate and unwrinkled. It looked exactly as it always did, as if nothing in her life had changed, and she had the dizzying urge to tear off the bedspread, throw the pillows onto the floor, dump out the dresser drawers, and knock all the pictures askew so the pristine room would match the uproar in her heart. Her shock was wearing off now that the necessary steps for the funeral were completed. She was starting to comprehend the enormity of her loss.

*A.B. can't be gone. He can't be!* She'd silently repeated the refrain on the endless train journey from Newport. But he was gone. Sylvia was alone. She would be from now on.

She went to the door leading to A.B.'s adjoining bedroom suite and peered inside. It still held his familiar scent. The clothes he'd always worn still hung in his wardrobe. The things he'd carried in his pockets lay on his dresser top, along with his gold watch and chain. But Sylvia couldn't bear to go inside his room. It was too soon. She closed the door again and sank down at her dressing table.

She hadn't had a chance to say goodbye to him. When he'd decided to return to New York, Sylvia had stayed in Newport, reveling in the parties, the sailing excursions, and the golden glow of summer by the sea. She'd been a little annoyed with him when he'd said he was leaving, because it meant she'd be without an escort at the Vanderbilts' summer ball. Now she would be without him forever. It was one thing to hold her head high and remain brave through the memorial service, the funeral, and the luncheon afterward. Sylvia wasn't sure she could continue the act for the rest of her life. She looked at her reflection in the dressing table's mirror. How was it possible that she was a widow at age forty-six?

"I should have come back to New York with him," she whispered aloud. She'd repeated those words countless times in the past few days. *"There was nothing you could have done,"* the doctor had said when she'd repeated them to him. His reassurances hadn't consoled her. She should have been at her husband's side when he'd died.

Sylvia stood and began to pace from the dressing table to the window and back again. She had no one to turn to in her time of sorrow. Her society friends were rivals more than confidantes, and Sylvia couldn't trust that her spilled secrets wouldn't leak into gossip. She'd always been distant from her bustling, self-assured mother-in-law, even though they'd lived beneath the same enormous roof all these years. Ernestine and Cordelia had married and moved away, leaving only Adelaide, a girl whose shy temperament was so different from Sylvia's. She would need to remain strong for Adelaide's sake.

She paused in her pacing and picked up the ivory fan she had used at the funeral. Sylvia had feared that the funeral would never end. It had unleashed an avalanche of memories reminding her of all the funerals she had endured, all the loved ones she had lost. She hadn't been prepared to bury her husband so soon—but then she hadn't been prepared to bury any of the others either.

What came next?

Sylvia didn't know. The family lawyer had assured her he would return to help her settle the estate. Maybe he would know what came next, aside from a year of mourning. A year of living in the shadows as she recovered from her grief while life went on around her. She felt angry with A.B. for suddenly leaving her. She'd lived comfortably under his protection, never giving a thought about money, enjoying status and power in New York society because of him. But all that was now threatened. The thought terrified her.

The dreadful changes she'd experienced as a child and again as a young woman had been out of her control. This time, she would make sure that she remained in control and that nothing would change. She'd built a good life with her husband, a life she loved. For Adelaide's sake, for her own sake, and as a memorial to A.B., she would make sure everything continued as before.

She crossed to her bed and lifted the photograph of A.B. that she kept on her nightstand. It shamed her to recall that she hadn't loved him when they'd married. For all these years, she'd kept the real reason why she had married him a secret. Yet over the years, her respect for him had slowly transformed into affection, then love. Had she told him lately that she loved him? Had she said those words when they were in Newport? Before he returned to New York? It pained Sylvia that she couldn't remember. How had she allowed days or weeks or even months to pass without saying those precious words?

Sylvia had struggled all day not to give in to the pain and loss she felt, not to let her daughters or the servants or anyone else see her weeping. Jealous rivals had nicknamed her the Ice Queen because of her pale beauty and fair hair, her cool, aloof demeanor. She had perfected that icy role because experience had taught her that it was better to stay distant and cold than to be vulnerable and risk pain. But grief now raged like a fire inside her, thawing the ice. Tonight, Sylvia Grace Stanhope's heart was breaking. She covered her face as a tide of painful memories welled up. She allowed them, at last, to overflow in tears.

# 2

⤞⤝

⤞ *Junietta* ⤝

Junietta stared at the wrinkled, gray-haired stranger in the mirror, barely recognizing her. In her mind, she didn't resemble that elderly woman but was the same woman she'd been at fifty, even forty years old, able to accomplish anything she put her mind to. It was her traitorous body that was the problem. She heard a soft knock on her bedroom door, and one of the servants entered. "Madame Stanhope, your family's lawyers have arrived. They're waiting in Mr. Stanhope's study."

"Thank you, Hattie. You're a dear."

She made her way carefully down the endless marble stairs so she wouldn't arrive out of breath. Her ankles were not too swollen today. And her heart was behaving itself, keeping a slow rhythmic pace, which was surprising, considering the heartbreaking wound it had suffered. She could hear the somber mumble of men's voices from outside the study and entered to greet the two lawyers. Mr. Wilson, the older one, wore outdated muttonchop whiskers and tiny spectacles. He was seated behind the desk, shuffling through a stack of papers, but he rose and bowed slightly to greet her.

"Good afternoon, Madame Stanhope. Please accept my condolences, once again, on your terrible loss." He gestured to the other lawyer, a much younger man with wide shoulders and thick ebony hair, who was busily arranging chairs in front of the desk for Junietta, Sylvia, and Adelaide. "This is my colleague, Howard Forsythe."

Junietta knew precisely who he was but pretended not to. "How do you do, Mr. Forsythe?"

"I'm honored to meet you, Madame Stanhope." She detected a smile in his blue eyes as he greeted her, and his friendliness pleased her. Lawyers were usually dour, and the reading of A.B.'s will certainly called for solemnity, but it pleased her that young Howard Forsythe didn't take himself too seriously.

Adelaide arrived next, and Junietta's heart swelled with love for her youngest granddaughter. The poor dear looked so detached, so austere, and she wondered what had happened to the gentle girl who would come into her bedroom suite asking a thousand questions. Junietta had neglected her these past few years, becoming so busy with her own work that she'd allowed Adelaide to slip away. Junietta had to remedy that. She wouldn't let her become like all the other Stanhopes.

"Put my chair closer to that window," she directed, brandishing her cane. Young Mr. Forsythe hurried to obey. "And kindly open those curtains and raise the sash to let in some air and sunlight. I told my late husband countless times that this room was too dark and gloomy, but he never cared much for my opinion. Well, it's clear that I was right and he was dead wrong, don't you agree, young man?" She smiled at Mr. Forsythe, who had managed to pull back the maroon velvet curtains, emitting a beam of dusty sunshine. He smiled in return before seeming to catch himself.

"It would seem so, Madame Stanhope," he replied in a properly somber tone. He turned back to the window, straining to open it, tugging almost comically until it finally inched open with a ragged scrape. Warm air drifted into the stuffy room, smelling faintly of fallen leaves. Mr. Forsythe smoothed his waistcoat back into place and wiped his brow.

"Thank you, dear boy." She patted his arm, then took her seat. "Of course, if you have dark, nefarious business to conduct, then I suppose you need a grim-looking lair in which to conduct it."

Mr. Wilson looked up sharply from his papers, shocked perhaps by the word *nefarious*. Shocking people with her bluntness was nothing new for Junietta. She'd spent her lifetime doing it. But judging by Mr. Forsythe's barely suppressed smile, he found her humorous.

"My son didn't do anything to change this dreary room when he took over his father's skullduggery," she continued, "but perhaps the room's next inhabitant will. Adelaide, dear," she said, poking Addy's arm with the tip of her cane, "put your suitors to the test when you choose one for your husband. Bring them in here and ask what their plans are for this hideout or whatever one chooses to call it. Then marry the man who throws open the windows and lets in air and sunlight. Better yet, marry the man who floods your life with air and sunlight. Promise me that much, won't you dear?" She gave her arm a second poke.

Addy rubbed the spot, her cheeks flushing pink, but before she could reply, Sylvia glided into the room with a rustle of black taffeta. Even in mourning, Sylvia Grace Stanhope was a beautiful woman, moving with the bearing and dignity of a queen wearing an invisible crown on her fair, fashionably upswept hair. Mr. Forsythe stopped admiring the intricately carved wooden ceiling and snapped to attention. Mr. Wilson quickly rose and hurried from behind the desk to guide her to her chair. "Good afternoon, Mrs. Stanhope. May I say, once again, how sorry I am for your loss. Your husband was a fine man and will be missed by all."

Sylvia returned his greeting with a slight nod. She had always kept herself at a distance, and Junietta barely knew her daughter-in-law. What would become of Sylvia now, without her husband? Junietta believed that Sylvia and Adelaide could both fly freely on their own if they could find the courage to escape from their gilded cages. All the more reason for Junietta not to give in to her illness or to her own grief.

"Shall we begin?" the older lawyer asked after Sylvia was seated. Again, she replied with a slight nod. "Mr. Stanhope's last will and testament is quite long and detailed," he said, gesturing to the inch-high ream of paper in front of him. "The relevant parties have already heard a formal reading of the business matters pertaining to Mr. Stanhope's will. According to his wishes, however, the private family details and bequests were absent from that reading. I would be happy to read the will in its entirety if you'd like, or I can simply explain the paragraphs which apply to the three of you." He looked up at them, his bristly eyebrows raised in question.

"We'll settle for the abridged version," Junietta replied. "None of us needs to hear all that fluff and blather."

"Very well." He pushed the pile to one side and cleared his throat as he lifted a single sheet from the top. "The original founder of all the Stanhope enterprises and investments, Arthur Benton Stanhope I, crafted his will in such a way that control of the company's holdings and the bulk of the family wealth could be inherited only by his male heirs."

Junietta thumped her cane on the parquet floor. "He was a bully! My father-in-law was a mean, greedy man who took great delight in ruining people's lives!"

"I . . . um . . . I wouldn't know about that," Mr. Wilson said. "It was before my time. Anyway, the founder's estate passed to his oldest son, Arthur Benton Stanhope II, when he died. That would be your husband," he said, gesturing to Junietta.

"Yes, and dear Artie did whatever his father told him to do, legal or otherwise."

Mr. Wilson's eyes widened slightly behind his tiny spectacles. He cleared his throat. "And when he passed, the founder's grandson, Arthur Benton Stanhope III, inherited the estate."

"Everyone called my son A.B.," she said. "It's less confusing."

"His current will must conform to the founder's original constraints, however. And since Arthur III did not have a brother or a male heir, control of all the Stanhope businesses, all of its many assets, and the accumulated family wealth and investments will now be inherited in their entirety by the founder's last remaining son, Roger Charles Stanhope."

"Roger! That weaselly old man? He's the least deserving of all the Stanhopes! Why, he'll gamble away the family fortune before Christmas!"

"Well . . . um . . . again, I wouldn't know about that." Mr. Wilson cleared his throat a second time as he looked down at the page.

"Are we to be at the mercy of fools? Can't something be done about this?"

"I'm afraid not. The deceased's inheritance will now be passed to his uncle, Roger Charles Stanhope, and eventually to his son, Randall David Stanhope."

"No," Junietta murmured. Her hands had begun to tremble. The mention of the name David had reminded her of how this unjust inheritance scheme had come to be written—and of the terrible part she had played in it. At the time, the guilt she'd felt had led her to start the Stanhope Charitable Foundation. Her heart began a clumsy, jiggety dance as she struggled to catch her breath. The thought of all her hard work now falling into Roger Stanhope's hands made her sick with dread. "Is . . . is any mention made in the will of our family's charitable foundation?"

"Not specifically in this will. But since the foundation is in the Stanhope name, it would be logical for Roger Stanhope to administrate it."

"Over my dead body!" Junietta whacked her cane against the side of the desk as if beating a drum, causing a hollow boom that made Mr. Wilson jump. "That foundation is the only good thing that was ever done in the Stanhope name. My late husband helped to endow it, then gave the operation of it to me. My son was a great supporter of all my charitable efforts and served on the board of directors. Do whatever you need to do, Mr. Wilson, but make sure the Stanhope Foundation remains independent and does *not* fall into Roger's hands!"

"We will look into it."

"Thank you. And let me know as soon as possible what I can do to ensure that it doesn't." She gave the side of the desk another boom with her cane for emphasis and sat back in her chair again, praying that her physical distress and weakness didn't show. Junietta cared little about losing the family wealth, but her foundation was everything to her, and she would fight for it.

Mr. Wilson straightened his glasses and his papers. "To continue, the bulk of the Stanhope wealth is tied up with the company and, I'm sorry to say, cannot be inherited by the three of you." He seemed to be bracing for another blow from Junietta's cane, but she refrained as his words slowly sank in. The enormous Stanhope fortune was no longer theirs. "However, Mr. Stanhope's will does provide his wife, Sylvia Grace Stanhope, and unmarried daughter, Adelaide Junietta Stanhope, with trust funds, much like the trust that his father provided for you," he said, addressing Junietta. "These trust funds could have benefitted from a few more years' time so the investments had a chance to grow and mature, but Mr. Stanhope couldn't have foreseen his untimely demise at the age of forty-six. With careful management, however, the dividends should provide a modest income on which to live in the coming years."

*A modest income?* Sylvia's financial situation was even worse than Junietta could have imagined. She couldn't refrain this time and banged the desk again. "Mr. Wilson! The future you're portraying is even darker than this room! Can't you and all those other clever lawyers find a way to stave off our imminent destitution?"

"Er . . . I'm afraid not." He drew another breath and hurried to finish. "As for Mr. Stanhope's property—as you're probably aware, the deceased's grandfather is the original owner of the summer home in Newport, Rhode Island, and so I'm sorry to say that the deed to that mansion will also pass to Roger C. Stanhope."

"What about this home?" Sylvia interrupted.

"Roger can't put us out of this home, dear," Junietta told her. "It belonged to my husband and was deeded to our son when Art died. This house has nothing to do with Roger."

"Yes, you're quite right, Madame Stanhope. I was getting to that. Your son deeded ownership of this mansion, all his personal property, and his yacht, the *Merriweather*, to his wife, Sylvia Grace Stanhope."

"Then why do I sense more bad news coming?" Junietta demanded.

"I'm simply explaining the main points of the will at the moment. I'll be happy to discuss the finer details at a later date, after you've had time to assess the future and—"

"Don't patronize us, Mr. Wilson! We want the cold hard truth, and we want it now. Should we be taking in washing to make ends meet? Delivering newspapers? Turning the west wing into a boardinghouse?"

"No, no, no. Of course not. But you may not realize yet what enormous costs are involved with keeping the *Merriweather* afloat, for instance. Or in maintaining a home of this size. Since there are only three of you living here—and Miss Stanhope will likely be wed within the next few years—you may want to consider a smaller home in order to reduce the number of servants and control expenses, in which case, we will be happy to help you make arrangements to sell—"

*Boom* went her cane on the side of the desk. "Is the income enough to live on or not, Mr. Wilson?"

"I'm afraid that some judicious pruning and careful management may be necessary—"

"And no more lavish parties?" she asked. The lawyer didn't reply.

Junietta glanced at her daughter-in-law, who had absorbed the news of her losses in stoic silence. Sylvia and her society friends were renowned for their extravagance when it came to entertaining, each competing with the next to produce bigger and more elaborate parties with mountains of exotic food, wagonloads of flowers, and elaborate decorations. They also strove to outshine each other in their expensive, diamond-bedecked ball gowns and dripping jewels, traveling to Paris each season to purchase the latest fashions. Sylvia's fame as a hostess was her life, her identity. She thrived on her unsurpassed reputation, and invitations to her events were prized among New York's high society. What could ever replace her role as hostess? Yet if Sylvia saw her world crumbling, she showed no sign of it. Her chin was still lifted high, her eyes dry.

"Our law firm will be happy to field all of your questions and manage all of your concerns in the coming months," Mr. Wilson finally said. "One of my colleagues will be at your disposal to help you navigate these legal and financial changes as the estate is settled, and to handle issues such as the sale of Mr. Stanhope's yacht and this mansion, when the time comes."

"I would like to ask that you assign Mr. Forsythe to help us," Junietta said, "since he already knows all the details of our losses." He blushed slightly as everyone turned to him, and let go of the plush velvet curtain that he had been fingering. He had been standing guard beside the window as if awaiting Junietta's further orders—or perhaps he was trying to stay out of the range of her cane. She thought she detected a hint of sympathy for their plight in his clear blue eyes. But even if he possessed first-rate legal and financial expertise, he couldn't possibly understand the elaborate inner workings of New York society or comprehend the family's social losses.

"Certainly, if you wish," Mr. Wilson said. "Now, unless you have further questions, we won't take up any more of your time."

Junietta thumped her cane on the floor. "Well, if we're paying an hourly fee for your services, then perhaps you should be on your way. And quickly."

"No, no, I assure you that isn't the case. I'll leave a summary of the will here for you to read at your leisure, but our law firm is at your disposal until the estate is settled."

"Thank you for coming," Sylvia said, rising to her feet. "May I speak with you in private for just one moment?"

"Certainly."

Junietta took the hint and left the study with Adelaide. Her heart continued to cavort and race and skip like a crazed goat, and she remembered the doctor's warning to get plenty of rest and avoid unnecessary strain and anxiety. But her charitable foundation! Junietta couldn't let Roger Stanhope get his hands on it. It was her life's work! If Junietta's heart was going to give out, then she needed to make sure the foundation was in capable hands before it did.

### ⤜ *Sylvia* ⤛

Gone. The millions of dollars the Stanhopes had amassed. Everything her husband had worked for. Gone. For the second time in her life, Sylvia was about to lose everything, and she could not let that happen. She needed to take control of the reins herself.

"How can I help you?" Mr. Wilson asked after Adelaide and Junietta had left the study. Sylvia took her time, choosing her words carefully in order to keep her emotions steady, and to avoid sounding needy and weak. Sylvia Grace Stanhope would not beg.

"I'm sure you must realize that my husband took care of all our family's financial concerns. He provided us with a generous living allowance, of course, and I felt free to ask for more beyond that. But the daily bookkeeping that kept our household running was handled by people in his office. I would like all of those accounts to be handed over to me, right away."

"Yes, of course. Your personal finances will need to be severed from the company's finances."

"And I would appreciate some assistance in learning to navigate those personal accounts from now on."

"I can set you up with a reputable accountant to do your bookkeeping."

"No, thank you. I would like to learn to manage it myself, Mr. Wilson." He looked surprised. And dubious. But she could not trust anyone with the truth of her financial losses. The gossip would destroy her. And it would ruin Adelaide's life. Sylvia had no idea if she truly was capable of handling the necessary accounts, but she was determined to learn whatever she needed to in order to take control of their future herself.

"As you wish, Mrs. Stanhope. Mr. Forsythe will secure the accounting ledgers right away and go over them with you."

"Thank you." After she'd escorted the two lawyers to the door, Sylvia wanted nothing more than to go to her room so she could fall apart, alone. But Adelaide was waiting for her, and she followed Sylvia upstairs to her bedroom suite as if she didn't want to let her mother out of her sight. Addy probably longed to hear reassurances that nothing would change, that their world wouldn't fall apart, that they would find a way to avoid social and financial ruin. But how could Sylvia do that when her own world had been knocked off its axis? She paused beside the second-floor railing for a moment, stalling for time as she corralled her emotions, running her hand along the polished wood. She gazed down at the vast marble foyer, remembering how she would stand down there beside her husband to greet their guests whenever she threw a party or a ball. Her daughters used to sneak out to this balcony and peek through the balustrades as laughter and music transformed their beautiful mansion into a fairy-tale castle. It would have been Adelaide's turn next to shine as the belle of the ball, but now she might never have that chance. The thought devastated Sylvia.

She lifted her chin for courage and strode into her bedroom suite, sitting down on the brocade settee and gesturing for Addy to sit beside her. Neither of them spoke for several minutes as Adelaide curled up beside her like a child. "Why does everything have to change?" she murmured at last. "Does this mean we can never go back to Newport?"

Sylvia traced gentle circles on Addy's back without replying. Their beautiful mansion on the sea, her family's refuge from the stifling city each season—gone. They had always looked forward to the cool Atlantic seacoast and the familiar round of summer balls and lawn parties and sailing excursions. But the loss of that mansion was just the beginning of their many losses. Sylvia felt irrationally angry with her husband for dying so abruptly and leaving them at the mercy of his uncle Roger. There was no love lost between his family and theirs, only years of resentment, suspicion, and jealousy. Sylvia agreed with Junietta's description of him as a weaselly old man. He had a habit of standing too close when talking to women and was notorious for pinching the maids on their bottoms. His son, Randall, was a shadowy figure whose various money-making schemes never amounted to much. She'd often heard A.B. refer to him as the family disgrace. It seemed outrageous that those two men would inherit everything.

"If only I'd been a son instead of a daughter," Addy said. "Father must have been so disappointed when I was born."

"He loved you, Adelaide. And he knew it wasn't your fault. Nor mine."

"Will we really have to sell this house like Mr. Wilson said?"

"Of course not." She made Addy sit up and face her. "But we'll need to be very smart, Adelaide. And very shrewd. I'm determined to salvage this mess that your great-grandfather's will created. I won't stand by and watch you lose everything. Especially this home. It's rightfully yours, and we're going to hang on to it and to the life that we have here. I'm going to make sure that you marry well. Very well. Nothing needs to change for you."

"But will my trust fund be enough to entice a suitor?"

"You have so much more to offer than money, Adelaide. Your beauty, your charm—and this mansion. Any suitor who sees this magnificent place will naturally want to become the master of it. It's the envy of everyone in the city, and will belong to you and your husband after you marry."

Adelaide nodded and tried to smile, but her tears continued to fall. Sylvia knew that Randall Stanhope's daughter, Cicely Stanhope, would quickly rise as Addy's greatest rival in attracting an eligible husband, now that her grandfather had inherited the family fortune. But Sylvia wouldn't worry about Cicely just yet. "I thought we would have more time for you to court and marry, but we'll need to work fast and start entertaining eligible suitors before news of our misfortune leaks out."

"How can we entertain guests? Aren't we supposed to be in mourning?"

Sylvia's mind raced to find a solution. "We can get around that if we act discreetly and invite people to call on us a few at a time. I'll start gleaning information about eligible suitors. But don't trust anyone, Adelaide. And don't reveal anything. Remember, your friends are your competitors."

"How will I meet suitors during the summer season without our home in Newport?"

Sylvia felt disheartened momentarily, but she bravely recovered. "I'll ask the lawyers to see what they can do about demanding our fair share of time there. Or maybe we won't need the Newport mansion at all.

We can do all our entertaining on the *Merriweather*. We'll make yacht parties the newest summer trend."

"But Mr. Wilson said that the yacht is very expensive, and—"

"Listen, Adelaide." She took Addy's face in her hands, silencing her protests. "I'm going to fight for us. You don't need to worry about anything that Mr. Wilson said. I'll fight for what's rightfully ours. Fight to keep the way of life your father always provided for us. If you trust me and do as I say, you'll have a secure future ahead of you." She kissed Addy's forehead and released her. "Now, go and get some rest so you'll look beautiful, even wearing ghastly gray. I'll start planning our next steps."

### ⸻ Adelaide ⸻

Mother didn't come down for the evening meal, but Grandmother did. The family dining room was a smaller version of the enormous formal dining room that could seat one hundred guests, but it was still a beautifully appointed room with damask drapes, a crystal chandelier, a ceiling of carved English oak, and an arsenal of silver serving pieces lined up on the sideboard. Adelaide was already seated at the dining table when Mimi Junie entered. "What a disastrous day!" she said as she dropped into her seat. "Such devastating news!"

"Mimi Junie, the servants," Adelaide whispered.

"They'll need to hear the truth sooner or later. After all, they might be looking for new employment soon." She unfurled her dinner napkin and spread it on her lap as the servants brought out platters of roast beef, potatoes, buttery rolls, and green beans. Addy chose only tiny portions, her stomach still in rebellion from the worrisome news.

"Things aren't really that bad, are they?" she asked with a nervous laugh. "Mother says she's going to fight for what's rightfully ours."

"Addy, dear. Your mother lost all her social status along with her husband and his millions. Don't be surprised if she no longer receives invitations to parties and balls."

"But Mother has so many friends—"

"An unmarried woman as beautiful as your mother is a threat to them. Now that Alva Vanderbilt and Charlotte Astor have made divorce acceptable, what's to stop Sylvia from stealing one of her friends' husbands away from them?"

Addy remembered Mother's fierce determination. Yet while she'd talked about finding Addy a suitor, she'd said nothing about remarrying herself.

"As for this house," Grandmother continued, "good riddance. There are ghosts everywhere. Some in this very room!"

"Mimi Junie, you sound a little deranged when you talk like that. Besides, I can't imagine living anywhere else but here."

"That's because you've been held prisoner here all these years."

"I'm not a prisoner—"

"Listen. What Mr. Muttonchops told us today was the best possible news for you. You're free now! You can go anywhere and be anything you want to be. This is our chance to look closely at our lives and decide what's important and what isn't. We can dream new dreams, look for new goals, pursue new adventures. You no longer have to live a life of mindless indulgence, conforming to a dull, unimaginative society."

"But Mother says that nothing is going to change and—"

"Your mother has lived her life, and it was a good one. She had wealth, privilege, prestige. She raised her three daughters and bolstered A.B.'s career. But now he's gone, and that life is over for her. It was the same for me when my husband died and I turned everything over to Sylvia."

"Mother isn't going to give up any of it, Mimi. She says if we work together, we can—"

"Get whatever *she* wants? Maybe that's true, but what do *you* want, Adelaide?"

"I-I want to help her. I don't want her to lose everything."

"That's very nice of you," she said in a tone that said otherwise. "But do you really want the burden of this place and all its secrets pressing down on your shoulders?"

"I don't know. I guess so. It's the only life I know."

Mimi wadded up her napkin and threw it at her. "Wake up, child!

Don't be such a mouse! You are a unique creation. A one-of-a-kind masterpiece with your whole life ahead of you. Think for yourself, for once!"

Addy looked away as tears filled her eyes. She had felt so reassured after talking with Mother, but now Mimi Junie was confusing her. "Don't I have an obligation to honor my mother?"

"That depends. What, exactly, is Sylvia asking you to do? Marry a wealthy man, I suppose?"

"Well—"

"Do you really want to marry a man you don't love and spend the next fifty or sixty years with him, just so you and your mother can live in this monstrous house and throw lavish parties and buy expensive ball gowns?" Addy didn't reply as she refolded Mimi's napkin into smaller and smaller squares. "Why not attend a nice women's college like Vassar or Bryn Mawr, and discover what your own interests are and what you're good at doing? More and more women are doing that nowadays. Or you could find a worthy man who loves you for yourself, not your money, and live happily ever after without all of this . . . this . . . pomposity!" She gestured to the row of silver serving pieces. "You could be free from everyone's expectations."

Addy shook her head to erase the picture her eccentric grandmother was painting. She had family obligations. Her mother knew what was best for her. "I need to help Mother," she said firmly.

"No, you don't. Believe me, she's quite capable of helping herself. She's a beautiful widow, still young enough to remarry. Let her secure her own future. But don't let her convince you to give up who you are."

"This *is* who I am, Mimi Junie. I'm a Stanhope. I'm my father's daughter."

Grandmother pushed back her chair and stood. "Come with me, Adelaide. I want to show you something."

"What? Now? We've just begun to eat. Can't it wait until after dinner?"

"No. This is too important." She waved her cane at the startled servant and said, "Jane, kindly put our plates on a tray and bring every-thing to my room, would you dear?" She prodded Adelaide with the tip of her cane until she stood up, then used it like a shepherd's staff to herd her out of the dining room and up the stairs. Once they reached her bedroom suite, Mimi Junie rummaged through the cedar chest in her dressing room and brought out a watercolor in a simple wooden frame. "Look at this," she said, handing it to Adelaide. It was an exquisitely painted woodland scene with mossy rocks and delicate wildflowers and trees that seemed to rustle in the breeze. A soft-eyed rabbit, a tiny mouse, and a spotted frog lay hidden among the ferns and leaves and grass. The artist had painted a world of lush beauty and life that seemed to beckon to Adelaide to enter.

"It's enchanting! Where did it come from?"

"Look at the signature."

In the lower corner were the initials *SGW*. Mother's initials. Her maiden name had been Woodruff. "This can't be Mother's work. She doesn't paint."

"You're right. She doesn't. And yet she once created that. Beauty flowed from your mother's heart and her hands, back when she was free to be herself." The painting was warm and alive, the very opposite of Addy's cool, aloof mother. She couldn't reconcile the two. And yet she thought of Mother's elaborate parties, the stunning tableaus and scenes she created to dazzle her guests, and realized they must spring from the same imagination that had created this painting.

Grandmother poked Addy's shoulder. "Somewhere in this house, hidden away in a dusty trunk, is a series of delightful children's books that your mother once wrote and illustrated. A dozen of them. Maybe more. Charming stories. Worthy of publication."

"Why would she hide them away?"

"Because her marvelous creations would be beneath the dignity of Mrs. Arthur Benton Stanhope the third."

"Did Father know about them?"

"I doubt it. If A.B. had seen them, he probably would have

encouraged her to continue painting. I came across them by accident years ago, and she let me keep that one. My point is, Sylvia sacrificed something she loved and that was so much a part of who she was in order to live this vacuous life. That's why she can't bear to lose it now."

"But you lived the same way, Mimi. In this same house."

"I didn't have a choice. She did. And so do you."

"Well, I owe it to Mother to help her keep our home and everything she loves."

"No, dear girl. She owes it to you to set you free."

Grandmother had spoken about freedom after Father's funeral, after her mysterious words about a second son. Were there more secrets Addy didn't know about? She tried to give back the painting, but Mimi held up her hands, refusing. "Keep it. Show it to your mother. See what she says."

"That would be cruel, I think."

"Suit yourself. But keep it anyway. Let it remind you of what you stand to lose."

The servants arrived in Mimi's room with two dinner trays, but Addy was no longer hungry. She picked at her food, wishing she knew what she was supposed to do and who she was supposed to listen to.

"I have been fighting my father-in-law, the first Arthur B. Stanhope, all my life," Mimi said. "And it looks as though I'll have to continue fighting him. It's too late for me to try to save anyone else from his greed and selfishness, but maybe I can still save you, Adelaide. You're the last Stanhope, and I'm going to do everything I can to keep you from becoming another one of his victims."

Addy carried her mother's painting back to her room when they finished eating. She had never imagined that Mother had lived a different life from this one. She and Mimi both had secrets, it seemed. Addy couldn't bear to think about the unknown, especially her own unknown future. She opened her wardrobe and stuffed the painting deep inside it.

# 3

## ~ Adelaide ~

The silk chiffon ball gown was as ethereal as fairy wings. Adelaide stood before her dressing-room mirror, holding the gossamer creation in front of her, longing to wear it to Ellen Madison's autumn ball tonight. She twirled from side to side, enjoying the fabric's swishing whispers. The pale blue color would look lovely on her, and with her chestnut hair swept up gracefully on her head, the low neckline would show off her slender neck and shoulders to perfection. She had looked forward to the ball when the invitation had arrived three months ago, seeing all her friends, dancing until dawn. Everyone was home from Newport or Long Island or wherever they had gone to flee the hot summer months, and the next round of society events had begun. But the dress would have to remain in her wardrobe until the mourning period for her father ended—at least six months for Adelaide, a year for her mother. By then, she would be six months older and inching toward spinsterhood, while her friends and rivals danced and flirted with all the eligible men.

The three months that Adelaide had already spent in mourning had been endlessly lonely. It was considered in poor taste to attend her usual club meetings and social activities, which meant long hours of solitude with nothing to do. Without guests to fill their sprawling mansion with laughter and gossip, the vast echoing rooms served no purpose. It was as if Addy's life had stopped along with her father's. But as Mother had promised, nothing had changed—for now. Aside from being in mourning, Adelaide had continued living in their vast mansion just as before.

"Kindly hang this up for me," she said, handing over the gown to her maid. "And do be careful. I hope to wear it someday." But not tonight. She appraised her appearance in the mirror a final time, smoothing imaginary wrinkles from her boring cloud-gray mourning dress. She had received a note from her mother on her breakfast tray, asking to meet in the morning room at eleven o'clock. The mansion was so vast that she and Mother often dispatched the servants in order to bring notes to each other.

Before the maid closed her wardrobe door, Addy spotted the painting she had stuffed inside and pulled it out to study it again. She noticed tiny beetles, crickets, and ladybugs cleverly hidden among the leaves and could almost smell the damp earth of the forest floor and feel the cushiony green moss. Why had Mother stashed away a painting she had every right to be proud of? Adelaide considered taking it downstairs to ask her, but in the end, she simply propped it against the mirror on her dressing table, waiting for a better time.

She took the back stairs to Mother's morning room, avoiding the marble staircase in the echoing front foyer, which always reminded her of a museum. For the past month, Addy had often thought of Mimi Junie's words as she'd struggled to fall asleep: *Do you really want to marry a man you don't love and spend the next fifty or sixty years with him?* Everyone knew that Consuelo Vanderbilt's mother had forced her to give up the man she loved in order to marry a British duke. Consuelo had been eighteen at the time, a year younger than Addy was now.

Adelaide knew almost nothing about love. She had observed her parents together, as well as her sisters with their husbands, and detected very little affection between any of them, let alone love or passion. Couples in their social class were rarely demonstrative. But what if Addy could fall in love as Consuelo had, and be allowed to marry a man who loved her in return?

No. The idea was outrageous, the chance of it happening in her present circumstances, nearly impossible. Mother had emphasized the need to hurry, to court and marry a wealthy man before news of the will leaked out, and she and Mother fell from favor in society. She wished again that she had been a son instead of a daughter. She could have inherited everything, and nothing would change.

The morning room was one of Adelaide's favorites out of the nearly seventy-five rooms in the mansion. It was filled with sunshine from an east-facing window that overlooked the garden, now bright with fall foliage. It was a cozy room even in the winter, with comfortable chairs facing the fireplace. The papered walls and painted ceiling were in soothing pastel colors that reminded Addy of summer dresses and lawn parties in Newport. "Good morning, Mother," she said, kissing her cheek. She looked beautiful and her fair hair smelled of roses. Adelaide had been in awe of her mother's beauty and poise her entire life.

"We need to talk about the dinner I plan to hold," Mother said after the maid poured coffee for Adelaide. "I wanted to explain—" They were interrupted by a loud thump as Mimi Junie pushed the door open with her cane.

"I've been looking all over for you two. Aren't I invited to be part of your scheming?"

"I don't know what you mean by *scheming*." Mother's tone was cool and calm. "We're simply talking about—"

"Ever since the will was read, you've been scheming to hang on to this house and all that goes with it. And you're planning to make poor Adelaide play a major role in that."

"We're all in this together, Junietta," Mother said. "Our husbands are gone, Adelaide's father is gone, and we have to make shrewd decisions from now on if we hope to survive."

"Then why not let me help? After all, I've managed to run my own life quite nicely for nearly seventy years—not to mention a charitable foundation that oversees millions of dollars."

The polite friction between the two women was nothing new. Addy had observed it all her life. For the most part, Mimi Junie remained in the background, adding color and spark at times, but she was rarely assertive. Adelaide had never seen her take control the way she had the day Father's will was read, speaking her mind and asking the lawyers questions. Mother had been the driving force in Addy's life and in her sisters' lives, calculating every move in order to see them successfully married and well provided for.

"Thank you, Junietta. We could use your experience." Mother gestured for Mimi to sit down with them and ordered the servant to bring another cup for her. "I'm sure you don't welcome these drastic changes any more than Adelaide and I do."

"Well, you can't prevent change. It's part of life. This cane was once an acorn, then a tree, then a stick of lumber," she said, waving it in the air. "Now it serves an entirely new role, propping up an elderly lady. Its usefulness came at the cost of a great deal of chopping and cutting and sanding, and we always abhor those painful processes, don't we?"

"We're people, not trees," Mother said. She took a sip of her coffee and returned the cup to its saucer before continuing. "Since you know so many people and have ties to all the important families, we could use your help in discerning the best suitors for Adelaide. The Stanhope name is highly respected and—"

"Ha!" Mimi Junie laughed. "*Feared* might be more appropriate than *respected*. It's lucky for the Stanhopes that ghosts can't talk. And that our skeletons have remained safely stashed away in our closets."

Mother gave a prim smile in response to Mimi Junie's colorful imagery. She had always been the more practical of the two women. In fact, Addy wouldn't have guessed that Mother had any imagination at all if she hadn't seen the watercolor for herself. "I've written to your sisters," she continued, addressing Addy, "and asked them to comb through their contacts and connections for families with eligible suitors. But letters take so long to get anywhere, and a family based here in New York is preferable to either Boston or London. We'll need to act quickly, before word leaks out about the will."

"And before 'Roving Roger' or his ridiculous son, Randall, bankrupts the Stanhope empire," Mimi added.

Mother continued, unruffled. "Adelaide's marriage will allow her to keep this house and her life here in New York."

"So this house is to be part of Adelaide's bridal dowry?" Mimi asked. "Where will it end, Sylvia? And how?" She turned to Adelaide, wagging her finger in warning. "Don't let yourself be bartered and sold like a rug in a bazaar. You deserve better."

Addy could tell by the pink spots marring Mother's alabaster complexion that she was losing patience. "I want the very best for Adelaide, just as you do, Junietta. And this is how it's always been done among our social class. Why are you challenging me?"

"We're talking about Adelaide's future. Your youngest daughter. Doesn't she deserve a better life than we had? As I told Addy, when changes come, they give us a chance to take a closer look at our lives and get a fresh start, keeping what's important and setting new priorities."

"I was very content with my life before my husband died."

"That's a curious choice of words, isn't it? *Content.* Why not *happy*? Why not *fulfilled*? Is that the most you want for yourself and Adelaide—contentment?"

"You're twisting my words."

"My hope for Addy is that she discovers who she is. And I believe she's so much more than a bargaining chip that will allow us to continue with the way of life that *we've* chosen. Why not let her choose for herself? Why not help her escape the mold you and I were forced to fill? Don't let her uniqueness be diminished into conformity, the way yours and mine were."

"I'm sorry if your life was a disappointment, but—"

"Why not let Addy marry for love instead of for wealth and social position?"

"You know that's not how it works for women in society. Love is the stuff of foolish romantic novels and silly poems. One can't survive on love. One needs food and clothing and a roof over one's head."

"Does one really need a house with a dozen bedrooms? And a dining room that will seat one hundred guests?"

"You're well aware that our husbands expected us to entertain important people. It was the role we played in the family business."

"But that's the point, Sylvia. The family business no longer belongs to us—or to Adelaide. We can reshape our lives any way we choose. If it turns out that we need to sell this house—good riddance! Mr. Wilson seems to think we could live on our inheritance if we're prudent."

Addy saw Mother's composure slipping. Her voice rose a notch. "I don't want Adelaide to be left out of everything important in New York society and sit in a cramped house all alone while Randall Stanhope's daughter takes *her* rightful place! After everything A.B. and I have worked to achieve for our family? I won't stand for it! It's especially unfair for Adelaide to be forced to change. She was born a Stanhope. This life is hers by rights."

"Is that what *you* want, Adelaide?"

Both women turned to her. She couldn't reply, unused to being asked her opinion.

"See?" Mimi said. "The poor lamb can't even think for herself. She wanders through life like a puppet on a string, doing whatever she's told, anxious to please you, never having a thought or an opinion of her own. Why not let her explore some alternatives instead of deciding her future for her?"

"There isn't time! Word about her father's will is certain to leak out, and Randall's wife will rush in to take our place in society, pushing her daughter, Cicely, forward—"

"Cicely also deserves the right to choose for herself."

"I'm sorry, but I don't have time for this." Mother stood. "We'll talk about the dinner party another time, Adelaide. Besides, the lawyer is coming this afternoon, and I have to get ready for him."

Mother gathered up her things to leave, but Mimi Junie raised her cane like a barrier, blocking her way. "Sit down, Sylvia. You have plenty of time. This is important, and you know it."

She sat, but Adelaide detected anger in her stiff posture and cold expression. The two women rarely interacted, living separate lives in their separate suites except for mealtimes and social events. Adelaide hated to see them arguing, hated that she was in the middle of their tug-of-war.

"Please don't argue over me," she said quietly.

Mimi reached for her hand. "I'm speaking up for you, Addy, because your future is too important for me to remain silent. I should have been more involved in your life these past few years than I have been. Your sisters' lives too. I got caught up with my foundation, which is important—its future is important. But not as important as your future. This is your chance to escape."

"That's carrying it a bit too far, Junietta. She isn't a prisoner."

"Isn't she? You and I each had a taste of a different life before we married into this family. Isn't it time we told Addy the truth about our pasts?"

The pink spots on Mother's cheeks deepened to red. "I don't know what you're talking about."

"Oh, come now. Does Ferncliff Manor on the Hudson stir any memories? Or any regrets?"

"Why are you doing this, Junietta? And why now, when our lives have been disrupted enough by A.B.'s untimely death?"

"I can't think of a better time. When you reach the end of the road, it's always wise to look back to where you've come from before deciding which way to turn next. Shall I spill my secrets first, Sylvia, or would you like to? Shouldn't Addy have the benefit of learning from our experiences? I've kept many things about my past a secret, mostly out of guilt

LYNN AUSTIN | 35

and shame. But I'm willing to share everything with the two of you if it will help you make wise decisions going forward."

"I'm not in the mood to play your games."

"Very well, I'll go first. And you'd better stay," she said, blocking Mother's path with her cane again. "I'll be unearthing secrets that you've never heard before."

"I should think it would be better to leave them buried."

"There's no longer any reason to hide them. All three Arthur Benton Stanhopes are gone—first, second, and third."

Addy moved to the edge of her seat, wondering if Mimi was going to talk about the other son she'd mentioned at the funeral.

"You've grown up with my stories, Addy," Mimi continued. "You already know that my father was a Van Buren and my mother was a De Witt. They were from the old line of Dutch families called the Knickerbockers, who trace their ancestors to the founders of New York—or New Amsterdam, as it was originally called. The Van Burens have owned land here since 1631 and were among this nation's founding fathers. We're related to Martin Van Buren, who was the president of the United States when I was a girl. Oh, how proud we all were to be Van Burens! Mama's family, the De Witts, are kin to Mary De Witt, mother of DeWitt Clinton. He was a senator, mayor, and then governor of New York. He ran for president before I was born but lost, sad to say."

Adelaide had, indeed, heard this recitation before, but she nodded politely.

"The Schermerhorns are another old Knickerbocker family. Lady Caroline Astor is a Schermerhorn." Mimi leaned closer to Addy as if to make sure she was listening. "Any Johnny-come-lately millionaire who wanted to be socially accepted in New York would try to marry a Knickerbocker. John Jacob Astor, a crude German immigrant and butcher's son, came to America with barely a penny to his name. When he died fifty years ago, he was the richest man in America. But his family didn't gain respectability until Caroline Schermerhorn married his grandson, William Astor. It was the same with your great-grandfather,

Arthur Benton Stanhope I. He wanted his son to marry me because I was a Knickerbocker."

Addy had never heard this part of the story and was paying close attention now.

Mimi sat back in her chair again and smiled. "By the way, not many people know that Arthur's real name wasn't Arthur Benton Stanhope at all. It was Gustav Steinhaus . . ."

# 4

NEW YORK CITY
JUNE 1849

### ❧ Junietta ❧

"Remember who you are, Junietta."

How I hated those words! I knew that if I looked over my shoulder as I hurried out of the house, Mama's stern warning would be accompanied by one of her equally stern stares. And if I didn't close the door quickly enough, I also knew which words I would hear next: *"You're a Van Buren and a De Witt. Do not bring shame to those good names."*

I walked swiftly until our family home was out of sight, then slowed my steps to enjoy the sweet spring morning. My great-aunt Agatha wouldn't notice if I was a few minutes late. She was a spinster who lived alone with her two servants in the De Witt family home, a short walk from ours. I had been given the role of her lady's companion. Visiting her had begun as a dreaded chore two years ago when I was sixteen, but had now become a welcome chance to escape the tedium of my home life. I had grown up in our moderately well-to-do home without a role to play. I was a useless extra daughter, the middle of three girls. My papa, who had filled a variety of political roles throughout my childhood, had become a New York State senator by the time of that fateful spring morning. He contented himself with grooming my two older brothers, William and John, for a future in politics, hoping that one of the Van Buren sons would achieve the fame and position that our relative Martin Van Buren had. Papa was either a hopeful optimist or a foolish dreamer, because I couldn't see how either of my dull, unimaginative brothers could possibly achieve anything worthwhile. William, who was five years my senior, never read anything more challenging than the daily newspaper. And John, three years my senior, couldn't add a column of numbers if someone held a gun to his head. What he'd been up to at Yale University, I couldn't imagine.

My sister Marietta, one year older than me, had chosen "being pretty" as her life's goal—another lost cause, in my opinion—and wouldn't dirty her delicate little fingers with any charitable duties, such as visiting Aunt Agatha. The baby of our family, my sister Chloe, had come along ten years and several infant deaths and miscarriages after me. She was far too busy being petted and spoiled by Mama and our two servants to even think about growing up. And so, as the nonessential extra sister, the task of visiting Aunt Agatha fell to me.

I had despised the job at first, sitting in stifling, overstuffed parlors as Aunt Agatha visited her arthritic friends, most of whom were so deaf they had to shout at each other over tea and canasta. In the afternoons, I would help with her correspondence and read aloud to her until she began to snore as loudly as her nasty little lapdog, Tibbles. But as time went on, I discovered two advantages to my otherwise boring assignment. The first was her library, which had once belonged to her father and grandfather. It contained a treasure trove of books on history, literature, plant life, geography, and even medicine, all of which I devoured hungrily. The second bonus was that reading aloud to Aunt Agatha invariably put her to sleep, giving me time to do whatever I pleased. At first, I used the time to explore her library, but as time passed and so did most of her friends, Aunt Agatha rarely ventured outside her home. The poor old dear dozed off so often and so soundly that I took advantage of her naps to sneak out the back door and explore the city. Her two servants were easily bribed to ignore my excursions and even made excuses for my disappearances if need be.

I loved the bustling, bumbling commercial district with its jumble of horses and wagons that would snarl into tangled, shrieking traffic jams. I explored the unseemly, overcrowded parts of town where feral pigs ate garbage in the streets, street vendors hawked their wares, and immigrants added colorful music and the cadence of exotic languages. Of course, Papa's daughters were never allowed into those areas of the city. Our servants purchased most of our daily necessities, and our dressmakers brought samples of cloth and lace and ribbons to our home so we wouldn't soil the hems of our gowns with the filth of the street. I even ventured as far as the city docks, where tall-masted sailing ships and passengers and goods from all over the globe landed in America. I had discovered a world of excitement outside my staid New York City neighborhood, and I longed to see all of it.

But even I wasn't fool enough to explore the city on that idyllic June morning in 1849. A plague of cholera, which had begun last winter, had now become a deadly epidemic. I had been a baby during New York's first wave of cholera in 1832, when thousands of people perished. They said the murderous affliction had originated in India, then spread to Great Britain, Canada, and eventually the United States. Now it was striking a second time. Experts said the scourge was caused by foul, stagnant air, and I knew how ponderous and fetid the air was in the city's working-class neighborhoods. I intended to order the servants to open all of Aunt Agatha's windows to the spring breezes as soon as I arrived at her house, and air out her blankets and featherbeds. But as I took a shortcut through the back lane and was passing my aunt's carriage house, the distinct sound of a baby's cry stopped me in my tracks. I stood for a moment, listening. There was no mistake. A small baby was definitely inside my aunt's stables, crying.

I wondered if it was a foundling. Desperate parents, unable to care for their children, would sometimes leave them on the doorstep of a wealthy home, hoping the owners would take pity. Orphanages were filled with such abandoned babies. I had inched closer to peek through the window when a voice behind me startled me.

"Good morning, Miss. Are you needing something?"

I jumped, then whirled around to face a young man in his early twenties wearing well-worn clothing. It took me a moment to recall that he was the new handyman and carriage driver that my uncle had hired last week to replace Aunt Agatha's aging one. I couldn't recall the man's name, but that hardly mattered at the moment.

"There's a baby inside the carriage house," I said. "I heard it crying."

He removed his cap, not in deference to a lady, which was proper, but to run his fingers through his hair. It was thick and curly and the color of mahogany. "Nay, Miss. I think you must be mistaken. 'Tis the cry of a bird you must be hearing."

I had learned from my brothers the futility of arguing with a man who was being stupidly contrary. I simply walked around to the side door and went inside. The cries had stopped, but I continued walking through the stables to where I thought the sound had come from. The new driver seemed to be making an unusual amount of noise as he followed me, stomping his feet as if his boots were coated with snow and talking nonsense about barn owls and cooing doves. I knew what I had heard. And sure enough, crouched in the back of an empty stall was a very frightened young woman with an infant clutched to her breast. "There's your mourning dove, Mister . . . ?"

"Galloway. Neal Galloway. Forgive me for doubting you, Miss De Witt."

"My name is Van Buren. Miss De Witt is my great-aunt and your employer."

"Right, then. I'll see to the lass and babe, Miss Van Buren. You don't need to trouble yourself any further."

I ignored him and stepped closer to the young woman. "What's your name?" I asked. She didn't reply. Instead, she looked up at Mr. Galloway as if for instructions. I knew then that he wasn't surprised in the least to find a mother and child hiding in the carriage house. "Do they belong to you, Mr. Galloway?" I asked, turning to him.

"Not in the way that you mean, Miss. The babe is me niece, and the lass is me brother Gavin's wife."

"What are they doing in my aunt's carriage house?"

He scratched his head and settled the cap back on his head as if stalling for time. "Are ye familiar with the story of how the Christ child started His life in a stable because there was nae any room for Him? And how He later fled the city when Herod's soldiers came after Him?"

"You don't expect me to believe this is another holy visitation, do you?"

"Nay," he said, laughing. "It's the 'no room' part of the story that I'm comparing this to. And the danger. The air is thick with cholera where Gavin and Meara are living. I only wanted to spare them and the wee babe."

"By moving them into our horse stall?"

"Aye. It's a step up for them, you see. And it's only until the air clears." There was something about his lilting brogue and the smile in his voice and in his hazel eyes that made it hard to be angry with Mr. Galloway. He had bucketsful of charm. And none of the dour Knickerbocker men of my acquaintance had even one ounce of charm. Even so, it was presumptuous of him to move his family into our stable a mere week after he'd been hired.

"And how long were you expecting this . . . arrangement . . . to last?"

He shrugged his broad shoulders. "Until the air clears. And the dying stops. That is, if it's fine by you."

"It's a little late to be asking my permission, isn't it?"

"Aye. I see your point." Mr. Galloway grinned and my breath caught in my throat. He was easily the most attractive man I had ever seen in my life. The young men in my world were all tightly buttoned from head to toe in stiff collars, starched shirts, vests, cutaway coats, frock coats, and gloves until not an inch of skin showed except on their faces, even on warm June days like this one. But Mr. Galloway—oh, my! Ruddy hair and tanned skin peeked from where his top two shirt buttons were undone. His sleeves were rolled up to reveal more tanned skin and ruddy hair. He had arm muscles that I'd seen only on marble statues. I knew I shouldn't stare, but I couldn't help myself. I wanted to be angry with him, but I couldn't manage that either.

"I'll look the other way until the epidemic ends," I said, conscious of the irony of my words and my weak-kneed inability to take my eyes off Mr. Galloway. "But if my uncle, Mrs. De Witt's son, catches you, I will deny any knowledge of this arrangement."

"Agreed. God bless you for your kindness, Miss Van Buren." I wanted him to call me Junietta. I wanted to hear my name roll musically from his tongue. But of course, it would be wildly inappropriate for him to do so.

I searched our attic when I returned home, looking for the trunk of baby clothing that had been worn by all the infants in our family. I smuggled the layette to Meara and baby Regan in a basket so no one would see it. I salvaged leftover food that Aunt Agatha had only picked at, and brought it to Meara. She let me hold tiny Regan in my arms and inhale her milky sweetness.

As the weather warmed, I saw more of Mr. Galloway in two respects. First, I saw more of his tanned skin and sculpted muscles whenever he removed his shirt to pitch hay into the loft or repair the roof or tend the garden. And second, I saw more and more of him in my day-to-day life as we became friends. The cholera plague had put an end to my explorations around town, so I had plenty of extra time on my hands. Aunt Agatha's cook and housekeeper, long bored with the tedium of an elderly woman's routine and also enamored with Mr. Galloway's endless charm, quickly embraced the novelty of having a mother and babe in our carriage house and befriended all three of them as well.

On one particularly fine day a week or so after Meara and Regan arrived, I brought a picnic lunch outside for Mr. Galloway and his sister-in-law, and we sat in the shade outside the carriage house to eat it. "This is ever so kind of you, Miss Van Buren, thank you," he said as he bit into his sandwich.

"You are ever so welcome, Mr. Galloway," I replied, mocking his formality. He grinned.

"I wish you would call me by my given name, Miss Van Buren. It's Neal. Mr. Galloway was me father."

"All right—Neal." I longed to have him call me Junietta but still didn't dare. "Am I right in thinking your accent is Scottish?"

"Aye. I crossed over to America with me brother two years ago, looking to make our way. Our farm wasn't prospering anymore, and there was no work to be found anywhere, so when our dad passed on, we decided to come here. Our mum was gone years before."

"And did you come over with Neal and Gavin too?" I asked Meara.

She shook her head. "I met Gavin not long after he arrived. I was doing cleaning and such in the rooming house where he stayed."

"Me brother fell hard for Meara, and that's the truth," Neal said, laughing. "After working at the docks unloading ships all day, Meara is a sweet sight for him to come home to. I'm happy for the both of them."

"Why aren't you working at the docks with him? Surely it pays better wages than my uncle does."

He studied me for a moment as if deciding something, then rose to his feet.

"Come with me, Miss. I'll show you another secret that I've been hiding from ye." My heart pounded foolishly as I rose and followed him into the carriage house. I don't know what I expected to find, but it wasn't a pretty little oak side table with gently tapering legs. I didn't understand what I was seeing at first and wondered if he had stolen it. Then I saw the tools spread out on the workbench and the wood shavings scattered across the floor. The air smelled of sawdust and turpentine.

"You made this table?" I asked stupidly.

"Aye. I love working with me hands. Always have. I'm thinking if I can make enough furniture and the like in my spare time, I can get a start on owning me own carpenter shop someday. Didn't our Lord and Savior get His start as a carpenter?" I stared, openmouthed at his impertinence. Then he winked, and I couldn't help laughing.

"Well, you do lovely work, Neal, if this is an example."

"Thank you."

"And if you decide to follow our Lord and Savior's example and walk on water, I hope I'm there to see it." His jovial laughter followed me out of the workshop.

As the spring days lengthened, I came up with the idea of taking Aunt Agatha out for a carriage ride every day. I told her and myself that it was in the interest of getting fresh air to ward off the plague, but the truth was, I enjoyed being in the company of her cheerful carriage driver. "I haven't seen much of these finer areas of town," Neal told me. "I feared I'd be taken for a vagrant or a thief if I strolled these streets without a purpose." He was as intrigued by the way we lived as I had been by the docks and poorer areas of the city.

"Would you look at that, Miss?" he would say, pointing out things that I took for granted and causing me to see my world through his eyes. He slowed to watch a group of pedestrians on the wooden walkway and said, "The dresses you fine ladies wear are as colorful and bright as a flower garden, aren't they now?" Sometimes he would bring the carriage to a halt, just to take it all in. And he did that very thing one day when we came to the row of new shops on Park Row that John Jacob Astor had just built. The building was five stories tall and the size of a city block, with shops that sold everything from boots and books to silks and stationery. "Would you look at that fine place? I think that's where I'll have me furniture shop someday." Having seen his skills as a carpenter and knowing his determination and charm, I had no trouble believing that he would.

Neal burst into song as he drove home, singing a ballad about bonny lasses and fair skies above the Scottish Highlands. He had a fine voice, but I had never had a singing carriage driver before, and I worried how Aunt Agatha would react. Even though she was growing deaf, she couldn't have missed hearing him.

"Was that him singing? The driver?" she asked in her creaky voice when he finished.

"Yes. His name is Galloway, Aunt Agatha." I held my breath.

"Well, tell him to sing another song. A little louder this time."

# 5

SEPTEMBER 1849

*Junietta*

Fortunately for me—and terribly unfortunately for Aunt Agatha—she became so frail and unsteady on her feet by September that she needed someone to stay with her throughout the night. I surprised my mother by volunteering. "That's kind of you, Junie," she said, "but you would be giving up so much. Wouldn't you rather spend more time with your friends?"

"Aunt Agatha has become very dear to me," I replied. And so had her handyman.

"But wouldn't you like to attend events with Marietta more often, where there are young gentlemen to meet?"

"If I'm going to meet any gentlemen, it won't be in Marietta's company. She isn't happy unless every man in the room falls madly in love with her. And they always do. None of them even notice me."

"You're every bit as pretty as she is, Junie."

I didn't believe her. She was my mother, and mothers always said things like that. If I stayed overnight with Aunt Agatha, I could sneak outside to the carriage house after dark and talk with Neal and read books to him while he worked on his furniture by lantern light. The smell of raw wood and lamp oil would forever remind me of him. The epidemic had eased, so Meara and her baby had returned to their apartment by then. Aside from Aunt Agatha's horses, we were alone.

I knew I was falling in love with Neal Galloway. And I suspected by the tender looks he gave me that he loved me too. But he made no move to declare his love, always careful to keep a respectful distance between us.

"Will you do something for me, Neal?" I asked one evening. I had closed the book I'd been reading to him with a snap that had made him look up.

"And what would that be?"

"Call me by my given name, Junietta."

"Ah, but that wouldn't be appropriate, Miss Van Buren. You're my employer, aren't you now?"

"No, I'm your employer's niece."

"'Tis the same thing." He had laughter in his voice and a sparkle in his eyes that told me he was toying with me. I slid off my stool and stood in front of him.

"Say it, Neal. Say, 'Junietta, my dear, how are you this evening?'"

"But I can see perfectly well that you're fine, Miss Van Buren." He grinned at me, then looked away to continue carving the new cane he was making for Aunt Agatha. Hers had splintered, so he was fashioning a beautiful new one for her with a lion's-head handle and carved vines and flowers spiraling down the shaft.

"Neal Galloway!" I said, stamping my foot. "As your employer, I order you to say my given name. It's Junietta."

"Aye, I know your name, Miss Van Buren, and if I may be so bold to say, your name is as beautiful as you are." He was still looking down, not at me. My heart galloped like a stampeding horse.

"Stop teasing and say it!" I reached out and covered his hands with mine, stilling them. Our hands had touched before whenever he'd helped me from the carriage, but I'd always worn gloves as a proper lady should. The moment I felt his warm, wood-roughened ones beneath mine, I understood why it was forbidden to touch each other barehanded. A sensation that I'd never experienced before shivered through me like liquid fire in my veins. I longed to hold him close, to feel his strong arms around me, his bearded cheek against my face.

He looked up at me and I stopped breathing.

"Junietta," he whispered.

I was undone, even before he took my face in his hands and kissed me. I had never been kissed before. It was the most wonderful, thrilling sensation I had ever known, and the liquid fire burned hotter. Neal Galloway's firm lips were pressed against mine, and I never wanted the kiss to end. But it did.

"I love you, Junietta," he whispered.

"And I love you." I could barely speak. I had no breath. "Please, Neal. Please kiss me again." He did, and this time his arms came around me, and mine surrounded him. It felt even more wonderful than I had imagined to be held in his arms. I felt his warmth, his strength, and my own fragility. But then he stopped suddenly and gently unloosed my arms, pulling away from me. "What's wrong?" I asked.

"Nothing. Everything." He backed away and picked up the cane again as if he might have to use it to hold me back.

"I don't understand."

"You surely know that we can never be together. There's a wide river between us that I can never cross. What happened just now—it shouldn't have. Forgive me, Miss Van Buren."

"Don't you dare call me that! You said you loved me!"

"Aye, and it was the truth. But I need to ask you to leave now, for both of our sakes." He still had the cane in one hand, and he picked up the lantern with the other. "I'll light your way to the door, Miss."

I was shaken and furious and trembling from head to toe. But I marched to the carriage house door and slammed it behind me in Neal's face.

I sat in my room in the dark, weeping as I gazed out at the carriage house where lantern light shone dimly through the window. Neal Galloway loved me, and I loved him. There had to be a way to build a bridge across the river that he believed was separating us. I would lay every plank myself, if necessary. And if he couldn't cross to my side, then I would cross to his. I didn't care if I had to live in a shoddy tenement or carriage house for the rest of my life, at least I would be with the man I loved. I planned and plotted and dreamed until my tears had dried and the light in the carriage house finally went out. I climbed into bed but I didn't sleep.

"Aunt Agatha and I would like a carriage ride this afternoon," I told Neal the next day. "Take us to the north side of Manhattan, if you please, into the countryside." I'd planned the ride for the time she usually took a long afternoon nap. And sure enough, by the time we'd left the city behind and reached farmland, the warm fall air and gentle motion of the carriage on the dirt road had lulled her to sleep. "You can stop for a moment, Neal."

"I was wondering when you would say that," he said. "If we drive much further, the horses will be needing to swim."

I smiled. He always made me smile. "Please turn around and look at me, Neal." He did, and his eyes looked as red-rimmed and swollen as mine. "That river you mentioned last night. The one that stands between us. There has to be a way to cross it. A bridge or a ferry. I'll even learn how to swim if I have to. I love you, Neal. And you said last night that you loved me too. Was it true? Do you love me?"

He nodded, as if his heart was too full to speak. His eyes glistened with tears.

"Then look around, Neal!" I gestured to the farmland on either side of the road. "You wouldn't have to live in my world, and I wouldn't have to live in yours. We could start a new life together in a place like this. We could get land out west in the territories—everyone is moving west these days. They'll need furniture when they get there, won't they?"

He almost smiled, then grew serious again. "Your parents will never let you marry me, Junietta, and I can't say that I blame them."

"Then we'll run away!" He slowly shook his head. "Why not?" His stupid Scottish stubbornness frustrated me.

"Two reasons, lass. I won't steal a daughter from her family without their permission. It wouldn't be right. The Good Book says we're to honor our father and mother so that it may go well with ye. How could it ever go well with us if I stole you away?"

I huffed, unable to argue with his reply. "And the second reason?"

"Because you deserve so much more than what I can provide for you. The frontier life is not for you, Junietta. I won't degrade the woman I love by making her scrub and scrape for all her days. I've seen the way your people live, haven't I? With fine houses and servants to cook and clean and drive their carriages for them. Your aunt's servants live better than you would if you married me."

"But you'll have your own furniture shop someday, and—"

"Don't be arguing with me about it. I won't hear it." His words were spoken firmly yet gently. He studied the grove of apple trees beside the road for a moment. I could smell the sweet, fermenting aroma of the fallen ones scattered on the ground and hear bees buzzing around them. "But you aren't the only person who has been looking for a way to ford the river, Junietta. If I were a wealthy man—well now, that would be a different story. Then your father couldn't say no to me."

"How do you intend to become wealthy?"

"I'll earn it. By hard work and the sweat of me brow. People leave everything behind and come to America because it's possible to go from rags to riches, as they say. Anyone can do it."

I thought of John Jacob Astor, who had died last year. He had arrived as a penniless immigrant and became the richest man in America. But it had taken him a lifetime. How long would I have to wait? "Neal, you put so much care and attention into each piece of furniture you make that it would take years to earn enough money to impress Papa. I want to be with you now!"

"I won't be building furniture, Junietta. They've found gold in California, haven't they? I'm going to go there and make my fortune, then come back for ye."

"No! That's much too dangerous! I don't want to be separated from you for even a day, let alone all the years it will take for you to find gold."

"I hate the thought of being apart too, but—"

"Then take me with you!"

"From what I hear, the gold fields are no place for a woman."

"They're no place for you either! Neal, listen to me!" I was almost shouting as I tried to make this stubborn man listen to reason. Aunt Agatha stirred and awakened beside me. She looked around, blinking her eyes as if she might still be dreaming.

"Junie, dear? Where are we?"

Neal jumped down from the driver's seat and began the process of turning the horses and carriage around on the narrow dirt road. "We're on the north side of Manhattan Island, Auntie," I said. "I thought you'd like to see the countryside. We're heading back home now."

Neal had made up his mind, and all my begging and pleading in the following weeks did nothing to make him change it. Gold fever was spreading as fast as the cholera plague, and he had a fiery case of it. So did his brother, Gavin, who had a friend waiting in San Francisco to partner with the two brothers. The three men planned to stake their claim together. Neal and Gavin would set sail as soon as they'd saved enough money for the ship's passage, leaving me, Meara, and baby Regan behind to wait.

"There are two ways we can get to California," he explained a few days later as I watched him saw a plank of lumber into pieces. "We can sail around Cape Horn at the tip of South America, then all the way up the coast of both continents to California. Or we can sail as far as Panama, then go overland through the jungle to the Pacific. The second way saves time and seems much shorter, but I'm told there are natives in those jungles, and strange fevers and wild creatures. There's also the chance of being stranded in that jungle if your guide turns out to be a crook who steals all your money and abandons you there."

"Is there any chance at all that I can talk you out of this foolishness?"

"Nay, love. Me mind's made up." He leaned over to where I was sitting and kissed me. Neal no longer kept me at arm's length now that he finally had hope of marrying me. He didn't hesitate at all to hold me and kiss me and tell me how much he loved me as we talked about our plans for the future. But at the end of every evening, he would always pry my arms away and say, "Ye better leave now, love, while I still have me wits about me."

The newspapers were calling it a gold *rush* because everyone was in a hurry to get to California and make their fortune. The urgent need for ships was so great that decrepit old sailing vessels were being dragged out of dry dock and put to use. That was true of a salvaged ship called the *Heiress*, which Neal and Gavin booked passage on. The fare was half the price of other ships because the skipper was young and had never captained a ship before. He planned to scuttle the *Heiress* in California like so many others were doing and go prospecting for gold himself.

"Gavin's friend says the harbor in San Francisco is packed with abandoned ships," Neal told me. "You can almost walk from one to the next like stepping stones. Gavin and I won't even be getting our boots wet."

We stayed awake the night before he left, knowing that neither of us would sleep. We held each other and talked about what our life would be like in the future. I begged him one last time not to go, but he assured me that he had every intention of returning to me as a very rich man. He talked of the diamonds and jewels he would dress me in, and the palace he would build for me. "You foolish man! Don't you know I don't want any of those things? I only want you!" I loved him. Oh, how I loved him!

I took a streetcar to the docks with him at dawn to watch his ship set sail. He had tried to talk me out of coming to see him off but quickly learned how stubborn I could be. "All right, then," he decided with a curt nod. "There's something I need to show you before I go." He took me to the one-room tenement apartment where Meara and Regan would live with Meara's parents and two younger sisters while Gavin was away. Her family had already left for work, even at this early hour, and Meara and Gavin were sharing a tearful farewell.

It was the apartment that Neal wanted me to see, a dark, cramped, airless room that was both kitchen and sleeping quarters. There was no running water, no toilet. Thin, ragged blankets covered the lumpy beds. It smelled of woodsmoke from the cast-iron stove, and of unwashed clothing and sweat. A pile of new woolen coats covered the splintery table—piecework, Neal told me. As Meara cared for Regan, she would sew on buttons for one penny apiece. The single window faced a narrow alley and another tenement ten feet away. That and an oil lamp provided her only light as she worked.

"Now do ye believe me, Junietta, when I tell you how much I love ye? Meara has never known anything different, but you have. Leaving you is the hardest thing I will ever do, but I'm determined to provide more than this for you when I come home."

I had hoped that Neal would change his mind at the last minute when he'd be unable to say goodbye and part with me for what would probably be at least a year. But I was still standing alone on the pier long after the *Heiress* disappeared from sight.

I received two letters from Neal as he sailed south and his ship stopped for supplies. He promised to write again after they'd sailed around the tip of Cape Horn, but there were no more letters. When one month turned to two and Neal should have arrived in California, I took a streetcar to see Meara, wandering through the maze of stinking streets and pitiful slums until I finally found her tenement. She hadn't heard from Gavin either. "But I did receive this, and I'm worried sick." She handed me a letter from Gavin's friend in San Francisco, asking if Gavin's plans had changed or if he'd been delayed, because the *Heiress* hadn't arrived. The dread I felt was indescribable.

I moved through the days and weeks and months, wondering where Neal was, murmuring useless prayers for his safety, trying everything I could think of to take my mind off him. Nothing worked. The newspapers printed fanciful stories describing life in the California gold fields and the perils would-be miners were experiencing in their quest for riches. Men were making—and sometimes losing—fortunes. And Neal was still missing.

Then the horrible day came when an article in the newspaper told of the fearsome storms that ships sometimes encountered as they sailed around the tip of Cape Horn. One lucky survivor told how he'd spotted three other ships battling the waves alongside his. The storm had tossed them around like corks throughout the night until he despaired of losing his life. In the morning, his battered ship was still afloat, but the other three had all sunk. Pieces of broken wreckage covered the churning waves all around him. Bloated bodies floated on the water. Only five survivors were found floating in the wreckage and were pulled onboard, all of them sailors, not passengers. The names of their sunken ships were the *Atlas*, the *Sea Quest*, and the *Heiress*.

I began to scream and couldn't stop. Aunt Agatha's servants came running to see what had happened. I was too incoherent with grief to explain. They gave me a dose of Aunt Agatha's laudanum and put me to bed.

For a long time, I refused to believe it. Neal would have survived. He had to survive! I couldn't function, unable to eat or sleep for days. When the shock began to fade, anger replaced it. I didn't care about jewels and diamonds and mansions; I wanted Neal Galloway—the man I loved! I roamed through the carriage house, willing him to be there, seeing him everywhere. I loved him, but he was gone.

When I could no longer deny the truth or expect a miracle, I went to see Meara and read the newspaper article to her. We grieved and mourned together as we faced the horrible truth that the *Heiress* had been lost. We would never see Neal or Gavin again.

I wanted to die and be with him. I imagined him saying, "Don't ye know what the Good Book says, love? There are bonny, grand mansions in heaven. We will be living in one together someday. I'll be waiting there for ye." I longed to die right now, but I wouldn't be allowed into heaven to be with Neal if I ended my own life.

I could no longer stay at Aunt Agatha's house where everything reminded me of Neal. My uncle hired a nurse to take care of her, along with a new carriage driver. I moved back to my parents' house. Neal was dead, and as much as I hated the thought, I had to go on living.

# 6

*Junietta*

"I think that's quite enough for today," Sylvia said, stopping Junietta midstory. "I won't have you putting silly thoughts into Adelaide's head with your talk of love and romance."

The morning room had grown warm as the autumn sun slanted through the windows. Telling her story had wrung much of Junietta's energy, but she believed it would be well worth it if she'd made an impression on her granddaughter. She wiped the tears that had fallen silently down her face as she'd relived Neal's death. Adelaide looked close to tears too, but of course Sylvia seemed unmoved. She stood as if determined to leave this time, even if it meant pushing Junietta's cane aside.

"You're idealizing a relationship that you've admitted was unacceptable and very unlikely to last," Sylvia said. "What could have ever come of it but a life of poverty?"

"He might have struck it rich in the gold fields."

"From what I heard, there were too many prospectors and too little gold in California. If Neal Galloway came home broke, like so many of them did, would you have been willing to live in the slums with pigs and cholera and who knows what other diseases?"

"He never would have allowed me to live that way. That's why he sailed off to California in the first place. He believed he could make his own fortune, and I believed it too. And why not? John Jacob Astor and Cornelius Vanderbilt are self-made millionaires, aren't they? It's the American Dream. We could add Addy's great-grandfather, Arthur Benton Stanhope I, to that list, too."

"Well, we've heard enough. I won't have you glamorizing inappropriate behavior, such as roaming the city without a chaperone. Not to mention fraternizing with the carriage driver." She swept from the room.

Addy rose to follow her but Junietta stopped her. "One final word about love, Adelaide. My heart was broken when Neal's ship went down. When you dare to love someone, you'll always risk the pain of loss. A broken heart, like a broken leg, will heal in time. You'll dance again someday. But the greater your love, the greater your limp will always be. You might even need one of these." She held up the cane for a moment, then lowered it so Addy could pass.

"Your cane, Mimi—is it the one Neal made for your Aunt Agatha?"

Junietta held it out to show her the exquisitely carved lion's-head grip, the delicate vines and flowers that spiraled down the shaft. "One and the same. It's why I always carry it wherever I go. It's my way of holding on to Neal." She reached to take Addy's hand. "Please think about what I'm trying to tell you, Addy dear. I pray that you'll dare to fall in love. Please don't settle for anything less, like your sisters did. In fact, ask them about love if you don't believe me. Ask if their beautiful homes and all their wealth is a fair trade for loving someone and being loved in return. Ask if they're happy and fulfilled."

Addy nodded and squeezed Junietta's hand before letting go. "Are you all right, Mimi? I think we've tired you out. You look pale. Do you want one of the servants to help you upstairs?"

"Nonsense. I'm fine. You go ahead, dear. I believe I'll sit here with my memories for just a bit longer." Addy kissed her cheek and left.

Junietta wasn't fine. It wasn't even midday, and she felt too exhausted to climb the stairs, even with the servants' help. She had been sneaking her doctors in and out of the mansion for the past few weeks, ordering them and the servants not to mention her illness to Sylvia and Adelaide—although they were much too preoccupied, and the mansion was much too large for them to notice what was happening in Junietta's life. The doctors had attempted to drain some of the fluid from her ankles, which had also drained her. They'd commanded her to rest. *Rest?* How could she rest when she still had a foundation to run? The charities it supported didn't stop needing help simply because Junietta's heart was acting jiggety. It required all her strength, but she still managed to oversee the foundation for a few hours every week and continue searching for her replacement. Her lawyers had assured her that, for now, the foundation was safe from a takeover by Roger or Randall Stanhope.

"The Stanhope Charitable Foundation is a separate entity from the rest of the Stanhopes' inheritance," Mr. Wilson had told her.

"So there have been no moves on their part to take it over?" she'd asked.

He'd given what might have passed for a smile. "From what I understand, your brother-in-law and nephew are working very hard just to take over the businesses they have inherited. I gather your son never gave them any part in running things?"

"No. And for a very good reason."

"The charitable foundation has a board of directors, as you well know, Mrs. Stanhope. Any changes in leadership would have to go through the board. I believe you're safe."

Junietta had yet to find a new board member to replace her son, let alone a strong, capable person to take her own place. She leaned back in her chair and closed her eyes, holding her cane tightly and thinking of Neal.

## ~ Sylvia ~

Sylvia had hurried from the morning room, unwilling to reveal how moved she had been by Junietta's story. It had brought back painful memories of her own first love, which had been even more inappropriate than Junietta's. She had no time for strolls down memory lane right now. She couldn't allow anything to distract her from her task of salvaging her family's future. The young lawyer, Mr. Forsythe, had been coming to meet with her every few days, patiently explaining the household finances to her, now that all the accounts had been handed over. Sylvia had found it overwhelming, yet she was determined to fight. She would not give up, even if worry kept her awake most nights.

Mr. Forsythe arrived on time later that afternoon, greeting her with his usual pleasant smile. He'd seemed very young to Sylvia—barely thirty, she guessed—but he was proving to be a wise and capable teacher. "In the past, your husband was the sole heir of all his father's and grandfather's assets," he had explained. "Expenses were paid directly from the company's bank accounts. Those accounts have now been inherited by your husband's uncle." As they had tallied all the monthly expenses, the cost of running this enormous mansion had stunned Sylvia. Now that she had a clearer picture of what she was facing, she was desperate for a solution.

"I know you've advised me against spending the money in Adelaide's and my trust funds too quickly," she told him as he sat down across the desk from her. "But I need to keep our household functioning normally for as long as I possibly can. I'm hoping you can help me find some alternative sources of income."

"Have you considered selling your family's yacht? I understand it's worth a fair amount."

For a moment, Sylvia pictured her husband standing in the bow as the vessel cut through the waves, the breeze tousling his hair. "A.B. was enamored with the *Merriweather*," she murmured. "He was never happier than when sailing aboard it. But after looking at the figures you gave me, I understand that the cost of operating it, compared to the number of days we actually sailed on it, makes keeping it impractical. I know we'll need to sell it—but not yet." He looked at her as if waiting for an explanation, but he was too polite to pry. Sylvia hated that anyone knew about her financial distress, but she felt she could trust this young man. "Selling it would send up a signal that we need money, you see, and I don't want to do that. Not until after Adelaide has found a suitor and I can be sure she will be taken care of."

"I understand. But perhaps we can make some discreet inquiries into potential buyers? I think people would understand that the yacht was your husband's hobby, not yours. And an asset like that may take some time to sell."

Sylvia closed her eyes for a moment, aware that this was probably only the first of many losses. Junietta had advised Sylvia to embrace change, to let go of all this and begin a new life. But how could she? How would she live? What would she do? "Very well," she finally said. "I could always explain that I couldn't bear to sail on the *Merriweather* without him."

He gave her a gentle smile and turned over a page in his notes. "And do you still want us to try to broker an agreement with Roger Stanhope for a share in the summer home in Newport?"

"No, I've given it some more thought, and after seeing how much it costs to run the summer mansion, I've decided to let it go. Besides, I trust that Adelaide will be betrothed by next summer. In the meantime, I need to find a way to continue living here and to continue the illusion that we aren't struggling."

He tapped his pen against the page of figures as he looked it over. "Fortunately, your husband didn't leave you with any huge outstanding debts. And the creditors who do remain will understand the need to wait until the estate is settled before demanding payment."

The thought of creditors hounding her made Sylvia feel ill. "Mr. Forsythe, please tell me. Do you think I'm being foolish for struggling so hard to keep this mansion?"

He paused before replying. "I think that's a decision only you can make."

"What would you do if you were me?"

"I . . . I suppose I would pray about it."

His answer startled Sylvia, but she tried not to show it. She simply nodded and looked down at the unrelenting columns of figures again, feeling dangerously close to tears. "I'll let you go for today, Mr. Forsythe, so you can look into selling our yacht."

"Very well."

Sylvia thought about his advice for a long time after he left. *Prayer?* It was something she rarely thought about aside from a Sunday church service. She was not on speaking terms with the Almighty, especially if it had been His idea to take away her husband so suddenly. And prayer had never done her much good in the past.

She swallowed her tears and stared at the figures again, aware of the need to cut more of her monthly costs. One enormous expense that jumped out at her was having gowns made for herself and Adelaide. They would need new mourning clothes, of course. And Adelaide would need a new gown to wear when she was introduced to potential suitors. In the past, they had often travelled to Paris to have their gowns designed by Charles Frederick Worth, but that was out of the question now. Even having original designs made here in New York would be expensive.

Sylvia's anxiety sprouted tendrils that squeezed her chest. *Prayer?* Was it blasphemous to pray about new clothes? Yet what else could she do? She was still pondering the question when a sudden thought struck her. Why not try to design some new gowns herself? She knew what all the latest fashions were. And she knew which design features would best flatter her daughter and herself. Sylvia wasn't sure where the thought had come from, but she decided it was a good one. She felt a tremor of excitement as she rummaged through her husband's desk drawers, finding sheets of paper, some sharpened pencils, and even a new Waterman fountain pen.

She shoved the ledgers with their endless rows of figures aside and began to sketch. The fresh white paper and the feel of the pencil in her fingers made her smile. The gown she pictured in her head took shape as she doodled and sketched and shaded. And along with her creation came so many memories.

### ⁓ Adelaide ⁓

A week crawled by in dreary boredom. Addy had little to do except stare at her calendar, longing to see her friends and take part in all the social events she was missing. She could almost understand how Mimi might be lonely enough to strike up a conversation with the carriage driver, especially if he was a charming Scotsman. Even worse than the boredom was the worry. Adelaide understood that their financial situation was precarious. She could solve their problems by marrying well, but how could she court a wealthy suitor when she was in mourning and unable to attend parties?

At last, relief from the tedium came one afternoon when Mother summoned her downstairs to Father's study. The family lawyer, Mr. Forsythe, was just leaving as Addy arrived. He had been coming and going often as he helped Mother sort out Father's will, and today he nearly bumped into Addy as he emerged through the study door.

"Oh! I'm so sorry, Miss Stanhope," he said, backing up a step. "I should learn not to be in such a rush."

"It's quite all right."

He hesitated for a moment as if wanting to say something more.

"Yes? What is it?" she asked.

"I don't believe I've had a chance to express my condolences to you, Miss Stanhope, at the loss of your father. I know that your family must still be grieving—a process that can seem as wearying and endless as crossing a vast desert. I just wanted you to know that my prayers are with you. I hope you find comfort and consolation in your memories of him."

It seemed like an extraordinary thing for a lawyer to say, yet his thoughtfulness touched her. Addy knew she had Mother's habit of ignoring the working people around her, and the lawyer had been no exception. Her grandmother, on the other hand, befriended everyone she met—including her carriage drivers. "Thank you, Mr. Forsythe," she finally said, unable to think of anything else. "Good day to you."

"Good day."

Mother beckoned to her from behind Father's desk. "Come in, Adelaide, and close the door." The heavy velvet draperies that had blanketed the windows were still drawn back as Mimi had requested on the day the will was read, and the study didn't seem nearly as dark and dreary as Addy remembered it in the past. "I've planned a very small dinner party to introduce you to some potential suitors. Only about fifty guests in all." Addy smiled. Leave it to Mother to call fifty guests a small party. "Let's not say anything to your grandmother about it for now, so she won't subject us to any more of her inappropriate stories."

"Do you think her stories are really true?"

"Who knows. She has always had a vivid imagination. Come look at this, Adelaide. Tell me what you think." Addy circled the desk to peer over Mother's shoulder at a sketch of an evening gown. It was so beautifully drawn that the gown's long sleeves and shoulder panels looked to be made from a translucent fabric like chiffon. The tightly fitted bodice resembled dark beaded lace. The long slim skirt looked to be of velvet.

"What a beautiful dress. Where did this come from?"

"Well, since we can't sail to Paris to consult a designer, I sketched it myself. I'm going to ask my seamstress to make it for me for our dinner party."

"It's beautiful!" Addy breathed. She meant the skill of the drawing as well as the gown itself. How had mother drawn and shaded the fabric so realistically?

"I may be required to wear black, but that doesn't mean I have to look drab and dowdy. I drew a gown for you too. Here, tell me what you think." She handed Adelaide a second drawing, and the gown was even more beautiful than the blue silk one that Addy had wanted to wear to Ellen Madison's ball. It had a flattering square neckline, gently puffed sleeves, and a flowing flared skirt that looked to be watered silk taffeta. She stared at the sketch, then at her mother as if seeing a stranger. Mimi's words came flooding back to her: *"Sylvia sacrificed something she loved and that was so much a part of who she was in order to live this vacuous life. That's why she can't bear to lose it now."*

"I've asked my seamstress to come today with some fabric samples," Mother said, interrupting Addy's thoughts. "I want to find just the right shade of gray for you. It needs to be a warm gray, so it won't make you look sickly. Almost a mauve, I'm thinking. She'll also be taking our measurements." She looked up at Addy, who was still staring at her. "You look thinner to me, Adelaide. You're not ill, are you?"

"I haven't had an appetite since Father died." How could she eat when her own future and that of her mother and grandmother were in jeopardy? She walked around the desk again and slumped down in the chair. She was about to comment on Mother's artistic ability, and how she'd never known of it before seeing her watercolor, when the door latch rattled noisily. Mimi Junie entered, pushing the door open with her ever-present cane.

"I was just talking to Mr. Forsythe as he was leaving," she said. "He told me I would find you two in here. More business with A.B.'s will?"

"Something like that." Mother hurried to hide the sketches, but Mimi was quicker. She pinned the drawings to the desk with her cane, then drew them over to her side to look at them.

"You've been leaving me out of your grand schemes again, Sylvia. One might begin to feel unwanted if this continues."

"It's not a secret. I'm having new dresses made for Adelaide and myself. Please bring Madame Stanhope an extra cup for coffee," Mother told the servant who had followed Mimi into the study. Addy rose to give Mimi her chair, then dragged another one over so she could sit beside her.

Mimi studied the sketches. "You drew these yourself." It was a comment, not a question. Addy heard admiration in her tone and saw it in her eyes. "Such talent. Are the gowns for a special occasion?"

"Yes. I was just telling Adelaide about it. I've planned a small memorial dinner for A.B.'s birthday in November. He would have turned forty-seven. Just a simple affair with some of A.B.'s associates and friends to honor his memory. There were so many people at his funeral that I didn't have a chance to thank them properly. I didn't think you would be interested in planning all the silly details with us."

"Not interested? A.B. was my son. If this dinner is to honor his memory, why wouldn't I be interested?"

"Of course, Junietta. You're welcome to join us."

"I thought we were about to become beggars," Mimi said as she sat down. "Where is all the money coming from for new gowns and a dinner party?"

"One must risk investing money in order to make money."

"*Make* money?" She looked from Mother to Adelaide, then back again. "Ah, I see. The birthday dinner is just an excuse. You're still plotting to find a wealthy suitor for Adelaide, aren't you? Well, go ahead. Continue with your party plans. Don't mind me," she said, settling back.

"It won't be a party, Junietta. It isn't appropriate to have music or dancing yet." The maid scuttled in with an extra cup, breathless from the long trip to the kitchen. The room was silent as she poured the coffee. "Thank you, Jane," Mimi said when she finished. Addy saw Mother flinch. It annoyed her when Mimi called the servants by name. Mother drew a breath and addressed Addy, ignoring Mimi Junie.

"A quiet dinner will give you a chance to mingle with your father's associates and meet new people. I've learned of two interesting potential suitors, and you will be seated between them at the dinner. I considered giving two separate parties and inviting these men individually but decided it would be better to spark a little competition between them. Men enjoy the challenge of a rival."

Mimi gave a short laugh. "Now you're the silver cup at the end of the horse race, Addy."

Mother didn't react. "It will be a challenge to keep both men equally engaged and interested in you over dinner, but I know you're up to the task. Keep in mind that it's never a good idea to talk about politics. And stay away from women's suffrage. Most gentlemen don't care for a woman who takes an interest in such unfeminine things. Don't talk about the war with Spain or about President McKinley, unless one of the gentlemen brings him up. But if they do talk about world affairs or things of that nature, be sure to ask good questions, as if their opinions fascinate you, and you want to hear more. Men like to appear knowledgeable and to show off. Don't ever let on that you know more about a subject than they do."

"The weather is usually a safe topic," Mimi said. "The record-breaking cold spell we had last winter is positively fascinating." Adelaide heard the laughter in her grandmother's tone and bit her lip to keep from smiling. "And why not ask his opinion on the newest states to join the Union? North and South Dakota are endlessly intriguing and certain to make any gentleman fall head over heels in love with you."

"Junietta, please."

"Whatever you do, don't mention any tragedies like that big hotel fire." Mimi added in a stage whisper, "That's still a *hot* topic."

Mother sighed. "I find it best in any good conversation to look to the future. What new innovations does one foresee? What are one's hopes for the new century that's on the horizon? Music is usually a safe topic, but be careful not to express too strong of an opinion. One never knows if you'll hit a nerve."

"In other words," Mimi said, "Adelaide is to reveal nothing of herself, her opinions, or her tastes. She is to be merely a pretty mirror that reflects her suitor's tastes, so he can gaze at himself like a preening Narcissus."

"You aren't helping."

"Well, if she can't be herself when she's courting, how will she ever become herself once she's married?" Again, Addy thought of how Mother had given up her artwork when she'd married.

"A wife's role is to support her husband so he can be successful," Mother said. "She—" One of the servants entered, interrupting her. "Yes? What is it?"

"Your dressmaker is here, ma'am."

"Send her upstairs to my suite."

"Thank you, Hattie," Mimi called after her. She winked at Adelaide as if taking delight in annoying Mother.

Mother stood, gathering up her designs and other papers. "Come, Adelaide," she said. "You're welcome to join us, Junietta, if you'd like to entertain my seamstress with your opinions."

"Another day, perhaps. By the way, if Addy's suitors turn out to be duds, have you thought about earning your living as a fashion designer?"

Mother didn't reply, but as Addy followed her out the door, she heard Mother mutter, "Certainly not!"

# 7

NOVEMBER 1898

*Adelaide*

On the night of Father's posthumous birthday party in November, Adelaide battled an attack of nerves that made her stomach cramp. The gown Mother designed had turned out beautifully, and as Addy admired herself in the mirror, she thought it showed off her graceful neck and slender waist to good effect. But she couldn't seem to sit still as Mother's maid swept her hair into the popular Gibson Girl style with dozens of hairpins. Her family's future depended on her.

Mother joined her as the maid was fastening the final hairpin. "You look beautiful, Adelaide. You'll take everyone's breath away."

"Thank you. You look lovely too, Mother." The black gown made her fair skin glow like mother-of-pearl. Mother stood behind Addy at the dressing table, talking to her reflection in the mirror.

"I want to tell you a little bit about the two new gentlemen you'll be meeting. Mr. George Weaver is a widower with three daughters. He's a millionaire, of course, but he hasn't had time to acquire all the trappings of one. You can provide those things for him, including this mansion."

"I assume he wants a wife who can bear sons and heirs?"

"Naturally." She tucked a loose curl of Addy's hair into place. "The other gentleman, Mr. Byron Albright, is younger and a bachelor. He comes from a fine family, but he has been sowing his wild oats, as they say, and hasn't settled down yet. His very wealthy father is eager for him to marry and take an interest in the family business. A sensible wife would offer stability."

"I'll do my best, Mother." She tried to sound poised and confident as her stomach cramped again.

"Good. Now, let's see if your grandmother will let you borrow her pearls."

"Is she joining us for the dinner?"

"Yes, and I hope she doesn't do something to disrupt the evening. She has been very outspoken since your father passed away." When they entered her suite, Mimi was sitting in her chair beside the window dressed in a plain black gown. Addy wondered if it was grief that made her look so weary and gray.

"You look beautiful, both of you!" Mimi gushed. "One would never guess in a million years that your gowns weren't designed by Charles Frederick Worth."

"You won't tell anyone, will you, Junietta?" Mother asked.

"I shall forget I ever knew their origin."

"I thought your pearls with the amethyst clasp and matching amethyst earrings would be the perfect complement for Adelaide's dress. May she borrow them for the evening?"

"I don't have them anymore."

Mother frowned. "Really? I thought they had sentimental value."

"I've never been a sentimental person."

"Well, you might have bequeathed them to one of your granddaughters."

"I might have—but I didn't."

Mother waited as if expecting an explanation. It never came. "I see.

Well, come to my room then, Adelaide. We'll find something else for you to wear."

⸺⸺⸻⸺⸺

The guests seemed to pour through the front door all at once, as if blown inside by the blustery autumn wind. Adelaide's memory was taxed as she labored to recall everyone's names and their places in society. The vast entryway had been decorated with a few garlands and flower-filled urns, but nothing at all like Mother's usual lavish displays. The same was true of the simple centerpieces on the dining room table, set for fifty people. Even with everyone seated, the table seemed to float in the cavernous room like a rowboat in the Atlantic.

Addy's stomach was still clenched like a fist as she greeted George Weaver, the widower. He was in his forties, much older than Addy had expected, and her vision of being a stepmother to three young girls vanished. It was possible that his daughters might be closer to her own age. "I'm so sorry about your father, Miss Stanhope," he said as he greeted her. "He was a great help to me when I was looking for investors to help expand my business. He will be missed."

The only word to describe the second gentleman, Byron Albright, was *arrogant*. As he sauntered into the foyer, he looked Adelaide up and down in a way that was nothing short of lewd. Rather than being dazzled by her as she tried to converse with him, he seemed indifferent, as if he saw through their families' schemes and wanted nothing to do with them.

Addy stifled yawns of boredom throughout dinner as Mr. Weaver droned on and on about the Spanish-American War. Not about the battles or the war itself, which at least would have been interesting. But about how advantageous the conflict had been for his company's profits. Mr. Albright talked about racing his motorcycle and seemed to know a great deal about the design and construction of Mr. Eiffel's famous tower in Paris. But he was dismissive of most of the conversations around him unless he was the center of attention. Addy had disliked Byron Albright within moments of meeting him, so the thought of courting him, let alone marrying him, made her shudder, as did the idea of marrying a man close to her father's age. But she would do whatever she had to do for her family's sake.

Throughout the evening, Mimi Junie sat at the far end of the dinner table, watching Addy. Her knowing smiles made Addy self-conscious and even more nervous. She had to admit that this ritual felt phony, the idea of pursuing a husband for his money dishonest. She remembered how joy had animated Mimi's face when she'd spoken of the carriage driver she'd once loved, and as the evening dragged on, Addy wondered what it would be like to fall in love and to be loved in return.

—⟨⟨⟨ *Sylvia* ⟩⟩⟩—

Sylvia had watched the evening's events unfold feeling as if she were holding her breath. Nothing less than her daughter's future was at stake. Adelaide had seemed nervous, but that was to be expected under the circumstances. The pressure on her was much greater than it had been on her sisters when they had begun courting. When the door finally closed on the last of their guests, she asked Addy to follow her to her bedroom suite, where her lady's maid was waiting to help Sylvia change from her evening clothes. "So, tell me, Adelaide. What did you think of the two gentlemen you met tonight?"

Adelaide stared at the floor, chewing her lip. "Mr. Weaver was . . . pleasant. Perhaps a bit older than I was expecting."

Older than Sylvia had expected as well. Closer to her own age than Adelaide's. "Marriage to a man who is more settled and mature could be a good thing." The maid helped Sylvia into her dressing gown, and she sat at her vanity as the girl removed her hairpins and brushed her hair. "What did you think of Mr. Albright?" Adelaide hesitated as if searching for a way to deliver bad news. "Never mind. I didn't like him either. He isn't worth our time, even with his piles of money." Adelaide's shoulders seemed to sag with relief. Sylvia wanted to remind her of the importance of good posture, but the poor girl seemed too weary to care. "You did wonderfully well tonight, darling. It was a very good beginning. And I learned the names of a few more interesting gentlemen to invite to our next dinner. Now, go get a good night's sleep. You've earned it."

"Good night, Mother." She kissed Sylvia's cheek and left the room.

"You may go too," Sylvia told the maid after she'd hung up the gown.

Alone again. Weariness filled Sylvia, yet she knew she wouldn't sleep. She crossed to the door to A.B.'s adjoining suite and peered into the darkness. His scent still hovered in the room. He always came to her after they'd hosted an event like this one, and they would talk and laugh together about everything that had transpired. A.B.'s comments and observations could be as sharp and impertinent as his mother's at times. Sylvia hadn't bargained on the waves of grief that had struck her as she'd presided over the evening for the first time without her husband by her side. And it would be this way for the rest of her life. Today was his birthday, the dinner in his honor, which had meant accepting her guests' condolences and listening to their well-meaning memories of him.

Tears blurred her vision as she closed the door again and went to sit on the edge of her bed. As far as the two potential suitors were concerned, the evening had been a failure. All that money and effort and worry for nothing. How many more dinners could she afford to host, and how many more obnoxious gentlemen like Mr. Albright would they have to endure before finding a worthy husband for Adelaide?

And once they did, what would come next in her own life?

### ⤙ Junietta ⤚

Junietta had marshaled all her energy to attend Sylvia's dinner party two days ago and had felt ridiculously weak ever since. Too weak to go to the foundation, which was still without a leader to replace her. Too weak to talk sense into her gold-digging daughter-in-law's head. God forbid that Addy married George Weaver, a man old enough to be her father. Or a man like Byron Albright who was too spoiled to behave politely. Junietta was used to charging through life with energy and purpose. Being ill was so frustrating!

She was surprised when Hattie brought her a note from Sylvia along with her breakfast tray that morning. She was being summoned to A.B.'s study at eleven o'clock. "I'll need you to help me climb out of bed and get dressed, Hattie."

"Are you sure you're feeling strong enough, ma'am?"

"Yes, dear girl. Don't you worry about me. But remember, you've given me your word not to tell anyone how much help I need."

"I won't, ma'am."

Junietta ignored her sputtering heart and painful ankles, determined to make her way downstairs if it killed her. She hobbled into the study at eleven o'clock sharp and surveyed the ledger books open on the desktop. "What? No sketches today, Sylvia? I was so looking forward to seeing more of them."

"We have business to attend to."

She spotted Mr. Forsythe, standing at attention near the window. "Good morning, Mr. Forsythe. How are you this morning?"

"I'm fine, Madame Stanhope. Thank you." His handsome grin charmed her. He held Junietta's chair for her as she sank into it with a sigh.

"Hold on to this for me, would you, young man?" she asked, handing him her cane. "And you may use it any way you'd like during our meeting, at any point that seems appropriate." He gave her a bemused look and took the cane from her as if flowers might pop out of it like from a magician's wand. "It makes a wonderful sound when you whack the desk with it," she added.

Adelaide arrived a moment later and kissed Junietta's cheek before sitting beside her. "Let's begin," Sylvia said. "I've been going over all our finances with Mr. Forsythe's help, and I've decided that the three of us will need to work together if we're going to continue living the way we're accustomed to. I know what my own trust fund consists of, and what Adelaide's does, so I'm going to be blunt and ask you straight out, Junietta—how much money do you have to contribute toward our living expenses?"

"None at all."

Sylvia leaned back in her chair. "Don't be ridiculous. I know your husband left you an inheritance, and you surely have a generous living allowance from that trust fund."

"What can I tell you?" Junietta said with a shrug. "The money he left me is long gone."

"Gone? Where?"

"I donated it all to the Stanhope Charitable Foundation. Heaven knows, there are plenty of poor souls in this city who needed it more than I did. Until his unfortunate passing, my son was supporting me quite generously."

Sylvia stared at her in silence for several moments. She had seemed so strong and self-assured when Junietta had first entered the study, but now she sagged like a deflated balloon. "That's very disappointing news," Sylvia said at last. "I was hoping we could use some of your inheritance to buy Adelaide some more time—"

"To ensnare a wealthy husband?"

"—but since you have nothing to contribute, I'll need to rely on my second plan."

"Which is?"

"I thought the three of us could go through some of the extra, unused rooms in this house and choose furniture pieces, artwork, and other valuables that we can sell to raise capital. Mr. Forsythe will help us get a fair price for everything at auction. And he promised to do it discreetly, so no one sees our household goods being taken away."

Junietta grinned with delight. "How very clandestine! Imagine! Handsome Mr. Forsythe in black clothing and a balaclava, sneaking our worldly possessions out of the house under the cover of darkness!"

Mr. Forsythe made a sputtering noise as if trying to stifle a laugh. "Sorry. Sorry," he said when everyone looked at him.

Junietta turned to Adelaide with a mock-serious expression. "Addy, you'll need to make sure that the wealthy gentlemen your mother dupes into courting you don't see all of our looted rooms until after your marriage vows have been spoken."

Sylvia huffed. "I don't think you're taking our situation seriously, Junietta."

"Oh, you're wrong, there. I do know how serious it is, believe me. But listen, you've subjected Adelaide to your little dinner party and your furniture-selling schemes, so now it's my turn. I would like to take her on a little excursion later this week."

"This isn't a contest."

She leaned forward to face Sylvia. "I love Adelaide as much as you do, and I have every right to help mold her opinions and show her some different options for her life. Fair enough?"

"After hearing how you roamed the city alone when you were Addy's age, I hope you know that it's still inappropriate for the two of you to wander around unescorted."

"You'll come with us to protect us, won't you, Mr. Forsythe?" Junietta asked, turning to him.

"Me?" He had looked as though he wanted to shrink into the woodwork after being caught snickering, but now he scrambled to attention, the cane propped against his shoulder like a soldier's rifle.

"Yes, my dear man. You. I believe that what I have in mind could fall under the heading of settling my son's estate."

"Well, in that case, I—"

"Good. We'll expect you here at one o'clock on Thursday." She prayed she would find the strength by then.

## Adelaide

Mr. Forsythe was waiting in the foyer Thursday afternoon when Adelaide came downstairs with Mimi for their mysterious excursion. He stood beside the statue of Aristotle, caressing the cool, smooth marble. "Would you like to take a tour of our cozy little mansion, Mr. Forsythe?" Mimi asked. Her voice echoed in the grand space. "You've been no further than our main entry and my son's dreary office down the corridor, have you?"

"I'm not sure that would be appropriate."

"Nonsense. There's a possibility that we might have to sell this house, isn't there? And if so, you'll be handling the transaction?"

Addy felt a wave of nausea at the thought of selling her home. The only thing she could do to prevent that from happening was to marry well.

"I suppose that's true," Mr. Forsythe replied.

"Show him around, Adelaide. I'm too lame for such a lengthy trek."

"Um, Madame Stanhope, it really isn't necessary—"

"Nonsense. Off you go. I'll wait here." She gave him a gentle push with her cane and sat down on one of the marble benches to wait.

"This way," Addy said with a sigh.

She led him through each of the grand downstairs rooms, walking briskly, hoping to get the tour over with quickly. She had to slow her steps several times because he kept stopping to gaze in open-mouthed awe at the elaborate hand-painted ceilings, the crystal chandeliers hovering above him, and the massive marble fireplaces. She heard him murmuring, "Wow!" and "Goodness!" beneath his breath. And she lost him altogether in the two-story library when he paused to scan the titles and admire her grandfather's globe. "It would take a lifetime to read all these wonderful books," he said in a hushed voice. "Do you know how many volumes there are, Miss Stanhope?"

"I have no idea." She was ashamed to admit that she rarely explored these shelves.

"Do you think your mother will sell some of these books?"

Addy felt a pang of regret at the thought. But what good were hundreds of dusty books when her family needed money? "I really couldn't say. Hopefully, our financial circumstances will improve before that becomes necessary." She turned and quickly moved on, hoping he would follow.

By the time they'd toured most of the main floor and returned to the foyer, Mr. Forsythe seemed overwhelmed. And he hadn't seen any of the mansion's other two stories.

"Well, what did you think of the house, Mr. Forsythe?" Mimi asked after they were settled in the carriage and on their way. The November afternoon was cold, and Addy shivered beneath the carriage blanket. "Adelaide and I would love to hear your honest opinion."

Mr. Forsythe paused as if reluctant to reply. "Well, I've really never seen anything like it. I've always wondered, you know . . . I mean, looking at a mansion like yours from the outside . . . I suppose I've wondered what it would look like inside."

"Do you wish you lived in a house like ours?"

His grin was quick and genuine. "I try to avoid the sin of envy. Not coveting is one of the Ten Commandments, isn't it? The Book of Proverbs warns that envy can rot the bones."

"You're avoiding my question, young man. I'll give you a five-dollar tip to be honest with me."

He looked down at the floor of the carriage, blushing. He seemed to blush a lot. "It won't be necessary to pay me, Mrs. Stanhope. Your home is very beautiful."

"But . . ?" She pressed her cane against the toe of his shiny black shoe. "Come on, let's hear the rest of it."

"Well, it doesn't really seem like a home. That is, like a place where a family could live." He glanced at Addy, and his cheeks turned a deeper shade of red. "Oh dear. I'm so sorry. I mean, you are a family, of course. But I can't picture children playing in all those huge rooms and endless hallways. It just isn't very—cozy. It seems like a small child could easily get lost. I would have been lost if Miss Stanhope had abandoned me."

Adelaide had feared that very thing when she was small. Her sisters had taken delight in luring her into an unfamiliar part of the mansion, then running off and leaving her there. She had been afraid to move, afraid that the house would swallow her up like the whale in Mimi's Bible stories had swallowed poor Jonah. She'd had to cry for help until one of the servants rescued her. Her sisters had also loved to tease her after she'd climbed into bed at night, telling her that the mansion's many statues came alive after dark and were going to creep into her room and turn her into stone like one of them. She shivered at the memory.

"You should see the mansions in Newport, Rhode Island, that our social set calls their 'cottages,'" Mimi continued. "We used to own one of them, as you may recall."

"Yes. That was a very unfortunate loss."

"Have you ever been to Newport, Mr. Forsythe?"

"No, ma'am."

"Alva Vanderbilt started the 'cottage' competition when she built Marble House with a mere fifty rooms. Then her brother-in-law, Cornelius Vanderbilt the second, decided to outdo her by building The Breakers with seventy rooms. And these are just our summer homes that we use for only a fraction of the year. Outrageously wasteful. Don't you think?"

He smiled. "It's . . . um . . . not for me to judge how other people live."

Addy thought he had a nice smile, sincere and friendly and warm.

"Of course it is! We all make judgments, all the time. Whether we say them out loud or not is another matter."

"I like to keep my judgments to myself. As the Good Book says, 'Judge not, that ye be not judged.'"

"My, my! A lawyer who quotes the Good Book. That's a first for me, young man."

He gave a shy shrug. "My father is a minister."

"Really? What made you decide to become a lawyer?"

"Well, an anonymous sponsor who had lost a loved one offered to pay for my education. For my two brothers' educations as well. Another anonymous sponsor recommended me to Mr. Wilson's law firm—and here I am."

"Do you enjoy what you do?"

When he hesitated, Adelaide decided to speak up. "Don't interrogate him, Mimi. It's really none of our business." Everything about this conversation seemed contrary to Mother's instructions for making polite conversation with a gentleman. Was Mimi doing it on purpose to prove a point? Addy needed to focus Mimi's attention elsewhere. "Where exactly are we going, Mimi Junie? You didn't say."

"You'll see. We're nearly there. Henry knows the way." The gentle carriage driver had worked for Mimi Junie for as far back as Addy could remember, taking care of their stables and horses. Henry was in charge of all the stable boys and drivers, but he drove a carriage only for Mimi Junie.

Addy wiped condensation from the carriage window and peered outside. They had traveled to a part of the city where she had never been before, and she was shocked when groups of dirty, raggedy children hurried to jog alongside their carriage. "Please, Miss, please," they begged, stretching their filthy hands toward the carriage. None of them were dressed for such cold weather.

Addy was about to ask Henry to go faster, worried the children would try to climb inside, but Mimi spoke before she could. "Stop for a minute, Henry. We don't want anyone to get trampled." Mimi must have been expecting to encounter the urchins, because she pulled a handful of coins from her pocket and opened her door. "Help me pass these out, would you, please?" She gave coins to Addy and Mr. Forsythe, then handed out the rest of them herself. "There, now. One for each of you. Don't crowd. I have enough for everyone."

"Poor little souls," Mr. Forsythe murmured. "I suppose these pennies are a lot of money to them."

"Mm. Indeed," Mimi replied. "And did you notice how young they are? Their older siblings are probably at work in a factory somewhere. They'll be working too, in another year or so."

The scene was repeated several times as they continued through the dreadful neighborhoods. The derelict tenements, which Mimi said housed dozens of families, looked ready to topple down. Lines of old women waited to draw water at the single spigot. The carriage bounced through potholes in the uneven streets. The stench of rotting garbage and filth and human waste became so foul that Addy pulled a handkerchief from her pocket to cover her mouth and nose. "What is that terrible smell?" she asked.

"It's a little bit of everything," Mimi said, "but today I believe that dead horse over there is contributing the most." Addy saw the carcass lying along the side of the street, covered with flies, and she quickly averted her eyes. But not before seeing several small children poking the corpse with sticks. "Trust me, it smells much worse on a hot summer day. It's hard to believe this is the same city where we live, isn't it?"

Addy didn't reply. She knew her grandmother was doing this on purpose, taking her through this terrible area to make some sort of point. She wanted to tell her she'd gotten the message and ask if they could move on now. But then they turned the corner into a slightly better area and halted in front of a large four-story brick building. Addy thought it resembled a train station, but she didn't see any rails leading in or out. A central steeple might have been a clock tower or bell tower, but it had neither. The building had plentiful windows for light and air, and open-air porches along the side of each floor. When the clomping horses stopped, Addy heard the squeals and laughter of children nearby.

"Now, Mr. Forsythe," Mimi said before they stepped down from the carriage. "You and Adelaide were both there when Sylvia asked how I had spent my inheritance. Well, this orphan asylum is one of my investments. I especially wanted you to see it, Mr. Forsythe, so you wouldn't judge me for being wasteful with my money. And I wanted you to see it, Adelaide, so you'll know there are more worthwhile things to spend money on than pearls and jewels and silk gowns."

Henry tethered the horses and helped Mimi and Adelaide alight from the carriage. A pretty middle-aged woman rushed forward to greet Mimi, taking both of her hands as they kissed each other's cheeks. Adelaide was astounded by Mimi Junie's easy familiarity with her.

"Harriet, I'd like you to meet my granddaughter, Adelaide Stanhope. And this is our family lawyer, Mr. Forsythe. Harriet Adams is my long-time friend and the assistant director here."

"I'm pleased to meet you," Addy said.

"Harriet, we were hoping you would show us around a little and tell us about this wonderful orphans' home."

"I would be happy to." Mrs. Adams led them through the warm lounges and gathering spaces on the first floor, greeting all the children they passed by name. They all wore green and red checked uniforms, the girls' dresses covered by white pinafores. Rows of long wooden tables filled the dining hall, with stools for the children to sit on. The wonderful aroma of baking bread drifted from the kitchen beyond. In the courtyard behind the building, a group of boys were pitching a baseball to each other and trying to hit it with a crude bat. When the batter swung and missed, the ball rolled over to land at Mr. Forsythe's feet. He smiled and tossed it back.

"Do you want to play with us, mister?" a boy asked him.

"Sure."

Addy watched as he strode over to the young pitcher, and the other boys quickly gathered around him. She couldn't hear what he was saying to them, but she judged by his gestures and the boys' rapt attention that he was giving them a few pointers. He laughed at something one of the boys said, and the hearty sound of it made her smile. Several minutes passed before he seemed to remember that he was supposed to be accompanying Mimi Junie. "I'm afraid I must be on my way," she heard him say. "I'm sorry." He hurried over to where Addy and Mimi were waiting. His dark hair had fallen over his forehead, and he raked it into place with his fingers, then straightened his overcoat. Addy thought he had looked more natural when slightly disheveled.

"I apologize for keeping you ladies waiting—"

"Think nothing of it," Mimi said. "I would play with these dear ones myself, if I were your age."

They returned inside to the main lounge. "Some of these children have living parents, but they're unable to care for them for various reasons," Mrs. Adams explained. "Others became orphans because of an outbreak such as cholera or diphtheria. We care for them until they're old enough to find work and live on their own. We're their family, you see." Adelaide did see. The older children watched over the younger ones with tender care. "The asylum was founded by three Quaker ladies in the late 1830s," Mrs. Adams continued. "I believe it's one of the first orphanages in America to care for Negro orphans. Before that, they were left to beg in the streets or were housed in jails, since no other orphanages wanted them. All our children receive an education through the sixth grade."

"I brought you here, Adelaide," Mimi Junie said, "because I wanted to give you some food for thought before you decide what to do with your inheritance. With what it will cost to run your mansion for a year, this home could feed and house these little ones for a dozen years."

Adelaide nodded, too embarrassed to reply. Thankfully, Mr. Forsythe broke the silence. "May I ask how you began supporting this place, Mrs. Stanhope?"

"The original orphan asylum burned to the ground during the draft riots in 1863," she said. "It was a terrible time, and the violence and loss of life were a disgrace to our city. I decided to help raise funds to construct this new building and continue the wonderful work they do."

When the tour ended, Mimi Junie thanked Mrs. Adams for her time. They were about to leave when one of the helpers hurried over. "Excuse me, Mrs. Stanhope. I thought you would like to know that Dr. Murphy is here today, checking on a few of our boys who've come down with measles. I know he would be very sorry to have missed you."

"Matthew? Why yes, I would love to see him!" A few minutes later, a well-dressed man in his late thirties came down the stairs with a medical bag. His face lit up when he saw Addy's grandmother, and he rushed over to embrace her warmly.

"Mama Junie! How wonderful to see you!"

"It's so good to see you, son. It has been much too long." The obvious affection between them shocked Addy. He had called her *Mama* Junie. Was it just a term of endearment, or could he be the mysterious son she'd mentioned at the funeral? Mimi gestured to Addy and said, "Matthew, I would like you to meet my granddaughter, Adelaide Stanhope. And this is our family lawyer, Mr. Forsythe. Dr. Murphy is a very special man and very dear to me."

"I'm pleased to meet you both," the doctor said.

"Would you two excuse Matthew and me for a moment?" Mimi asked. "I'll be right back, and then we'll be on our way." She pulled the doctor aside to talk in private, and Addy heard them laughing with delight a moment later. She gazed around the main lounge while she waited and noticed a framed watercolor on the far wall that looked oddly familiar. She went to look at it more closely and was astounded to see her mother's initials, *SGW*, in the corner. The scene had the same leafy background and color palette as the picture Mimi had given Addy, but in this one, the mouse, rabbit, and frog were having a picnic.

"Does Mother know you gave her painting away?" she asked when Mimi came to stand beside her a few minutes later.

"I asked her if I could have it, and she told me she didn't care. Come, dear. I'm ready to leave."

Addy had a lot of questions for her grandmother, but she didn't want to ask them in front of Mr. Forsythe, fearing the answers might shock him. Mimi was an expert at shocking people. Instead, Addy waited until they were home again and Mr. Forsythe had driven away.

"Tell me more about Dr. Murphy. He called you *Mama* Junie."

"He's a darling man, isn't he? And a very gifted physician. Do you know he does all the work at the orphanage for free?"

"But who is he? How is it that you know each other so well? Is he . . . is he your son?"

Mimi laughed and took Addy's face in her hands to kiss her forehead. "I would love to tell you all my secrets, my dear child. But before I do, there's something I would like to say to you." She suddenly grew serious.

"What is it, Mimi?"

"I have no doubt at all that with your beauty and charm, you could find a wealthy husband who will support you and your mother in the style to which you are accustomed." She tenderly brushed a lock of hair from Addy's forehead, fallen loose after she'd removed her hat. "When you do marry, I hope you'll use your beauty and charm to convince your wealthy husband to support a worthy charity like the orphan asylum."

Before Addy could reply, Mimi saw one of the servants standing off to the side as if waiting to be noticed. "Yes, Betsy? Did you want to tell me something?"

"Mrs. Stanhope asked to see you and Miss Adelaide as soon as you return, Madame. She is in the east wing on the third floor."

"She probably wants to make sure I didn't turn you against her plans," Mimi told Addy. "You'd better hurry along so you can tell her where we've been. I'll join you in a few minutes."

"But you haven't answered my questions, Mimi."

"I will, dear. All in good time."

### ⟡⟶ Junietta ⟶⟡

Junietta sank down on a gilded chair in the foyer as soon as Adelaide was out of sight. The maid hovered over her, looking concerned. "Are you all right? Can I get you anything, ma'am?"

"You can help me navigate all these stairs in a minute so I can find Sylvia up on the third floor. But I'll need to catch my breath first." She wished her heart would slow its frantic pace, but there was nothing she could do about it. "Too bad my father-in-law didn't have the foresight to install an elevator when he built this monstrous house," she sighed.

With Betsy's help, Junietta slowly made her way up the endless stairs and found Sylvia in one of the spare bedroom suites, tying a yellow tag onto a Victorian side table. Yellow tags dangled from items all over the room—end tables, lamps, paintings, a pitcher and bowl set, a gilded mirror. The room felt cold, and Junietta guessed that the heat had been turned off in this and all the other unused rooms to save money. "I see you've been busy while we were gone," she said as she lowered herself onto a chair.

"Yes. But I felt I should ask your permission before putting these items up for sale. Would you kindly look them over, Junietta? I believe all these furnishings once belonged to you."

"I didn't buy any of them. My father-in-law hired the services of a decorating expert. I heartily approve of the sale—good riddance to all that clutter! But I do not necessarily approve of what you plan to do with the proceeds."

"I plan for the three of us to live off those proceeds."

"Yes, yes, until you can dupe a millionaire into marrying Addy and taking care of us in style. I know."

"You keep insisting that Addy marry for love and not for money, but isn't that what you did? Why did you agree to marry Art Stanhope if you weren't in love with him?"

"You asked an honest question, so you deserve an honest answer, and here it is: I had no choice. Arthur Stanhope wanted his son to marry a Knickerbocker, and so I was bartered for and bought. It was my own fault, really, for ending up in that position."

Sylvia and Adelaide stared at her, waiting. The time had come for Junietta to tell them the rest of the story about her past. She could only pray that the truth would influence their decisions about the future. "You see," she began, "three months after Neal Galloway drowned on his way to find his fortune in California, I discovered that I was pregnant with his child."

"Junietta!" Sylvia gasped. "Do not say another word!" She glanced around as if to make sure none of the servants had overheard her, then continued in a hushed whisper. "I won't have you talking to my daughter about such things."

"Oh, calm down, Sylvia." Mimi said with a gentle push of her cane. "Adelaide is an adult. And I sincerely hope you aren't going to wait until her wedding night to teach her about the birds and the—"

"Junietta!"

"Especially if she'll be spending it in a virtual stranger's bed. When I think of our dear Addy with an old man like Mr. Weaver—"

"That's enough! The intimacies you're discussing belong within the bounds of marriage. I won't have you regaling Adelaide with tales of your grand love affair and glorifying a relationship that the church clearly calls immoral."

"I'm well aware that it was immoral, Sylvia. And I paid a huge price for my sin. My story is meant to be a cautionary tale so young Adelaide will see what happens when one strays beyond the bounds of biblical morality . . ."

# 8

JANUARY 1850

*Junietta*

In January of the new year, I awoke for the third morning in a row feeling so nauseated that I vomited into the wash bowl. My younger sister, Chloe, ran from the bedroom we shared to fetch our mother, shouting, "Mama! Mama! Junie is dying!" Mama hurried upstairs to see for herself. She rested her hand on my forehead.

"No fever, but I'll send for the doctor right away. I just pray to God that another cholera outbreak isn't upon us." She turned to hurry away, but I stopped her.

"Wait! Before you send for the doctor, I need to tell you something."

"What is it, Junie?" she said impatiently. "There's no time to waste. I have the health of all the other people in our household to consider."

I made a shooing motion to my sister. "Go away, Chloe. Leave us alone for a minute." She rolled her eyes and took her time slouching from the room. "And close the door," I called after her.

"What now?" Mama asked once my sister had left the room.

I lowered my voice, knowing that Chloe was surely listening with her ear to the door. "I haven't had my womanly curse for three months." It took Mother several moments to comprehend what I'd said, but when she did, her knees gave way and she sank down on the bed.

"Merciful heavens! How—?" She turned so white I feared she might faint. I scrabbled around on the nightstand for the vial of smelling salts that Chloe always kept nearby. I offered it to her, but she pushed my hand away. "How could this happen? Please don't tell me it was that immigrant boy—the one who works for Aunt Agatha. Your uncle said he seemed overly friendly for a carriage driver."

"We were only . . . that way . . . one time. The night before he left, we—"

"Stop!" She clapped her hands over her ears. "I'll hear no more of this! How could you do such a thing to our family?" She was shouting.

"Shh, Mama. Chloe will hear you. So will the maid, and she'll tell the whole world. You know how she loves to spread gossip."

"Is this Irishman going to do the honorable thing and make you his wife?"

"He's Scottish, not Irish—"

"As if that mattered! I suppose your father could find a decent job for him, and—" She halted when she saw my eyes fill with tears. "What now? Your father can have him arrested if he refuses."

My tears rolled down my cheeks as I shook my head. "Neal is dead, Mama. His ship was wrecked on the voyage to California and . . ." I couldn't finish as my grief overflowed. Mother moved away from me, refusing to offer any comfort for my broken heart.

"Are you certain he hasn't simply absconded?"

"No. He's really dead." I could hardly bear to say the words.

"Well. Your father will need to be told. We'll see what he has to say." She strode from the room, nearly knocking over my sister who stood just outside the door. I buried my face in the pillow and wept. Chloe tiptoed into the room.

"Junie, what's wrong? Are you really dying?"

I wished I was. "Just go away, please."

My father let me know how terribly disappointed he was in me. "You'll bring shame on our family name if this ever gets out. My political career would be ruined by such gossip, not to mention your mother's and sisters' reputations." From that day forward, he never looked at me the same way, and I was forever sorry for that. "You will stay with Great-Aunt Agatha until other arrangements can be made."

"Are you going to tell her the truth?"

"And have her die of shame? Never! We'll find another place for you before . . . you know . . . it's time."

In my mind, I planned to keep Neal's baby and raise him on my own. Our child was the only part of Neal that I had left. But until I could figure out a way to do that, I had to do whatever Papa said. I had no way to support myself, much less a baby. I moved in with Aunt Agatha again and went into hiding, a captive inside her house. I was ordered to avoid talking with her nurse or any of her servants, as if my condition was contagious. I felt like a prisoner. Two months later, when my clothes had become too tight to button properly, Papa came to see me one afternoon for the first time.

"Pack your things. I've made new arrangements for you. You'll be leaving early tomorrow morning."

I snuck out of the house after Papa left and rode an omnibus to see Meara Galloway. I hadn't spoken with her since I'd told her that Neal's and Gavin's ship had gone down, but she was my last hope now. Thankfully, she and Regan still lived in the same one-room apartment with her extended family. The air in the cramped space made me gag, so I suggested we sit outside on the cold stoop. The air out there was no better, stinking of garbage and human filth. I cringed to see little Regan toddling around in it. Neal had been desperate to protect me from this.

"Meara, I came to tell you that I'm expecting Neal's child." Her head jerked back, and she gaped at me in shock.

"What are you going to do?"

"That's why I came to see you. I thought we could find a place to live together. Take care of each other and our two babies."

"How? Where?"

"I don't know. I'm not sure yet." But not here. Neal didn't want me living here, and I didn't want his child to live here either. "We could find work—"

"You have no idea what you're talking about. No idea what my life is like. Neither one of us could ever find a job with a baby to look after. I won't leave Regan in a foundling home. She's all I have now that Gavin is gone, and I won't let her out of my sight."

"What will you do then?" I asked, figuring that I could do the same thing.

"The only thing I can do once the money that Gavin left me runs out. I'll find a man to take care of us."

"You mean, get married again?"

"No, Junie. Most of the men I'm talking about are already married." I didn't understand what she was saying until she blushed and looked away.

"Meara, no. There must be some other way."

"Well, there isn't!" she said sharply. "And you're not going to stoop as low as me, are you? Even if it is the only way to keep Neal's baby?"

She was right. I could never do what Meara planned to do.

"Now, go away and leave me alone. And don't come back here again. You don't belong here."

Neal had loved his brother and had helped him protect Meara and the baby from the cholera epidemic. For his sake, I had to help them too. "Meara, listen. I want to help you. I'll give you some money so you and Regan can get by. But please, promise me you won't do what you're thinking of doing. Promise?" I continued coaxing her, and in the end she agreed. I gave her all the money I had with me and promised to send more. I was already thinking of a few things I could sell.

I packed my bags and left with Papa in the morning, boarding a train headed north out of Manhattan. I gazed from the coach window as we juddered along, wishing that the gray waters of the Hudson River or the forested green mountains all around us would swallow me up. I hadn't slept, still pondering my dilemma and trying in vain to come up with a plan. I couldn't live with Meara, but there must be some other way to support myself and my baby. Maybe we could tell people that my child was a foundling, abandoned on our doorstep, and that Mama hadn't been able to part with the poor babe. But no, if there was even the slightest chance that the servants or nosy neighbors would figure out the truth, Papa's reputation would be ruined. For now, the story was that I was ill, and I was going into seclusion to keep from spreading the illness to my family, hoping that the mountain air would cure me. I had four months to figure out a solution, and I was determined to find one. I could feel the little one moving inside me now, which made him very real. He was part of me, part of Neal.

Papa left me at the train station in Tarrytown and continued north to Albany. He had learned of a midwife who helped girls in circumstances like mine, and she met me at the station. I rode in her wagon to a cottage on the edge of town where I would stay until it was time for my baby to be born. She told me to call her Elizabeth, and I was to be known only as "Mary." I could almost hear Neal saying, *"Don't you know that the mother of our Lord and Savior was also called Mary? And that she wasn't a married lass, either?"*

Elizabeth's cottage was rustic, with an open hearth for cooking and a cramped storeroom with a bed in it where I slept. Out back, there was a vegetable garden, apple trees, a yard full of chickens, and an outhouse. She expected me to help with the chores and wash my own clothes. Once again, I became a prisoner who couldn't be seen. I ventured only as far as the backyard, and only after dark.

Elizabeth's work as a midwife kept her busy, tending to mothers and delivering babies in the surrounding villages. We didn't become friends. Elizabeth didn't speak with me any more than necessary, and those months of solitary waiting were the loneliest ones of my life. As the days passed, I read every book I had brought with me, twice, and all three of the books in the cottage, one of which was a Bible.

At first, I avoided reading the Bible, knowing from my lifelong church attendance that God would surely condemn me for my sin. The child growing in my womb was visible proof that I had broken one of His commandments. I imagined that if I tried to approach Him, I would receive the same shocked reaction that I would if I paraded into my parents' church on Sunday morning in my condition. And yet something drew me to finally open the Bible one day. Elizabeth had gone to deliver a baby and I knew I would be alone for several hours. She kept the book on a small table beside her chair and I gingerly picked it up, as if it might burn me. I didn't even sit down to open it but remained standing, ready to close it and return it to its place at any moment.

A tiny bouquet of pressed flowers—lavender, I believe—caused it to open to the Gospel of St. John. I started to read, and I was still standing, still reading, when I came to the verse that read, "For God sent not his Son into the world to condemn the world; but that the world through him might be saved." The words stunned me. Could it be true that God wasn't standing over me, ready to condemn me?

I had never read the Bible before. What little I knew of Scripture I had learned from Sunday sermons, and to be honest, I had never paid very close attention to them. I finally sat down in a chair near the window where the light was better and continued reading. I got as far as chapter 8 and read the story of the woman who'd been caught in adultery. I held my breath as she was made to stand before Jesus. He seemed uninterested at first, then finally gave the order to stone her to death as the law demanded. But He said that only those men who had never sinned were to throw rocks at her. Like magic, the men who'd condemned her vanished. And then came Jesus' amazing words, "Neither do I condemn thee: go, and sin no more." I closed the book, went into my tiny bedroom, and wept.

Three days later, I was still trying to convince myself that the words I had read were true. That afternoon, when Elizabeth left to deliver another baby, I wrapped my cloak around myself, hiding my head and shoulders, even though the spring afternoon was warm. I left the cottage in the daylight for the first time in more than a month. I knew there was a church in the village, because I'd heard the bells tolling each Sunday morning, so I headed in that direction. The steeple soon became visible through the trees. I kept my head down, not looking at anyone, and finally reached the church. The door was unlocked. I went inside and saw a man in a dark suit and clerical collar standing on a ladder, changing the numbers on the Sunday hymn board.

"Excuse me," I said. He turned quickly and nearly lost his balance. He had been humming to himself and must not have heard the heavy door close behind me. "I'm sorry. I didn't mean to startle you."

"It was my own fault. I was woolgathering. I'm Reverend Cooper," he said, climbing down. "How can I help you?" He was in his late thirties, I guessed, with dark hair and a round, clean-shaven face. I was grateful that he hadn't pasted on a phony pastoral smile, but neither did he seem forbidding and unapproachable.

"I'm . . . um . . . Mary," I said, nearly forgetting. "I have a question. From the Scriptures. Is there a Bible . . . ?"

He gave a small smile. "I think I can find one. Give me a moment." I had remained in the rear of the church, not daring to move up the aisle into the sanctuary. The church looked old, with stiff, boxlike pews with small wooden doors so parishioners would have their own family section, closed off to outsiders. Reverend Cooper disappeared into the vestry for a moment before returning with a Bible in his hand. He walked the length of the sanctuary to where I waited and gestured to the usher's bench. "Please, have a seat, and I'll do my best to answer your question." He handed the Bible to me, then sat down as well.

I quickly turned to the eighth chapter of St. John. He had to notice that my hands were trembling, making it hard to turn the thin pages. Finding the spot, I turned the Bible around and handed it back to him. "A woman committed adultery and was brought to Jesus. He refused to condemn her. He forgave her." I hadn't asked a question, but he seemed to understand.

"He did. It's one of my favorite stories. I beg your pardon, Mary, but I couldn't help noticing that you're with child. Are you wondering if Jesus will also forgive you?"

I nodded, looking down at my lap, unable to meet his gaze. "My child's father is dead. Otherwise, he would have married me. I know it doesn't excuse what we did, but . . . I also know that it was a sin."

"True. But it's not an unpardonable sin. Sin is sin, and we all do it. Every one of us. Yours is just a bit more obvious than mine. No one can see me coveting the fine horses and carriages that fill the churchyard every Sunday morning, but even so, coveting, like adultery, is also a sin." He closed the Bible but kept his finger in place. "The original meaning of the word *sin* is similar to the expression 'missing the mark.' Imagine shooting a bow and arrow at a target and missing the bull's-eye."

"Or missing the target altogether?"

"Mm. It happens."

I liked him but still couldn't look up at him. "I know I've missed the mark."

"So you've recognized your sin and confessed it to me. And to God?"

"Yes."

"Now you need to ask God to forgive you. Then it's done."

"You make it sound simple."

"Simple but very costly. God forgives you because of Christ's death on the cross. He died in your place, took your punishment. Our sins cost Jesus His life."

I had heard the story retold every Easter, all my life, but it had never made so much sense to me before. But I still felt ashamed, remembering my mother's shock, my father's stern disappointment. I know they felt as though they had failed. "What happens then?" I asked, finally looking up. Again, he smiled faintly.

"Now you can live a forgiven life. I believe Jesus told the woman, 'Neither do I condemn thee: go, and sin no more.' That's the meaning of the word *repentance*. We turn and go, walking in a different direction."

"I'm not going to make this mistake again," I said, resting my hand on my middle. "But how will I know which direction to walk?"

"Simply follow Jesus. He's always going in the right direction. And He asks only two things of us. First, that we love God with all our heart. Putting Him first in everything we do, letting Him direct our life, worshipping Him alone instead of money or success or fame. And second, that we love our neighbor as we love ourself. Not turning away from someone in need. Forgiving people who have hurt you. Doing the loving thing, even at a cost to ourselves." Again, these were words I had heard all my life, but they had never seemed so important.

"Thank you, Reverend Cooper." I started to stand, but he stopped me.

"One more thing, Mary. Our sins are forgiven by a loving God, but they sometimes have consequences. You're facing one of them now, I believe." He gestured to the baby in my womb. "God forgave King David for his adultery with Bathsheba, but David had failed to restrain his passions for many years, and he'd failed to set a godly example for his sons. Those failures had painful consequences for him. If you do suffer for your mistake in the future, please don't ever let the enemy tell you it's because God hasn't forgiven you."

I pulled my cloak over my head again as I hurried back to Elizabeth's cottage, wondering if the shame I still felt was one of those consequences. I continued to read Elizabeth's Bible each day and slowly began to believe that I was forgiven. But I was no closer to finding a solution for my baby's future or my own.

My son's birth, when it finally came on a sweltering July afternoon, took nearly two days. Elizabeth said the difficulty was with my narrow pelvis and with the way the baby was positioned. I learned later that I had nearly died. But at last, I heard my son's cries, and Elizabeth placed him in my arms. She told me to nurse him, that it would be good for both of us. Then she gave me something warm to drink, and I fell into an exhausted sleep. When I awoke the next morning, my arms were empty.

I sat up, my entire body aching, and looked around. There was no sign of my baby. I screamed Elizabeth's name.

"What is it?" she asked from the doorway.

"Where's my son? I want to hold him. I need to feed him."

She shook her head.

"He's already gone. Adopted by a good family."

"What? Where? You have to tell me where he is!" I threw the covers aside and tried to get out of bed, but Elizabeth was at my side in a flash, holding me down with surprising strength.

"You will bleed to death if you try to get up. Stay in bed!"

"You can't take my son away. You can't! I'm his mother!"

"It's already done. It's what your father asked me to do."

"No! Tell me where my baby is! Please!" I continued struggling to get up, but she held me down against the pillows, speaking sharply.

"Stop fighting and listen to me!" I had to do what Elizabeth said because I was too weak to fight. "You have no husband, and nothing to offer your son except the shame of his birth. No name to attach to him except *bastard*. Now, suppose there is another grieving mother. She has a husband and a loving home and a name to give your son. A very fine name. But her arms are empty. She grieves because her little ones die before they ever take a breath. Can you imagine the joy such a woman will feel when your baby is placed in her arms?"

"No! Please, please, don't give my baby away."

"Now, if you love your son, and I believe that you do, which future would you want for him? One with a father and a home and a name? Or one with poverty and shame and rejection?"

"I want my son!"

"I'm sorry, but your father has already made the decision."

I felt the grief of Neal's death all over again. I had lost him and now his child. Our baby had been my only link to the man I loved, and taking him from me had been unspeakably cruel. Once again, I wished I had died. My chest burned with pain as my milk came in, reminding me of my loss. I mourned alone, beaten down. I remembered Reverend Cooper's words about being forgiven yet suffering the consequences.

A week later, Elizabeth took me to the train station and I returned home. I was destined to remain a spinster like Aunt Agatha and take care of my parents in their old age. I didn't mind my fate. I didn't ever want to fall in love again or get married. I would never love anyone as much as I had loved Neal Galloway. And I never wanted to experience the pain of losing him and our child again.

# 9

SEPTEMBER 1850

~ *Junietta* ~

Two months after my son was born and taken away from me, Aunt Agatha passed away quietly in her sleep. I was truly sorry to see her go. My uncle made plans to sell her home, so I would no longer be able to go back to the carriage house where my memories of Neal remained so vivid. My great-aunt had left me a small amount of money and some jewelry in her will, which I used to keep my promise to Meara and Regan.

Papa called me into his library a few days after the funeral, telling me to close the door and sit down. I braced myself to hear what he had to say. I hadn't spoken to him since he'd taken me to Tarrytown, and I still hadn't forgiven him for giving away my son.

"Arthur Stanhope paid me a visit today," he began. "Do you know who he is?"

"I've heard the name."

"He's a self-made millionaire and a ruthless businessman. He came into my office and asked to speak with me in private." Papa drew a breath, then released it with such a painful sigh that I thought he must be ill. I sat forward in my chair.

"Papa?"

"Somehow, he knew all about you and your baby, Junietta. He hires brutish men to do all his dirty work, and they must have bribed someone to find out the truth. Stanhope didn't exactly smile when he told me, because Arthur Stanhope never smiles, but he wore such a smug look on his face that it made me hate him even more. I asked him what he wanted, and he said, 'I'm looking for a wife for my oldest son. I don't mind that your daughter is . . . soiled.' That's the word he used, Junietta. *Soiled.*"

I slumped back in my chair, the wind taken out of me. I had heard of Arthur Stanhope, of course. Everyone had. No one seemed to know where he had come from or how he had gotten his start in business. There were rumors of shady dealings, so no politician wanted to be associated with him, regardless of how much money he offered to donate to his campaign. My father's words and the grim way he had spoken them made me sick to my stomach.

"Are you going to make me marry Arthur Stanhope's son, Papa?"

"No, Junietta. I would never force you to marry against your will. But Stanhope reminded me that he owns a daily newspaper. He has the power and the lack of moral scruples to ruin our family's reputation and probably my political career. Your brothers' futures would be ruined as well. Your sisters would never find respectable husbands." He closed his eyes for a moment and ran his hand over his face as he struggled with his emotions. "Do you see how the consequences of your immoral choices have affected all of us?"

I lowered my head as my tears fell, remembering Reverend Cooper's words. "Yes, Papa. I do see. And I'm so sorry."

"I abhor the thought of being blackmailed this way. And I cannot imagine turning you over to such a despicable family."

If only Neal had let me go with him to California a year ago. We could have died together when the ship sank. I had been happy for such a short, fleeting time, and I already knew that I would never be happy again. I looked up at my father. "Tell Mr. Stanhope that I'll marry his son."

"Junietta—"

"I've already ruined my own life, and I couldn't live with my guilt if I ruined everyone else's."

"Take some time to think about it. I want you to be certain."

"I am certain. Tell him I'll do it." Because if Arthur Stanhope knew all about me, he might also know who had adopted my son.

<hr/>

I met Arthur Stanhope's son Art a week later when he took me to the theater. He was a pleasant-looking man with mud-brown hair and hazel eyes. Tall and slim, he was able to afford fine suits and expensive barbers to keep him looking dapper. If his father hadn't been Arthur Stanhope, the young women my age would have been fighting over Art and the wealth he could provide. At age twenty-two, he was three years older than me. His brother David, a year younger than Art, was his fiercest rival for power and position in their father's business enterprises. Arthur had set the rivalry in motion to keep his sons motivated and vigilant. Their mother had died giving birth to their youngest brother, Roger, who was twelve.

Art and I had a short but suitably proper courtship where we were seen together at the theater, in box seats at the opera, and at dinner parties with his father's colleagues. I learned that the gossip about me was that I had suffered from rheumatic fever and had rested in a private sanatorium. The gossipmongers watched my return with curiosity, so I did my best to appear healthy and cheerful in public, and to carry on animated conversations everywhere I went. I heard no hint of gossip about the true reason why I had been away. A pregnancy in the venerable Van Buren family was unthinkable.

I had expected Art Stanhope to be boorish and obnoxious after the way his father had blackmailed mine into this arrangement, but Art was very different from his father. Like me, he seemed intimidated by him. Art was quiet and rigidly polite, as if unsure how to converse with a woman. "I've been too busy with the business world to take time to court anyone," he told me. I found him so intense and serious that I made it my goal to make him smile whenever we were together. I sometimes succeeded.

On a Sunday afternoon carriage ride in his father's expensive four-in-hand coach, he proposed to me with a diamond and ruby ring that would feed Meara and Regan for years.

"Yes, Art. I'll marry you," I said, aware that I was sealing my fate and setting the course I would follow for the rest of my life.

"Good. I'm very pleased, Junietta. I've already asked your father for your hand, and he has agreed." Art slid the bulky ring onto my finger, then gave me a stiff embrace. I wondered if he knew the truth about me and my baby. I needed to find out so I would know where I stood with my future husband, and how much control he held over me. I decided to raise the issue delicately.

"Art, you know that your father chose me for you, right?"

"Yes. Of course."

"Did he give you a reason why he chose me?"

"He gave me two reasons. First, because you're the daughter of one of New York's oldest Knickerbocker families, and our marriage will raise my family's standing and prestige here in New York. The very best people will now attend the social events you and I will be hosting. And second, because your father has political connections that will be advantageous for our family."

Maybe Art didn't know the truth.

"My father also said that you were very pretty," he continued. "And spirited. And I agree. You *are* very pretty, Junietta." He smiled one of his rare smiles and kissed my hand.

"What if I had been an ugly hag with bad teeth and a sour temperament?" I teased. "Would you have still married me?"

"Of course." He didn't smile when he said it, and for a moment, I forgot to feel sorry for myself and began feeling sorrier for Art.

"Your father has that much control over your life?"

"Weren't you also taught to obey your father?"

"I was taught to respect him, yes. But he wouldn't force me to marry against my will. The choice to marry you or not was always mine."

"And yet, you just said yes." That small smile again.

"I did." I looked down at the ring on my finger and thought of Neal.

"You're a smart girl, Junietta. And you're about to become a very wealthy one too." I looked up at him again.

"Is that why you think I'm marrying you? For your money?"

"Of course. Why else? I've noticed that you enjoy the finer things that money can buy, like box seats at the opera. Your father will appreciate the Stanhope millions as well. It's costly to run a political campaign or to lobby Washington for the things you want."

It hurt me to think Art believed that of me, and even more to hear Papa's character being tarnished that way. I bit my tongue to keep from blurting the truth, remembering Meara and her baby, knowing that I would be able to support them with some of Art's money. I might even be able to hire someone to find my baby. I would become Art's wife, but my heart still longed for Neal and for our son.

"I expect I will be given a living allowance," I said, regaining my composure, "but I would prefer not to have to give an account for every penny I spend. Would that be acceptable to you?"

"My father doesn't care what you do, Junietta, aside from your duties as a hostess and as the mother of my heir. I don't much care either." Unless Art was concealing another side of his personality, marriage to him might not be as bad as I'd feared.

I realized that Arthur Sr. would always be in control of my life, as he was of his son's life. And I suddenly understood why he hadn't told Art about my illegitimate baby. Arthur would hold on to the truth like an ace up his sleeve in order to keep me in line. If I didn't do everything he commanded, he would tell my husband the ugly truth. And no doubt he would make it seem as if he had just discovered it, rather than knowing about it before we were married. I would be the villainess who had entered the marriage under false pretenses. I might never have a loving relationship with Art, but what little trust we did have would be destroyed.

"You won't regret accepting my proposal, Junietta," he said when he brought me home again. He gave me a brief kiss, our first. His mustache and beard tickled my face. I held back tears, longing for Neal.

⌒◦⌒

On a crisp January morning in 1851, Art and I were married in spectacular style, and presented to New York society in an extravagant reception at the Metropolitan Hotel. The newspapers announced these important events, and people lined the streets outside the church and reception hall, blocking traffic, in order to glimpse New York's royalty in their jewels and gowns. Arthur Sr. insisted that all the finest Knickerbocker families be invited, along with Papa's political cronies. I became Mrs. Arthur Benton Stanhope II, and one of the wealthiest women in New York City. We left for Europe on a steamship the following day, to tour London, Paris, and Rome.

Lying in bed in our luxurious stateroom the first night at sea, I made an important decision about life with my new husband. I sat up on one elbow and looked down at him in the darkness. "Art, may I ask a favor of you?"

"That depends what it is."

"I don't expect you to ever love me, especially since you didn't choose me for yourself. But I would like it very much if we could be friends. And for our friendship to continue, even after I give you an heir. Especially then." I reached down to stroke his beard, enjoying the softness of it.

"Friends?"

"Yes. Instead of living separate lives like most society couples, I would like us to be able to talk to each other and share little things about our lives. I would like you to feel that you could come to me for more than . . . you know." I pulled my hand away, suddenly shy. "It would be nice if you even grew to value my perspective and wanted to hear my advice."

"What an interesting request."

"I don't know much about how marriages work among most rich people. I do know that my grandparents truly cared for each other because I watched them together. I've also seen the affection my parents have for each other, and I know that my father relies on Mama in many ways." I swallowed a knot of sorrow, realizing again how much I had hurt my parents. "I think . . . I would really like it if our marriage could be based on friendship, like theirs is."

"Come here." He pulled me down beside him again and kissed my forehead. "Having a friend is something new for me. I don't think I've ever had a friend."

"Not even your brother David?"

"Especially not David. Father deliberately pits us against each other, making us compete in everything we do. It has always been that way, and it always will be, I suppose. In fact, I'm worried that David will gain an advantage over me while I'm away on this trip, since he'll have our father all to himself."

"Then why take this trip?"

"Father insisted. That's the way he is. He likes to keep David and me on edge all the time, so we're always looking over our shoulders."

"Will David be pressured to marry an even more advantageous wife than me?"

"He won't have any more choice in the matter than I did. But I'm already ahead of David as far as the potential to produce an heir is concerned."

His words brought me back to reality and told me exactly where I stood. I would be foolish to hope for affection or friendship in our marriage. I wasn't Art's partner or even an individual person, simply a womb to carry his son. I hated that it may never change. Then I had another thought.

"Art? What would happen if you and David decided to work together instead of competing? What if you became partners and refused to play your father's games?"

"Simple. He would disinherit both of us and start grooming Roger to be the next mogul."

"Would that be so bad? To be disinherited? You seem like a bright, capable man. And you must have learned a lot about doing business from your father. Why couldn't you make it on your own? We might never be millionaires, but at least you could be your own person and—"

"You don't know what you're talking about!" His tone turned brusque. I felt a cool distance open up between us even though we lay side by side. I instinctively shrank back, my heart beating faster. "I appreciate your blind confidence in me, Junietta, but my life isn't as simple as you naively believe. And don't ever let my father hear you talking such nonsense either."

I sensed that if Art ever grew truly angry, he would become a different person from the self-contained man I knew. We were both silent for a moment before I spoke again. "Thanks for the warning."

We lay in silence, miles apart. Then Art said quietly, "The answer is yes. I'll agree to your favor. I could use a friend, Junietta."

❧

We visited places on our wedding tour through Europe that I had never dreamed I would see, places I had only read about in books from Aunt Agatha's library. But my enjoyment was marred by Art's growing anxiety and restlessness as time passed. I was grateful that he'd told me about the relentless competition between him and his brother, because I recognized that his unhappiness had nothing to do with me. "Let's go back to New York," I told him one morning in Rome. I'd been sitting with him at a little table in a bustling piazza, watching the worry lines in his brow deepen as he read a London newspaper. "We've had a good trip, Art. Let's save all the other sights for next time."

"How will we explain to Father why we're back earlier than expected?"

"Tell him I'm tired. It's the truth. I need to conserve my strength for childbearing." I smiled and rested my hand on his arm. He almost smiled in return. He went to the steamship office that afternoon and booked our passage home.

I was glad that I'd had time alone with Art to get to know him better, because after we returned, his father demanded all his time. Art sometimes worked fourteen-hour days, seven days a week, and would be exhausted when he returned to the limestone mansion we shared with his father and two brothers. He would come into my bedroom suite and lie down beside me, asking only that I hold him, unable to voice his frustrations or his true feelings toward his father. I grew to hate Arthur Stanhope Senior. He told his sons what to think, what to say, and how to act, dictating every aspect of their lives. He never praised Art for doing well, only belittled him if he made a mistake. I grew so tired of living under my father-in-law's dictatorship that I longed to simply walk away with Art and start a new life for ourselves someplace else. In the western territories, perhaps. But I never suggested it again, knowing that if Art and I did try to leave, Arthur would tell him the truth about why I had married him, and the slender bond of our friendship would be severed. It often seemed that my friendship was the only thing holding Art together.

I was given a generous living allowance and the role of the Stanhope family's hostess. "I want you to plan a spring ball, Junietta," Arthur Sr. told me. "Spare no expense. Invite everyone you know. See to it that the social events we host are the ones that all of New York society envies and longs to attend."

It was a very tall order for a woman barely twenty years old. My Calvinist upbringing had taught me moderation in all pleasures and to be a good steward of money and possessions. Now my father-in-law was ordering me to spend more than the yearly wages of a dozen working men on a single party, simply because he wanted to be accepted into New York society. Thankfully, he hired someone to help me plan everything, from the engraved invitations addressed to four hundred select people, to the desserts that would be served at the end of the evening. I threw myself into the task, propelled more by boredom and a desire to have a purpose than by genuine interest. Like his sons, I also feared the consequences of failing Arthur B. Stanhope.

After returning from Europe, I embarked on another ambitious project that was much more important to me. I hired a cab and traveled to the part of town where Meara and Regan lived, finding them exactly as I had left them four months earlier. I turned down her offer of refreshment, and she returned to her piecework, bending over each garment in the near darkness of the tenement, sewing with nimble, pinpricked fingers. I told her how I'd been forced to give up Neal's baby, and how his father had blackmailed me into marrying Art.

"I may have sold my soul to Arthur Stanhope, but at least some good will come of it, Meara. I'll be able to support you and Regan from now on, like I promised. But not only the two of you. I've come up with a plan."

She didn't look up at my announcement, continuing to work as if sewing on buttons for a penny apiece was her only hope. Her voice was dull as she asked, "And what might that be?"

"I've hired an estate agent to find a boardinghouse I can purchase in a better part of town. I would like you to live there and manage it for me. It will be for women only, and especially for women who find themselves in the same circumstances you and I were in—on our own with a young child to care for. If the women who come to us are able to work, we'll charge a minimal fee for their room and board. And those who are still nursing babies can watch over the other children so they will be cared for in a clean, healthy environment. You can all work together doing the cooking and keeping house."

Meara finally looked up. She had tears in her eyes. "Why would you do that for us?"

"Because I know what it's like to have a child I dearly loved and wanted to raise but with no way to provide for him. If there had been a place like the one I'm proposing, my life would have been very different. I may never get my son back, but I would like my loss to count for something good. Will you work with me, Meara?"

She rose and silently embraced me in reply.

After much searching, a property agent found the perfect building and negotiated its purchase. It cost more money than I had planned to spend, but it had been difficult to find a place in a suitable area with clean water and safe streets. I could make do with last year's gowns to economize, and perhaps enlist the help of other wealthy women in my social circle to create a charitable trust. But for now, the project was underway. Meara and Regan moved into their new home, as did four other young women and their children. I was pleased with what I had accomplished. And I also had the pleasure of telling my husband that we were expecting our first child.

Arthur Benton Stanhope III was born in November, two years after I'd held Neal Galloway in my arms for the last time. I called my baby A.B. for short. Again, I nearly died in childbirth, and this time the doctor advised me not to risk another pregnancy. I had to tell Art the news when he came to see me and his new son. He stood over my bed, frowning slightly as he looked down at the fair-haired baby in my arms. I wondered what he was thinking.

"Are you very disappointed that you won't have a houseful of sons?"

"I only need one heir." His frown deepened. "Is he all right? He looks . . . scalded."

"All babies look that way at first." Tears sprang to my eyes as I remembered my first son. His head of wispy hair had been the same mahogany color as Neal's. He would be more than a year old by now, and calling another woman "Mama."

"Are you all right, Junietta?" He reached out hesitantly and brushed away my tears.

"Yes. He's a lovely, healthy boy."

Art heaved a sigh. "Good. I've been worried. About you, I mean. My mother died giving birth to Roger, you know. So, maybe it's for the best that you won't have more children. You . . . you've become a good friend."

"I'm glad."

He was growing emotional, so he cleared his throat as if to change the subject. "At least I beat David. My son is the firstborn in the third generation of Stanhopes."

David was still unmarried. Arthur was holding marriage out as a prize, making him wait until he did something to earn it. Art and I would never have a home of our own where he could escape from his father's domination. Arthur demanded that his sons be available to do his bidding at the snap of his fingers.

"To tell you the truth," Art said, "I never wanted to be a father. Not if it makes me like him."

"It doesn't have to. You aren't at all like him, Art."

"I don't know how to be a good father. I've only had my own."

"What if you tried to be the kind of father you wished you had?"

He seemed to ponder my question for a moment. Then he bent over me, kissed my cheek, and left the room.

# 10

NOVEMBER 1898

~ *Junietta* ~

Junietta had to pause in her storytelling to pull a handkerchief from her pocket and wipe her tears.

"Are you all right, Mimi Junie?" Adelaide asked.

"Yes, child. It's good to remember your past sorrows and joys. It puts today's trials into perspective."

Addy fingered one of the yellow tags dangling from an end table near her chair. "I know you're against me marrying a wealthy man just so we can keep this house, but you just told us how you married your husband in order to save your family. Isn't it my duty to do the same thing?"

"It isn't the same thing at all, dear girl! I dug the trap that my family was caught in, so yes, I had a duty to help. You did nothing at all to cause our present circumstances."

"Except being born a girl." Addy gave a weak smile.

"You know that wasn't your fault. But listen, at least I had Neal

Galloway in my life, and a chance to learn what true love was, if only for a little while. And that's what I wish for you."

Addy huffed as if frustrated. "You keep telling me to marry for love, but it sounds like you eventually grew fond of your husband. Not all arranged marriages have to be bad, do they? Can't fondness grow?"

"Yes, fondness and friendship can grow with a little work on your part. But you haven't heard the end of my story, dear."

"Well, there won't be time for it today," Sylvia said. If she had been moved by Junietta's story, she was doing her best to brush it off, like snowflakes from a coat sleeve. "I think that's all the items I want to tag in this room. We'll tackle another room tomorrow. Thank you for your help, Junietta."

She gave a wry smile. "Why do I get the feeling I'm being dismissed?"

"I don't mean to sound dismissive, but Adelaide and I have other things to do, and I'm certain you do too."

"At the moment, not one of them is more important than encouraging Adelaide to think for herself. You only have one life, Addy. The decisions you make today will reap a lifetime of consequences tomorrow. And probably more than a few regrets."

"Yes, I'm sure that's true," Sylvia said, but her breezy tone seemed to cancel the weight of Junietta's advice. "But this is the life that Adelaide was born to, and she deserves to continue living it. She shouldn't have to give up any of it because of her great-grandfather's unfortunate will. Marriage to a man from her social class will ensure that she won't have to. We simply need to find the right man for her. Come, Adelaide. There's something in my suite I need to show you."

Junietta remained seated for a few more minutes after Addy followed her mother from the room, trying to muster her strength for the walk downstairs to her suite. Reliving the past combined with their outing to the orphanage had exhausted her. Was she getting through to Adelaide at all? She couldn't tell. Addy still seemed to believe she had to secure her future by marrying a rich man. And the dear girl had seemed more disgusted than moved by the poverty they'd seen in the slums earlier today.

At the same time, Junietta had been very impressed by young Howard Forsythe today. She was so proud of the fine man he had become and the part she'd played in it. Howard was bright and personable and hadn't seemed at all repulsed by the sights and smells of poverty. Instead, he'd shown compassion and had even taken a moment to play with the children at the orphanage. The memory made Junietta smile—and wonder. Might Howard be the right person to take her place at the Stanhope Charitable Foundation? For the first time in weeks, she felt a glimmer of hope.

## Adelaide

November turned into December, a cold, lonely month for Adelaide, whose days seemed empty of life. She missed being able to attend the glittery whirlwind of holiday parties and balls, and worried about her future as she huddled in her drafty mansion. Ever since Father's will was read, she'd felt as though she was being tossed back and forth between Mother and Mimi Junie. Her grandmother had revealed a lot about her past, causing Addy to realize how little she knew about her mother's past. Did she have regrets for the choices she'd made? If so, she wasn't saying.

Finally, the year changed to 1899, the last year of the century. Mother called Adelaide into her bedroom suite on a snowy afternoon, and she seemed unusually cheerful. She asked the maid to bring tea, and they sat together in Mother's sitting area, a charming room in one of the mansion's turrets that always reminded Addy of a castle in a fairy tale. She remembered visiting Mother's suite as a child along with her two older sisters and being fascinated by the antique Belgian tapestries that warmed the walls. She had studied the elaborate woven figures closely, trying to unravel the stories they portrayed.

"This arrived for you in the morning mail," Mother said, smiling. She handed Addy a letter addressed to her. The embossed return address told her it was from George Weaver. Addy stared at it for a long moment, remembering the boring middle-aged gentleman. Her stomach squeezed with dread. "Well, open it!" Mother said. "I'm curious to hear what Mr. Weaver has to say."

Addy loosened the seal and pulled out the handwritten card. The message was printed in neat, precise writing and finished off with a flamboyant signature. Her stomach squeezed again after she read it. "Mr. Weaver has tickets for the theater in two weeks. He would like me to attend with him and have dinner at Delmonico's afterward." She looked up to see Mother's reaction. She seemed pleased. "Do you think I should accept?"

"That's entirely up to you. But I don't see any harm in getting to know Mr. Weaver a little better."

"Is it too soon? I mean, after Father died? Aren't I meant to be in mourning?" She found herself hoping it was. Had Mimi Junie felt this way when told she should court Art Stanhope?

"Not at all. Six months is an appropriate period for a daughter. You can wear your new gray gown, if you're worried what people will think. But it's very important that you start to be seen in society again. You don't want to be forgotten. Perhaps you'll attract the interest of a few other gentlemen while you're with Mr. Weaver."

She was to be put on display—like a rug in a bazaar, as Mimi Junie would say. No wonder Mother had asked to speak with Addy in private. She must have noticed Addy's hesitation because she added, "It's not as if he's proposing marriage. It's only the theater."

"I'll write back and accept his invitation right away."

Mother rested her hand on Addy's shoulder. "Adelaide, the important thing to remember is that Mr. Weaver found you fascinating and attractive, and he wants to spend more time with you. And perhaps he's afraid that someone like Mr. Albright will beat him to it."

"Someone younger, you mean. How old do you think Mr. Weaver is? In his midforties?"

"Certainly no older than that. Listen, I know your grandmother has been filling your head with her radical ideas and trying to undermine my efforts. But you mustn't think less of a suitor simply because he happens to be wealthy. They say that the best marriages are between people from the same backgrounds because they'll have things in common. It's why your grandmother's romance with her impoverished immigrant never would have worked."

"I understand. But it's just that . . . it seems wrong to pursue a man or agree to marry him for no other reason than that he's wealthy." Yet it was what her sisters did. What all the young women she knew did. It had never seemed wrong to Addy before Mimi Junie started telling stories.

"You're looking at it the wrong way," Mother said. "You have many wonderful qualities to bring to a marriage. You should be very proud that a gentleman like Mr. Weaver recognized some of them and wishes to pursue you. You'll have much to offer him in return—this home, your abilities as a hostess, your place in society. Please don't ever get the idea that I want you to adopt a phony façade to entrap a husband. Simply be yourself and let everyone see your attractive qualities. I'm quite certain that the wisest gentlemen will soon be fighting over you."

*Be herself?* As Mimi Junie had pointed out so precisely, Addy wasn't sure who she really was. All her life she had done whatever she'd been told, going to places chosen for her, wearing gowns that others had selected for her, befriending girls who'd been deemed suitable, even reading books that others had approved. She didn't have a favorite color or favorite flower or favorite song. She couldn't paint like Mother, and only played the piano and danced well because Mother had made sure she'd taken lessons. When she thought about it, Addy didn't know how to do anything well except smile and make polite conversation and dance at parties and balls.

"Adelaide?" Mother squeezed her shoulder, bringing her back. "I also want you to know that Mr. Weaver won't be your only choice. I've planned a second dinner party, and I already have the names of two more gentlemen who have been recommended for you to meet." Addy wanted to ask how Mother could afford to host another big dinner, but she held her tongue. "And my friend Dorinda Rhodes has agreed to hold a party for you in the spring and invite several eligible men to fill your dance card. I helped her daughter Ionia find a suitor, remember? She owes me a favor. I think enough time will have passed by then that you can wear your new blue gown."

Mother tossed out all these plans as if discussing items on a menu. Addy wouldn't have thought twice about these schemes if Mimi Junie hadn't made her question everything. There were so many things Addy wanted to ask her mother. Did she still mourn for Father? Had they truly loved each other? Did she regret marrying him? Mother was such a private, self-contained person that Addy knew better than to ask. Mother always found a way to avoid answering her questions.

⁓

Adelaide's evening at the theater with Mr. Weaver was her first social outing since her father had died, and it felt good to be back in the exciting swirl of chattering voices and elegantly dressed acquaintances. From their box seats, she and Mr. Weaver could not only view the play but could be seen by the rest of New York society. The play had a romantic storyline, telling a tale of true love that Mimi would have applauded heartily. In the past, Addy would have dismissed it as fanciful fiction, but she viewed it differently after hearing Mimi Junie's love story with Neal Galloway.

"Are you enjoying the play, Miss Stanhope?" Mr. Weaver asked at intermission.

"Yes, very much. And you?"

He made a face. "The plot is somewhat far-fetched, and the dialogue is tedious, but I'll reserve judgment until the end. Come, I'll buy you a drink, Miss Stanhope."

Why hadn't she ever noticed how stiff and awkwardly polite social dialogue was—*Miss* Stanhope and *Mr.* Weaver. As they stood in the crowded lobby, sipping their drinks, she tried to imagine being held in Mr. Weaver's arms and being kissed by him. She gave a little shudder, finding the idea repulsive. He was too old for her. Their marriage would be for the wrong reasons on both their parts. She wondered if she could be as courageous as Mimi Junie had been, asking him on her honeymoon if they could be friends.

Her thoughts were interrupted by a well-dressed but slightly drunk young man with fair hair and a roguish grin who staggered against Mr. Weaver and slapped him on his back. "George Weaver! How are you, my good fellow? I haven't seen you in months!"

"I've been well, Charles. I would like to—"

"Say! Is this one of your daughters? How did an ugly mug like you produce such a beauty?"

Mr. Weaver's pale cheeks flamed. Addy felt the heat rush to her own face as well. "Charles Durand, I would like you to meet my guest for the evening, Miss Adelaide Stanhope."

"How do you do," Addy said politely. Mr. Durand stood uncomfortably close, and she smelled alcohol on his breath.

"I do very well," Mr. Durand said, laughing, "But obviously not as well as my old pal, George!"

"If you'll excuse us," Mr. Weaver said, tugging Addy away from him, "there's someone I must speak with."

"Robbing the cradle, you old fox!" he called after them. Heads turned in their direction as Mr. Durand trumpeted the words loudly enough for everyone to hear. Mr. Weaver ignored him as he took Addy's elbow and guided her through the jostling crowd, greeting people, introducing them to Addy, and making polite small talk. She knew she should be taking note of them, but their names flew in and out of her mind as swiftly as he spoke them. She made the mistake of glancing over her shoulder and wished she hadn't. Mr. Durand was still watching them. And still smirking.

"I apologize for my rude friend, Miss Stanhope," Mr. Weaver said when they'd taken their theater seats again. "He usually isn't so impolite."

"Think nothing of it." Yet she couldn't stop thinking of it. Was the rest of society also laughing at them behind their backs?

Mr. Weaver nodded off during the second half of the play, snoring softly and missing the tender love scene near the end where the hero pledged his eternal love as he lay dying. Mimi Junie would have nudged

Mr. Weaver awake with the tip of her cane and fired off one of her lively comments like "I thought only infants and ancients needed naps." Addy fervently hoped another suitor would appear soon so he wouldn't be her only choice.

After the final applause, Mr. Weaver mingled with the crowd once again as he had at intermission. She worried that they would encounter Mr. Durand and was relieved when they didn't. Mr. Weaver seemed to know a great many people, and he introduced Addy to each of them, saying, "And of course you must know Miss Stanhope." Many of them had known her father and offered their condolences.

Their breath fogged the air as they emerged from the theater, and a light dusting of snow frosted the pavement. Addy and Mr. Weaver joined the others who were waiting for their carriages beneath brightly lit electric lamps. "I have been thinking of buying an automobile," Mr. Weaver said as they waited. "I understand your family owns one."

"Yes, Father had it shipped over from France. He says automobiles are really catching on over there, and he believes they will soon become just as popular here. He wants to be one of the first, and—" She caught herself speaking of Father as if he were still alive and halted suddenly.

"I'm sorry. It was rude of me to remind you of your recent loss. Please forgive me."

"Of course. No harm done."

Mr. Weaver's carriage finally arrived, and they drove to Delmonico's. The great restaurant was jammed with the after-theater crowd, and again Mr. Weaver paused to speak to many people, if only for a moment. After hearing Mimi's stories of Arthur Stanhope's ruthlessness, she was relieved to see that Mr. Weaver was so well liked and highly regarded.

He had booked a reservation at a lovely, private table, but her food seemed tasteless. For some ridiculous reason, she remembered the rows of tables in the orphanage and the aroma of baking bread that had wafted from the kitchen. Mimi Junie could probably tell her how many orphans could be fed for the price of her meal, and Addy felt absurdly angry with her grandmother for ruining her enjoyment. Even more so when she remembered that Mimi had never told her whether the doctor they had met there, Dr. Murphy, was her lost son.

It seemed the evening would never end. Addy's face felt stiff from smiling politely and feigning interest in everything Mr. Weaver said. It was very late and she was weary when he finally escorted her to her door. A waiting servant opened it, and they stepped into the foyer. "Thank you for a lovely evening, Mr. Weaver." Her voice echoed in what she now realized was a ridiculously large space.

"I enjoyed myself very much. You are a charming companion, Miss Stanhope. May I call on you again?"

Her stomach protested but she answered politely. "I would be delighted, Mr. Weaver." He smiled, a prim, tight smile that showed no teeth. Addy had the absurd thought that perhaps he didn't have all of them, or they were rotting in place. "Well, good night, then," she said.

"Good night."

She climbed the stairs to her bedroom, wondering what to tell her mother about her evening with Mr. Weaver. Mother was certain to advise her to continue seeing him while they waited for a younger gentleman to come along, but that seemed deceitful. Yet her family's financial need must be urgent if they had to plunder all the extra rooms in their house. Grandmother advised Adelaide to let this house go so she would be free to fall in love and find a sense of purpose. What purpose could Addy possibly pursue?

She reached the top of the stairs and gazed down at the cavernous foyer. Which woman should she listen to? Each was equally determined to win Addy to her side. She wished she could find a patch of middle ground where she could make both women happy, but that was very unlikely. Addy would have to choose. And the thought of making a mistake paralyzed her.

One of the servants was waiting to help her hang up her gown and unpin her hair. What was her name? Betsy? Jane? Mimi would know, of course. Adelaide bravely held back her tears, waiting until she was alone in the dark to finally cry.

## ~ Junietta ~

Junietta found Sylvia and Adelaide in the morning room, sipping coffee and quietly conversing. A tray held a plate of fresh croissants. "How was your evening with George Weaver last night?" she asked.

"It was fine, Mimi. The play was enjoyable. And Mr. Weaver was a pleasant companion."

Junietta made a show of giving a polite yawn as she sat down. "What a tepid reply. It sounds like there were barely any sparks, let alone fireworks."

"And why should there be?" Sylvia asked. "These things take time."

"Especially when the fuel is old and a bit soggy," Junietta said.

"Adelaide and I were just talking about the next dinner party I'm planning," Sylvia said. "It will be in A.B.'s honor again, so it's appropriate for his mother to be there."

"Well, in that case, I wouldn't miss it. I'll enjoy sizing up the next batch of fish intended for your net." She looked at Addy and winked. "Let's hear who you've invited to the second round of this fishing expedition. I hope they're livelier catches than the first two flounders were."

Sylvia sighed. "I've invited a gentleman acquaintance of Mrs. Rhodes named Mr. Charles Durand—"

"Oh, no," Addy groaned.

"What's wrong?" Sylvia asked.

"I met Charles Durand last evening at the theater. He mistook me for one of Mr. Weaver's daughters and embarrassed both of us with his rude comments."

Junietta laughed and thumped her cane. "I daresay he won't be the only one to make that mistake if you continue courting a man old enough to be your father."

"I'm surprised to hear that," Sylvia said. "Charles Durand came very highly recommended."

"For his money or his manners?" Junietta asked.

"Must we invite him?" Addy asked. "I think it would be awkward for both of us to meet again."

Sylvia's shoulders sagged. "I've already sent out the invitations. It's too late to cancel them now. But listen, I've invited a second gentleman for you to meet named Henry Webster. At least the evening won't be a total loss."

"Is he related to Marcus Webster?" Junietta asked. "If so, the Websters are what they call 'new money.' It's ironic that the Stanhopes were once 'new money' too, and determined to marry their way into respectability. And now, three generations after Arthur Stanhope got his start, the tables are turned. Who knows how many people Marcus Webster stepped on as he made his upward climb, or what sort of family he comes from? No one knew the dirty truth about Arthur Stanhope in my day."

"I'm sure there will be plenty of time to learn about Mr. Webster's background if he's interested in courting Addy."

"Don't you mean, if Addy is interested in courting him?" Junietta asked. Sylvia looked away. Junietta wasn't getting through to either of them. "Listen, since you're planning a second dinner party, I've decided to plan a second trip with Adelaide. To broaden her perspective on life, you might say."

"This isn't a contest, Junietta."

"Maybe not. But I'm wondering how long you can afford to give parties and have gowns made before Adelaide will be forced to choose."

"I'm simply trying to help my daughter take the next step in her life, and this is the way it has always been done. Parents arrange dinners and parties so young people have a chance to meet and mingle."

"We're at the dawn of the twentieth century. Times change, Sylvia. Customs change. And they should. My era was different from yours, and Addy's will be different again. She'll have more freedom than we did, so why not let her explore and grow and live in her own times in her own way? Heavens, we light our homes with electricity now, not candles and gas lamps. We can cross the continent by train in a matter of days. If that had been possible when I was Addy's age, then Neal could have gotten to California safely, and none of us would be sitting here discussing this."

"Would you really have married him, Mimi? Even though he was poor?"

"Absolutely. I told him as much, but you know men and their silly pride."

"Well, regardless of modern advances," Sylvia said, "this is still how proper young ladies find acceptable suitors."

"If you weren't in such an all-fire hurry to snag a rich husband to support us, Addy might meet someone suitable on her own. He might not be wealthy, but at least he would be someone she'd be happy to spend the next fifty years with. Although I daresay you won't have fifty years if you marry George Weaver, dear—which might be one advantage in his favor, now that I think about it."

"Ignore her, Addy," Sylvia sighed. "There are plenty of eligible gentlemen out there. I'm sure we'll find one who suits you."

"But she's fishing in a pool that's stacked with your choices, Sylvia. You're restricting her prospects to men who are wealthy. How is that a choice?"

"I'm sure you want Adelaide to be well provided for, don't you? And for that, she needs a wealthy husband."

"I wish that wasn't true," Junietta said. She leaned back in her chair, frustrated by what couldn't be changed. "The problem is that the majority of women are still dependent on their husbands for everything, even at the dawn of a new century. Whether we're rich or poor, it's still the same. We're helpless when it comes to supporting ourselves, and therefore all the important decisions are still being made for us. I wish we could be seen and appreciated for ourselves. Not as a bearer of children, not as a decoration on our husband's arm or as his trophy, but as an individual with value. I want that for all women. And I certainly want it for Adelaide."

Junietta slowly rose to her feet, praying that her heart would behave, and that she would be strong enough to make it upstairs—not to mention well enough to take Adelaide on another excursion this week. "I'll get out of your way now and let you finish your plans." She walked as far as the door, then turned around. "Am I allowed to invite a dinner companion to your party, Sylvia?"

"Who do you have in mind?"

"I'll let you know. Just reserve a place, please." She turned again and left the room.

# 11

FEBRUARY 1899

*≈ Adelaide ≈*

"Mr. Forsythe will be here at one o'clock for our excursion," Mimi Junie told Adelaide at breakfast. "Please be ready. His time is costing us money, you know."

"I'll be ready." She wondered what her eccentric grandmother was up to now in this tug-of-war between her and Mother. If only Adelaide had someone to confide in who could help her wrestle with all her confusing thoughts. But that was the problem with being caught in the middle between Mother and Mimi. She couldn't truly confide in either one because each was trying to sway Addy to her side. The second dinner party was tomorrow night, and Addy felt queasy at the thought of meeting loudmouthed Mr. Durand again.

The process of finding a husband hadn't seemed this confusing and stressful for her two sisters. They had enjoyed the parties and balls and had been content with the suitors who'd proposed. *Content*, yet not necessarily *in love*, Mimi would point out. But Father had been alive when her sisters were courting, and she and Mother didn't have the added financial pressure they now were under.

Addy was waiting in the foyer when the lawyer arrived, a few minutes before the hour. The late-winter day was overcast, and Addy found the view from the front window of barren trees and scattered piles of dirty snow disheartening. But Mr. Forsythe was beaming with good humor as he came inside to wait for Mimi Junie.

"I love the eve of springtime, don't you, Miss Stanhope? There's such a promise in the air of renewed color and life. And new beginnings."

His words and bright smile made Addy take notice of him. She usually paid the family lawyer no more mind than she would the servant who'd opened the door for him. But here he was, pleasant and cheerful as he prepared to escort her and her grandmother this afternoon. And, she noticed for the first time, he was surprisingly good-looking. She quickly dismissed that thought as irrelevant.

"I find spring to be a fickle season, Mr. Forsythe," she replied. "As changeable as a Greek goddess." He gave her an odd look, and she realized she had replied to his cheer with the sort of tepid response she might have given to a gentleman at a society function, revealing her classical knowledge yet offering a neutral response to his enthusiasm. There was an awkward silence, mercifully interrupted when Mimi Junie swept into the foyer.

"I see everyone is ready. Wonderful! Henry has just brought our carriage around."

If Mimi Junie had wanted a lively traveling companion, she couldn't have chosen a better one than Mr. Forsythe. He listened and laughed and offered his own keen observations as the conversation rambled through a variety of topics. Addy didn't join in as they drove across the city, brooding about her future and her failure to find a good suitor.

Their first stop was the Five Points House of Industry, a multi-purpose charity that Mimi supported in the Five Points neighborhood. "This was once the most despairing slum in the city," Mimi lectured as one of the caretakers showed them around the huge brick building. "The Methodist clergyman who founded it as a Christian mission, soon realized that along with the residents' spiritual needs, their physical needs were also very great. And so for the nearly fifty years since, they've offered food, schooling, jobs, and a refuge for children whose parents can't or won't take care of them."

Would it be so terrible, Addy wondered as she half listened, if she and Mother did move to a smaller, more affordable mansion? Maybe that could be the middle ground between what Mother wanted and what Mimi Junie did. But Mother would probably say that such a move would send a signal to society that their circumstances had lowered.

They were about to leave the building when a group of two dozen small children, no more than two or three years old, toddled past with their caretakers like tiny ducklings in a row. Addy and the others stood aside to let them pass, but a ragged brown-haired child who was staring at the visitors instead of watching his step, suddenly stumbled and fell. Before the caretakers could react, Mr. Forsythe swooped up the boy and set him on his feet again. "There you go," he said with a gentle pat. "Mind your step, now." Addy tried to imagine one of the young gentlemen in her social circle doing the same and couldn't. In fact, if they came here to the mission at all, she could imagine them holding their noses at the institutional stench of the place. Mimi may have intended for today's excursion to inspire Addy, but instead it depressed her. She couldn't wait to escape the suffocating poverty she saw all around her, but Mimi wasn't finished.

Their second stop was the Children's Aid Society headquarters, another charity in the city's slums that was overwhelmed with needy children. The scale of the work that needed to be done seemed mountainous. When they arrived at the headquarters, the stairs leading into the building were blocked by a dozen school-aged boys in well-worn clothing, bags and bundles of belongings in hand. "Are you off to the train station?" Mimi asked the man who'd been issuing instructions to the boys.

"Yes. We have a great adventure ahead of us, don't we, boys?" Addy thought the lads looked more frightened than excited.

"Where are they going, Mimi?" she whispered as the boys followed their leaders down the steps and away. Tears shone in Mimi's eyes as she replied.

"I have such mixed feelings about this, Addy. They're leaving on an orphan train, where they'll be taken to live with families on farms and homes in the Midwestern states. The poor little dears know nothing of country life or farm work. Their entire world has been here in the slums and tenements. The Children's Aid Society has been finding homes for orphans this way for more than forty years now, and thousands of children have found new families out west. But I wish the need wasn't so great. I wish they weren't forced to leave their sisters and brothers and the only homes they've ever known."

"I've heard of those trains," Mr. Forsythe said. "I was told that a great deal of care goes into finding new homes. Even so, it seems so heartbreaking."

"We can only pray that the homes they find will be loving ones," Mimi said.

By the time they finished touring inside, Addy felt bone-weary. The sight of so many orphans was breaking her heart. If Mimi Junie's plan was to make Adelaide feel guilty for her indulgent, wasteful life, it was succeeding. "Can we please go home now?" she asked.

"I have one more donation to deliver, dear, and then we're done for the day. This one goes to the Foundling Asylum." Addy had noticed Mimi discreetly passing envelopes to the directors of the first two places but hadn't realized she was delivering charitable contributions. Addy wondered how much money had been in the envelopes—and how much money Mother was spending on her next dinner party so Addy could get acquainted with Mr. Durand and Mr. Webster. How could she enjoy herself with such a load of guilt piling upon her shoulders? She wished she had never agreed to come with her grandmother.

"The interesting thing about the Foundling Asylum," Mimi said as they traveled there, "is how it began. After the Civil War, hundreds of infants were being abandoned in New York's streets and there was no place to care for all of them. So, three nuns put a cradle on the doorstep of their home and said they would take in any unwanted child. Hundreds have been left in that cradle over the years. Some of the dear babes had notes pinned to their blankets from destitute mothers, pleading with the sisters to take care of their child. It was heart-wrenching. The need was so great that the nuns eventually had to move to a larger space."

Addy was relieved to see that the building was sparkling clean and had large windows to let in light and fresh air. But the rows of infants lined up in their iron beds, and the sad-eyed toddlers reaching out for attention, tore at Addy's heart. "Will these children eventually be adopted?" she asked.

"We're able to find homes for most of the younger ones," the director replied. "And we now have a care center where mothers who need to work can leave their little ones for the day and know they will be cared for." Once again, Addy saw her grandmother slip an envelope into the director's hand.

She sighed with relief when Mimi told Henry to drive them home. It wasn't that she had no sympathy for these pitiful children—she did! But Addy had nothing to offer them. Perhaps Mimi should take Mother on these excursions from now on, instead of her.

"Thank you for opening my eyes to the enormous need," Mr. Forsythe said on the way home. "I won't soon forget what I've seen."

"I think you can tell that I have a special place in my heart for orphaned children," Mimi replied. "I would have adopted a dozen of them myself, if my husband would have agreed. Heaven knows, our mansion has plenty of bedrooms to spare."

"You've made your point, Mimi Junie," Addy said. "It really isn't necessary to take me on any more outings. And I understand why the plight of orphans is so important to you after what happened years ago." She longed to ask Mimi if she had ever found her son, but Mr. Forsythe was listening.

"Oh, but you still haven't seen the work being done in charity hospitals such as Bellevue or Sloane Maternity Hospital or the Lunatic Asylum on Blackwell's Island."

*Lunatic asylum?* Addy recoiled in dread at the mere mention of it. "That won't be necessary, Mimi Junie. You've convinced me that the need among the poor in our city is very great. And I'm glad that you and others are doing something for them."

"But . . . ?" Mimi gave her a poke.

Addy lifted her shoulders and let them fall with a sigh, something Mother would have scolded her for. "All I can think about right now is our own family's situation. I know that makes me sound spoiled and petty, but I need to find a solution to our own problems before we lose everything. Once we're on our feet, I'll be happy to give to charity."

"We spend more money to run our household in a month than most people make in a year."

"I know, I know."

"We could live comfortably on what your father left us, according to Mr. Wilson, if we did some careful pruning. It's a matter of priorities, Addy. And while I have great respect for your mother, I'm trying to show you that her priorities are quite different from mine. You don't need to adopt mine or hers, though. More than anything else, I want you to start thinking for yourself."

Addy lapsed into silence for several minutes as she tried to make the adjustment between the dreadful poverty she'd just witnessed, and the return to the excesses of her life in her mansion. She had to admit that such a large, expensive home was too much for three women. But how could she convince Mother without hurting her?

Adelaide had all but forgotten that Mr. Forsythe was in the carriage with them until Mimi suddenly turned to him. "Tell us about your upbringing, Mr. Forsythe. From the looks of you, you seem to appreciate many of the finer things, like a good barber and a nice suit and a good job. Is your father also a lawyer?"

"No," he said, laughing. "He's a minister."

"That's right, I believe you've told us that before. I want to thank you again for accompanying us, Howard. May I call you that?"

"It would be a relief, actually. Too much formality makes me uncomfortable."

"And why is that?"

"It creates distance between people and keeps them from becoming friends in a natural way. And I think that's a shame. There are enough divisions between people without adding more."

"Well said! Now tell me, Howard, how would you like to work for me?"

"I already do, don't I?"

"You work for Mr. Wilson's law firm, and they work for the Stanhopes. But I need a bright, able-bodied person to help me administer my charitable foundation. You didn't know it, but when I asked you to accompany us, I was trying you out. I wanted to see your reaction to the places we've visited and some of the charities the Stanhope Foundation helps. And you've exceeded my hopes and expectations."

"Oh . . . well . . . thank you."

"You seem comfortable with the lower classes of society that are different from your middle-class upbringing. Why is that?"

He grinned. "My mother is the first generation of her family to be born in America, and she's quick to remind me of her humble immigrant origins. Many struggling parents dream that their children will have a better life and more opportunities than they did, and it proved true in my case. Also, my father's church has always welcomed people of all backgrounds. Our congregation is involved in many charitable enterprises too."

"And what about the wealthy class? Are you comfortable with us as well?"

"To be honest, I didn't have much interaction with millionaires until I started working for Mr. Wilson's law firm. And I've only worked there for a short time. I'm not even a junior partner yet."

"I see. One more question. Are you married, Howard?"

"Mimi! It's none of our business!" Her grandmother's very personal questions had made Addy uncomfortable, but the last question had gone too far.

"I know that sounds very personal, but if Howard decides to accept my offer, I will need to know how much time he has to spare. I don't wish to take him away from his family responsibilities. I believe a husband should have time at home with the family he loves instead of working night and day."

"It's okay, Miss Stanhope. I don't mind answering. I'm not married."

"And is there a sweetheart in your life?"

"I'm afraid not."

"Because you haven't had time for one?"

"Mr. Wilson keeps me very occupied."

"Well, please take as much time as you need to think about my offer, Howard. I can send you some information about the Stanhope Foundation in the meantime, if you'd like, and you're welcome to visit our offices. I don't need a decision right away, but I'm feeling my age more and more every day, and it would be nice to know the foundation will end up in good hands."

As soon as they arrived back at the mansion, Mother whisked Mr. Forsythe away to discuss the furniture sales with the auction house. "I've prepared an inventory of what I've selected so far . . ." Addy heard her say before she and Howard disappeared into the study.

"I'm going upstairs to freshen up," Adelaide told her grandmother. "I feel so . . . gritty."

"We'll talk some more at dinner," Mimi said.

### ～ Junietta ～

Junietta didn't think she had enough strength to climb the stairs to her room, then come back down again for dinner. Yet she had to talk with Adelaide about today's experience while it was still fresh in her mind. The excursion had nearly defeated Junietta physically, yet she was buoyed in her spirit at the thought of Howard Forsythe taking her place at the foundation. How wonderful he would be for the job—young, bright, compassionate.

She allowed Betsy and Jane to help make her comfortable downstairs in the morning room instead of attempting the stairs, and after a cup of tea and a short nap by the fire, she was able to make her way to the family dining room at suppertime. Sylvia and Addy were already seated when she arrived, and she sat down beside them, feeling a little breathless. "Did Adelaide tell you where we went today, Sylvia?"

"No, but I'm sure it was fascinating," she said dryly.

"Please, Mimi. I'd rather not relive all the tragic scenes of sad-eyed orphans that we witnessed," Addy said. "But if you don't mind, I'd very much like to know if you ever found your son who was given up for adoption."

"I don't mind at all. But in order to answer your question, I'll need to back up and tell you a little more about my life with Art and our son, A.B.—your father. Would you like to hear it?"

Mother held up her hand. "Not if it's going to be shocking. The servants have ears, you know."

"Then they'd better leave the room and wait in the kitchen," she replied, laughing. "Hattie and Betsy, you're excused for now. We'll ring for you when we've finished talking." They quietly left the room, but Junietta wouldn't have been at all surprised—or upset—if they stood just outside the door, listening.

"Now as you already know," she began, "my sin forced me to make a deal with Arthur Stanhope. And I was faithful to keep my end of the bargain. I gave parties and balls with New York's finest families in attendance. Arthur and his sons received invitations to the wealthiest homes, including the Astors and the Vanderbilts. I presented Arthur with a grandson and heir, A.B. So, as time passed, I felt I had a right to demand something in return. And what I wanted more than anything else was information about my first son. Neal Galloway's son. I knew that Arthur did business by unearthing damaging information about people, then threatening to expose it in order to get his own way. So I watched and listened and waited for an opportunity to learn something damaging about my father-in-law, so I could get my own way. But my patience ran out after a terrible scene at our family dinner table one night . . ."

# 12

*~~~*

1852

*~~~ Junietta ~~~*

The gold-rimmed dishes and sterling silver place settings glittered
beneath the ornate chandelier. Our servants glided silently in and out of
the room as they removed the remains of the five-course dinner, which
had included oysters, watercress soup, and rack of lamb. There were only
four of us at the table—Arthur, my husband Art, his brother David, and
me—and I couldn't imagine what the cringing waiters must have thought
of the venom that had spewed from Arthur Stanhope's mouth and soul
throughout the long, agonizing evening. I hadn't enjoyed any of my food
as I'd sat rigidly in my chair, gritting my teeth, trying in vain to close my
ears to Arthur's caustic words. They were directed against his sons Art
and David, who sat in stoic silence, not daring to utter a sound in reply.

After two years of marriage, I'd learned to dread the family dinners
that Arthur commanded me to attend. Thankfully, I endured them only
once every month or so. The rest of the time, Arthur worked long hours,

seven days a week, and expected his sons to do the same. I had never heard him praise his sons at any of these meals. Instead, he recited a litany of their failures and faults, and tonight he had been particularly brutal. Something had obviously gone wrong at work. I couldn't make sense of it and I didn't want to, but Arthur spent the entire meal chastising Art and David, mocking them cruelly and threatening to disinherit them. If my husband had stood up and said, "Fine! Disinherit me! I've had enough!" I would have cheered. We could have taken our year-old son and made it on our own somehow. But of course, Art didn't dare. The jealousy that Arthur had fostered between the two brothers was so intense that Art and David held their anger and frustration inside, not daring to respond to their father's humiliating treatment and give the other brother an advantage. When I could take no more, I rose to leave.

"Where do you think you're going?" Arthur bellowed.

"You're discussing business, so I thought—"

"Sit down! You need to know what a worthless dunderhead you married."

I sat, my stomach churning with fear and hatred. Arthur ranted for another hour before he excused us.

I retreated to my room on trembling legs, longing to pack my things and leave for good. But where could I go? Divorce or even marital separation was still a scandalous undertaking, and I feared it would lead to my family's disgrace. Besides, neither Arthur nor Art would ever allow me to leave with my son, and I couldn't leave A.B. behind.

After a while, I heard the door to Art's adjoining bedroom open and close. Glass clinked as he poured himself a drink from the liquor bottles he kept in his room. Then the floorboards creaked as he paced. I waited, hoping he would come to me so I could offer my friendship and comfort, but he didn't. At last, I went to our adjoining door and knocked.

"Art, it's me. May I come in?"

"No. Go away."

I stayed by the door for a long time, listening, hoping he would change his mind. But he didn't. And that night I vowed to find a way for my husband and me to get out from under Arthur's control. If we didn't escape soon, it would be only a matter of time before Arthur began bullying our son the same way he bullied Art, David, and Roger. And maybe if I helped my husband find a way to escape, we would grow closer. Maybe I could finally tell him about my lost son, and he would be so grateful for my support that he would help me find him.

⁂

Months passed as the growing tension in the household became nearly unbearable. Something had to change. I couldn't stand living in such an atmosphere of recrimination and hatred, nor did I want my beloved son to grow up in it. Desperate, I began watching my father-in-law closely, listening from behind closed doors, waiting for my chance to learn one of his secrets so Art and I and our son could break free from Arthur's tyranny.

Most of my father-in-law's mail went to his office, but I ordered our housekeeper to let me see anything that arrived for him at our house. The servants were on my side. They hated and feared Arthur as much as I did. I felt close to the breaking point when, miraculously, the letter that changed everything arrived in the mail. It stood out from the rest of Arthur's mail because of the homemade envelope and childish writing. It was from someone named Helmut Steinhaus in a town I'd never heard of in Lancaster County, Pennsylvania. I considered steaming open the envelope but didn't dare. Instead, I copied down the return address and asked the chambermaid to bring me the contents of Arthur's wastepaper basket every day. I had no idea how explosive the contents of that letter would prove to be until I read the crumpled letter the maid rescued from the trash.

> *Gustav,*
> *Mother is in her last days and would like to see you.*
> *She wants to tell you that all is forgiven.*
> *Please come so she can rest in peace.*
>
> *Your brother,*
> *Helmut*

I waited for Arthur to announce that he was going away for a few days to see his dying mother. When he didn't, I made plans to go to the mysterious address myself, aware that the only way to play Arthur's game was by his rules. If I could learn some of my father-in-law's secrets, perhaps he'd be forced to set Art and me free. I told my husband that I was going to visit my sister for a few days and left A.B. with his nursemaid. Then I went to see Meara, my closest and most trusted friend, at the boardinghouse. She agreed to leave Regan with the other women for a few days and accompany me to Pennsylvania.

With multiple stops along the way, the train took all morning to travel the ninety miles from New York City to Allentown, Pennsylvania, then the remainder of the afternoon to reach the town of Lancaster. Meara and I spent the night in a small inn, then hired a carriage and driver the next morning to take us to the return address on Arthur's letter. After stopping twice to ask directions, we pulled up to an aging farmhouse from the last century, surrounded by cluttered outbuildings, animal pens, a barn, and cultivated farmland. A snarling dog sprang from hiding, keeping us inside the carriage until a woman finally emerged from the house to quiet him. My heart thudded with fear and hope, anticipation and dread, as the driver helped Meara and me from the carriage and we walked toward her.

"Good morning. My name is Junietta Stanhope, and I'm looking for Helmut Steinhaus. Is this his farm?"

She gave a curt nod. "What do you want with him?" Her suspicion was obvious from her stance and tone, and I wondered if she would set the dog loose on us if I gave the wrong reply. I had worn a plain traveling dress, but the difference between my clothing and her stained, homespun skirt and apron was still obvious.

"I would like to speak with him about a letter he sent to my father-in-law." I didn't know if I should call him Gustav, as the letter had. It seemed to take the woman an endlessly long time to reply—or was it just my unease?

"I'll have to fetch him," she finally said. "You can wait in the house."

She directed the driver to a trough where he could water the horses, then motioned for us to follow her. The squat, one-story, stone farmhouse was dark and smoky inside, and it took a moment for my eyes to adjust. An open fireplace filled one wall, and it appeared from the glowing logs and the cast-iron pot dangling from the crane that all the cooking was done on that hearth.

"You want coffee?" She pointed to an enamel pot on the edge of the coals. "There might be some left."

"No, thank you. Please don't trouble yourself. Our errand shouldn't take long." Meara and I pulled chairs from beneath the wooden table and sat down to wait while she disappeared outside again.

"What do you make of this place, Junie?" Meara asked in a whisper. Neither of us were sure if we were alone in the house, but it seemed quiet.

"I honestly don't know what to think. It doesn't seem possible that Arthur could have grown up in a house like this, but the letter seemed to have come from his brother."

The woman returned five minutes later with a man who resembled Arthur so strongly that I knew they had to be related. But Arthur was always expensively barbered and attired, while this man wore laborer's clothes. His grizzled face was brown from the sun, his dirty hands rough and calloused. Even with the wary look he gave us, he seemed like a much nicer man than Arthur.

"I'm Helmut Steinhaus," he said. "And who are you again?"

"Junietta Stanhope. And this is—"

"Stanhope! Did Gustav send you?"

"He's my father-in-law. I saw the letter you wrote to him about your mother and—"

"You're too late. She passed away two days ago."

"Oh. I'm so sorry." Although I hadn't come with the hope of meeting her.

"Gustav could have made an effort to come. He owed her that much and a lot more, besides. I don't know how she could forgive him after what he did, but our mother was a good Christian woman and not one to bear a grudge. I'm surprised my high-and-mighty brother could find it in his heart to send you, even."

I assessed his bullish stance and the anger I heard in his tone and decided to take a chance with the truth. "He didn't send me. I came on my own after I saw your letter. To tell you the truth, my father-in-law is not a very nice man. He bullies my husband and his other two sons, and everyone he does business with. I thought if I came here to meet his family and to see where he came from, it would help me understand him—"

"Understand him? Nobody has ever understood him, least of all his family."

"Well, would you mind . . . ? I mean . . . can you tell us a little more about him? He never talks about his past, even to his sons, and I'm hoping you can help us get to know him a little better."

"I have nothing good to say about my brother. Nothing. But if you want some dirt to help bury him, I'll be happy to give you plenty of it!"

It was exactly what I had come for, but when he put it so starkly, it made me feel dirty myself. Especially after Helmut's words about his forgiving Christian mother. I would have denied my motives, expressed my condolences, and gone home if it hadn't been for my two sons. I wanted A.B. to grow up free from Arthur. And I was convinced that Arthur knew who had adopted Neal Galloway's son.

I drew a deep breath and said, "Yes. Thank you."

Helmut had been standing in the doorway all this time, but he crossed the wide-plank floor and pulled out a chair at the table across from Meara and me. His wife quietly poked the coals in the fireplace and stirred whatever was simmering in the pot as we talked. I didn't know how long Helmut's anger toward his brother had been simmering, but it took no prompting on my part to make it boil over.

"His real name is Gustav Steinhaus, and he has plenty of dirty secrets. One of them is the truth about our father, Gerhard Steinhaus. He was a good man and didn't deserve a son like Gustav, but our father had secrets too. He came to America in 1776 as a Hessian soldier and fought for the British during the war."

My mouth fell open in surprise. Arthur Stanhope was the son of a hired mercenary? No wonder he didn't want his background known. Families like the Van Burens and De Witts had lost loved ones in America's battle for freedom from British tyranny. Their memories were long, their loyalties strong. Arthur never would have gained acceptance among them if they'd known he was the son of a Hessian soldier.

Helmut must have seen my shock because he spread his hands and quickly said, "It wasn't the way you must think. Our father was a good man, a farmer's son from the German state of Hesse. That's why he and the other soldiers were called Hessians. It wasn't in him to be a soldier, but he had been drafted into the army and required to serve. When his country's leaders decided to rent their army to the British to fight against the Americans, the soldiers had no choice in the matter. They weren't for the king or against the rebels. Our father was eighteen years old and was forced to do what he was told."

"I understand. But that isn't the way most loyal patriots would see it. There's still a lot of bitterness against the British and their Hessian mercenaries, even after all these years. The second war forty years ago brought it all back to life again."

"That's true in these parts too."

"So what happened to your father?"

"He fought in the Battle of White Plains in the fall of 1776 and was taken prisoner. They brought him here to Lancaster County, where he was eventually made to do farm work when the need for laborers became great. Many of the farmers in these small communities spoke German, and they knew that the German mercenaries weren't their enemies. Our father was put to work here on this farm, which belonged to my grandfather. Opa loved his farm, but he only had daughters to help him. My father fell in love with the oldest one and married her when the war ended. He deserted from the army and led the British to believe he had died. He never returned to his homeland and eventually inherited this farm."

The incredible story left me momentarily speechless. That it was

Arthur B. Stanhope's story made it almost unbelievable. "Where do you and Arthur—I mean Gustav—fit into the family?"

"My father and his first wife had seven children, although not all of them lived to grow up. After his wife died giving birth to the last one, he needed help with the house and all the children, so he married my mother, who was several years younger than he was. Gustav is the oldest of her three children, and I'm the youngest. We have a sister in between."

I tried to take this all in, but I had trouble imagining Arthur growing up in this primitive farmhouse on a struggling farm. Yet I easily imagined the reaction of New York's high society if they learned the truth. "What was he like back then?" I asked.

"Gustav was always different from everyone else. Never content. Always reading and studying things. He learned how to bully everyone, even our older brothers, and he did it well. Everyone feared him. He got whatever he wanted."

I wasn't surprised to hear that Arthur had always been a tyrant. I might have felt sorry for him if it had been tragic circumstances that had hardened him and turned him into one. But that wasn't the case. "When did he leave home?" I asked.

"Gustav was itching to leave and make a name for himself from the time he was twelve years old. But we were poor, and he didn't have a way to make it on his own. Then our father died of pneumonia when Gustav was sixteen. He bullied our brothers and sisters into letting him handle his affairs and transfer the deed to this farm to our oldest brother. Instead, Gustav sold off most of the acreage in a secret deal and skipped town with the profits."

"He stole money and land from his own family?"

"He did. Without enough land to make the farm prosper, our older brothers were forced to leave home and look for jobs in Philadelphia to support their families. I was fourteen, so I stayed to work what was left of the land and take care of our mother. Later on, I heard that Gustav had changed his name and used our inheritance to buy a factory of some sort. Then he doubled his wealth during the War of 1812 and moved to New York. They tell me my brother is a very rich man now."

"He's a multimillionaire." How I wished I could wash my hands of him and his filthy money. But at least I had an arsenal of ammunition to use against Arthur now. I thanked Helmut for telling me the truth, then Meara and I climbed back into the hired carriage.

"What do you make of all that, Junie?" she asked along the way.

"I think I hate him more than ever, if that's possible."

"Don't be doing that, Junie. There's no end to hate once it starts growing."

"Well, I've made up my mind to give away every penny that my father-in-law gives me. And the first people I'm giving some of it to is Helmut and his family."

I decided not to tell anyone what I had learned. I would keep the information like an ace up my sleeve, waiting for the right time to tell my husband. More than anything else in the world, I longed for Art, A.B., and me to be free from Arthur Benton Stanhope.

# 13

1853

*~ Junietta ~*

A light shone through the crack beneath Art's bedroom door. I could hear him pacing on the other side. I knew from the inky darkness outside my window that it was the early hours of the morning. For the past two weeks, Art had been wound so tightly I worried he'd explode. I knew it had something to do with work, because David seemed just as anxious, walking through the hallways white-faced, barely hearing when someone spoke to him.

I climbed out of bed and put on my dressing gown. My rapping on Art's door sounded thunderous in the quiet house. "It's me, Art. May I come in?"

He opened the door. "What do you want?" He hadn't changed out of his trousers and shirt but wore a smoking jacket on top of them against the chill from the open window. Cigarette smoke hovered in the room. The ashtray was filled with butts. The liquor bottle on his side table was empty, the sticky glass leaving a ring on the wood. I could tell by his disheveled hair that he'd been running his fingers through it.

"Can't you tell me what's making you so upset?" I asked. "Maybe it will help to talk about it."

"I doubt it." He gave me a dismissive look, as if he thought me incapable of understanding, let alone helping.

"Try it." I came into Art's room, closing the door behind me, and sat down on his bed, waiting. The alcohol Art had consumed helped to loosen his tongue, and he soon began to share his heart with me as he continued pacing the room.

"My father's second-in-command is retiring because of poor health. David and I are competing for the chance to replace him. I've worked all my life toward the goal of taking over this position, and I want it badly, Junietta. But so does David. We're supposed to come up with ideas and strategies for going forward. So far, Father has rejected everything I've proposed. I have no idea what David is up to, except that he's probably stabbing me in the back. Everything is at stake! My entire future! My livelihood!"

I thought of my own siblings and felt badly that these two brothers, so close in age, so much alike, could never be friends. I thought, as I often did, that Art and David should work as a team and outsmart their father instead of letting him manipulate them. "Would it be so bad if David won?" I asked.

He turned on me angrily. "What do you think! I would be ruined!"

"But at least you'd be out from under Arthur's thumb. You could move someplace else. Find another job or start your own business."

"Neither my father nor David would ever allow it. I know too much about how Father runs his business. He would pursue me to the moon and back and try to destroy me. Besides, I've worked hard. I deserve the top position in this company."

It was time to use Arthur's secrets against him. I stood and went to Art, touching his arm to halt his restless marching. "Listen, Art. You need to approach this problem the same way that Arthur would. He's able to control people because he holds damning information over them. He threatens to expose their secrets if they don't do exactly what he says." I waited until he focused on me.

"Go on."

"I know some of your father's secrets. Do you want to hear them?"

He nodded. I took his hand and led him to the bed, sitting down beside him. The glee I felt at finally getting my revenge against Arthur made me smile. "I came across a letter from Arthur's brother, so I went to Pennsylvania to visit him. I found out that Arthur's real name is Gustav Steinhaus. His father was a Hessian mercenary who fought for the British during the war for independence."

I watched Art digest this news. "Are you sure?"

"Positive. The fact that he's the son of a Hessian mercenary who later deserted from the British army is damaging enough. But when his father died, Arthur defrauded his own brothers out of their land and their inheritance. He stole from his family, including his own mother, in order to get his start in business. His brother still lives as if it's the eighteenth century while Arthur lives like a millionaire. It's unforgiveable."

Art was suddenly sober. He studied me as if trying to see inside my thoughts. My husband had a brilliant mind, and when he pulled his hand free from mine, I suddenly feared I had given away too much.

"You didn't go all the way to Pennsylvania to find out this information just for my sake, did you?"

"I hate the way Arthur treats you."

He hesitated a moment, then asked, "What is my father holding over you, Junietta?"

Was I going to trust Art or not? Were we really partners and friends, or would he reject me because I hadn't told him the truth about my past? I should have realized how jealous and insecure Art was, his paranoia fed and stoked by Arthur all his life. But I took a chance that Art would be grateful to me for helping him, and that he would help me find my son in return.

"Tell me!" he bellowed.

A chill chased up my arms. Art knew me well enough to know if I tried to lie. In that moment, I felt afraid of him, sensing that he had the ability to be as fierce and ruthless as his father. I could lose my son A.B. just as I had lost my first son.

"There was a man I once loved," I said quickly. "He went to California to prospect for gold, but his ship was wrecked and he died. I had his son—"

"Out of wedlock?"

I nodded. "My father gave my child up for adoption. Arthur found out, somehow, and used my disgrace as a weapon against me and my family."

Art's shock registered on his face. Then I saw the shock change into anger. Again, I feared this man. "He blackmailed you into marrying me, didn't he?"

"Yes. But you and I have become friends, Art. We're allies. Please believe me when I say I want to help you get out from your father's control as much as—"

"But you want power over him too. What are you really after, Junie?"

It was useless to lie. "Arthur must know where my son is. I want to find him and see how he is, see if he's loved and cared for. I won't tear him away from his new family; I just need to see him, even if it's from a distance. Will you help me, Art? I just helped you—"

"In order to use me!" he shouted. "You wanted to use me to find your lover's bastard child!" He felt betrayed, by his father and now by me. Perhaps he sensed that he would lose me once I found my son, and he was probably right. "So all of this talk about wanting to be friends with me has been a lie?"

"No! I felt so alone after I left home, and I needed a friend! And we are friends, aren't we? We're A.B.'s parents. We're partners. That's why I just told you about Arthur's past. I want to help you."

"But you kept the truth from me about your past. Friends don't keep secrets, Junietta. How can I ever trust you again?"

"You know me, Art. We've been married for two years."

"I thought I knew you, but I guess I was wrong. Get out of my room."

"Please, listen—"

"I said, get out!" He pulled me to my feet and shoved me roughly through the door.

I didn't know what to do. I was barely twenty-two years old and condemned to spend the rest of my life with a husband who hated me. And with his vicious father. I would have stolen A.B. from his crib and disappeared somewhere, but I knew that Arthur would use his endless wealth to search the ends of the earth to find his heir. My plan for revenge had backfired. I was trapped in my own net.

❦

The days passed in agonizing tension and silence. I wondered when and how Art would use the information I had given him against his father. I was terrified that he would reveal my part in obtaining it. The simmering hatred in our household had become nearly unbearable, a loaded gun, cocked and aimed. To my dismay, Art finally used his weapon at our next family dinner. Arthur had spent most of the meal taunting him and David, threatening to cut off both of them and hiring a general manager from the outside. I saw Art's hand shake as he lifted his wineglass and took a fortifying gulp. Then he set it down and said, "You're going to hire me, Father."

"Oh, you think so, do you?"

"I know secrets about your past. I know your name is Gustav Steinhaus and that your father was a traitor to the revolution. A Hessian mercenary. A deserter." Art stared down at the table as he talked, fingering the stem of his wineglass as if not daring to look up at his father. "I know you got your start in business by cheating and defrauding your family. You stole from your own mother."

Arthur leaned back in his chair and folded his arms across his chest. "Is that so?" His expression was unreadable.

Art finally looked up. A trickle of sweat ran down his face. "Appoint me second-in-command. Then change your will and designate only me and only my son as your heirs. David and Roger get nothing." He wore a slight smile on his face as he glanced at David. "If you don't, the world will soon learn about your origins. How will that sit with the old Knickerbockers, whose families fought and died fighting against the British? Or with the fine churchgoing men you do business with every day? Do you think they'll want you to invest money in their businesses when they hear where it came from?"

The room grew very still. Art and his father stared at each other. I held my breath, unable to guess how Arthur would react to his son's ultimatum. I wondered if Art had overplayed his hand.

Then Arthur laughed out loud, and it was such a cruel, humorless laugh that I wanted to cover my ears to escape it. "I'm not afraid of what people say about me," Arthur said. "You've greatly misjudged me if you think gossip like that will make me give in to your demands." I couldn't breathe, fearing for my husband and for myself. "Nevertheless, I'm going to agree to your terms. Not because I'm afraid of you or your threat to cause a scandal. But because you just proved to me that you have the guts and the ruthlessness that are necessary to succeed. If you would try to blackmail your own father and disinherit your two brothers, then you won't think twice about dirty deals with strangers." Arthur reached out and shook Art's hand in what looked like a bone-crushing grip. "We'll outdo the Astors and Vanderbilts and all the rest, Son. You're now my second-in-command. And you," he said, turning to David. "You, my sorry excuse for a son, will not only spend the rest of your life serving your brother, but you won't get a dime of my money when I die."

David rose to his feet. "In that case, I don't intend to work for either one of you a day longer." He tossed his napkin onto the table and started for the door.

"If you think anyone else in this city will hire you, you're mistaken," Arthur called after him. "I'll tell them exactly how worthless you are."

"I don't care!" Tears glistened in his eyes and made his voice tremble.

"Are you going to cry, little baby brother?" Art asked.

I rested my hand on my husband's arm. This had gone too far and had to stop. David was his brother! I was appalled by what I had put into motion. "Art, please don't—" He shook off my hand.

"You like my money too much to ever leave and go off on your own," Arthur shouted at David as he left the room. "You wouldn't know how to live without servants to wait on you."

I left the room, too, and fled upstairs. I couldn't stop crying as I relived David's utter devastation. I had wanted a weapon to use against Arthur, not him. I needed to plead with my husband and beg him not to punish his brother, so I waited for Art to come upstairs. But I cried myself to sleep long before Art finished celebrating with his father and came to bed.

Early the next morning, one of the grooms found David Stanhope hanging from a beam in the carriage house. He had tied one end of the rope around his neck, the other to the beam, then had jumped to his death from the loft.

I screamed in horror when the chambermaid who brought my breakfast tray told me. I was appalled by what I had done. I had provided the ammunition and loaded the weapon that had killed David. His death was my fault. I was no better than Arthur, who took pleasure in plotting to hurt people and destroy their lives. My husband had become like him too. What would stop my beloved son, A.B., from growing up to be just like his father and grandfather—and like me?

I couldn't face my husband or Arthur, or even our servants. I needed to get out of the house and go somewhere, anywhere, as long as it was far away from them. I didn't even pack a bag, but simply walked out the door and hailed a cab to take me to the train station. I boarded the first train that arrived. It was northbound, leaving Manhattan Island and traveling through the peaceful countryside. Within a few minutes, the gray expanse of the Hudson River was flowing alongside me, the mountains were surrounding me, and the filthy city and the Stanhope mansion were far behind me.

I knew I could never find forgiveness for what I had done, but as the train approached the station in Tarrytown, twenty-five miles outside the city, I remembered Reverend Cooper and his kindness to me. I got off the train, then stood watching its plume of dark smoke until it faded from sight. The Hudson River docks were a short distance away, and I considered walking out into the dark water and allowing the tide to pull me under, but what would become of A.B.? Then I looked in the opposite direction and saw a church steeple. I started walking toward it.

The pain and guilt I felt over David's death multiplied with every step. I relived Neal's death four years ago, and the loneliness and isolation I felt as I had hidden away in shame in Elizabeth's cottage. I recalled the pain of my son's birth, then the even greater pain when he'd been taken from my arms. Now there was new pain, new shame and loneliness. I didn't know how I would ever find joy or hope again.

The church sanctuary was unlocked but empty. The space smelled of wood polish and musty hymnbooks. I sat down in an empty pew for several minutes, but couldn't find any words to say to the Savior who had forgiven me once before. At last, I went next door to the stone parsonage and knocked. A servant in a white apron and cap answered. Children's voices rippled in the background. "I'm looking for Reverend Cooper," I told her.

"Come in. I'll fetch him."

"I would prefer if he came out here." The maid disappeared inside, leaving the door open. Reverend Cooper appeared a few minutes later. He smiled when he saw me.

"Your name is Mary, if I remember correctly?" It took me a moment to recall my lie. "You came to me a few years ago with a question."

"I-I have another question for you, Reverend Cooper, if you can spare the time."

"I'll try. Please, come in."

"Could we talk inside the church again?"

"Of course." He led me down the walkway and through the rear door into the church. We sat on a pew in the empty sanctuary.

The words squeezed painfully from my heart. I told him how much I hated my father-in-law for blackmailing me into marrying his son. I explained how far I had sunk in my thirst for revenge. I confessed how I had used my husband's hatred and jealousy as a weapon, and how he had then turned that weapon against his brother. And I covered my face and wept as I told him about David's suicide. I felt Reverend Cooper's hand on my shoulder.

"I'm so sorry, Mary," he soothed.

At last, I lifted my head to wipe my tears. "I'm so sorry for all the pain and destruction I've unleashed. I only wanted to find my son, the baby I was carrying when I was here three years ago. My papa gave him away to be adopted as soon as he was born, and I was certain that my father-in-law knew where he was. But I've done a horrible, horrible thing, and now David is dead, and it's all my fault. I'll never forgive myself."

He was quiet for a moment before saying, "It seems to me that two other people also played a part in David's unfortunate death."

"That doesn't make me any less guilty." I paused to form my question, staring at the shadow patterns on the floor as light streamed through the tall windows. "You convinced me that I could be forgiven for having a baby out of wedlock. But now I've done something so much worse. Once again, I've missed the mark, only this time someone died because of me. How can I ever make up for that? I would do anything to be able to undo what I've done, but I know it's impossible."

"You're right," he said softly. "It can't be undone. And I suspect that you'll suffer guilt for the rest of your life. But feeling guilty doesn't mean that God still considers you guilty. As I explained once before, if you confess your sin to God and plead for His mercy, He will forgive you."

"But how can He forgive me when I can't forgive myself? I'm as selfish and vindictive as my father-in law."

"And you deserve to be punished. But Christ was condemned in your place. He willingly took on the punishment for your sin. You've been set free."

He let me think about that for a moment, but I couldn't take it in. I silently shook my head as I pictured Jesus on the cross. I felt so ashamed. "I'm not worthy of His forgiveness."

"Nobody is. That's the point. Everyone alive is a sinner. Listen, I can tell that you're genuinely sorry, and that you don't want to continue sinning. By confessing, you can accept the forgiveness that God freely offers you. The Bible promises that God doesn't punish us as our sins deserve, but 'as the heaven is high above the earth, so great is His mercy toward them that fear Him. As far as the east is from the west, so far hath He removed our transgressions from us.' Every time you look up at the heavens, you can remember those words and believe that you are forgiven."

I covered my face and cried for a few more minutes, aware that it might take much longer this time for me to feel forgiven. Every time I walked past the carriage house or saw David's empty seat at the table, I would question God's willingness to show mercy. I longed to get back on the train and keep running forever, but where would I go? I didn't want to go home to my husband. I couldn't go home to my parents. And I had no way to get by on my own. I sighed and looked up at him again.

"Reverend Cooper, you warned me about facing the consequences of my sin the last time we spoke, and I'm terrified to face them again this time. I know divorce is wrong, but I can't go back. I don't want to live with my husband or father-in-law anymore. Yet I have a little son who I love dearly. They would never let me see him again if I left. I-I just don't know what to do."

"From what you've told me, it sounds like love is absent in your household."

"They don't know the meaning of the word."

"And yet, your husband and father-in-law aren't beyond the hope of Christ's redemption any more than you are. As long as we have breath, there's hope that repentance will bring forgiveness and lives will be changed. God can redeem any situation and bring new life from it, even yours and mine."

I silently shook my head, finding it impossible to believe that the Stanhopes could ever change.

"Now that you've experienced Christ's love," he continued, "you can be an example to them of what love means. The Bible says that unbelieving husbands can be won over to God by the loving behavior of their wives. I urge you to continue showing him the love of God, regardless of how you feel toward him. Show it to your son as well. Christ showed His love for us by laying down His life, and He sometimes asks us to lay down ours. He can bring good from your mistakes if you ask Him to guide you."

"How . . . ? Where do I begin?"

"We all begin by loving God with all our heart. And then by loving our neighbor. Do all the good that you can, any way that you can, to whoever you can. But don't do it to buy God's forgiveness—forgiveness is free. Do it to show your gratitude for being forgiven."

I knew my passion would always be to help mothers and their children. Yet it seemed as though no matter how much good I tried to do, or how much money I gave away, it would never be enough.

"May I also offer you some advice about your first son, Mary? The one who was given away for adoption?"

I nodded. How my heart squeezed whenever I thought of him!

"Do you know the story of how Abraham offered his son Isaac to God? He was the most important person in Abraham's life, but he offered him because God was even more important to Abraham than his child. Can you give your missing son to God the way Abraham did? If God wills that you'll meet your boy again, then He will arrange it. If not, can you let him go and trust him to our Father's hands?"

It was a question that I couldn't answer . . . yet.

The train stopped dozens of times on the way home, giving me time and space to think about Reverend Cooper's words. He was right. It was going to take a long time for me to feel forgiven. And for me to learn how to show love to Art and his father the way that I should. I remained in my room for the next two days, eating my meals there, not speaking to anyone. I didn't see Arthur or my husband again until we stood together at David's funeral. It was a small, private affair. Only the servants knew the truth about how he had died. If Art or his father felt any guilt or remorse for their part in his death, I saw no sign of it. They remained dry-eyed throughout.

The next time I saw Art was a week later when we attended a ball together. We had accepted the invitation weeks ago and were obliged to attend. Art looked handsome and distinguished in his tuxedo, and he carried himself with more confidence now that he ran his father's business. But I saw no softness in his eyes when he looked at me. I knew the cruelty he was capable of—that I was capable of. I didn't speak a word to him all evening, but on the carriage ride home as the dawning sky grew light, I summoned enough courage to confront him.

"I want to start a charitable foundation to give money to the poor," I said. "Your father never gives away a cent, but you're in control now. Help me set up a charity in the Stanhope name."

"Why should I do that?"

I blurted every reason I could think of. "Other wealthy families are philanthropists. It will reflect well on you as the new head of the company. You'll become well known and admired for your generosity. You don't want to inherit your father's reputation for being ruthless and tightfisted, do you? You can win respect in this city and, more importantly, in the eyes of our son by helping the poor. Remember, your grandfather was also a poor, penniless immigrant."

"I'll have someone look into it when I have time." He sounded bored. I leaned across the space that separated us and forced him to face me.

"Don't try to shove me aside, Art. The wealth that you and Arthur have accumulated is blood money. Arthur stole from his family and left them destitute. And now you've robbed your two brothers. Remember, I know the truth about how David died."

"Are you trying to blackmail me? Did you forget about your own sordid past?"

"I haven't forgotten, and I'm not blackmailing you. I'm simply saying that this family needs to make atonement for our wrongdoing."

He was quiet for a moment. I listened to the rhythmic cadence of the horses' hooves on the cobblestones, wondering what Art was thinking. "I'm not happy about what happened to my brother," he finally said. "I never intended for things to go that far. My father convinced me that David was my enemy, and I saw him that way all my life. When I finally had an opportunity to defeat him—"

"You need to confess to God, not to me, Art." He made a mocking sound as if he thought I had made a joke. I hurried to finish as we neared home, not wanting to be with my husband any longer than necessary once we arrived. "Get one of your lawyers to help me set up a foundation and make me the administrator. There are dozens of worthy causes to contribute to. But I need your answer now. Tonight. It makes me sick to my stomach to think of how much money our hosts just spent on this evening's ball."

"I don't like to be pressured."

"And I don't like to be ignored or silenced." We halted in front of the mansion and the coachman opened the door of our carriage. I was supposed to alight first but I remained in place, waiting.

"Very well. I'll send one of our lawyers to the house to help you set it up."

# 14

### ~ Sylvia ~

The candles on the dining room table had flickered down to stubs by the time Junietta finished her story. Her revelations left Sylvia feeling numb. Like Junietta, she also had secrets in her past that needed God's forgiveness. She had been able to ignore them while A.B. was alive, her mind busy with all the distractions and indulgences her wealthy lifestyle provided. Now her mother-in-law seemed to think they should all reshape their lives with new priorities, as Junietta had done after David's suicide. Where would Sylvia even begin?

"The Stanhope Foundation now distributes millions of dollars each year," Junietta continued. "We've invested in dozens of worthwhile projects over the years, and I've made it my life's work. But I'm getting too old and too tired to administrate it anymore. That's one of the reasons why I've been showing you the many needs in this city, Adelaide. I would like to think that some of my passion for the work will carry on after I'm gone. It's up to each of us to find ways to show our love to God and our neighbors. That's really all He asks of each of us."

Adelaide looked to Sylvia as if expecting her to reply or argue in return, but she felt too exhausted by her mother-in-law's revelations, and the truth about the Stanhopes' millions, to engage with her. She also realized why Junietta was so different from the rest of the family, rarely attending parties and dinners, and never making social calls like her peers. Sylvia had assumed that Junietta was just too old or too reclusive to do all those things, never realizing just how much work she had been doing with her charity all this time.

Everyone seemed to be waiting for Sylvia to speak. "I was always led to believe that David had died in an accident," she finally said.

"That's because the Stanhopes had enough money and power to reinforce that belief. Very few people ever knew the truth. And if they did suspect suicide, they didn't know the terrible reason why David had taken his own life."

"Did A.B. know the truth?" Sylvia asked.

"I don't know if Arthur or Art ever told him, but I certainly shielded him from it. No child needs to know his parents are capable of driving a man to kill himself. I told the two of you the truth because I wanted you to understand why I don't want this house and why I am so determined to give away my share of the Stanhopes' money."

"But this is my home, Junietta. And Adelaide's home. It wasn't even built when David took his life. What happened in your past doesn't affect the way Adelaide and I feel about our home."

"I understand. But it's only wood and stone. Love makes it a home, and love has always been in short supply around here."

"I'm sorry you feel that way." Sylvia stared down at her cup, gently swirling the remaining dregs of coffee and grounds. "I love my daughter, and therefore I cannot, will not, stand by and watch Adelaide lose everything. The only thing a mother in my position can do is make sure she marries a wealthy husband. And this mansion is the only bargaining chip we have left."

"Well, I'm sorry too," Junietta said. "If only my husband was here to see how his jealousy and hatred have backfired against the three of us. If he hadn't convinced Arthur to change his will so only the oldest son could inherit, the estate would have been divided equally between his three sons, and we wouldn't be in this predicament."

"But here we are," Sylvia said firmly. "And now it's up to me to figure out what to do about it."

"Well, please don't involve me in any of your schemes to keep this house. I don't want any part in them. Mr. Wilson said we could live comfortably in a smaller home with the inheritance that A.B. left us, and I, for one, would be quite comfortable in one of those new luxury apartment buildings. I forget what they're called."

"You don't mean the Dakota?"

"Yes, that's it."

"Heaven forbid!"

"I've seen those apartments, Sylvia. They have central heating, electricity, servants' quarters, and all the amenities the three of us would ever need. And it wouldn't drain our finances to live there. At least think about it, please."

Sylvia rang the silver bell, summoning the servants to clear the table, then pushed back her chair and stood. Junietta held up her cane to stop her. "One more thing, dear ones. Do you see a pattern in the stories I've been telling you? Arthur's lust for wealth caused him to steal from his own family. My husband's drive for wealth and power caused his brother's death. Even my beloved Neal died because of his desire for riches. I would hate to see the two of you destroyed because of money too."

Sylvia lay awake in bed that night, trying to dislodge the thought of David Stanhope's suicide. It reminded her, much too painfully, of her own past losses—losses which she had been unable to control. She had to hang on to the reins of what she could control, so she concentrated on her upcoming dinner party, going through a mental checklist to make sure every detail was covered. She must make sure that this dinner party was worth the expense and provided a step forward for Adelaide's future.

But Junietta's words continued to seep between the cracks of her own worried thoughts. She remembered Mr. Forsythe's advice to pray and wondered if God was truly interested in her problems, especially since she had done very little to show love for Him or for her neighbors all these years. But surely, she could pray for her daughter's future, couldn't she? Would God answer a mother's prayer to provide a wealthy husband for her daughter? Sylvia whispered one anyway. Hoping, even if not quite believing. She couldn't recall ever feeling so alone.

## Adelaide

Addy didn't sleep well the night before Mother's dinner party and awoke later than usual that morning. When she arrived in the breakfast room, Mother and Mimi Junie had just finished eating. "Shall I ring for the servants, dear?" Mother asked. "Would you like coffee? Something to eat?"

"Just a cup of tea, please."

"You aren't anxious about tonight, are you?" Mother asked. "There's no need to be."

"Yes, perhaps you'll meet your handsome prince tonight," Mimi said, "and we'll all live happily ever after in our fairy-tale castle."

"It's too early in the morning for sarcasm," Mother said.

Adelaide took a sip of her tea when it arrived, wishing she really could meet someone wonderful tonight and relieve the pressure she was under. But after hearing Mimi's stories about her own marriage, she had no illusions about living happily ever after with anyone, no matter how wealthy he was.

"By the way, Sylvia, did you set aside a seat for my guest tonight?" Mimi asked.

"Yes. Tell me his name so I can put it on the place card."

"His name is Mr. Forsythe."

Mother looked at her blankly, as if scanning through a roster of society families and not finding his name. "Do I know him?" she asked.

"Well, I should hope so. He's your lawyer. You've been going over the household accounts with him and conspiring to sell off our furniture under the cloak of darkness."

"*That* Mr. Forsythe? You must be joking."

"Why? Howard is a bright, engaging young man, isn't he, Addy? Quite nice-looking too, if an old woman is allowed to have an opinion on such things."

"Next you'll want to invite the chauffeur or one of the footmen to sit down at our table."

"What a marvelous idea! I'm certain they would have some very lively stories to add to our conversation."

"Seriously, Junietta. Mr. Forsythe will have no clue how to act among polite society."

"That's a good thing, as I see it. I've known some very wealthy men who behaved quite badly. And if you're worried that Mr. Forsythe won't know which fork to use to eat his oysters or what to do with his finger bowl, seat him beside me and I'll coach him."

"It's so much more than etiquette, and you know it. I would hate for him to feel uncomfortable and out of place among our other guests. Whatever will he find to talk about?"

"I'm quite certain he knows how to read a newspaper. And as a lawyer with high-society clients, he likely knows more about what goes on in their bedrooms and boardrooms than you or I do. And by the way, why aren't you just as concerned about Adelaide feeling uncomfortable and out of place among your guests? Does she know either of the 'gentlemen'—and I use the term very loosely—that will be seated alongside her? At least she has gotten to know Mr. Forsythe. They've had some very interesting adventures together, haven't you, Addy?"

She was taken off guard and scrambled for a reply, hating being the cause of their disagreement. But Mother answered first. "Is that what this is about? Are you using Mr. Forsythe to prove some sort of point to Adelaide?"

"Listen to yourself, Sylvia. You're outraged to think that I would have an ulterior motive in inviting a young man to dinner. What are your motives for asking your young gentlemen to dinner?" She thumped her cane on the floor for emphasis, then rose to kiss Addy's cheek. "I wish you luck tonight, my dear. You'll need it. And do try to be kind to Mr. Forsythe, Sylvia, in spite of his lack of millions."

The day had just begun and Addy already felt weary. Mother turned to her after Mimi Junie left. "Do you think Mr. Forsythe is going to cause a disruption at our dinner? He has seemed polite and discreet while I've been working with him, but you've spent time with him when he was with your grandmother."

"He has excellent manners, from what I've seen. I've never felt uncomfortable with him. He's genial and polite." Which was more than she could say for inebriated Charles Durand or arrogant Byron Albright. Addy would much prefer sitting next to Mr. Forsythe for the evening than them. She remembered his easy smile and quiet sense of humor as he'd talked about growing up in the parsonage and learning to help the poor. She recalled him spontaneously playing ball with the boys at the children's asylum and helping a small child in the foundling home who had stumbled and fallen. "I can't see Mr. Forsythe causing a problem. But I'm not too sure about Mimi Junie," she said with a smile.

"She does seem determined to undermine all of my efforts." Addy had hoped to make Mother smile too, but she still appeared distressed. People called her the Ice Queen behind her back because she always seemed so calm and unruffled. Now Mimi had disturbed her equilibrium. She'd disturbed Addy's too.

The closer the hour came for their dinner guests to arrive, the more Addy worried about meeting Mr. Durand again. She tried to appear serene as she stood beside Mother in the cavernous foyer, welcoming everyone. Mimi hurried over to greet Mr. Forsythe when he arrived and swept him away to the conservatory. Addy glimpsed at least an inch of shirt cuff sticking out beyond his coat sleeves and guessed that he was wearing a borrowed tuxedo jacket. Henry Webster, one of the gentleman Addy was supposed to charm, arrived shortly after Mr. Forsythe. He didn't make a good first impression as they were introduced, striking

Addy as the type of man who is good-looking and knows it. When all their guests had arrived except for Mr. Durand, Addy felt relieved. He wasn't coming after all. The party moved into the conservatory for drinks.

Adelaide was beginning to relax as she mingled there with her guests when Charles Durand finally made his entrance. He was breathless, his fair hair a little disheveled, his cocky grin firmly in place. "Hey, everyone!" he called out. "I'm here!" The scattered conversations halted as people turned to stare at him. "Sorry I'm late. What did I miss? Did anyone get engaged? Divorced? Drunk? Ah, but the night is still young for getting drunk. Come on, someone tell me the latest gossip." A few of the other guests chuckled as if they found his antics charming, but Addy thought him loud and rude. She forced a smile as she went to greet him.

"Mr. Durand. I'm pleased to see you again."

"And I'm happy to see that Old Man George isn't hanging all over you this time. Don't get me wrong, Weaver is a good friend of mine. But he's much too old for a lovely young thing like you."

Addy scrambled for a polite reply. "I had a very enjoyable evening with Mr. Weaver. But tell me, what did you think of the play we saw that evening, Mr. Durand?"

"You really want to know? I thought it was a cartload of romantic manure. No one marries for love these days, am I right? I mean, you of all people must surely know that, Miss Stanhope."

Heat rushed to her face to hear the truth stated so bluntly. She stammered for a reply. "I-I'm not sure I know what you mean."

He made an elaborate show of pulling Addy aside and speaking confidentially, but she was uncomfortable with his closeness, and his breath smelled of alcohol. And he still spoke loudly enough for everyone around them to hear. "Look, no one is fooled by your mother's dinner invitations that supposedly honor your late father. It's quite clear that she's inviting potential suitors for you. And wealthy ones, at that."

Addy pulled away from him. "You're being very rude, Mr. Durand."

"Am I? I thought I was being honest. Why else would a loving mother allow a man as ancient as George Weaver to court you? Does she really think there's any chance the two of you will fall in love? Mind you, George is also guilty of ulterior motives. His enjoyment of pretty little playthings is not a very well-kept secret—"

"Mr. Durand! I will thank you to stop this conversation immediately. I will hear no more of it. Did you accept Mother's invitation so you could come here and mock us?"

"Not at all. I came because I heard she employs an excellent cook."

Thankfully, Mother hurried over to rescue Addy. "You must be Charles Durand," she said. "I'm Mrs. A.B. Stanhope. I'm so glad you could join us tonight. Come, I would like to introduce you to some of my other guests. And how about a drink before dinner?"

"I thought you'd never ask."

Addy's hands were trembling so badly she had to set down her glass. She dreaded having to sit beside Mr. Durand all evening at dinner. If only there was a way to get rid of him altogether. When she felt calm again, she looked around for Henry Webster, the other gentleman she was supposed to get to know tonight. She found him standing before the conservatory's wall of windows, smoothing his hair as he gazed at his reflection. She drew a steadying breath and walked over to him.

"What do you think of our collection of plants, Mr. Webster?"

"Impressive. Indeed, this is a beautiful room in a beautiful home. The perfect setting for a beautiful woman like yourself."

"Thank you. You're very kind." Mimi had said the Websters came from "new" money, but he'd obviously been well coached and seemed the perfect gentleman. Addy pointed out some of the more exotic plants and the figs that were forming on one of the trees, but Mr. Webster seemed uninterested in them. He had a habit of repeating fussy little gestures, such as smoothing his waistcoat and his mustache, and dusting his lapels. When dinner was announced and they made their way to the dining room, she caught him looking at himself in a gilded mirror as they passed it.

Then, a miracle! They took their seats at the table and Addy was relieved to see that Mr. Durand was no longer seated beside her. The place cards had been switched, and he was now seated at the other end of the table beside Mother. He was still being loud and rude, but Mother was doing a masterful job of controlling him. Addy could concentrate her efforts on Mr. Webster.

"Our family deeply regrets the loss of your father, Miss Stanhope," Mr. Webster said after the soup course had been served. "We did business with him, and I admired him a lot."

"Thank you. I understand that your family owns sugar refineries?"

"Yes. Stanhope Investments provided a good deal of the capital. We consider the Stanhopes our business partners."

Addy wondered if Mr. Webster shared Mimi's dire predictions of what would happen to the company now that Uncle Roger and Cousin Randall had taken over. She put it out of her mind and concentrated on being a charming dinner companion to Mr. Webster, while taking care not to ignore the gentleman and his wife who were now seated on her other side. Late in the evening, when the dessert course was being served, Mr. Webster turned to her and said, "I can't help noticing the fine artwork displayed in this room. Someone has good taste, judging by the selection of artists represented on these walls."

"I believe my mother chose these pieces from our gallery collection."

"If I'm not mistaken, that landscape across from us was painted by an artist from the Hudson River School."

Addy had no idea what he was talking about, but she smiled and said, "You're welcome to take a closer look after dinner. And I'll be happy to give you a tour of our gallery, if you're interested."

"I would be very interested. I collect artwork as an investment. I'm not interested in the styles or subjects at all, only their monetary value. It's a skill I've been developing and that I've become quite good at. I can predict which artists and their work will bring a good return on my investment, and I can assure you that your mother has excellent taste in art."

Addy immediately thought of her mother's beautiful, original watercolor, still hidden away in her bedroom. "I also admire her taste and these beautiful pieces she has collected, but I'm sorry to say I'm not very knowledgeable. I would love to learn more."

"Splendid. Then perhaps you would like to accompany me to the celebration of new acquisitions at the Metropolitan Museum of Art sometime? I'll be happy to advise you on which artists' works are likely to increase in value in the next few years."

"That sounds lovely, thank you." She returned to her dessert, feeling that she had accomplished an important first step by getting an invitation from him. She would have to ask Mother to prepare her with some questions to ask him about artworks.

Addy also had watched Mr. Forsythe throughout the dinner and noticed that he seemed to be having a wonderful time. Mimi Junie had him and everyone around them laughing with delight. If he'd felt uncomfortable with the array of stemware, knives, forks, and spoons that surrounded his plate, he'd shown no sign of it. Observing the lively chatter at that side of the table, Addy wished for a less boring table companion.

Mr. Webster offered Addy his arm after dinner as they circled the dining room to view the paintings. "Aha! See that signature?" he crowed. "Just as I suspected. This is a Thomas Cole. He was the first artist of the Hudson River School, paving the way for a generation of artists who painted scenes of untouched America. This painting is worth quite a bit of money, by the way." Addy wondered if Mother knew its value. As far as Addy was concerned, there were so many other paintings in this house that this one would never be missed if Mother sold it. The sale could buy Addy some time until a better suitor came along.

She escorted Mr. Webster through the enormous gallery next, listening to a monologue of his skills as an art investor. He didn't seem to care about the beauty of the individual paintings, only what they would be worth if sold to a collector or an art museum. The more he talked, the more boring he became. He was obviously very enamored with making money. Later, as the guests all began to depart at the end of the evening, Addy realized that Mr. Webster had talked exclusively about himself. He hadn't asked Addy any questions about herself or what her interests were. If one evening with him had wearied her, what would a lifetime with him be like?

She had just bid him good night, and Mother was saying goodbye to the rest of their guests, when someone came up behind her and put his hands over her eyes. "Guess who?" a man's voice asked. There was a strong smell of alcohol on his breath. She recognized the voice and felt a surge of panic. "Take your hands off me, Mr. Durand!" She twisted away.

"But the night is still young, Miss Stanhope. Let's you and me hit a few night spots. What do you say?"

"I say no, thank you." She tried to squirm away, but he was too quick. He smoothly trapped her against one of the pillars.

"Come on. I haven't been able to get my hands on you all evening. And I'm sure I was meant to be in the lineup of wealthy gentlemen who've been chosen to court you."

"You are no gentleman, Mr. Durand. I believe it's time for you to leave."

"You don't mean that. I really am fantastically rich. And I wouldn't mind sharing this house and its many bedrooms with you. But your mother will have to move out. She's a bore and has no sense of humor at all."

"Move out of the way and let me go." She would have pushed him away, but she didn't want to touch him.

"Don't you know it's a challenge when you play hard to get?"

"I'm not playing at anything, nor am I trying to present a challenge. You are extremely rude, and you drink too much."

He inched closer still. "I love a woman with sass."

Addy wondered if she would have to scream or cry out for help. Everyone else was on the other side of the foyer, too far away to see what was happening. She had begun to panic when, thankfully, Mr. Forsythe suddenly appeared.

"I think you'd better be on your way now, sir." He was taller than Mr. Durand by at least four inches and looked menacing enough to make Durand's lewd grin disappear. As Mr. Forsythe gripped his arm and propelled him to the door, Addy stumbled to a marble bench and sank down on it, her knees trembling.

"Are you all right?" Mr. Forsythe asked when he returned from his errand. "He didn't harm you, did he?"

"I'm fine. And no, he just frightened me. Thank you for rescuing me."

"Glad I could help."

Addy had been certain that she would be fine now that Mr. Durand was gone, but in the next moment, as she realized what a waste of time and money the evening had been, she lowered her head and covered her face with her hands. Mr. Forsythe sat down on the bench beside her murmuring, "There, there," as if he had no idea what else to do or say. He had been so chivalrous a moment ago, but now he seemed helpless in the face of her tears. At last, he pulled a handkerchief from his pocket and handed it to her. "Here. Take this."

She looked up at him, and for some reason, the absurdity of this dinner party and the dreadful men she'd been paired with in the hunt for a wealthy suitor suddenly struck her as ridiculous. She began to laugh through her tears.

"Did I say something funny?" he asked in bewilderment.

"No, it's just that . . . Is this your first high-society dinner party in a millionaire's mansion?"

"Well . . . I must confess that it is."

"And what is your opinion of us, Mr. Forsythe? We're ridiculous, wouldn't you agree?"

"Only the gentleman who just left, Miss Stanhope. Otherwise, I had a wonderful evening. I won't soon forget it."

"I wish I could forget it," she murmured, and felt her tears starting again.

"If something is troubling you, Miss Stanhope, I would be happy to listen. Perhaps I can even help you find a solution."

"That's very kind of you, but—" She stopped. Why was she being so polite? She had wished for someone to confide in, and here someone was, ready to listen. Mr. Forsythe already knew the details of her family's financial problems. Perhaps he could offer her a better solution than a lifetime of marriage to a man she didn't love. "I'm sure you know why

Mother is holding these dinner parties," she began. "Mr. Durand was one of the wealthy suitors who Mother hoped might rescue us if I married him. Mr. Webster, the vain, boring man seated beside me at dinner, was another one. And I met two more gentlemen a few weeks ago who were no more appealing. I know I need to do what I can to help Mother keep our home. It's all she has left, but—oh, never mind."

"No, please go on. I'm listening."

Addy sighed. "You've seen all the places my grandmother has taken me. She's trying to show me how wasteful our life is and to talk me out of marrying someone for his money." Addy gave a little laugh and added, "She thinks I should only marry a man I'm madly in love with."

"And what do you think?"

"That's the problem, don't you see? I don't know what to think. Mimi is too romantic and Mother is too practical. I can see both points of view, but I . . ."

"Yes?"

"They're both right, and yet they're both wrong. Oh, see how mixed up I am?"

"I wouldn't call it mixed up. You love both women very much, and you're discovering that you can't possibly please both of them at the same time."

"Yes. Exactly. But what should I do?"

"You're the only one who can answer that question, Miss Stanhope. But if you want my advice . . ."

"Yes. Please."

"I would say to give yourself more time before you make any decisions. I'm sure you don't want to make one that you'll come to regret."

"But you know all about our financial distress. You know how much it's costing us to continue living here."

"That's true. But after tonight, I think even your mother will agree that the situation isn't quite so dire that you must run into Mr. Durand's waiting arms." Addy managed a smile at the way he'd phrased it. "And as time passes, perhaps your mother may come to agree that this house isn't worth clinging to."

"I'm beginning to feel that way about this house already, even though it's the only home I've ever known." Addy noticed Mother eyeing them with alarm from across the foyer and quickly stood. "Thank you for your help and advice, Mr. Forsythe. You've given me much to think about. I'm sure you must be eager to be on your way."

For a brief moment he looked surprised by her sudden coolness, then he gave a slight bow and said, "It's my job to offer your family advice and help. Thank you for a very pleasant evening."

Adelaide said a quick good night to her mother and fled to her room before Mother could ask her opinion of the evening's events. She would brace herself to face her and Mimi Junie tomorrow morning. No matter what, she made up her mind to tell Mother her true feelings about her two newest suitors.

### ∞ Sylvia ∞

Sunshine streamed through the window in the morning room as Sylvia waited for Adelaide to join her for breakfast. Yet shadows hovered over her when she thought of her daughter's unease at last evening's dinner party. Inviting Mr. Durand had been a horrible mistake. All of Sylvia's careful planning, all the money that had flowed through her hands like water, had been for nothing. She was no closer to finding a suitor for Adelaide. Her older daughters' courtships had gone so smoothly. What was wrong this time?

Of course, with Cordelia and Ernestine, Sylvia had been able to spend money freely, without a second thought. Now she counted every penny just to continue running this mansion, not to mention courting potential suitors in style. A buyer for A.B.'s yacht still hadn't come forward, forcing her to deplete her remaining inheritance.

Her worrisome thoughts were interrupted by Junietta, who marched into the room out of breath, her cane thumping. She sat down at the table with a wheezing sigh. "This is one of the few rooms in this monstrous house that I actually enjoy being in. Perhaps it's because it's small and intimate and doesn't make me feel as though I'm being swallowed alive or suffocated by layers of draperies and bric-a-brac."

Before Sylvia had a chance to reply, Adelaide hurried in, looking as though she hadn't slept. Sylvia reached to take her hand. "Adelaide, I need to apologize to you for inviting Mr. Durand last evening. He's a dreadful man, and as soon as I spread the word about him, he will never be invited to another dinner party or ball again. He was insufferably rude." She glanced at Junietta, expecting a comment, but she sipped her coffee, saying nothing. "Now, tell me what you thought of Mr. Webster. I saw you escorting him around our gallery, and he seemed pleasant enough when I spoke with him."

"He was very interested in your art collection. It seems he considers himself somewhat of an expert when it comes to investing in artwork. He recognized the artist of the landscape that's hanging in the dining room."

"You mean the Thomas Cole?"

"Yes, that was it. Mr. Webster said something about a school on the Hudson River and seemed to think your painting was worth quite a bit of money."

Sylvia sat back in her chair and closed her eyes for a moment as a ripple of pain ruffled her composure. "It isn't for sale."

"Addy," Junietta said, "it isn't a school with a building and teachers. The Hudson River School is a group of artists who were loosely associated with each other and who painted in a similar style. Many of them chose scenes along the Hudson River."

"I see. Anyway, Mr. Webster seemed interested in seeing me again. He invited me to accompany him to view the newest paintings at the Metropolitan Museum of Art, although he didn't mention a specific evening."

Sylvia managed a smile. "I'm not at all surprised that he found you fascinating and attractive. You have so much to offer any gentleman."

"But our conversation was all about him last night. He wasn't interested in finding out about me, what I liked and didn't like."

"There will be plenty of time for him to get to know you if you go out with him again."

"He just went on and on about himself, and he couldn't stop admiring himself in the mirror. He was just so vain and boring."

"Perhaps he was nervous. After all, he was meeting you for the first time."

"Or perhaps he is just a vain and boring man," Junietta said.

The room fell silent. The maid entered with the coffeepot, offering to refill their cups, but no one wanted any. Adelaide waited until she left, then said, "I had a brief talk with Mr. Forsythe about our finances last night. He seems to think that our situation isn't critical just yet, and if that's the case, I'd rather not raise Mr. Webster's hopes any further by agreeing to see him again."

"Listen, I wasn't impressed by your father the first time we met, but once I got to know A.B. a little better, I—"

"Sylvia," Junietta said quietly. "Listen to what Addy is saying."

She raised her hands in surrender. "Very well. We'll forget about Mr. Webster."

"I'm sorry we had to waste so much money on him," Adelaide said.

Sylvia forced another smile. "You don't need to worry about that. I know we haven't gotten off to a very good start in finding suitors, but let's hope for better results from the spring party that Mrs. Rhodes is throwing for you. There will be more young people your age, and the atmosphere will be sprightlier with an orchestra and dancing."

Addy nodded, then turned to Junietta. "And will we be going on another excursion into the city's slums again, Mimi?"

"Why do you ask?"

"Well, you and Mother seem to be taking turns in your campaigns to influence me, and I suppose it's your turn next."

Junietta chuckled. "No, dear. I think you've seen enough. I didn't take you with me to make you feel guilty and depressed, but to open your eyes to a world outside of this one. And with the hope that you'd be grateful for all you have."

"I am grateful, Mimi. And I've learned a lot from hearing all the stories about your life."

"Good. I would hate to see you make the same mistakes that I did. And Sylvia," she said, turning to her, "I hope my confessions helped you understand the reasons why I seem to be opposing your efforts."

"Yes." It was all she could manage to say, feeling emotional for some reason.

"I see the strain you're under, Sylvia. And I know it's made worse by the grief you're still struggling with. Jesus was right when He said we can expect sorrow in this life. But those painful times in my life were when I changed and grew the most. And they are the reason why loving God and my neighbor became so important to me."

Sylvia felt close to tears and didn't want to give in to them. "It seems like the more stories you tell," she said, trying to make her tone light, "the more questions you raise."

"Mother's right. You still haven't told us if you ever found your son, or why Dr. Murphy called you Mama. Is he Neal's son, or isn't he?"

Junietta laughed. "I'll be happy to answer your questions if you have time to listen. But I don't want to keep either of you from more important tasks." She looked at Sylvia expectantly.

"I could use your help going through the rest of the spare bedrooms," she replied. "But not today. I'm much too tired after last evening." She didn't add that seeing the rooms being emptied had brought painful memories of seeing her own childhood bedroom being emptied. She wished she had her brothers' resilience in embracing change.

"Well, then," Junietta said. "Let's get Hattie to refill our cups and bring us some more of those lovely pastries, and I'll be happy to tell you all about Dr. Matthew Murphy. But in order to do that, I'll need to take you back in time to the War between the States . . ."

# 15

## ~ Junietta ~

A.B. found me at my desk in the drawing room, catching up on my correspondence. He tugged on my sleeve as he pleaded with me. "May we please go to the park today, Mama? Please? I want to watch the soldiers drilling again." I couldn't resist the urge to ruffle his curly brown hair, so like my own in color and texture. He had his father's dark eyes, but thankfully without the hard coldness that always reminded me of lumps of coal. I made the most of every opportunity to be with A.B. and to cuddle him, knowing that at age ten, he wouldn't suffer my mothering much longer.

"What does your tutor say? Is your schoolwork finished for the day?"

"Yes, Mama. You can ask him. He'll tell you I finished all my work very quickly and very well." Art had wanted our son to attend the boarding school in Connecticut that he had attended as a boy, but he relented after I pointed out all the problems his younger brother Roger

had encountered in various boarding schools. Of course, Roger had been
the cause of most of those problems, but he'd settled down after Arthur
hired an excellent private tutor to come to our home, the same man who
now tutored our son. Meanwhile, Roger, who was now twenty-three,
had been working for his father and Art for the past few years after failing to finish his studies at Princeton.

"I have a few more thank-you letters to write, but we can leave when
I'm finished," I said. "We can't stay too long though. I have a meeting to
attend at Bellevue Hospital later this afternoon." A.B. did a little dance
of glee before skipping away.

The chauffeur drove us to Central Park, and we stood at the edge of
the meadow, watching the new recruits run through their drills. We'd
brought our own small flags to wave, like the hundreds of other people
around us were doing. Patriotic fervor was running as high as a river in
flood stage this first summer of the war, and my son was eager to jump
into the current. More flags waved from lampposts, houses, stores, and
every public building in the city. You could hardly turn a corner without bumping into a Union soldier. A.B. especially loved watching the
parades of soldiers marching up Broadway to the beat of military drums.

"I wish I was old enough to be a soldier," he said as the wind carried
the drill sergeant's commands across the green. A chill shivered through
me. *God forbid.* I put my arm around his shoulders.

"I know it seems exciting, A.B., but the reality is that many of the
young men you see marching here will soon be tramping hundreds of
miles to go into battle, and sleeping outdoors in all sorts of weather,
and—"

"That sounds like fun!"

"And unfortunately, some of them may end up as casualties. That's
why I've been helping to set up that military hospital. Remember the
one I showed you?"

"With all the beds and bandages and things."

"Right." I had the urge to tell him about his great-grandfather,
Gerhard Steinhaus, who had been forced to fight for a cause he didn't

care about. But I resisted, knowing that my bright, inquisitive son wouldn't rest until he'd heard the entire story. That piece of his past was better off laid to rest. "I wish we didn't have wars, A.B. I wish our leaders could have found a way to settle our differences peacefully, but it wasn't possible. Remember what I told you about slavery?"

"That it's wrong to own people as slaves because we're all God's children."

"Yes. It's been against the law here in New York for more than thirty years, and it should be outlawed everywhere. All men are created equal by God."

He watched in silence for a moment, his foot tapping to the beat of the drums. "But we aren't really equal, are we, Mama? We live in a big house on a nice, clean street and have servants to do everything for us, while the people who live in Five Points have houses that are crowded and poor and dirty. And it smells terrible down there."

"We may not be the same in those ways, but we *are* equal because we're all made in God's image. What you saw in Five Points isn't inequality, it's injustice, and that is caused by a lot of different things. You could have been born into a poor family and be living in a tenement, just as easily as in our mansion."

"I'm glad I wasn't!"

"And because we're wealthy, we have a responsibility to use our money to help people in need."

"Like you do?"

"Yes, like I try very hard to do. I hope you'll remember that when you're all grown up, someday." The soldiers pivoted on command, then pivoted again. A.B. watched in silence until they had marched past us.

"I'm going to work in a big office like Father does and make lots of money, someday."

"Is that your idea or your father's?"

"He said I could have the office right next to his."

I didn't reply. I knew A.B.'s future was probably as inevitable as Art's had been, but it grieved me just the same to think he had no choice. A few minutes later, as the drums faded and the soldiers had marched out of sight, A.B. looked up at me. "Can we go to the confectionery and buy some candy now?"

"Sure. Let's go." He slipped his hand into mine as we walked to the candy store, whistling a little tune as he skipped along. I prayed that my son might always be this innocent and happy and carefree. So far, he hadn't been forced to endure the terrible family dinners that his father and David had suffered through. And I had been able to shelter him from the worst of Arthur's ranting wrath. Art barely paid attention to his son, so it surprised me to hear that he had shown A.B. the office where he would work someday. The older A.B. grew, the harder I prayed that he wouldn't become like his father and grandfather.

I sent A.B. home with the chauffeur after he dropped me off at Bellevue Hospital for my meeting. I had been gathering with a group of like-minded women to form the Women's Central Relief Association for the purpose of providing aid and assistance to our soldiers and their families. Our inspiration came from the Scripture that says, "Pure religion and undefiled before God and the Father is this, To visit the fatherless and widows in their affliction." Together, we worked with the U.S. Sanitary Commission, a civilian relief agency created by the federal government. But I longed to do more than simply sit in church halls and private homes rolling bandages and knitting socks. Today, a pleasant, well-dressed woman with a crisp British accent bustled into the room to address our gathering.

"Good afternoon, ladies. I'm Dr. Elizabeth Blackwell, and I'm very pleased to be here today to tell you about the new nursing program we're starting here at Bellevue Hospital. We'll soon be enrolling students and offering nurses' training to middle-and-upper-class women like all of you. We're already seeing the huge toll this war is taking on our young men, and so the need for volunteer nurses at Union hospitals is becoming greater and greater."

She went on to explain more about the new program, and I became so excited I could barely remain in my seat. This was exactly the sort of purposeful work I longed to do. When Dr. Blackwell finished, I was the first one to go forward to introduce myself, eager to enroll in her nursing program. "How old are you, Mrs. Stanhope?" she asked.

"I'm thirty."

"Are you married?"

"Yes."

"And are you squeamish about seeing blood and tending to grievous wounds?"

"I suppose I won't know for certain until I try. But I'm so bored with the usual tasks that have been allotted to women like me, and I've been wishing there was something more I could do for the war effort."

She looked down at the enrollment forms in her hand and seemed reluctant to offer me one. "Might you need time to consult with your husband before volunteering? The training schedule will be quite rigorous and intensive. And once you complete the course, the nursing shifts will cover all hours of the day and night."

It hadn't occurred to me to ask Art's permission or even to tell him what I would be doing. He lived his life and I lived mine. They intersected very infrequently. "I'm sure my husband will approve," I said, aware that I had no idea if he would or not. "But once I'm trained, I'm afraid I will only be able to volunteer in hospitals here in the city. We have a ten-year-old son at home, you see."

"That won't be a problem. If you will kindly complete this form, I will sign you up to be among our first nursing students."

I quickly learned that I did enjoy nursing work, and that I wasn't squeamish, and that Dr. Elizabeth Blackwell was an amazing and inspiring person. She was the first woman in the United States to receive a medical degree, having overcome obstacles of bias and prejudice at every step. She still remained one of the very few female doctors at a time when the need for physicians had never been greater.

For the next several months, I juggled my charity work with the Stanhope Foundation and my duties as Art's hostess with my nurses' training, and

I was pleased to successfully accomplish all three. I mentioned to Art what I was doing one morning at breakfast when Arthur wasn't there, but he seemed uninterested. The day after I received my certificate, I began nursing part-time at Bellevue Hospital.

A year quickly flew past. Casualties now filled every available hospital bed and spilled into the hallways, but the war was no closer to ending. I had worked extra hours one evening because the hospital was short-handed, and arrived home after dark, tired and bedraggled, to find Art waiting for me by the front door, wearing evening attire.

"Where have you been?" he shouted. "We're supposed to be at the Harrisons' dinner party in less than an hour, and look at you!"

"I'm sorry, Art. I completely forgot about the dinner." I was weary, my feet ached, and I wanted to soak in a hot bath and go straight to bed. "Can't you go without me this once?"

"No, I cannot! General Burke will be there from Washington. Our company is vying for some crucial military contracts. This is important. You need to be with me." He pulled out his pocket watch and opened it. "If you hurry and pull yourself together, we might still make it in time."

"You're joking. Do you have any idea how long it takes to have my hair dressed and pinned properly, let alone put on corsets and hoop skirts and—"

"Stop arguing and start dressing! Where have you been all this time? You're a filthy mess."

"At the hospital—"

"Doing what? You look like you've been scrubbing floors."

"Nursing wounded soldiers."

He looked incredulous.

"Art, I told you months ago that I was taking a nursing course at Bellevue. I've graduated and I'm attending patients now."

"Never!"

"Well, it's true—"

"No one with the Stanhope name will ever do the filthy grunt work of a servant."

"But nursing is a very respectable profession. I'm not the only woman from a prominent New York family who—"

"I don't care if President Lincoln's wife works there. I will not have you lowering yourself to take care of a breed of low-class men in a charity hospital!"

His attitude surprised and worried me. I tried to remain calm and reason with him. "Rich or poor, all men bleed and die the same way."

"Well, from now on, they'll have to bleed and die all over someone else's wife. Not mine."

A tremor of anger swelled inside me like a thunderhead. "I'm your wife, not your employee. I have as much right to pursue my chosen work as you do."

"That's true. You do have a choice," Art replied. His anger was as cold and stinging as sleet. "But if you choose to continue working as a nurse, you'll have to leave my house and live someplace else. Maybe you can find a room in one of those squalid tenements you're so fond of visiting. But you'd better think it through, Junietta, because if that's what you decide to do, you'll never see my son again."

"Art, please listen—"

"You have a choice right now, as well. You can hurry and get dressed and come to the dinner with me, or you can walk straight out that door."

I hated my powerlessness. I hated my husband. But I loved my son. I went upstairs to my room, my tears falling as my lady's maid quickly dressed me in my chemise, drawers, corset, crinoline, petticoat, and evening gown. My reflection was blurred by tears as she hurriedly pinned up my sweaty hair and covered it with a fine silk hairnet and bonnet. Then I dried my eyes and went downstairs, determined not to let my husband see my tears.

I resigned from my work at Bellevue Hospital the following day. I missed nursing very much at first, but I still had plenty of other work to do. The war that was taking such a terrible toll on our young men was also taking a financial toll on the city's poorest citizens. The cost of everything increased, from the price of rent and coal to the price of food. Families struggled to purchase basic commodities like flour and milk as prices doubled. Thousands of soldiers had died, leaving behind destitute widows and orphans. I saw more and more children living in the street, and an alarming number of infants were being abandoned on doorsteps by widowed mothers who had no place to live and no way to care for them. When the New York Foundling Hospital had been converted into a military hospital, the abandoned infants had to be brought to the city's almshouse on Blackwell's Island, where many of them died. I helped to convert a former mansion at Eighth Avenue and Fifty-eighth Street into an orphanage and school for soldiers' children, but it quickly filled to capacity.

The Stanhope Foundation's funds were stretched to the limit as all these needs mushroomed. I added every penny to it that I could spare from the living allowance Arthur provided. The war had brought him even greater wealth and prosperity, and the divide between rich and poor widened.

On January 1, 1863, the Emancipation Proclamation went into effect. Slavery had finally come to an end. If only the war would end, as well. But battles were still raging, casualties were mounting, and the need for fresh troops was escalating. In March, the government enacted the Conscription Act, making all men between the ages of twenty and forty-five eligible for the draft. My husband was thirty-five and his brother Roger, twenty-five. In July, shortly after we heard the news of the devastating Union losses near Gettysburg, Pennsylvania, the first names were drawn.

I was in the breakfast room with A.B., eating a quick meal before we left to help distribute food, when Art strode into the room. He usually left for work around dawn, and it surprised me that he had returned home. "Where are you going, Junietta? I saw the coachman preparing your carriage."

"I have plans to visit several charitable institutions today with the Women's Central Relief Association."

"Cancel your plans. Don't leave the house, and don't let A.B. leave, either."

"Why? What's going on?"

"A mob of protesters set the draft office on fire. They're on a rampage, and the rioting is out of control. They've attacked the mayor's house and Newspaper Row among other places, and now they're looting shops."

"Surely the police will stop them."

"There aren't enough policemen left in the city since so many of their kind are off fighting the war. The number of rioters is in the thousands. Stay inside until I tell you it's safe."

"If I can't leave, will you at least bring me a newspaper so I'll know what's going on? I care about what's happening to the people that our foundation serves."

"Your precious 'people' are trying to burn down our city and destroy everything I've worked to build."

I did as Art asked, remaining inside for the rest of the day. And he did what I had asked, bringing me copies of the latest newspapers so I could follow what was happening. Since the uproar seemed to be caused by the immigrant population that I had long been trying to help, I suspected that Art's gesture may have been motivated by a gloating desire to show me how wrong I'd been about them. I was, in fact, appalled by the violence. As days passed with no end to the rioting, the city asked the government to send troops to quell it.

According to the reports, what had begun as a protest against the draft law and the unfair advantage of the wealthy class, had transformed into something much worse. With so many working-class men being sent off to fight, resentment between Irish immigrants and New York's Negro population had escalated. Both groups were exempt from the draft and were competing for the same jobs. Dozens of Negroes were being beaten and killed. Innocent Negro men had been lynched in the streets. And I was horrified to learn that the Colored Orphan Asylum had been deliberately set on fire.

I couldn't sleep for two days until finally learning that all 233 children had miraculously survived. Superintendent Davis and head matron Jane McClellan had quietly led the orphans out through the back door of the burning building while the firemen battled the flames in front. The children had been taken to a nearby police precinct at first, then relocated to Blackwell's Island. I wasn't able to bring any help to them until five regiments of Union troops succeeded in stopping the riots. The damage to our city and the deaths of more than a hundred people during the riots shocked everyone.

After the city was calm again, A.B. asked to come with me when I went to check on the orphans. I hesitated to take him, knowing how his father would feel about it. But A.B. had visited the orphan asylum with me before the fire and had been following the newspaper reports of the violence along with me. The driver took us to the ruined site, first. Clearly, the orphanage could not be rebuilt. I stared at the still-smoking ruins, wondering how anyone could destroy the only home these innocent children had, simply because of the color of their skin. "This is what evil looks like," I told A.B. "And this is where hatred always leads. I hope you'll remember these ruins whenever you're tempted to hate someone."

Afterward, we drove to the almshouse on Blackwell's Island where the orphans were being housed. A.B. remained with the carriage while I went inside to ask Superintendent Davis what the orphans' most pressing needs were. When I came outside again, A.B. was talking with one of the orphans, a boy a few years younger than himself.

"I see you like horses," A.B. said as the boy gazed in admiration at the one pulling our carriage. The boy nodded.

"Would you like to come closer and pet him?"

"Sure would!"

"What's your name?"

"Henry."

"Mine's A.B." The driver held the bridle while A.B. hoisted Henry up so he could stroke the horse's muzzle, then his neck and flank.

"Thank you, sir," he said after A.B. set him down again. "My pa took care of horses, and that's what I'm gonna do, someday." He saw me approaching and backed away a little.

"It's all right," I said. "I'm A.B.'s mother. If you still want to work with horses in a couple of years, Henry, I'll pay you to come after school and help us with ours. Our head driver, Mr. Crain, will teach you everything you need to know. What do you say?"

"I say I would like that just fine!"

# 16

~~~

1864

Six months after the draft riots, I was sitting at my desk at home, poring over the latest requests the foundation had received for assistance, when our housekeeper brought me the morning mail. Among the envelopes addressed to me was a letter for Art from the U.S. draft board. I wouldn't open his mail any more than he would open mine, but I was certainly curious about the contents. We would be attending an event at the Academy of Music that night, so I waited to show him the letter until we were both dressed in our evening clothes and riding in our carriage. I knew I would have his full attention and he wouldn't be able to walk away from me.

"This letter came for you today," I said, pulling it from my reticule. "It was mixed in with my mail and I've been curious about it all day. It's from the draft board."

"And you're just now giving it to me? On our way out for the evening?"

"If it's what I think it is, your name has been drawn for conscription.

There's only one way to find out." I could tell by the smell on his breath that he'd had his usual evening drink, and I was counting on it to calm him enough to be patient with me. He sighed, slit the envelope with his forefinger, and pulled out the letter. He tilted it to read by a passing gaslight, then tossed it onto my lap. "Your guess is correct. I've been drafted to serve in the United States Army."

"What are you going to do?"

"You don't really expect me to put on a uniform and go off to fight, do you? I'll get a stand-in. My work as a civilian is vital to the war effort."

"I figured as much, but I'm curious to know how that works. How do you go about finding a man who is willing to fight and possibly die in your place?"

"Are you trying to make an issue out of this? Because if you are, Junietta, I'm not interested in taking your bait."

"No, I'm serious, Art. I would honestly like to know how this works."

He studied me with a frown before he seemed to decide that I was sincere. "There are lists of immigrants who are willing to be substitutes. They aren't citizens and therefore aren't subject to the draft. I hand over my summons and three hundred dollars, and the man enlists in my place. That's the end of it for me."

"But only the beginning for him," I mused.

"They do it for the money, Junietta. To people like that, it's a quick way to make a buck. He'll probably receive a signing bonus along with what I pay him, and I've heard that some of these fellows then scamper off with the money and are never seen again. But if he goes through with it, he'll get all his meals for the next two years, along with a new pair of boots, a warm uniform and blanket, and a regular monthly salary."

I had seen soldiers at Bellevue Hospital who'd suffered horrendous wounds, losing arms and legs. I couldn't imagine that any amount of money would be worth taking such a risk. Art had turned to stare out the window as if not interested in further conversation with me. It had rained, and the carriage wheels hissed through the puddles. The streets glistened in the lamplight.

"I would like to meet him," I said.

"Meet who?"

"The man you're going to hire to be your stand-in."

"Oh, good heavens, Junietta. Why?"

"Let's just say I'm curious. People intrigue me. I would like to meet a man who is willing to put a three-hundred-dollar price tag on his life."

"He will be a gullible fool, trying to make some money and have an adventure in the bargain. The type of person who likes a good brawl now and then. He doesn't really believe he could die in battle. The guy firing a gun alongside him or in front of him will die, not him. And as I said, a lot of times these people take the money and run."

"What happens then? Are you responsible for getting another substitute if he disappears?"

"Not if the stand-in has signed the enlistment papers. He would be guilty of desertion in that case, which is punishable by firing squad."

"Well, when you go down to meet whoever you hire to replace you, may I come along?"

"I have neither the time nor the interest to be bothered with this business. I'll send someone from the office on this errand."

"May I tag along with him?"

"Why are you pestering me about this? I don't want to hear any more about it tonight."

"Fine. I'll hang on to this for you." I folded the draft notice and tucked it into my bag.

When Art's clerk came to fetch the draft notice, I made him take me along to meet the stand-in. Ian Murphy was a young Irish immigrant, twenty-three years old, who reminded me, painfully, of Neal. In my heart and mind, Neal Galloway hadn't aged a day in the past fifteen years, remaining the same handsome young man he'd been on the day his ship had set sail.

"I'm grateful to you for taking my husband's place," I told young Ian. "But may I ask why you're doing this?"

"It's not a lark. I'm married, you see. My Kate will be putting the extra money away until I come home, and we can start a new life for ourselves. Maybe out west where there's land to be bought. Kate and our boy will have my Army pay in the meantime."

I wanted to tell him Neal's story and beg him not to do it. No amount of money in the world was worth risking his life. No loving wife would ask him to do it. But I sensed Ian's determination and knew he probably would volunteer to be a substitute for someone else, if not for Art. I had worked with new immigrants long enough to know that many of them saw America as the land of opportunity, a land where a poor man could become a millionaire, just as Arthur Stanhope and so many others had. Having been born into a life of privilege, I had no right to lecture Ian on the snares of wealth.

"So, you have a family, Ian?"

"Yes, and if you're truly grateful, Mrs. Stanhope, will you do something for me?"

"If I can."

"Will you check on my wife and babe now and then, and make sure they're taken care of while I'm gone?"

"Of course. It's the very least I can do." He gave me Kate's address. I told him I would send letters and packages to him, too, if he stayed in touch with me. "After all, I would be sending packages to my own husband if he was away in the army instead of you."

I took a much keener interest in the war and in the battles being fought after that. I had the name and face of a real soldier who was now involved in the fight. Ian and I exchanged letters and I sent the promised packages. I visited Kate and the baby every few weeks too, and made sure they had everything they needed. And I prayed for Ian every day, this man who was fighting a war in my husband's place.

In the spring of 1864, I helped the other ladies in the Women's Central Relief Association organize the enormous Manhattan Sanitary Fair. The fair featured a huge bazaar, musical entertainment, and dramas

presented by a theater company. We were raising funds for medical supplies, aid for injured soldiers, and food and clothing for their loved ones
who were struggling back home. The fair ended with a glittering ball,
something I was experienced at organizing. The work exhausted yet
exhilarated me. I looked around at the ballroom when everything was
ready, and felt proud of the work we had accomplished. We ended up
raising one-million dollars for our cause.

And still the war dragged on.

The newspapers reported the grim statistics each day, including the
more than seven-thousand Union soldiers who had died within twenty
minutes in the deadly Battle of Cold Harbor in Virginia. I hadn't heard
from Ian in a few weeks, so I went to Kate's tenement to see her and the
baby one rainy, spring afternoon. To my surprise, Kate flew at me in a
rage the moment she opened the apartment door and saw me.

"How dare you come here and show your face! Get out! Get out!"

"Kate, what is it? What's wrong?"

"He's dead! My Ian is dead, and it should be your husband lying in
that cold grave, not mine!" I tried to defend myself from her pummeling
fists, yet I knew she was right. A mere three hundred dollars had kept
Art from suffering Ian's fate.

"Oh, Kate! I didn't know! I'm sorry. I'm so very, very sorry." I began
to weep along with her as the baby wailed in the background.

"My Ian should be here at my side, helping me raise our son!"

"I'm so sorry."

"Don't try to tell me you care. If you cared about the baby and me,
you wouldn't have let my husband enlist in the first place. We're not even
citizens of this god-forsaken country. He didn't have to fight."

When her anger was finally spent, I gently eased her into the apartment and closed the door behind us. I lifted the baby from his crib and
rocked him to soothe his tears. "Tell me what happened, Kate."

"I got a letter saying he died in a battle down in Virginia, somewhere. I don't even know what it was all for. Did his death do anybody
any good?"

"It does look as though we're winning this terrible war. The Union will be restored. The innocent people who were held in bondage as slaves will all go free."

"But that won't give my son a father. Or me a husband. What are we supposed to do now?" She finally let me hold her, and the three of us clung to each other, crying.

"I promised Ian I would take care of you and little Matthew if anything happened, and I intend to keep my promise. First of all, there's a place where the two of you can live from now on. It's a boardinghouse for women and their children. The other ladies will take care of you until you get back on your feet. My friend Meara, who is also a widow and also an immigrant from Ireland, runs it with her daughter, Regan."

"That won't bring my Ian back."

"No, it won't. The only man I ever loved is also gone, and so is his son. Now we must wait for the world-to-come, when we'll be together with our loved ones again. You and I are sisters from now on, Kate. Matthew will be my son as much as he is yours. I'll make sure he always has everything he needs, and the very best education that money can buy."

I sent my carriage and driver home, telling him to return for me in the morning so I could stay and grieve with Kate. I spoke with Meara the following day and arranged for Kate and Matthew to move into the boardinghouse. It still didn't seem like enough.

A week later, I waited for Art to return from work in the evening so I could tell him about the man who had died in his place. I knocked on his bedroom door and asked if I could come in and talk without Arthur or Roger there.

"I need to tell you about something that has happened," I began. "May I sit down?"

He nodded and gestured to the small seating area in his suite as he unbuttoned his suitcoat and loosened his tie. He looked weary and older than his thirty-eight years, worn down by the pressures of his work. And undoubtedly by his father. For all of Art's labor, he seldom had a chance to enjoy the huge sums of money he was making.

"What's on your mind?" he asked after removing his jacket.

"I've learned that the man who went to war in your place has been killed in battle. His name is Ian Murphy, and he left behind a wife and small son."

I read several emotions in Art's expression—surprise, concern, anger—before he turned away. "I'm sorry to hear that."

"You and I were once friends, Art, and although we haven't been close for a while, I still couldn't help thinking that it might have been you. I could be that widow, and A.B. the fatherless son. I thank God that it wasn't you. That you're still here with us." I rose from my chair and went to him as my tears fell. He took me in his arms and let me hold him.

"How did you find out about him?" Art asked.

"I met Ian when he enlisted in your place. He asked me to look after his wife while he was away, so I have been. She told me the news. I promised Ian that I would take care of Kate and the baby if anything happened to him, and I intend to keep that promise. I wondered if . . . if you would like to stay in touch with them, too. Help them get by."

Art released me and took a few steps backward to sit down on his bed. "I suppose I owe him that much," he said softly.

"I keep thinking, what if you had been born poor? What if you hadn't been able to pay for a substitute? It could be you in that grave in Virginia. But it isn't. Aren't you grateful to God that someone could fight in your place?" He didn't reply. "To meet a man who was so young and alive—and to know that he's gone—it really brought home to me the story of how Jesus died in my place. I guess I've never had such a vivid example before, of the sacrifice He made for me. I'm grateful for that. And I can't seem to stop crying."

"Come here, Junie." I went to sit beside him on the bed and he wrapped his arm around my shoulders. "You have a heart as big as the ocean. I hear nothing but admiration from my colleagues and their wives for the good work your foundation does."

His praise surprised me. I gave a little laugh and said, "It's our foundation, Art. It bears the Stanhope name."

"We'll do whatever we can for this man's family. I promise you."

And for a time, Art and I were closer after that night.

# 17

1867

## ~Junietta~

I was getting ready to leave for church with Art and A.B. on a cold January morning when Arthur stopped us at the door. "You won't be going to church today. You're going to see my new house instead. The carriage is waiting."

"Couldn't we go after church?" I asked.

"We're going now. It will take time to travel there, and then all afternoon to see everything." He even demanded that Roger, who had been carousing until the early morning hours, get up and come with us.

Arthur had been building his new mansion for the past year and a half, but I had yet to see it. I couldn't imagine a house so large that touring it would take all day. I was in for a surprise. It wasn't a house, or even a mansion. It was a palatial castle.

Arthur had become a multimillionaire during the war, and had decided to construct a huge mansion uptown, where New York's wealthiest citizens were moving. Cornelius Vanderbilt had a 130-room Renaissance-style chateau on Fifth Avenue, so Arthur wanted to keep up. He would be seventy-seven years old this year, and although he occasionally complained of aches and pains, he was as cruel and ruthless as ever. He had wanted a part in every aspect of construction, making sure every detail was to his liking, from the paintwork on the coffered ceilings to the intricately carved fireplace mantels. Several construction foremen had quit during that time, unwilling to put up with Arthur's bullying for any price.

The five of us climbed into Arthur's carriage and headed to upper Manhattan. The city had spread far to the north in the past twenty years. I remembered riding up this way with Neal and Aunt Agatha and seeing nothing but farmland. The son I'd had with Neal would turn seventeen this year, nearly the same age I had been back then.

When I caught my first glimpse of Arthur's massive limestone fortress, I nearly laughed out loud. It filled a city block and was ornamented with turrets, balustrades, carved pediments, and gargoyles. A tower on each of its corners was topped with a conical spire. Our carriage halted in front, and we made our grand entrance through an arched portico leading to huge, carved oak doors. I could see the glee on Arthur's face as he watched the four of us, as if expecting to see slack-jawed looks of awe. I was in awe, but not in the way he had hoped. It amazed me to think that a man could be so arrogant that he would build a monstrosity like this purely for his own enjoyment. This was Arthur's house, not ours.

A servant opened the door. Arthur had hired servants to work here already, along with the ones who would be moving with us, later. Our first view of the echoing, two-story foyer stopped fifteen-year-old A.B. in his tracks. "Why do we need such a huge house?" he asked.

"We deserve it," Arthur said. "My hard work built this place."

A.B. didn't seem to hear him. He wandered around the space, feeling the smooth marble of the pillars and benches, gazing up at the high arched ceiling, then at the broad staircase and upper balcony. "Wow!" he finally said. "Mother and I have visited tenements that are half the size of this house, yet dozens of families live there."

Arthur's face darkened. "I started out just as poor as they are and worked hard all my life. I earned all of this, and they can do the same."

"It doesn't seem right—"

"Don't tell me what's right and what isn't! Do you hear me?"

I tried to signal to A.B. not to question his grandfather any further, but he didn't seem to notice my frantic signs. My curious son was always asking questions, and once he started, he wouldn't stop until he was satisfied with the answers.

"But there are rooms in our current house that we never even use. What are we going to do with even more rooms?"

"Whatever I please!"

"Which way shall we explore first?" I asked, desperate to stop A.B.'s questions. Arthur didn't move.

"Where else has your mother been taking you besides those filthy tenements?"

I felt sick. A.B. didn't see it as a trick question or understand that Arthur was about to attack him—and me. I had long feared the day when Arthur would bully A.B. the way he had bullied Art and David, and I felt helpless to stop him. I knew Art wouldn't intervene, so I decided to speak up.

"I've been showing A.B. some of the places that the Stanhope Foundation supports—"

"Stay out of this, Junietta. Let the boy tell me where he's been."

My son was getting nervous now, as if afraid he might say the wrong thing. "I-it's like Mother said. We've gone to see the work that the foundation is doing at the new orphans' asylum, the House of Industry, the Children's Aid Society—places like that."

"And I suppose she's been filling your head with stories of how wealthy people like us are evil for making money? How we should give away all our hard-earned money to degenerates who drink away their paychecks and have litters of children and then expect to receive handouts? Or how we need to let in even more immigrants so they can bring diseases and fill our city with their violence?"

"N-nothing like that, sir."

"Well, I think it's time you cut your mama's apron strings. From now on I'll expect you to spend your spare time with your father and me, learning what the family business is all about. Learning how to work hard so you can spend your money on whatever you please."

A.B. looked at me as if he didn't know how to reply. "Don't look at your mother!" Arthur bellowed. "I'm talking to you!"

"Y-yes, sir!"

"Good. Now I'm going to take you on a tour through your new home and don't you dare ask me again why we need so many rooms. I expect to command respect in this city, and this is the way it's done. I need a house that befits my standing in the business world."

Most of the main rooms on the first floor were already completed and furnished with curtains, rugs, and even statues and other ornaments. Arthur had hired decorators to choose everything, and I found their taste gaudy and ornate. When we reached the immense, two-story ballroom Arthur turned to me and said, "I want to see this space filled as soon as possible with five hundred members of New York's highest society in their gowns and jewels. There's room on that balcony up there for a full orchestra. Send out the invitations and plan the evening for me, Junietta. I expect the best of everything for our guests—flowers, food, wine, music."

I hated that Arthur's demands and expectations as he showed off his new mansion would keep me from the work I loved, probably for the next six months. But I had no choice. He continued his tour, showing us the drawing room, gallery, formal dining room, and the conservatory, which already contained trees and exotic plants. All the rooms had abundant windows and tall ceilings, but I still felt as though I was suffocating.

Back home, I sought out my husband to talk with him in private. "Is there any way we could live in this house for a little longer? Just you and me and A.B.? We've been married for sixteen years and we've never had a home of our own. Let Arthur and Roger have the new house. This is our home. And A.B.'s home."

"Don't be absurd. The Stanhope empire has outgrown this house. Why do you think there's a huge ballroom in the new one? And a much larger dining room? As head of the company, I'm expected to entertain guests in style."

"You mean, show off your wealth?"

"You can leave anytime, if you're unhappy. The scandal of desertion will fall on you, not on A.B. and me. Then what will become of all your charity work?"

I had expected his reply, but it made me sad just the same. "What does Arthur plan to do with our old mansion?"

"The real estate it sits on is worth more than the mansion itself. It will be torn down so the land can be developed." I shook my head at the waste.

A week later, I moved into my new bedroom suite in Arthur's new mansion where everything from the draperies and bedspread to the ivory-handled hairbrush on the vanity had been chosen for me. My sitting area had an imported French escritoire that was already filled with my own engraved stationery and personal wax seal. I sat down at the desk with sullen resignation and began planning Arthur's grand housewarming ball.

Once his castle was complete and had been inaugurated with a series of balls, parties, and elaborate dinners, Arthur began constructing a forty-room 'cottage' in Newport, like many of New York's other wealthy families were doing. The Rhode Island coast was becoming the summer playground of the very rich. Arthur took A.B. and his tutor with him as he traveled back and forth to watch the mansion's progress, then added trips together to the shipyard where his new yacht was being constructed. I saw less and less of my son, which was Arthur's intent. When I did see A.B., I noticed how much he was changing. He was taking sailing lessons now, and had fallen in love with life on the sea.

"When grandfather's ship is finished, we'll be able to sail it all the way to Europe," he told me. Arthur gave him one thousand dollars for his sixteenth birthday and taught him how to invest it in stocks and bonds. When A.B. quickly doubled his investment, Arthur praised him in a way that he'd never praised any of his three sons. But Arthur was aging and slowing down. He developed a cough in the winter of his eightieth year that he wasn't able to shake. It developed into pneumonia, and his doctor ordered a team of nurses to stay with him day and night. The doctor visited Arthur every day, sometimes twice a day, trying every cure and remedy in his arsenal, but my father-in-law's condition didn't improve. Arthur Stanhope was dying.

I debated a long time about whether or not I should talk to Arthur about his spiritual condition before he died. I didn't want it on my conscience that he'd passed away before he'd had a chance to repent and receive forgiveness. I thought about asking Reverend Cooper to come down from Tarrytown and explain God's grace to Arthur the way he had twice explained it to me. But I had a feeling that the reverend would refuse, and would encourage me to be the one to talk to Arthur, instead. On a bitterly cold afternoon in February, I waited until the doctor left, then went into Arthur's bedroom.

He looked shrunken in the enormous room and massive canopied bed. Dark, heavy draperies shut out the winter sunlight. A sprawl of medicine bottles cluttered the bedside table. I could hear Arthur's wheezing breaths from across the room. He opened his eyes when I stopped beside his bed and gave me his usual glare. His illness hadn't softened him. He spoke in a near whisper, with none of his usual volume, but with all his customary venom. "What do you want?"

"I came to see you, Arthur."

"And gloat because I'm dying?"

"You and I have been through a lot over the years, but I'm not gloating. I'm very sorry you're ill. I've come to wish you peace."

"What's that supposed to mean?"

"Peace with God."

He gave a derisive snort, which caused him to start coughing.

I waited until he stopped, then hurried on. "I know that I committed a sin when I had a child out of wedlock. And I've missed God's mark in many other ways in my lifetime. But a wise pastor helped me see that if I repented for what I'd done and put my faith in Christ, God would forgive me. I would be accepted as His child and have the right to enter heaven."

"You believe in heaven?"

"I do."

"Then you're a gullible fool."

"Arthur—"

"Get out and leave me alone."

I did as he asked, but I had a hollow ache inside, knowing that Arthur would die unrepentant. I had lost Aunt Agatha and other relatives over the years, but I had always known that they'd been believers and had entered eternal life. Arthur's situation felt horribly different.

I stayed up late that evening until Art returned from work, then went into his suite to see him. "If you have anything to say to your father, Art, you'd better go in and say it. He's dying."

"Did the doctor tell you that?"

"He didn't need to. I went to see Arthur today. I don't think he has very long."

"Considering the enormous fees the doctors charge, they should be able to cure him."

"No amount of money in the world can help Arthur live forever."

He exhaled and said, "I suppose you're right."

"Your father has treated you very badly over the years, Art. In fact, I can't say that I've ever felt any love for him. But he's dying, and when I talked to him about repentance and forgiveness and finding peace with God, he said I was a fool for believing in heaven, and he told me to get out."

"Typical," he said.

"Do you think we should ask our minister to come and talk with him?"

"It wouldn't do any good."

"The thief on the cross repented as he was dying, and Jesus promised he would be with Him in paradise."

"Fine. I'll send for him, then."

"I also think that if there's anything you need to say to your father, if you want to make peace with him . . ."

Art didn't reply. He had crossed to the window and parted the drape to stare into the darkness. I could only imagine the complex emotions he was experiencing.

"You should probably let Roger know, too," I said. "And maybe we should fetch A.B. home from Princeton so he can say goodbye."

Art still didn't reply, so I left the room. That night, Arthur Stanhope died alone in his massive bed in his enormous bedroom suite, in his monumental new mansion. Rich or poor, everyone returns to dust.

# 18

MARCH 1899

### ~ *Sylvia* ~

Junietta seemed wrung out by the time she finished her story. Her shoulders slumped wearily, and her hands lay limp in her lap. She sighed as she faced Adelaide and Sylvia. "I've lived in this enormous house for more than thirty years now, and I still can't say that it has ever truly felt like home to me. In my mind, it will always be a monument to Arthur Stanhope's pride and arrogance."

Sylvia had her own reasons for hating Arthur Stanhope, and Junietta's stories had added more fuel. But this mansion rightfully belonged to her for reasons that Junietta didn't know about. She hoped Adelaide wouldn't be persuaded to hate it as much as her grandmother did. Yet after poring over all the accounts, Sylvia knew that some other source of income would be necessary in order to continue living here. Finding a suitor for Adelaide—and quickly—seemed to be the only answer.

"So, the doctor I met at the orphanage?" Adelaide asked. "Is he Ian Murphy's son?"

"Yes. Dear Matthew. His father had died in battle, and it might have been my husband if Art hadn't been wealthy enough to pay for a substitute. It was truly 'a rich man's war and a poor man's fight.' I kept my promise to Ian, and I still visit his widow, Kate. Art kept his promise too, and paid for Matthew's education so he could become a doctor. Matthew is like a son to me, and I'm so very proud of him."

"And Henry, your driver? Is he the little boy from the orphanage who liked horses?"

"One and the same. Henry is in charge of our carriage house and all our horses, now. He has plenty of helpers who could drive me around, but Henry always insists on doing it himself. He and A.B. remained friends, and before he died, A.B. taught Henry how to drive his new automobile. Your father believed horses and carriages would be as obsolete as kerosene lamps, one day, and he may be right."

They were interrupted by a maid with a message for Sylvia. "Your dressmaker and seamstress are here, ma'am."

"Oh, I completely forgot!" Sylvia didn't know what was wrong with her, lately, to make her so forgetful. She needed to remain in control if she and Adelaide were going to survive, but she felt so weary most days that she hated getting out of bed in the morning. And so overwhelmed by the burden of the future that she found herself close to tears at the oddest moments. Like right now, for some inexplicable reason. She rose from her chair, smoothing her skirts, and turned to her mother-in-law, hoping she wouldn't be obstinate and block her way with her cane again. "Please excuse Adelaide and me, Junietta. We have some things to attend to."

She and Adelaide spent the rest of the morning going through their wardrobes and planning alterations for gowns they had worn last year. It was another cost-cutting measure that had come to Sylvia on a sleepless night after seeing how much money she typically spent every year on new dresses. Together with the dressmaker, they came up with ideas on how to combine fabric from two dresses, add new lace or ribbons, and create a new gown that resembled the latest fashions in the dressmaker's pattern books.

"You won't tell anyone what you're doing for us, will you?" Mother asked the dressmaker. "I would rather not endure anyone's pity because our family's state of mourning has prevented us from shopping in Paris this year."

"No, ma'am. I admire your design ideas a great deal," the dressmaker replied. "Your gowns will be every bit as lovely as any Paris gown. No one will ever know you haven't been abroad."

She felt close to tears again by the time the dressmaker and seamstress left. One particular gown that would now be altered had been a favorite of A.B.'s last season. He'd told her how beautiful she looked in it as they'd waltzed together at the Astors' Christmas ball. She remembered the warmth of his arms, the brush of his face against her cheek, the spicy scent of his imported cologne, and longed for just one more day with him. One hour. One minute. She closed her eyes against the pain. Her year of mourning would end, eventually, and she would wear her remade gowns as she rejoined the social whirl. But nothing would ever be the same without A.B.

~~~

The next morning when Sylvia joined Junietta for breakfast, she and Adelaide found handwritten invitations at each of their places, printed on Junietta's stationery. Sylvia picked hers up to study it. "What is this, Junietta?"

"Well, I understand we're on a tight budget, so I thought I would save the cost of postage and deliver them myself. Go ahead, open them."

Sylvia broke the seal on hers and found an invitation to a dinner party that her mother-in-law was hosting here at their mansion.

"I don't understand. Are you mocking me?" she asked.

"I would never do that, Sylvia. I'm perfectly serious about this dinner. As long as we're still living in this huge house, I thought I may as well take advantage of it to entice two new prospective board members to become part of my charitable foundation. I would be pleased if you and Addy would join me that evening and help me entertain these gentlemen." Her plan sounded innocent enough, but Sylvia couldn't help wondering if she was up to something.

"Will you be inviting these gentlemen's wives, as well?" she asked.

"As it happens, neither gentleman is married. Mr. Alberts, the king of all curmudgeons, is a lifelong bachelor and will be seated next to me. Mr. Timothy Barrow is a widower, and I'm hoping you'll be kind enough to entertain him, Sylvia, and do your best to charm him. Both gentlemen are quite wealthy, and I would love to have them as part of the foundation. My other board members and their wives will be there to support us, as well. And you needn't worry about the cost. The dinner won't be extravagant, and all the costs will be paid for by the foundation."

"I suppose you've contrived to seat Adelaide beside someone of your choosing too?"

"As a matter of fact, yes. Mr. Forsythe."

"Oh, for heaven's sake. This is getting ridiculous with him showing up everywhere."

"I'm not playing matchmaker. As Addy already knows, I'll be stepping down as the chairman of the Stanhope Foundation soon—"

"Stepping down?" Sylvia couldn't imagine her tireless mother-in-law ever giving up the position she loved.

"Yes. It's time. So, I've asked bright young Mr. Forsythe to take my place. And while he still is considering it, I know our Adelaide will do an excellent job of helping him feel comfortable with all the other board members."

Sylvia started to protest, but Addy interrupted her. "It's all right, Mother. I really don't mind. Mr. Forsythe seemed to have a nice time at your last dinner party. And I'm still grateful to him for rescuing me from Mr. Durand."

"So, what do you ladies say? Will you be accepting my invitation?"

"It would be very ungracious of us to refuse, Junietta. Of course, we'll come. I'm always happy to help the Stanhope Foundation, especially since I'm not in a position to make a donation at this time. Now, if you aren't otherwise occupied today, I could use your advice and help later this morning. I'll be going through a few more rooms on the third floor. In the west wing this time."

"Poor Arthur must be rolling over in his granite mausoleum," Junietta said with a laugh. "I would have gotten rid of all his bric-a-brac and folderol years ago if it had been up to me. Of course I'll help you."

"I'll help too, Mother," Adelaide said.

"Maybe we'll get lucky and find a pot of gold," Junietta said with a chuckle. Sylvia could only wish that they would.

<hr/>

### ⁓ *Adelaide* ⁓

Adelaide made her way up to the third-floor wing later that morning, and as she wandered past the endless rooms, she felt as if she were in someone else's house. She remembered visiting this part of the mansion only once before, when she'd gone exploring with her sisters as a small child. They had crept down the carpeted hall, peering into room after room, and then, as now, the larger pieces of furniture had been covered with dust sheets. Ernestine and Cordelia had teased Adelaide so unmercifully, telling her that the shadowy white shapes were ghosts, that Addy had run back downstairs to the safety of her bedroom and hadn't ventured up here since.

The chambermaids helped Mother open the draperies and remove the sheets, unleashing clouds of dust that danced in the sunbeams and made Addy sneeze. Then Mother sent the maids away. "The less they know about what's going on around here, the less chance there is of them spreading gossip," she said.

Mimi laughed. "They aren't blind and deaf, you know. I'd wager they know perfectly well what's going on. And they have a right to know. Our future is their future too."

Mother dismissed her comments with a wave. "Anyway, my plan is to clear away most of the unnecessary décor, along with any extra furnishings, yet still have bedrooms that will function for guests."

"Guests? Even if we did have out-of-town guests in need of a bed, there are some perfectly lovely hotels in the city. I hear that the Waldorf is quite luxurious."

"Please, don't start, Junietta."

"You have to admit that owning all this space is a waste."

"There was a time when we used all these rooms, remember? A.B. and I would host house parties that would last for two or three days, and we would invite dozens of friends and guests." Mother's wistful tone surprised Adelaide. She was usually so brisk and businesslike. "And it wasn't very long ago that Ernestine got married and we were able to host her husband's relatives from London. Some of Cordelia's in-laws from Boston stayed with us too, when she got married. Who's to say we won't be filling these rooms with friends and family once again? Perhaps for Adelaide's wedding." Adelaide's stomach clenched at the thought of it.

"I'll say no more," Mimi said, tapping her lips as if to seal them. She crossed to the fireplace, which had a towering set of shelves above it filled with vases, figurines, and decorative bottles. "I can't imagine what a task it was for Arthur's decorators to buy all these things and have them shipped here and put into place," she mused. "Velvet chairs from France, marble sculptures from Italy—money was no object back then. Did you know that he had artisans create our drawing room over in France, carving the ceiling, fireplace mantel, cornices, and all the wood paneling? Then they took the room apart and shipped it over here so the workmen could put it back together again."

"But that drawing room is huge," Addy said.

"This house cost Arthur millions of dollars, and he didn't even blink. He believed his palace would give him status and power, never realizing that character and integrity are worth more than anything money can buy. And poor Arthur never knew love. Can you imagine living your entire lifetime without ever being loved or giving love in return?"

"I think we've heard quite enough about Arthur Stanhope, if you don't mind," Mother said. "Adelaide, help your grandmother take down most of the items on those shelves. Leave just a few things so the shelves don't look entirely bare."

Addy worked for more than two hours, piling items on one of the dust sheets that the maids had spread on the floor. "I feel a bit like a Viking looting Constantinople," Mimi joked as they worked.

They moved to a second bedroom, and Addy was gathering figurines from the top of a vanity when she noticed a painting hanging alongside the mirror. It reminded her of the one in the dining room that Mr. Webster had said was valuable. The signature wasn't Thomas Cole's, but the painting was a realistic depiction of a river that resembled the Hudson, surrounded by forested mountains.

"Come and look at this, Mother," she said. "I'm no expert, but this painting looks like it might be by one of the Hudson River artists. If so, perhaps we can sell it."

Mother barely glanced at it before turning away and saying, "You're right. It is one of theirs. But it isn't for sale."

Mimi Junie walked over to look at it too. "It's by Willard Eastman," she said, reading the signature. "I've heard that his work is in demand. Where did you get this, Sylvia? And why is it hiding in an unused third-floor bedroom?" She and Addy both turned to Mother, waiting for an explanation. Mother didn't face them.

"Mr. Eastman asked my father for permission to paint the view from our lawn at Ferncliff Manor. He spent the summer with us and completed several works. He gave us this one in gratitude."

"This was really the view from your home?" Addy asked. "It's magnificent!"

"Ferncliff Manor was our family's country retreat, thirty miles upriver from Manhattan. Father found it very restful. By the time Mr. Eastman came there to paint, we were living there year-round."

"A lot of people built second homes in the countryside to escape the summer heat," Mimi told Addy. "That was before the really rich started building summer mansions in Newport."

Being reminded of the loss of their summer home made Addy angry. "I wish there was a way to fight Uncle Roger and get our home in Newport back."

"I asked the lawyers to see if there was a way, but they haven't found one," Mother said.

"Well, will we be able to go to Rhode Island at all this summer? You originally thought we might live on the yacht, didn't you?"

"The *Merriweather* is simply too costly and too complicated to operate, so Mr. Forsythe is looking for a buyer. Besides, I will still be in mourning until July."

Addy swallowed her bitter disappointment. As the losses piled on, she was starting to better understand Mother's determination to hang on to this house and some semblance of their former life.

"This is a beautiful painting," Mimi said. "By a renowned artist. Why isn't it on display downstairs in the picture gallery, Sylvia?"

"I never cared much for it."

Addy thought that was odd. To her eye, it was very similar to the one that hung in the dining room. The view was different, but the beautiful, realistic way the river and mountains and trees were painted seemed nearly identical in style. "In that case, why don't we sell it, since we need the money?" she asked.

"I don't want to sell it, either."

"That makes no sense at all," Mimi said. "If you don't like it, and—"

"That's enough work for today," Mother said, cutting her off. "I'll have our lawyers send someone to collect these things and take them to auction." She swept from the room before anyone could comment. Mother was hiding something. What other reason would she have for not selling a valuable painting that she disliked? Addy was more curious than ever to find out about her mother's past and why she had stopped painting.

After changing out of her dusty work clothes and washing up, Addy went in search of her grandmother. She found her in her room, sitting by the window with her eyes closed and her feet propped on a hassock. She looked pale and tired. Addy was about to ask if she was unwell, but then Mimi smiled and the life returned to her features. "What brings you here, my darling girl?" she asked after Addy kissed her soft cheek.

"Mimi, am I the only one who thought Mother was being very evasive about that painting this morning?"

"She clammed right up, didn't she?"

"Do you know why? Is she hiding something?"

"I have no idea, dear. Sylvia has always been a closed book. Maybe your father knew some of her secrets, but I don't."

"I keep thinking of the beautiful watercolors Mother painted. And you mentioned that she had written and illustrated some children's books. Do you have any idea where they are?"

"In this monstrous house? Who knows? They could be anywhere."

"Do you remember where you found her two paintings? The one you gave me and the one that's hanging in the orphans' asylum?"

"Hmm. Let me think. That was years ago . . ." She stared off into space as if trying to peer back in time. Addy was about to apologize for bothering her and find something else to do, when Mimi said, "Ah! I remember now. Not long after Sylvia and A.B. were married, the foundation put on a play for charity. None of you girls had been born yet, and Sylvia was still eager to help me back then, so we went up to the attic together to look for furniture and things to use for props. Sylvia had offered to paint some backdrops for us, and she thought some of her old paints and brushes might still be usable. We found a steamer trunk with her maiden name and the Ferncliff Manor address on it. The paints and brushes were inside and also—much to my astonishment— the marvelous set of children's books she had written and illustrated. Her two watercolors were there too, unframed and all rolled up. Sylvia pulled the books from my hands and shoved them back inside the trunk, saying they were nothing. But she let me keep the watercolors. I had them framed and gave one to the orphans' home."

"Do you think she would mind if I searched for the books?"

"She has probably forgotten all about them by now. Be sure to take a light with you if you go up to that attic. And take one of the servants too. It's very creepy and cobwebby up there."

Mimi Junie was right about the cobwebs. They hung from the rafters above Addy's head like lace curtains. Barely any light penetrated the grimy windows, making the space dark and shadowy. She stood in the attic doorway with the scullery maid, getting her bearings and waiting for her eyes to adjust. "Hold the light a little higher, please." The girl lifted it and shone it around in an arc. Addy had been amazed by how much furniture and miscellaneous items had been crammed into the downstairs rooms, and now here were even more belongings, looming in the shadows and piled in crates and boxes. She stepped forward into the space, wondering if some of these possessions might have come from the Stanhopes' first mansion. Perhaps some of them could be sold too.

"Come on," Addy said shuffling into the gloom. "Hold the light so we can see where we're going."

The girl remained rooted in the tiny doorway. "They say it's haunted up here."

"Who says that?"

"The other maids."

"They're teasing you. There's no such thing as ghosts."

"A-are you sure, Miss?"

"Positive. There's nothing up here but a lot of old things. Come on."

Addy inched her way forward with the quivering maid, taking only a cursory look at some of the items as she searched for Mother's steamer trunk. The attic space was nearly as large as the building's footprint, and much of it was lost in darkness from where Addy stood with the feeble kerosene lamp. It would require an expedition to explore the entire space above the mansion and its two wings. But Mother had been the last person to move into this house, so it made sense that her belongings would be closest to the attic door.

Two steamer trunks had Uncle Roger's name on them. A third

had belonged to Addy's father. She spotted another trunk half-buried beneath some hatboxes and motioned to the maid.

"Put down the lamp for a minute and help me shift these boxes."

The girl shuffled closer, her shoulders hunched. "You don't suppose there's spiders up here, do you, Miss? Or rats?"

Addy shivered. She had been so intent on her task that she hadn't thought of either. "Mice, maybe," she replied. "But I don't think this mansion has rats." She would try to forget about spiders and search for a few more minutes before quitting. They stacked the hatboxes in a tottering pile and wiped the dust off the top of the trunk to read the shipping label.

Miss Sylvia G. Woodruff
Ferncliff Manor
Village of Sing Sing
Westchester County, New York

"This is it! I think I've found what I was looking for."

"Saints be praised, Miss Adelaide. Can we go now?"

"Hold up the lamp so I can look inside." Addy fumbled with the trunk's latches and opened the lid. The wooden tray on top contained tubes of dried-up paint, used brushes, paint palettes, spatulas, and an array of half-used pencils and charcoal sticks. Addy's heart sped up as she lifted out the tray. Beneath it was an unfinished canvas oil painting that looked oddly familiar in the dim light. She lifted it out and set it aside. And there were the children's books, hand-bound and neatly stacked. She opened the first one and saw the same charming animals as in the paintings: a rabbit, a frog, and a mouse. She quickly leafed through the pages, and it was like stepping into one of the paintings and entering a rich green woodland world of moss and ferns and wildflowers. Even in the feeble light, Addy found the illustrations charming.

"Okay," she said, closing the book again. "Help me drag this trunk closer to the door, please. We'll take this canvas and as many of these books as we can carry, and return later for the rest."

Back in her room, Addy carried the oil painting to her window seat so she could study it closely in the daylight. One corner of the sky was unfinished, and there was no signature, but she was certain that it was the same view of the Hudson River and surrounding mountains that she'd seen in the third-floor bedroom. She hurried upstairs to compare the two. The unfinished one was smaller, but it was as if the two artists had stood side by side, painting the same scene together. A more skilled artist had painted the framed picture, so might the unframed canvas be Mother's? There was no doubt that she had artistic talent, so might she have painted it alongside the master painter, Willard Eastman, that long-ago summer?

Addy could hardly contain her excitement as she looked through the children's books. The first one told the story of three woodland friends, Missy Mouse, Harry Hare, and Freddy Frog, who were always trying to outwit wily Nanny Fox. Missy Mouse was afraid of everything, including her own shadow. Harry Hare, who was something of a daredevil, tried to coax her into doing daring things. "You may need to be brave someday, Missy," he told her. "If you practice taking little risks, you'll know that you can be courageous when the time comes." With her friends Frog and Hare cheering her on, Mouse slowly overcame some of her fears. Then one day, Hare became trapped in a hunter's snare. Frog told Mouse that only she could rescue him by chewing through the binding. But first she had to sneak past the hunter's dog. With Frog helping to distract the dog, Mouse gathered her courage and bravely saved her friend Hare.

Addy quickly read a second book, then a third and a fourth. The characters were charming and real, the storylines captivating. Addy couldn't recall ever reading books as engaging as these as a child. If she hadn't known for a fact that the books were her mother's creations, springing from her imagination and brought to life through her artistic talent, Addy never would have believed it. The mother she knew and loved seemed so different from the woman who had created these books. Yet Addy had seen signs of her talent in the sketches Mother had made of the evening gowns. Addy took the unfinished canvas and one of the books, and went in search of Mimi Junie—not an easy task in a mansion this size. She found her in a small smoking room off the library, sipping a cup of tea.

"Why, Addy! Would you like to join me? Shall I ring for Jane to bring you a cup?"

"Yes, please." She sank down in a wicker chair beside Mimi.

"What do you have there? Oh my! You found your mother's books."

"They were where you said they'd be, in a trunk in the attic. And I found this canvas there, too." She showed it to her grandmother. "I compared it to the one we found this morning on the third floor, and it's the same view but smaller and obviously by a different artist. It isn't signed. Do you suppose it might be Mother's?"

"I wouldn't be at all surprised. And it would explain why she wouldn't sell the other painting. It might hold memories for her."

"I read a few of Mother's books too," Addy said, handing one to her. "There's a dozen more of these at least. The stories are really very good. And the pictures are amazing! I think she should have them published."

"I doubt if Sylvia would consent to that." The maid entered with a cup for Addy and filled it from the teapot.

"Do you know Mother's story, Mimi? She never talks about herself or says anything about her past."

"Only bits and pieces of it. She came to the city to live with her aunt when she was maybe a year younger than you are now, and she quickly took New York's high society by storm. She was so beautiful and mysterious that every gentleman wanted to meet her. She could have had her pick of husbands, but she chose your father, who had been smitten by her beauty as well."

"You've been so honest in sharing your story with us, but I don't suppose Mother will ever share hers."

"There may not be anything to tell," Mimi said with a laugh. "I was a bit of a rebel earlier in my life, but your mother has always played by the rules."

"Even so, I would like to hear more about the books she wrote, and who they were for, and where she learned to paint so well, and why she gave it up."

"You're absolutely right," Mimi said after a moment. "Since Sylvia is asking you to give up your freedom and marry some wealthy dupe in order to save this house, she owes it to you to tell you why she made the choices she did. Let's talk with her." She shifted forward in her seat as if preparing to rise and go immediately.

"Mother and I are receiving callers in the drawing room this afternoon."

Mimi gave a little groan and rolled her eyes. "Ah, I remember that tedious, useless practice. The only purpose was to bore each other to tears, spread the latest gossip, and show off your daytime finery. I never had much patience for all that nonsense."

"Mother says it's a traditional social custom."

"For women who have nothing better to do with their time, yes. Tell me, don't you sometimes wish you had something purposeful to do?"

*Purposeful?* Mimi was the only person she knew who talked as if Addy was supposed to do something grand and meaningful with her life. Was she truly missing something?

"Never mind," Mimi said when Addy didn't reply. "When do you think the last of the boring callers will be departing?"

"Around four thirty, I would think."

"Perhaps I'll pay a call on you and Sylvia then, and we'll have a little chat about the past." Mimi's plan made Addy uneasy, but she reluctantly agreed.

The afternoon began pleasantly enough as Addy and her mother greeted friends they hadn't seen in a while, and visited over tea and sweet cakes. Mrs. Rhodes and her daughter Felicity described the next party they were planning, and gossiped about the people they planned to invite, particularly the gentlemen. But as the hands on the case clock

ticked closer to four thirty, Addy grew restless, having heard enough
of the latest news. It had been nice to visit with her friends again, but
they had talked of superficial things, not the worries and concerns that
occupied Addy's thoughts and pressed on her heart. Mimi Junie's flip-
pant summary of the tradition had proven too close to the truth as the
ladies had shown off their new hats and day dresses while whispering
the latest gossip.

The last callers hadn't left yet when Mimi Junie swept into the
room. Mother's polite smile seemed stiff as Mimi sat down with a cup
of tea to converse with them. When the guests finally departed, Mimi
heaved a sigh. "I thought they would never leave! You can relax now,
Sylvia, and spend a few minutes with us. There's something I think we
should discuss."

"Will it take long?" she asked, glancing at the clock. She was still
standing after escorting her guests to the door.

"I'm not sure. But I've had a peek at your calendar, and I know for a
fact that you don't have any other plans this evening."

Mother closed her eyes for a moment as if conceding defeat, then
sank down on the sofa beside Addy. "What do you want to discuss?"

"Sylvia, I know how important this house is to you, and that you
don't want to give it up. But you're asking Addy to make choices that
will affect the rest of her life. I believe it would help if you could explain
to her why you don't want to move. Is it because the house has so many
memories, or is it the beauty of the rooms and furnishings? We can
make new memories somewhere else, you know. And you can keep any
furnishings and artwork that are special to you."

Mother paused before answering. "It's difficult to put into words."

"I think you should try. For Addy's sake. She has the most at stake."

"What do you mean by that?"

"I mean she's only nineteen years old. If she marries someone just so
the two of you can keep this house, she could well be living here with
that husband for a very long time after we're dead."

"Mimi! Don't talk of dying!" Adelaide said.

"I'm sorry. I don't mean to be morbid. But I've already shared some of my memories of this house. I've given balls and parties and dinners here with Art, pasting on a smile and pretending we were the perfect family when all along it was merely an act. I'm glad that you have happy memories of this very same house. But you have no way of knowing whether Addy's life here will be as happy as yours or as dreadful as mine. I do know that Addy needs to make her own decision. I would hate for her to resent either one of us, someday, for influencing her to go in the wrong direction."

"Do you consider your life wasted, Junietta?"

"Not at all."

"Neither do I, and we've lived in the same house in much the same way."

"Then why don't you try to explain to Addy and me why it's so important for you to stay in this house?"

Mother was still for a long moment. Adelaide was surprised to see tears fill her eyes. When she spoke, her voice trembled with controlled emotion. "More than anything else, I want Adelaide to be able to continue with the life she was born into. I made sure her sisters married well so they would always be cared for, and I want the same for Adelaide. I know what's at stake if we lose everything, which is why I'm fighting so hard to keep it. I know what it's like to lose my family home and to be forced to move to a vastly different place. I know what it's like to borrow and beg and scrape in order to keep living in the manner to which you're accustomed. And I swore that I would never live that way again. Or let any of my children lose their home the way I did."

Mimi reached over and laid her hand on top of Mother's. "Perhaps it's time we heard your story, Sylvia."

# 19

1857

~ *Sylvia* ~

I watched with envy as my brothers slid down our mansion's winding banister. Ten-year-old Harry went first, as he always did, followed by eight-year-old Freddy. The stairwell filled the center of our home, and when I peered down the shaft from the second floor, I felt dizzy. My brothers were very brave and daring. I was only four, and I wasn't brave at all.

"Come on, Missy Mouse, try it!" Harry called from the bottom. I shook my head, hugging myself as if that would keep me rooted in place. "Freddy and I were your age the first time we did it."

"But you're boys," I replied. "Nanny would say it's unladylike." Being a young gentleman seemed so much more exciting than being a young lady. They could wear trousers, while I had to wear petticoats and bloomers and stockings and dresses and pinafores, all layered on top of each other, making it impossible to run as fast as they did.

212

"Nanny will never know," Freddy called up the stairs. "Quick! Slide down before she sees you."

"Yes, hurry," Harry said as he started climbing to the top again. "I'll stay right beside you. You have to try it."

"Why?" I glanced down the dizzying hole again and backed away, hugging myself tighter.

"Because it's fun. And because you can't be scared all the time. Someday you might need to be brave, and when you remember how fearlessly you slid down the banister, you'll find your courage."

"What if I fall?"

"You won't fall. Watch me again. I'll show you how easy it is."

"Harry Elton Woodruff!" a voice behind me roared. I jumped in surprise as Nanny's hand clamped onto my shoulder. She could appear out of nowhere, as quick and sly as a fox. "What do you think you're doing, young man?"

Harry halted halfway up. He winked at me, then straddled the rail and slid all the way to the bottom again. "See you later, Missy!" he called. He and Freddy took off at a run, faster than Nanny could ever catch them.

"Don't you dare do that, Sylvia Grace! Ever! You'll fall to your death and break your dear parents' hearts."

Our parents' hearts were the threat by which Nanny controlled us. When we were obedient and sedate, we would bless their hearts. If we were disobedient and rowdy, we would break them. I grew up fearfully aware of the power I wielded over their vital organs. I'd observed Father's displeasure when he'd had to discipline Harry and Freddy for their mischief. And I'd seen how a good report from their private day school could make Father glow with pride. Harry thrived on mischief. Freddy was more studious, but he idolized our older brother and followed him on all his daring escapades.

Nanny's hand was still clamped on my shoulder. "Your brothers are naughty rascals whose deviltry will be the death of your saintly parents. Now, come to the nursery with me, Miss Sylvia. You can play with your dollhouse or perhaps your paints. Make a pretty picture to please your mother."

I didn't know it, but that afternoon had been my last chance to slide down the banister and show my brothers how brave I was. The following day, the servants draped the railings with pine branches and ribbons for Mother's annual Christmas party. I loved the excitement that overtook our house whenever my parents entertained. And my father, the proprietor of Imperial Flour and Grain Company, had many powerful, important people to entertain. I loved to peek down from the top of the stairs to see my mother and all the ladies in their fancy gowns, my father and the other gentlemen in their elegant evening clothes. My mother was the most beautiful woman of all, like the princess in a fairy tale. Daddy was her handsome prince, and our gracious stone mansion their palace. I also didn't know it at the time, but this would be my last Christmas in my beloved home.

But what a memorable Christmas it was. The house smelled of pine and cinnamon. A towering evergreen tree filled a corner of our drawing room, with brightly colored parcels for Harry, Freddy, and me crowded tantalizingly beneath it. The servants polished our sterling silver until it gleamed, and prepared our spare bedrooms for our out-of-town guests. Daddy's sister, Aunt Bess, was coming with her new husband. Mother's party promised to be bigger and more dazzling than ever before, and I loved all of it—the bright laughter, the sound of tinkling glasses, the music from the string orchestra that filled our home. How I longed to be old enough to wear a ball gown and waltz with my own handsome prince to the lovely music.

On the night of the party, Nanny dressed Harry, Freddy, and me in our finest clothes and we were allowed to go downstairs and be introduced to the guests. "What a beautiful child," one of them remarked when she saw me. "Her hair is like spun gold. She will be a beauty like you, one day," she told Mother. Daddy ordered the orchestra to play a waltz, and he scooped me up in his arms and danced with me. He smelled wonderfully of cigars and bay rum. Freddy waltzed with Mother, and Harry with Aunt Bess. Then Nanny spoiled it all by making us go back upstairs and eat our dinner from trays in the nursery. I was put to bed, but I couldn't sleep as sounds of the joyous party drifted upstairs.

Suddenly, my door opened a crack. "Missy Mouse? Are you awake?" Harry whispered.

"Yes! Oh, yes! Come in!" Harry tiptoed into my bedroom with Freddy right behind him, both in their nightshirts and caps. "Tell me a story," I begged as they clambered onto my bed. They were both wonderful storytellers. Freddy's tales were beautifully detailed as he took me on journeys with the great explorers Lewis and Clark. Harry's imaginative accounts of daring sea pirates and their adventures on the high seas edged deliciously close to giving me nightmares.

I drifted off to sleep, the happiest girl alive, unaware that my fairy-tale world already had begun to crumble into dust four months earlier. That was when the country's oldest flour and grain company and Daddy's biggest rival, had gone bankrupt, helping to trigger what became known as the Panic of 1857. Investors went on a selling spree that grew worse in September when the *SS Central America* sank in a hurricane. The ship had been carrying a cargo of gold worth millions of dollars, destined for New York City's banks. Our family's slide from the heights of prosperity was as swift and dizzying as the ride down our banister.

My gregarious daddy no longer smiled. He spent hours and hours at work. Mother grew silent and reclusive. She no longer gave parties or called on her friends or went shopping for beautiful things. Nanny Fox and many of the other servants resigned to find work elsewhere. A deep sadness fell over our home, and I didn't understand why.

Then Daddy stopped going to work altogether. One day, I crept downstairs to his study where I wasn't allowed to go, longing to hear his assurances that everything would soon return to the way it used to be. His study door was ajar. Daddy didn't see me peeking inside. But I saw him and the empty liquor bottle in front of him. He sat slumped with his arms folded on his desk and his head lowered. He was weeping as if he might never stop.

I turned and ran up the stairs, deeply shaken, and nearly collided with Harry and Freddy, who had just returned home from school. Harry caught me in his arms. "Where are you scurrying off to in such a hurry, Missy Mouse?" Then he saw my tears. "Hey, hey, what's wrong?"

"Daddy didn't go to work today, and I just saw him in his study, and . . . and he's crying!"

"Oh, no," Freddy groaned. Harry lifted me in his arms and carried me into the bedroom he shared with Freddy. My brothers' faces had suddenly turned so sad that I feared they might start crying too.

"Listen," Harry said as he smoothed my hair from my face. "I won't lie and tell you that everything's fine, Missy, because it isn't. Father's business is in trouble."

"What do you mean?"

"Mother and Father think we don't know about it," Freddy said. "But we do. Some of the older boys at school have been ridiculing us, saying Imperial Flour and Grain is bankrupt, and we'll soon have to go begging in the streets."

"We didn't want to believe that it's true," Harry added. "But businesses everywhere have been failing, and if Father is weeping . . . well, things must be really bad."

They were. My parents scrambled for ways to cut back on expenses. The boys were taken out of their school. All but a handful of servants were let go. I missed Nanny Fox and all the attention she paid me. Harry and Freddy tried to take over for her, creating games for the three of us to play and making me laugh. We played hide-and-seek among the crates and boxes of our belongings as they were packed up and sold. But we played quietly, so as not to distress our parents and further injure their breaking hearts.

Then the day came when the last of my dresses and toys were packed and taken away. Harry had warned me that we would be moving out of our house soon, and the day had finally arrived. My echoing bedroom seemed empty and bare. I wandered into my brothers' room, clutching

Annabelle, my doll, and found it barren as well. Freddy was packing the last of his books, Harry his tin soldiers and toy sword.

"When will we move home again?" I asked.

Harry's voice was gentle. "Never, Missy Mouse. Our house has been sold. We aren't rich anymore."

"Father's business collapsed," Freddy added.

"Like the houses you make out of cards?" I asked. Freddy could build towering structures with his steady hands, but they always fell flat in the end.

Harry smiled. "Not exactly like that." He patted my hair, which often remained tangled and uncombed for days now that Nanny was gone and Mother stayed in her room. "It means he lost everything. All our money."

"Can't we help him look for it? You're good at finding Freddy and me when we play hide-and-seek."

"If only it was that easy," he said with a sigh.

"Father explained it to us this way," Freddy said. "He borrowed money from a rich man so he could make his flour mill bigger. Now the rich man wants all his money back, and Father can't pay him. So, the rich man took over Father's company. But that still wasn't enough to pay all his debts, so we had to sell our house."

"Father swears he'll get back on his feet," Harry said. His expression had turned hard and determined. "Then he's going to get even with that greedy old man who ruined us, and Freddy and I are going to help him do it, right, Fred?"

"You bet!"

I was trying very hard to be brave like my brothers and not cry, but my stomach ached from holding all my fear and sadness inside. I looked around at the empty room and asked, "Where are we going to live from now on?"

"Do you remember Grandfather's home in the country?" Freddy asked. "Ferncliff Manor?" I shook my head.

"She's too young," Harry said. "We haven't gone there in a long, long time. Not since Nana and Grandfather died."

"Ferncliff is the house where Father and Aunt Bess grew up," Freddy said. "It's on a hill above the Hudson River, and you can watch the ships sailing past all day. Grandfather's original gristmill is still there on the creek, but no one uses it anymore."

"And there are woods all around Ferncliff where we can play," Harry said. "We'll have all sorts of adventures. It'll be fun!"

We took a carriage to the train station and traveled north off Manhattan Island. I had never been on a train before, and when I first saw it crouched in the station, making a monstrous noise and puffing smoke and steam, I thought it was a dragon. I sat on Harry's lap, holding his hand for courage as we chugged out of the city. Later, we disembarked in the village of Sing Sing, which I thought was a lovely name for a town. But it was very small and nothing at all like the big city that I was used to. My brothers didn't tell me at the time because they didn't want to frighten me, but there was a famous prison in our new town. We hired another carriage when we arrived, which took us down a dusty road, past fields and pastures and woods. Everything looked strange. There was too much sky. Too many towering trees. The forest reminded me of Freddy's tales of pioneers and Indians, and I shivered as we rode through it.

We halted at last in front of an odd-looking house with what looked like steps on the roof. "We're here! This is Ferncliff Manor," Harry said. I saw his excitement as he jumped down, then he lifted me down as well. The stone house had a steep gabled roof with a small lookout tower at the very top. A profusion of overgrown vines made it hard to see the windows or front door. It reminded me of a house I had seen in Freddy's book of Grimms' *Fairy Tales*. I had never read any of those stories because Nanny said they were too scary. The pictures alone had convinced me she was right. The house seemed large and spacious enough for all of us, but it looked lonely sitting on a patch of ground with no other houses around it. It was so unlike our mansion, which sat snuggled up against the surrounding buildings. I was afraid to venture past all the creeping vines to go inside.

"This is only temporary," Daddy declared as he pushed the greenery aside and fumbled to unlock the door. "Just until our country's financial situation improves."

Mr. and Mrs. Davies, our new housekeeper and gardener, had made the place ready for us. They lived in a tiny cottage up the lane on the edge of our property. Freddy took my hand and tugged me inside, following Father. The original house was more than one hundred years old, with two newer additions added later. The furnishings and rugs looked old and well worn. Some of our belongings and crated household goods had arrived ahead of us, shipped by train, then carted out to Ferncliff in a local delivery wagon.

"Let's explore," Harry said. My brothers and I wandered through the rooms, which seemed cold and dark and very dusty. Our chambermaids would have had the place sparkling and smelling of lemon oil in no time, but of course we no longer had chambermaids. We found the two upstairs bedrooms that would be ours, and our familiar bedding from home was already in place. Neither room could hold much more than our beds and a dresser.

"I wish I could sleep in your room, with you," I said.

"Don't worry, Missy Mouse," Harry said. "We'll be right next door." We found a third bedroom beneath the eaves that would serve as our playroom. Then the boys climbed a set of steep, spooky stairs to the lookout tower and claimed it as their own. "This will be our hideout," Harry decided. "Come on up, Missy, and see this." Mrs. Davies hadn't thought to clean the tower, and it was very dusty and cobwebby. Freddy sneezed three times in a row. Harry spit on his handkerchief and wiped grime from one of the windows. "Look at that view! There's the Hudson River. And you can see into the distance for miles and miles."

The next few days were busy ones as Mr. and Mrs. Davies helped us unpack everything and rearrange the furniture to try to make it fit. The rooms ended up looking like a jumbled mess, with pieces from our mansion looking out of place and much too elegant crammed alongside the old-fashioned, threadbare ones. Mother remained in her room for much of the day, her mahogany wardrobe stuffed with beautiful gowns and hats and fur capes that she would have no use for in the nearby village. Father took over the smaller living room as his office because it had shelves filled with Grandfather's old books. I would sometimes find him sleeping on the sofa in there when I got up for breakfast in the morning.

Outside, Mr. Davies had cleared a patch of lawn to give us a beautiful view of the winding Hudson River and the surrounding mountains, which curved down to the river's edge. It was springtime when we moved, too late in the school year for the boys to start classes in the village, so the three of us were left to occupy ourselves all day. Freddy and Harry set off to explore the woods and spent their days following deer paths through the forest or playing down by the river. I was too frightened to join them, so I sat on a rusting wrought-iron bench in what had once been a formal garden, and watched ships and boats of all sizes sailing up to Albany or down to the city. I drew pictures of the world that I remembered, a world of beautiful ladies in gowns who lived in fairy-tale castles.

I was upstairs in the playroom one rainy day, whispering secrets to my doll, Annabelle, when I heard my parents' voices downstairs. They spoke to each other so rarely, not even at dinnertime, that I was curious to hear what they were saying. I crept downstairs. Mother stood in the doorway to Father's study, and I could tell by the way she'd planted her hands on her hips that she was angry. "Why aren't you out looking for a job?" she demanded. I couldn't hear Father's reply, but Mother's voice grew louder as she stepped inside his office and said, "How are we supposed to live without an income?"

I tiptoed closer to hear Father's reply. "I told you, I'm leasing the farmland around Ferncliff and collecting rent." He sounded angry as well. "And I'm going to have someone take a look at the mill and get it functioning again." Harry, Freddy, and I had gone down to see the remains of the old mill by the creek. The stone foundation was crumbling like stale cake, the machinery had turned to rust, and the mill itself with its missing windows and rotting wood leaned precariously as if a strong wind might topple it. The creek that once powered the mill wheel was a mere trickle that the three of us could wade across and catch minnows in.

"Do you honestly think being a farmer's landlord or resurrecting an ancient flour mill will support your wife and children?" Mother asked. "When we're used to having so much more?"

"Once the economy improves, I plan to sell part of the land and invest the money—"

"The same way you invested all our other money?"

"I wasn't the only one who lost everything."

"How long are we going to be forced to live in this godforsaken place?"

"Only a year or so. Maybe less. But in the meantime, we can still attend parties and concerts and events in the city. We're only a short train ride away."

I heard Mother's bitter laughter. "Don't be a fool. No one is going to invite us to their dinner parties. Even if you do manage to recover a portion of what we once had, we'll never recover from the scandal of bankruptcy. We can't even show our faces in the city."

"Our friends know it wasn't my fault. That unprincipled scoundrel could have extended my credit. I only needed another month or two. He did it purely for spite, I tell you, not because he needed the money. The man's a stinking millionaire! He ruined us on purpose!" Father was shouting, his voice quaking with fury. I heard words I'd never heard before as he cursed his enemy's name. "I'll pay him back for what he did to our family, I swear I will!"

I scurried back upstairs, unwilling to hear more. Somehow, I knew, even at such a young age, that my life would never be the same.

# 20

### ❦ Sylvia ❦

When I turned six, I started attending the village school with my brothers. The students were all crammed into one room under the keen eye of the rat-faced schoolmaster, Mr. Radcliffe. I had heard of his reputation for using a leather riding crop on disobedient students, and had worried and fretted about going to school. "Don't worry, Missy Mouse. We'll protect you from him," Harry assured me. My brothers didn't seem to mind the occasional lashings they received for their pranks and mischief, insisting they were well worth the fun they'd had. My courage grew as I watched and admired them.

Freddy had already taught me to read and do numbers at home, so I was ahead of my classmates. Mr. Radcliffe let me draw pictures when my schoolwork was finished, and I became popular with the other students when I gave away my drawings. My brothers encouraged me, too.

"You're a really, really good artist, Mouse," Freddy said. "Don't ever stop drawing." He helped me find the paints that Nanny Fox had given me, packed away in one of the boxes from home. Harry bought me a second set of paints when those colors ran out. I never learned where he'd gotten the money for them.

I started writing stories to go with my pictures after I learned to spell. At first, I painted our old life in the city from memory, recreating the beautiful gowns and opulent rooms. Our mansion became a fairy-tale castle, where the king and queen lived with their two princes and little princess. Then an evil sorcerer tricked them out of their kingdom and stole it away from them. They were left with nothing and forced to live in a tumbledown cottage in the woods. But the two princes swore revenge, and one day they convinced a witch to cast a magic spell and give them enough power to defeat the evil sorcerer. They won back their kingdom, the princess married a handsome prince, and they all lived happily ever after.

I showed my book to my brothers when it was finished. We sat in their bedroom and I watched them read it, waiting eagerly for their response. "It's beautiful, Missy," Freddy said. "These are your best pictures yet."

"I like it too," Harry said. "But do you really want to go back to New York City to live?"

"Don't you?"

Harry thought about it as he leafed through my drawings again. Then he shook his head. "No, I like it here. I used to hate it when Nanny made us get all dressed up in our stiff, fancy clothes. This is much better. We don't even need to wear shoes."

"You should paint the woods, Missy," Freddy added. "The trees and birds and wildflowers and things."

I took their advice and began studying the forest world more closely. I would sit with a pencil and sketch pad, and fill page after page with drawings of the forest around me. I learned to sit very still, barely breathing, so I could watch the animals without causing them to scurry away and hide. I drew rabbits, chipmunks, squirrels, frogs, and mice, practicing until I could make them more and more lifelike. I filled a second pad, then a third. Before long, I grew to love the woodland world as much as my brothers did.

We settled into a routine at Ferncliff Manor, and it became our home. At Christmas, Harry and Freddy and I tramped through the snowy woods to cut down a tree, decorating it with bits of things we gathered in the woods. Our parents rarely left the house, so we chose our own Christmas gifts from the village mercantile. Mine were new art supplies. Mrs. Davies planned and cooked our meals, having the groceries delivered by wagon each week along with a steady supply of liquor. My parents were seldom without a glass of it in their hands.

Father spent his days—and sometimes his nights—in his study, going over his ledger books, keeping track of the rent he received from the land, and paying our household accounts. He paid Mrs. Davies to cook and clean, and her husband to keep up with the property, making sure the view of the river was clear. But it was too much for one aging gardener. The forest slowly crept toward the house while Father read the newspaper and ranted about stock prices and shady business dealings. "I'm waiting until the time is right to make my next move," he insisted. "That scoundrel will be sorry for ruining me. I'll ruin him!"

Mother continued to fade like the once-vibrant curtains had faded in the sunlight. We saw less and less of her color and beauty as time passed. Even when she was in the same room with us, it was as if she wasn't there. Her resentment toward Father increased. She rarely spoke to him, and she looked through him at the dinner table as if he was invisible. Then her mind began to fade as well. "Get our trunks down from the attic, Harry," she would tell my brother. "It's time to pack our things and go home. Our vacation will soon be over, and there are things in the city I need to do." She would plan grand parties, making lists of guests to invite, and elaborate, multicourse meals for the cook to prepare. None of it would ever happen.

Yet Harry, Freddy, and I were happy at Ferncliff. Summer was the best time of all. I was no longer afraid to go exploring, and followed my brothers barefooted along the paths through the woods. One led down to the river, where we would collect interesting bits of things that washed ashore. We would pretend we were pioneers or explorers or sometimes Indians. We were always discovering little nooks and crannies among the rocks and trees to turn into our hideouts.

Harry made swords and spears and bows and arrows. Freddy loved to search for interesting leaves and insects and other specimens for his growing collection. He catalogued everything by their Latin names, using the crumbling botanical books from Ferncliff's library for reference. I helped by drawing pictures of all his discoveries. "Someday, we'll explore the jungles of South America together," Harry promised, "and discover new species."

They built a raft out of logs and paddled along the shores of the river. They were careful to steer away from the middle, where the tide and currents were sometimes strong. I was frightened to sail with them at first. But eventually, they coaxed me into overcoming my fear and taught me how to paddle.

In the spring of 1861, our nation went to war. Mr. Radcliffe insisted it would end quickly. Father insisted that all the northern mills would go bankrupt without cotton from the South.

We watched and waited as a year went by and the war dragged on. Some of the young men from the village had signed up to fight. As we walked home through the woods after school one day, Harry talked of becoming a soldier and going off to fight too. "You're too young," Freddy chided. "You're only fifteen. You have to be eighteen to enlist."

"I could pass for eighteen."

"Could not."

"What do you think, Missy? I look old enough, don't I?" Harry was big for his age in size and strength, and more mature than other fifteen-year-olds. He had effectively become the man of the house these past few years. Freddy was thirteen and had long surpassed Mr. Radcliffe's knowledge of science and botany. I was only nine, and I couldn't bear the thought of either of them leaving me.

"Please don't go, Harry," I said, taking his hand. "Freddy and I need you."

"It's true, Harry. We do."

"All right, Missy Mouse. I'll stay, just for you, until your handsome prince comes to take you to his castle."

That summer, Harry took a job to earn a little extra money, helping a neighboring farmer bring in his hay crop. He returned after a long, hot day and coaxed Freddy and me to go down to the river with him to cool off. I was never brave enough to swim in the Hudson, but I liked to wade in the shallows and watch from shore as my brothers splashed and swam.

As the afternoon shadows lengthened, I scented rain in the air. The wind picked up, whisking my straw hat from my head. I chased it down the shore, and when I caught it and turned back, I saw that the sky in the west had begun to darken. "Better come in before it rains," I shouted to them.

Freddy got into trouble first. I heard his frantic shouts. "Harry! Harry, help me! The current's too strong!" Harry dove into the water and swam out to help Fred. They would be fine, I told myself. My brothers were strong swimmers. They would be fine. But I watched with growing terror as Harry seemed to be making no progress. The current pulled Freddy farther and farther away from him. Soon they were both flailing, their heads disappearing beneath the waves for longer and longer stretches of time.

"Help!" I screamed. "Somebody, help them!" But there was no one around to hear my cries or help my brothers. I had to help them myself.

I spied their raft beached onshore, tethered to a tree. I untied it with trembling fingers, still hollering for help as I did. It took all my strength to drag it across the pebbly ground and push it into the water. The raft wobbled as I climbed onboard, nearly pitching me into the cold water, but I held on. I felt the current tugging me toward the middle, and I used every ounce of strength I had to paddle toward Harry and Freddy. I could still see them bobbing between the waves, but each time they disappeared, it seemed like minutes would pass before they reappeared again, coughing up water. I screamed their names as their cries for help became weaker. The current was pulling them farther out. At the same time, it was carrying me away from them and I couldn't paddle fast enough. The raft rocked and pitched beneath me, the waves soaking me, but I was more terrified for them than for myself.

"Harry!" I screamed. "Freddy!" I searched the river where I thought I had last seen them, waiting to see their heads bob above the surface. But there was no sign of them. I screamed and screamed for them.

But they were gone.

At last, I stopped, my throat raw. I heard someone calling from onshore. "Miss Sylvia! Miss Sylvia, come back!" It was Mr. Davies, beckoning to me. If only he would jump into the river and save my brothers. But he was old and would never survive the current either. It was too late. I was too late. If only I had found my courage and reacted sooner. Maybe I could have saved them. But they were gone. Harry and Freddy were gone.

I sat hunched on the raft and wept as the waves tossed it aimlessly. I no longer cared what happened to me. Eventually, the wind and current washed the raft ashore, a little farther downstream from where I had put it in. Mr. Davies followed my progress down the beach, and he waded into the water to grab the raft. I was soaked and shivering when he lifted me into his arms and carried me home.

My parents heard my grief-stricken cries before we reached the house and were waiting by the drawing room doors together. Thunder grumbled in the distance, and it had begun to rain. "What's wrong? What happened?" Mother cried. She was as pale as paper. Mr. Davies set me down and I ran to her, clinging tightly to her and sobbing.

"It's the young men," Mr. Davies said, his voice quivering. "I heard them hollering and saw from the top of the hill that they were in trouble. I ran down to the river as fast as I could, but they had already gone under. Missy used the raft to try to save them, but she was no match for that current. I'm sorry. I'm so sorry."

"My boys?" Mother whispered. "My boys are gone?"

"I'm so sorry, ma'am," poor Mr. Davies repeated. His wife had come into the room and she began to wail as well.

"No!" Mother breathed. "No!" She pried my arms loose and pushed me away. Then she turned and climbed the stairs to her room as if walking in her sleep. It was the last time I saw her alive. My brothers, who had always held her heart in their hands, had broken it beyond repair. She wrote a note, saying she was going away with them.

The village men found my brothers' bodies downstream. My father held a funeral for all three of them, burying Mama alongside Harry and Freddy in the village churchyard.

I returned to Ferncliff afterward, wondering how this could have happened. My brothers had always been so alive and vibrant. How could they be gone? Aunt Bess came from New York for the funeral, and she sat down in the drawing room with Father and me to talk.

"You and Sylvia need to sell Ferncliff and come back to New York with me. You can stay with me until you get back on your feet."

"There's nothing for me in New York anymore," Father said. There was very little of him left in the hollowed-out shell that had once been my father.

"You can't stay here," Aunt Bess insisted. "You shouldn't stay here."

Father turned to me, his eyes swollen and red. "Do you want to go back with her, Sylvia?"

If she had asked me five years ago when we'd first arrived, I would have said yes. But Harry and Freddy had convinced me to stop thinking about New York and the life we'd lost. I had long since forgotten what life in the city was like. My brothers had taught me to really see Ferncliff and to love it. Now they were gone, yet I saw them everywhere I looked. I needed to stay here in the place they had loved.

"I want to stay here with Father," I told Aunt Bess.

And so I did.

Father and I let the vines grow over the house and the forest slowly overtake us, hiding us and keeping the world outside. For a long time, we were captives of our grief.

Then one day I sat down and created a story about my brothers, painting the adventures of Harry Hare, Freddy Frog, and Missy Mouse. I had discovered a way to keep them alive forever. I longed for a world where everything turned out happy in the end, because nothing in my world was right. And so I created one.

I went to and from school on the narrow path through the woods. I painted my stories. Father paid the bills and drank.

Together, we lived in lonely grief for the next nine years.

# 21

※

1871

~ *Sylvia* ~

It was so unusual for visitors to disturb the peace of Ferncliff Manor that I heard the squeak of wagon wheels and plod of horses' hooves before the vehicle came into sight. Mrs. Davies was busy making breakfast and Father was still in his room, so I wrapped my shawl around my shoulders and went outside to see who it was. I recognized the hired delivery wagon from town but not the gentleman in the plaid cutaway coat and peaked cap who was climbing down from the seat.

"Kindly wait a moment," I heard him tell the driver. Then he strode confidently toward me. He was in his early thirties, I guessed. Very tall, with wavy brown hair, eyes the same gray color as the river, and a handsome, clean-shaven face. "Good morning, Miss," he said, sweeping off his hat. He looked me up and down in a manner I was quite unused to, the way Mrs. Davies might examine a melon she was considering buying. "I understand this is Ferncliff Manor? Might I speak with Mr. Woodruff?"

"Mr. Woodruff is my father, and he's . . . unwell. Perhaps I can help you? I'm Sylvia Woodruff."

"Yes, perhaps you can." He had finished scrutinizing me, and now his gaze scanned our vine-covered house and the gray sliver of the Hudson River, visible from there. "I'm Willard Eastman, the artist. Perhaps you've heard of me?" I hadn't. When I didn't reply, he frowned slightly. "I was told that Ferncliff Manor's views of the Hudson are unsurpassed. I would like to see them for myself, and if they are as magnificent as I've been led to believe, I would like your father's permission to set up my easel and paint here this summer." His request was so unexpected, so out of the ordinary, that I wondered if he might be joking. Before I could reply, he took a few long-legged paces past me, toward the river. He stopped in the spot near the corner of the house where the vista opened, and spread his arms wide. "Ah yes! This is glorious!"

"I'll go and speak with my father," I called to him. I had no intention of inviting him inside our house, embarrassed by the state of it as Father's mind continued to slip away and his habits became slovenly.

"Miss Woodruff, wait!" he said, striding back. "Anticipating your father's good reply, I believe I'll stay here this morning and sketch. The weather is so favorable, and since I'm already here, I'll just get my things from the wagon and send the driver back to the village." He was already pulling a bag and a folding easel from the wagon as he spoke. His self-assurance and forward manner irritated me. Part of me hoped Father would refuse, and our quiet life at Ferncliff Manor could continue undisturbed. But another part of me was intrigued by Mr. Eastman—a genuine artist, possibly famous. I wanted to see how he worked and what his paintings were like.

I found Father eating toast in his disheveled bedroom, wearing a threadbare bathrobe over his pajamas. He hadn't washed or shaved or combed his hair yet, and his eyes were still bleary from all the liquor he'd consumed last night. As always, my love for him and my disgust at his state tugged my heart in opposite directions. "Good morning, Father,"

I said quietly. He hadn't noticed me entering and I didn't wish to startle him. "There's a gentleman outside, a Mr. Willard Eastman. He's an artist, and he would like your permission to paint the view from our yard."

"Eh? He what?"

"He wants to sit outside and paint a picture of the river." I spoke a little louder, although I knew Father hated loud voices or noise of any kind. "Would that be all right with you?"

"As long as he's not a bother . . ." His voice trailed off in a string of mumbled words I didn't understand.

"I'll go tell him. I'm sure he'll be grateful." I returned outside using the French doors in the drawing room and found Mr. Eastman perched on a folding stool in front of his easel. He shot a quick glance at me before returning to his sketch, intent on his work.

"I hope you don't mind, Miss Woodruff, but I couldn't resist this glorious sunlight. And the curve of the river, just there," he said, pointing. "It's magnificent! Like the curve of a woman's body." His words made me blush. I wanted to leave, but I couldn't tear myself away as I watched his swift, broad strokes in speechless fascination. The familiar view of the Hudson quickly came to life in charcoal on the page.

"I spoke with my father," I finally said. "He granted his permission."

"Mm."

"Would . . . would you mind if I watched you work, Mr. Eastman?"

"It's your property," he said with a shrug.

I don't know how long I sat on the grass and watched him. At least two hours, maybe more. His dexterous hands wielded the charcoal expertly, shading, smudging, drawing, sketching. He was married, I noticed, judging by the gold wedding band on his finger. As the sun grew warmer, he removed his jacket, unbuttoned his waistcoat, and rolled up his shirtsleeves, leaving dark fingerprints on the white linen. Every once in a while, he moved his easel and stool to a new spot, starting a new sketch each time. Neither of us spoke a word in all that time. I thought his work was beautiful, so it surprised me when he suddenly stopped, tossed his charcoal into his box of paints, and swore.

"What's wrong?" I asked. He turned and looked at me as if he'd forgotten I was there.

"The sun is too high, don't you see? The shadows, the light—they've all changed." I didn't understand his anger and surprise. Didn't the sun travel across the sky the same way every day, changing the shadows, shortening then lengthening them? Yet Mr. Eastman seemed offended by the sun's fickleness. I turned to go, unwilling to witness his silly tantrum, and saw my father emerging through the drawing room doors, still disheveled, still in his robe, and wearing slippers on his feet. I hurried toward him, hoping to coax him back indoors, but he brushed me aside as he limped toward Mr. Eastman.

"I thought I would come out and see what you're up to, young man," he said in his rusty voice. His hand had a tremor as he extended it to Mr. Eastman. "I'm Richard Woodruff."

"Willard Eastman. Nice to meet you. Thank you for allowing me to work here. Your view is spectacular."

"Yes. Yes." Daddy peered past him to examine the sketch for a moment. "You look warm, Mr. Eastman. Why don't you come inside out of the sun for a few minutes and let me pour you a drink?"

I cringed and held my breath, hoping, praying, that he would refuse. Not only was I ashamed to have him see the state of Ferncliff Manor, but I had left my watercolors spread out on the drawing room table to dry. I was appalled to think he might see them. But Father was already gesturing for Mr. Eastman to follow him into the house, and he was obliging, using his handkerchief to wipe smudges of charcoal from his fingers as he went.

"What can I fix you to drink?" Father headed straight toward his liquor supply after entering through the French doors.

"Just a glass of water, please."

"Go get it for him, Sylvia." I nodded and hurried toward the kitchen. Mr. Eastman was scanning the room as if taking note of every cluttered detail. I needed to hurry back and distract him before he saw my paintings. But I was too late. My father, proud of my amateur dabbling, had led him straight toward my work area. "My daughter, Sylvia, is also an artist," he bragged.

I quickly handed the glass of water to Mr. Eastman and took Father's arm. "Let's all sit down over here. I'm sure Mr. Eastman isn't interested in my silly little hobby." Mr. Eastman took a gulp of water and set the glass on my worktable. Then he picked up my paintings, one after the other, and tilted them toward the light to view each one.

"Mm," he grunted. "Mm." I didn't want to know what he was thinking.

"She's good, eh?" Father asked. I had led him to his chair and helped him sit, but I returned to the table, holding my breath as I watched Mr. Eastman's expression.

"Mm. Quite good," he finally said. I felt a flush creep across my face. "Where did you learn to paint? Who have you studied with?"

"No one."

He looked up from the painting to stare at me. "You taught yourself?" I nodded. "You have a natural eye for color. And for perspective. And for framing a subject."

"Thank you."

"If all of this is self-taught, imagine what you could do with professional instruction. How old are you, Miss Woodruff?"

"Eighteen."

"You should attend art school. Or at least be part of an art colony so you can learn from other artists."

"That isn't possible," I said, lowering my voice. "I take care of my father." I had stopped attending the village school when I'd turned fourteen. There was nothing more Mr. Radcliffe could teach me that I couldn't learn from the books in Father's study.

He finally set down the last of my paintings and picked up his glass of water, staring out at the river as he sipped it. Then he turned and walked over to where my father was, and sat down on our settee. "I would like to suggest a business proposition, Mr. Woodruff. If you will allow me to stay at Ferncliff Manor this summer and paint, I will give your daughter art lessons in return. She can sit beside me, and I'll teach her to paint with oil."

Once again, I felt my heart being tugged in opposing directions. As excited as I was at the prospect of professional art lessons, I was appalled to imagine an accomplished artist staying in our sad, muddled household. Yet he'd said my work was good. *Quite good.* And I wanted to learn everything I could from him.

He turned to me. "I would like to see for myself what you can do with a little guidance. I think you're capable of much more than rabbits and toadstools."

"I-I don't have any oil paints. Only watercolors."

"I'll order some for you." He addressed my father again. "What do you say to my proposal, Mr. Woodruff?"

Father raised his glass in salute. "We have a deal."

<hr>

I helped Mrs. Davies scrub and dust and air out Harry and Freddy's bedroom for Mr. Eastman. We carried the rug outside and beat it. We washed and pressed the bed linens. Father and I hadn't eaten a proper sit-down meal in the dining room since my brothers died nine years ago, but that would soon change. "You'll have to cook for Mr. Eastman for the next two months," I told Mrs. Davies. "I'm sure he'll expect three meals a day. And he may need his clothes laundered too."

Mr. Eastman returned three days later with his luggage, easel, canvases, paints, and brushes. He brought extra supplies for me, and for the first week, I sat beside him as he faced the river, sketching with charcoal and watching him work with oils. When he finished his first painting, he moved to a new location, and this time he set up a second canvas for me beside his own. The view he'd chosen was beautiful, but it overlooked the place where Harry and Freddy had drowned. I was embarrassed to explain why I didn't want to paint there, fearing Mr. Eastman would get angry and tell me to leave, yet I wanted desperately to learn to paint like him. I consoled myself with the idea of painting that river scene as a memorial to my brothers.

I was afraid of the large canvas at first, so much larger than the smaller pages I was used to. Mr. Eastman coached me through the process, step by step. "Don't be so timid, Miss Woodruff. Use broad strokes. Let your arm sweep freely across the canvas, like this." He stood behind me and took my hand in his, our bodies touching. My heart raced so fast I found it difficult to catch my breath. I had never experienced such a thrilling sensation. My hand continued to tremble for several minutes after he released it, making it hard to control my brush. For days afterward, I couldn't erase the warmth and scent and nearness of him from my mind. I made a nuisance of myself, following him everywhere, drinking in his every word and gesture. The way he raked his wavy brown hair from his forehead with his long fingers. The impatient way he rolled up his sleeves as the sun warmed us, revealing thick brown hair on his forearms. The way he dipped his brushes into the daubs of paint. I wanted to be near him every minute.

We began each day early in order to capture the morning light, quickly gulping the eggs and toast and coffee Mrs. Davies prepared. Mr. Eastman often asked her to pack a picnic lunch and we would stay outside when the weather permitted, painting side by side until late afternoon. Mrs. Davies had brought our dining room back to life, and Mr. Eastman ate dinner there in the evening by lamplight with Father and me. I stayed up late with him and Daddy as they drank and smoked cigars.

"I can't get the shading on the trees quite right, Mr. Eastman," I said one day as we worked.

"Let me see." He stood behind me, studying my canvas. His warm breath tickled my neck and made me shiver. "It looks fine," he finally said. "Perhaps a bit more cadmium there and there." Then he rested his hands on my shoulders and made me turn toward him. "Listen. You must call me Will, from now on. And I'm going to call you Sylvia. It's a beautiful name. It reminds me of sylphs. Do you know what they are?"

"I don't think so."

"They're invisible beings of the air. Somewhat like nymphs, I suppose, which in Greek folklore are beautiful maidens of the woods and trees. They are nature itself, sprung to life. That's why you paint nature so well, Sylvia. It's as if you're part of it." His hands had remained on my shoulders as he spoke, and when he released them and sat down again, I felt a loss. We never talked much as we painted, but I loved the sound of his deep, cultured voice, and I longed to hear more from him.

"You never told us where you're from, Mr. East—I mean, Will."

"I have a home in Boston. Beacon Hill."

"Is that where your wife lives?" He gave me a questioning look. "I assumed by your ring that you're married. Do you have a family?"

"Yes, a son and a daughter."

"Do they mind that you're away from them all summer?"

"My wife knew when we married that I would be away much of the time. This is how I make a living. She takes the children to her parents' summer home in Maine."

"I've heard that Maine is very beautiful too. Why not paint there?"

"I already have." He leaned closer to the canvas, concentrating so intently on his work that I knew our conversation was finished. I had ruined the moment by asking about his wife, but I was falling in love with Will and I needed to know about her.

Will worked faster than I could and had already finished three paintings while I still labored away on my first. His were beautiful works, so much better than mine, and would fetch great sums in the city. We ventured farther and farther from the house, painting down near the river or in the woods, always just the two of us, alone. He was so handsome I could hardly keep from staring at him. He had allowed his beard to grow out that summer and it looked as thick and soft as moss. I began to sense by the long looks we exchanged and by the warmth I saw in his gray eyes that things were changing between us. I was in awe of him, not only of his skill but of his gentlemanly manners and self-assurance, which some might have called arrogance.

"If you're good and you know it, never apologize or be ashamed to admit it," he told me. "Accept the accolades—and you will receive many of them one day, my sweet Sylvia. Of that I have no doubt."

The companionship we shared had become soul-deep, even though we spoke little while we painted. When he was near me, I felt the same breathless sense of danger I used to experience when doing something daring with Harry and Freddy. I sketched Will's face from memory when I was alone in my room at night. I missed the sound of his voice and his easy laughter after we parted to sleep. I couldn't wait to wake up early and paint beside him all day.

One humid summer afternoon as we worked, the sky began to darken with clouds, and we heard the rumble of thunder as a storm began building above the mountains. "We'd better go inside," I said, gathering my things.

"No, no. Not yet. I want to capture the exact shade of that sky." Will continued painting, quickly capturing the billowing gray clouds on his canvas until a nearby crack of lightning made the hair on my arms stand on end. The rain began pelting us in cold drops. Only then did he scoop up his things.

"Run, Sylvia! Run!" he shouted above the booming thunder. We sprinted to the safety of the drawing room, soaked and laughing. Then he stood at the open French doors and watched the storm swirl above the Hudson. "Come here and watch the clouds with me, Sylvia." He wrapped his arm around my shoulders and pulled me close, describing the colors he saw in the sky, and deciding which shades of paint he would mix to achieve each color. He taught me to see the sky the same way Freddy had taught me to see tiny insects and mushrooms and woodland animals. "If only I could capture the energy of the storm," he murmured.

"Shall I make you some hot tea?" Mrs. Davies suddenly asked from the drawing room door. Will's arm fell from my shoulders, not in haste or guilt, but with casual ease.

"That would be nice," he replied. "And fetch us some dry towels."

When I followed her into the kitchen to help her, Mrs. Davies gripped my arm and pulled me aside. "You be careful of him, Miss Sylvia," she whispered. "I don't like the idea of you spending so much time alone with him—and him a married man."

"He's teaching me to paint. That's all."

"Well, you just be careful, and don't let him take any liberties."

Little did she know that I dreamed of him taking liberties. I was in love with Will, and I longed for him to hold me close and kiss me the way I had read about in romantic novels. It was easy to forget he had a wife and family, easy to believe the summer would never end and we would always be together. But the evenings were growing cooler. Summer was fading. Will would be leaving soon. I didn't want him to go.

I returned to the drawing room with towels and the tray of tea. Rain streamed down the windows and thunder rumbled, making the glass rattle. Will watched me as I crossed the room and his gaze made me feel naked. He continued watching me as we dried off and sipped our tea, and when we were finished, he said, "Sit over there by the window and let me sketch you." He posed me in place, then picked up his sketch pad. I had taken down my hair to towel it dry, and it laid damp and heavy on my shoulders. Will's gaze traveled back and forth from my face to the page, his hands moving rapidly as his charcoal scratched against the paper. I didn't know why my heart pounded so hard when all I was doing was sitting still by the window.

"Do you know that you're a very beautiful woman, Sylvia?" he suddenly asked. He had paused in his sketching and his gaze met mine. "It makes me wonder what you're hiding."

"I don't know what you mean. I'm not hiding anything."

"Then why does a beautiful young woman of some means live alone in the countryside, far from the excitement of the city?"

"We had a home in the city, but we moved to the country fourteen years ago when Father suffered some financial setbacks. We discovered that we enjoyed it here, and so we've stayed." Indeed, my life in the city now seemed like a long-ago dream that I could barely remember.

Will showed me the sketch when he finished. "I can't do you justice,

Sylvia. It would take Renoir or Vermeer to do that." He had drawn the face I saw in the mirror every day quite accurately, and yet it wasn't the same face at all. Will had drawn me through the eyes of love, making me truly beautiful. I couldn't speak as tears rolled down my cheek. Will reached for my hand.

"Come outside with me," he said, pulling me to my feet. "The rain has stopped." We had removed our wet shoes when we'd come inside, and now we walked barefoot through the grass to the wrought-iron bench near the tangled, overgrown formal garden. Will sat down and pulled me onto his lap. His arms surrounded me and he pulled me close until our lips met in a gentle kiss. "I've been wanting to do that all summer," he murmured. "I hope you don't mind." I couldn't speak, so I simply shook my head. I wished he would kiss me again. As if reading my mind, he took my face in his hands and kissed me again. Not gently this time, but with all the passion and longing that had been slowly building in both of us over the past two months. I don't know how long we kissed. It felt like a lifetime. It felt like an instant.

At last, he pulled away. We were both breathless. I hungered for more and I sensed that Will did too, but he slid me off his lap and set me on my feet, then stood and took my hand. We started walking back to the house. "Summer will soon be over, Sylvia. I've decided to go out west to paint."

"Why go west when there's so much beauty right here?"

"I want to capture the unspoiled grandeur of America before it's gone. Before men with their greed and lust for power spoil the wilderness and tame it with their railroads and bridges. Our nation is nearing the end of something great, we're on the brink of change, and artists like you and me have the opportunity to capture the beauty for posterity." He halted and tipped my face toward his. He kissed me again. "Come out west and paint with me, Sylvia."

I could think of a dozen reasons to say no. I needed to stay here and take care of my father. I had never traveled before, and it frightened me to think of leaving idyllic Ferncliff. Exploring had been Harry's and Freddy's dream. Could I really run away with an itinerant artist and roam the vast country, painting pictures? I could almost see Harry's grin and hear him say, *"Do it, Missy Mouse! You can't live your life by being afraid."*

But Will was married.

"Don't answer now," he said when I didn't reply. "Think it over for a few days. I'm leaving for Boston tomorrow." He didn't mention his wife or say that he was going to see her and his children. Just that he was leaving for Boston. "I'll come back for you in a week, and we'll head west together. In the meantime, I'll miss you."

"And I, you."

He leaned close and kissed me again, leaving me hungry for more.

We ate our last meal together in the dining room that night, conversing with Father, who seemed to drink twice as much as usual after Will told him he was leaving. Early the next morning, Will walked to the village train station, taking only a small bag. I knew he would return for me because he'd left all his paintings and art supplies behind. I had one week to decide whether I would go out west with him or not. I had no one to confide in to help me make that decision.

I loved to paint, and I was eager to learn more techniques from Will, to become an even better artist. He could show me new lands, beautiful lands. Mr. and Mrs. Davies could take care of Father while I was away. Will said it would only be for a year. I wanted to be with Will Eastman. Forever. I couldn't bear the thought of being apart. And yet I couldn't forget that he had a wife and children.

I ate my breakfast in the kitchen with Mrs. Davies the morning Will left, then carried Father's tray up to his bedroom. He wasn't in his room. I carried it back downstairs to his study and the tray nearly slipped from my hands when I saw him sprawled on the floor beside the sofa. The stench of vomit was strong in the room. I set down the tray and ran to him, crouching beside him, shaking him. "Papa! Papa, wake up!" His body felt cold and rigid. His eyes were open, staring. He was gone.

Mrs. Davies came running when she heard my screams. Mr. Davies sent for the doctor, even though we all knew it was hopeless. The doctor pronounced him dead. He said my father had choked to death on his own vomit.

Once again, I plunged into a river of bottomless grief. All thoughts of Will Eastman fled my mind. The pastor of the village church walked me through the funeral arrangements and helped me send a telegram to Aunt Bess with the news. She arrived the next day and seemed astounded to see Ferncliff Manor in such a state of disarray. "Why didn't you send for me sooner? Your letters led me to believe everything was fine, and that you loved it here in the country."

"I do love it here. That's why I wanted to stay after Harry and Freddy and Mother died."

"Well, you can't stay here now, Sylvia. I'm taking you to New York to live with me. By the time your father's estate is settled and Ferncliff Manor is sold, you'll have a better idea of what you want to do with your future."

"What if I don't want to sell Ferncliff? What if I want to live here?" There were memories of the family I loved here. Memories of Will.

"You can't stay. This place is crumbling down around you, and there's no money to repair it. I won't let you live here all alone. You're only eighteen years old, for heaven's sake. You have your whole life ahead of you."

"And yet I feel so old."

Aunt Bess's taffeta gown rustled as she pulled me into her arms. Her perfume smelled of lilacs. I thought of my mother, the way she used to be, not as she was near the end. "I'm going to take care of you from now on," Aunt Bess said. "I should have done it a long time ago. You deserve the life you once had before your father lost everything."

"Can I still paint if I go to New York with you?"

"Of course. It will be nice to have a hobby to keep you occupied."

Aunt Bess went back to the city the day before Will was due to return. I told her I would join her in a week after packing my things, putting Ferncliff Manor in order, and saying goodbye to my home for the past fourteen years, the home where all my family members had died. Father's sudden death had left me free to choose my own future. I could travel with the man I loved and learn to paint, or return to the life I'd once had in New York before my father's enemy had ruined him. I paced through the empty house all night, torn between the two choices. A full moon bathed the distant river with light and streamed through the drawing room doors. I studied Will's magnificent paintings in the moonlight alongside my own. My work was whimsical and childlike, born of the dreams and fantasies of my childhood, and my grief for my brothers. And as the moon set and the sun rose, I made my decision. I had compared his paintings to mine, and realized that he wasn't taking me along so he could teach me to paint. I would never become a great artist.

Will arrived at Ferncliff later that morning. He pulled me into the kitchen and kissed me until I could barely breathe. "How I've missed you!" he said. "Are you ready to go? The driver can load your bags onto my carriage." I nearly changed my mind in that moment, drawn by a power I didn't understand. I loved him, and the thought of Will going away was another grief I didn't think I could bear. Yet I knew he would never divorce his wife and marry me. I would always be his mistress.

I swallowed a knot of sorrow and said, "Will, my father died the day you left."

"Oh, my darling. I'm so sorry." He pulled me close again. "But see? Now there's no reason at all for you to stay here. We can leave on the afternoon train to Albany."

I wriggled free to look up at him. "My Aunt Bess came for Father's funeral. She wants me to go back to New York to live with her."

"Don't do it, Sylvia. You're such a beautiful, sensitive soul. I've no doubt that your beauty will fascinate every man in New York. But they'll see only your outward beauty. You need a man who knows your heart."

"And that would be you, I suppose?"

"Yes. Come out west with me. I'll take care of you, Sylvia. We'll paint together like we did all summer."

"My work will never be gallery-worthy."

"I've fallen in love with you, my beautiful sylph. You're my muse. I've done the best work of my life this summer. I need you beside me."

If Will hadn't been married, I might have decided differently. But he was. I slowly shook my head. "Go west and paint without me, for now. Seek your fame and fortune—"

"That's not fair. You know I'm not seeking those things in themselves. Only because they will allow me to make a living doing what I love to do. What my soul and heart and very being were created to do."

"I'm going to New York to live with my aunt because I need time to grieve, not only for my father but for Ferncliff. Come back for me next summer, on this day one year from now. We'll meet on the back lawn overlooking the river where we painted together. I'll be ready to go with you by then."

He kissed me and held me close. "Sylvia," he murmured. "My beautiful Sylvia. If I spend one last day with you here at Ferncliff, may I come to your bed tonight?" In spite of my love and curiosity and longing, I shook my head. He had stolen my heart but I wouldn't let him take my virtue.

Will packed up his paintings and art supplies, and left right away. I walked down the path to the river alone while he gathered his things, unwilling to watch him leave. When I returned to the house, I found his finished painting of the river where Harry and Freddy had died, propped beside my unfinished one. His note read:

> *Darling Sylvia,*
> *Use this to finish your own painting while you're in New York.*
> *I'll return to Ferncliff for you next summer on August 31.*
>
> *Love,*
> *Will*

I tucked his note inside my sketch pad where I could look at it whenever I wanted to remember the man I had loved. I wondered, as I packed all my belongings to move to New York, if I would ever love anyone the way I had loved Will Eastman.

# 22

❧

❧ *Sylvia* ❧

Sylvia had been so deep into her memories that she was taken by surprise when the maid entered to clean up the tea things, breaking the spell. "Oh, I'm sorry, ma'am," the girl said when she realized she'd interrupted. "I thought your callers were all gone by now."

"They are. And we're finished as well." She rose and smoothed her skirts as she prepared to leave. Adelaide touched her arm.

"Mother, wait! Did you return to Ferncliff Manor a year later to meet Mr. Eastman?"

"By the time a year passed, I had grown up," she said with a sigh. "I realized that what I had mistaken for love was an adolescent infatuation. Will was a married man who had tried to take advantage of a lonely, naive girl. He never would have left his wife and family for me." She started walking toward the door again.

246 | ALL MY SECRETS

"It makes sense now, why you hold the notion of marrying for love in such low regard," Junietta said. "Your first love was fleeting and heart-breaking. But wouldn't you like Addy to know what it feels like to fall in love? Doesn't she deserve the chance to find out?"

Sylvia wanted to leave. She didn't want to think about these things or be reminded of Will Eastman. And A.B. "Love can grow between two people, given a chance," she said. "And you have to admit that marriage works best if a man and woman come from the same background."

"I'll admit no such thing," Junietta replied. "But I have another question. Why did you stop painting?"

Sylvia paused for a moment, unwilling to admit, even to herself, how good and natural it had felt when she'd designed and sketched the two evening gowns. She'd been happy for those few hours, able to forget her grief and the unending worries about money. Yet the truth was painful to admit. "Because I knew I would never be a real artist. At best, I was merely a talented amateur."

She tried again to leave, but Junietta kept poking at her pain. "Losing your childhood home that way must have been devastating."

Sylvia turned to face her, anger simmering as she relived it. "My father didn't fight for his family. Both of my parents gave in and didn't even try to recover their losses. They withdrew from life in shame and let the gossip win. That's why I'm determined to fight for Adelaide and for her future."

"What about your brothers? If they had lived, do you think they would have wanted to return to your former way of life in the city? It sounded as though they'd loved living at Ferncliff."

"It doesn't matter because none of us had a choice."

"Then why not give Addy a choice? Why make her rush into a marriage she may regret?"

"I want her to have choices, but we're running out of time. It's taking all my efforts to balance the books and keep this household running. If we show any signs of loss, the suitors will scatter. We'll lose this house, which is a huge part of her inheritance."

"And after she chooses a suitor—what's next for you, Sylvia? Once all three of your daughters are married and this house is saved, will you return to a life of balls and parties and gossip? Don't you ever wish for something more?"

She did. But Sylvia couldn't face the emptiness that loomed in her future without A.B. For now, she had to keep busy so she wouldn't think about his abandoned room beside her own. Or face the emptiness inside it. "It's Adelaide's future that concerns me at the moment, not my own," she replied and hurried away before Junietta could say anything else.

### ⚞ *Adelaide* ⚟

On the day of Mrs. Rhodes's ball, Adelaide awoke with both excited anticipation and uneasy misgivings. She had attended other balls and had enjoyed the splendor and excitement, but back then she hadn't been in desperate need of a suitor. The May morning was sunny and mild, the weather perfectly balanced between the cold bite of winter and the humid heat of summer. A perfect day for a ball. Addy was no longer in mourning and could wear the new pale blue chiffon gown that had hung in her wardrobe all these months, along with Mother's sapphire and diamond earrings and necklace. She would meet potential suitors tonight, hopefully ones who were younger and more promising than arrogant Byron Albright, middle-aged George Weaver, opinionated Marcus Webster, and the insufferable Charles Durand. After hearing the story of her mother's tragic losses, she was determined to marry well and secure a home for her. Ten months had passed since Father had died, yet their lives were still shaken by uncertainty.

Mother fussed over her as she waited in the foyer for the carriage to fetch her, fluffing Addy's gown and straightening the jewels that adorned her neck. "You look so beautiful, Adelaide. You'll be the loveliest girl there."

The mirror in her bedroom had told her the same, yet Addy still felt like an item for sale in the marketplace, going to the highest bidder, as her anxiety lingered. She struggled to pull on her gloves over sweating palms.

"You seem nervous," Mother said.

"I am, a little."

"There's no need at all to be nervous. I want you to forget about everything else tonight and enjoy yourself."

"But I want to help you. I know how much this home means to you, and—"

"Your happiness is important too. You deserve to have a good time with your friends after all these months in mourning. Mrs. Rhodes has invited a dozen young men for you to dance and flirt with and get to know. Any one of them would make a fine suitor, so you can afford to be discerning. See which gentlemen are drawn to you and which ones you find attractive. You do have a choice, Adelaide." Mother was beginning to sound like Mimi Junie. Addy remembered her grandmother saying that Mother had dazzled New York society at her debut.

"Was that the way it was for you after you came to live with Aunt Bess? Mimi said you could have had your pick of suitors."

"Yes, it was. These should be the happiest years of your life, when you get to be a princess at the ball, dancing with a roomful of handsome princes."

"But I need to choose quickly, don't I? I don't want us to lose our home and wealth the way your family did."

Mother's smile seemed forced as she pressed Addy's hand between her own. "Mr. Forsythe has assured me that our finances will be fine for a few more months. Our items sold well at auction. Now, promise me you'll forget about our worries and enjoy yourself tonight. Promise?" She tipped Addy's chin up and met her gaze.

"I promise."

"Good. Now, let me see your beautiful smile."

Addy managed one, already feeling more lighthearted. The carriage arrived out front at that moment and whisked her off to the ball like Cinderella.

Mrs. Rhodes had spared no expense in decorating her mansion with flowers and greenery. She looked like a queen in her glittering silver gown and diamond tiara as she greeted her guests. "Here's our favorite young lady," she beamed when Addy arrived. "You remember my son Alfred, don't you?"

Addy had nearly forgotten that Mrs. Rhodes had an older son, and wouldn't have recognized the tall young man on her own. He looked to be in his midtwenties, and although his nose was a bit too large to make him classically handsome, he was still nice-looking and well built, with light brown hair and blue eyes. "Alfred will escort you to the ballroom, my dear, while my husband and I finish greeting our guests. Alfred, be a love and make sure Adelaide has a glass of punch, then introduce her to all your friends."

"With pleasure." He offered Addy his arm, and they strolled through the mansion toward the sound of a string orchestra playing a waltz. "You've grown up since I last saw you, Adelaide Stanhope. I remembered you as Felicity's friend and schoolmate, and now I see you've become a lovely young woman."

"Thank you. It has been several years. You were leaving for college, I believe, the last time we met."

They reached the ballroom, a smaller version of the one in Addy's mansion, yet still beautifully luxurious. Crystal chandeliers sparkled with prisms of light. The high, beamed ceiling, painted a kaleidoscope of sumptuous colors, was trimmed with gold leaf. Elegant brocade draperies adorned the palatial windows. The magnificent room already crackled with energy and laughter as ladies in splendid ball gowns and gentlemen in white shirts and black evening suits mingled and flirted against a background of lush music. Addy felt alive and excited for the first time in a long time as she made her entrance down a sweeping set of stairs on Alfred's arm. This was what Mother remembered from her childhood, before her family had been bankrupted by an unscrupulous creditor. No wonder she wanted this life for Addy, as well as for herself. Truth be told, in that moment, Addy wanted to hang on to all of this too.

Alfred released Adelaide's arm when his sister Felicity, who was seventeen, rushed over to greet her. "I'll fetch you some punch, while you ladies catch up," Alfred said. "But you must promise to waltz with me later."

"I would love to."

"Isn't this wonderful?" Felicity gushed. "Did you ever see so many handsome men? I plan to dance with all of Alfred's friends!"

Addy shared Felicity's excitement. The ball seemed like a magical, swirling dream, and she was thankful Mother had told her to forget her family's precarious finances and enjoy the evening. She felt lighthearted and beautiful as she waltzed with one gentleman after another, all of them charming and eager to get to know her. She danced with Alfred several times and found herself drawn to him more than any of the others, her heart skipping just a bit faster as she waltzed in his arms and looked up into his blue eyes. Several of Addy's longtime friends had been invited, and when the orchestra took a short break, she went with them and Felicity and her older sister, Ionia, to the bedroom the ladies were using to freshen up. Addy laughed with them, her cares forgotten as they admired each other's clothing and jewels, then gossiped and giggled about the gentlemen they'd met.

"Alfred likes you, Addy, I can tell," Felicity told her. "Just think—if you married him, we would be sisters!"

Addy smiled. "It's a bit early for wedding plans. But I like him too."

"Don't let him monopolize all your time," Addy's friend Frances advised. "There are plenty of other fine gentlemen to flirt with. Give him some competition. Make him chase after you."

"They all seem so . . . confident," Addy said. "Perhaps even a bit arrogant."

"They have to be arrogant to make it in the business world," Frances replied.

"Mother says that the more self-assured a gentleman is, the better businessman he'll make," Ionia added.

"And the richer their wives will be?" Frances asked.

"Yes! After all, we're used to this life, right?" Felicity said. "I can't imagine any other."

"By the way," Ionia said, "I was introduced to Cicely Stanhope at a party recently. Are you two related?"

Addy's stomach did a small turn. "Cicely is my second cousin—or something like that. Our grandfathers were brothers."

"I figured she was related, since she said her family was going to stay in your Newport home this summer." Addy fought a surge of anger at how her grandfather's will had robbed her of that lovely summer mansion.

"We missed you after you left last summer," Clara said. "The parties were outrageously fun! Are you coming again this year?"

"It's still too soon after Father's passing for us to go," she replied. Addy wondered if she would ever be able to go to Newport again.

"I'm sure you'll run into Cicely everywhere, now that you're attending events again," Frances said. "She's being pushed forward to become part of our social set by some very influential people." As Addy had feared, she and Cicely would be competing for the attention of the same gentlemen. Cicely's father may have inherited the family business, but his mansion couldn't compare with Adelaide's. Her beautiful home lifted her a step above her cousin, giving her another reason to fight to hang on to it as Mother was so desperate to do.

Ionia motioned for Addy to lean closer. "I think you should know that Cicely is spreading gossip about you."

Addy's stomach turned again. "What's she saying?"

"That you and your mother are bankrupt, and that you'll have to sell your mansion."

"Don't worry," Felicity said. "No one believes her." But Addy's friends eyed her curiously, as if waiting for her to confirm or deny the gossip. She forced a smile.

"Well, I assure you that we do not have to sell our home. Listen, it sounds like the orchestra has returned. Let's go dance with all those handsome men."

Alfred hurried over to ask Addy to dance as soon as she reentered the ballroom with the other girls. She wondered if Mr. and Mrs. Rhodes knew the truth about her financial situation, and if they would encourage their son to court her if they did. She did her best to engage Alfred in bright conversation as they waltzed, but a shadow had been cast over the evening. Addy had been reminded of Cousin Cicely and the need to secure her family's future quickly.

Before the ball ended with a splendid buffet dinner in the early hours of the morning, Adelaide had danced with every young man in attendance, and with Alfred several times. He was charming and attentive and an excellent dance partner. Mimi Junie would have approved of the way he'd asked Addy about her interests and opinions as they'd browsed the buffet together. She wished she could get to know him without feeling like she was bait in a trap being set for him.

Addy thought about Alfred and all the other gentlemen she'd danced and flirted with as she lay in bed in the early morning hours. Every one of them had seemed more interested in having a good time than in searching for a suitable wife. She also thought about the worrying news of Cousin Cicely's gossip. Like it or not, Addy was running out of time and would need to find a serious suitor soon. The ball had been a timely reminder of how much she enjoyed her life of wealth and privilege, and how much she stood to lose if she failed. She rolled over in bed, unable to get comfortable. The sun would rise soon. Light was already sneaking around her bedroom curtains. Mother's tragic story had intrigued her, yet it left so many unanswered questions. How had she adjusted to life in the city after spending so many years at Ferncliff? How had she met Father and decided that he was the man she would marry? Had they fallen in love?

Addy tossed and turned until the bedsheets were a snarled heap. She needed to decide how to describe the evening to Mother and Mimi Junie in the morning. How could the two women she dearly loved be so different in their opinions and approaches to life? They couldn't both be right, could they? Maybe they were both wrong. Or was it a combination of the two? No matter what, Addy knew it was going to be impossible to please them both.

# 23

MAY 1899

### ~ Sylvia ~

Sylvia stood in the echoing foyer with her daughter and mother-in-law, waiting for the Stanhope Foundation's guests to arrive for Junietta's dinner party. Junietta was beautifully but simply dressed, beaming with an inward glow that outshone any absent jewelry. "Now, don't forget, I'm counting on you two ladies to use your charm to sweet-talk Mr. Barrow and Mr. Alberts into supporting the foundation," she said. "And if you can help me convince Mr. Forsythe to take my place as the chairman, that would be an added bonus."

The dinner would be a smaller and much simpler affair than the two dinners Sylvia had given, but was still elegantly and tastefully arranged. Sylvia had the opportunity to witness Junietta's social artistry, and to see Junietta herself in a different light. She was skilled at making each individual feel welcomed and valued, whether they were wealthy prospective board members like Mr. Alberts and Mr. Barrow, or as modest and unpretentious as Mr. Forsythe. And she did it all without drawing any attention to herself the way most social matrons did at their events. Sylvia also noticed that Junietta was walking slowly as if it pained her to move. She leaned heavily on her cane—the cane Neal Galloway had carved—as if holding Neal's hand.

The widower, Timothy Barrow, turned out to be younger than Sylvia expected, in his early fifties, she guessed. He looked more like a university professor or philosopher than a business tycoon, with his tall lean frame, graying blond hair, and neat goatee. "We're very glad you could join us tonight, Mr. Barrow," Sylvia said as she greeted him.

"I am too. I've been looking forward to this event ever since I received the invitation."

"Do you know much about the Stanhope Foundation?"

"My wife served on the board of directors. She spoke so highly of your mother-in-law's work with the foundation, that I decided to learn more about it to honor her memory."

"I'm sure my mother-in-law will be happy to answer any questions. In fact, she's hoping you'll consider taking your wife's seat on the board."

"Yes, Mrs. Stanhope did mention that in her note." Sylvia could tell by his gentle smile and the warmth in his voice that she would enjoy giving him her full attention tonight. "I've had time to rethink my priorities since losing my wife," he continued. "I hope to leave a better legacy to my children than just money."

"May I ask, how long has Mrs. Barrow been gone?"

"Nearly three years. I can speak of her without pain now." That gentle smile again. "I used my work as a distraction at first, cutting myself off from the rest of life. But I feel it's time to attend parties and dinners again, mainly because I know she would want me to."

"Yes." And A.B. would want the same for her. But it was still much too soon.

"I was so sorry to hear of your husband's death, Mrs. Stanhope. And it was so tragic for your mother-in-law, as well, to lose her son."

"Thank you, Mr. Barrow. I know you understand what the loss of a spouse is like."

"Indeed. Grief is such a fickle enemy, isn't it? Just when life seems to be going well, it sneaks up from behind when one least expects it. It's a powerful force and can knock the unsuspecting off their feet." Sylvia swallowed a knot of sorrow, keenly aware of what he described. "I hope you'll be ready to enjoy life again too, one day, Mrs. Stanhope. I know that it's still much too soon for you, but perhaps when the time comes, we might enjoy it together, as friends and companions in grief."

His words took her by surprise. She had thought she would spend the rest of her life alone, excluded from social events without A.B. by her side. Between running this house and finding a suitor for Adelaide, she'd had little time to consider what would come next in her own life. His kind offer gave her hope. She returned his smile. "Thank you. I would like that very much."

Suddenly, Sylvia saw Junietta's cunning in planning this evening and nearly laughed out loud. She was playing matchmaker too! What better way to take pressure off Adelaide to find a husband than to introduce Sylvia to a wealthy widower? She glanced over at her mother-in-law. *You sly old fox!* Junietta met her gaze and winked at her.

She turned her attention back to Mr. Barrow, who was examining the foyer with undisguised admiration. "You have such a magnificent home. I confess, I always feel tempted to covet when I happen to drive past it."

"Would you care to take a quick tour? We have time before dinner."

"I would love to. Thank you."

She took his arm as she led him into the drawing room.

### ⤙ *Adelaide* ⤚

Addy was waiting to greet Mr. Forsythe when he arrived, aware of how much her grandmother was counting on her to help him feel at ease. She was glad she had gotten to know him a little better on Mimi's excursions. It would make her job much easier. "Welcome, Mr. Forsythe. It's so nice to see you again."

"Thank you, Miss Stanhope. It's good to see a familiar face." Mr. Forsythe greeted Mimi Junie, as well, who welcomed him like an old friend. But Addy could tell he was nervous, tugging on his coat sleeves as he looked around at the millionaires laughing and chatting in the foyer, the ladies' jewels sparkling in the chandelier's light. He still wore the borrowed jacket that was a little too small, and she couldn't help comparing him to the wealthy young gentlemen at Mrs. Rhodes's ball in their impeccably tailored evening suits. Yet their self-assurance had skated close to arrogance, making them seem cold compared to Mr. Forsythe with his utter lack of pretension. He reminded her of a boy playing dress-up, yet not in an awkward or rude way. She couldn't put her finger on it until she remembered Mother's mischievous brothers, Harry and Freddy. She was unable to imagine Alfred Rhodes and his friends ever sliding down the banister, but she could easily picture Mr. Forsythe being playful, as he'd been when he'd played ball with the children at the orphans' home.

Addy noticed him admiring the foyer's sweeping staircase and asked, "Did you have a second floor and a banister at the parsonage, by any chance?"

His smile was quick and genuine. "What an interesting question. Actually, we do have one."

"Did you and your brothers ever slide down it?"

"All the time!" he said, laughing. "Whenever we could get away with it. Why do you ask?"

"I grew up in this mansion with its three stories of stairs and banisters, but I confess that I never had the courage to try it."

Mr. Forsythe glanced around. Mimi had invited everyone to follow her into the conservatory for drinks and hors d'oeuvres, and they were trailing off behind her. "Shall we do it now?" He grinned.

Addy laughed. "No, of course not. I don't know what made me ask. But thank you for the offer."

"Well, let me know if you change your mind. It looks like it would be quite a ride!" His eyes sparkled with laughter, and she was glad she had put him at ease.

"Shall we join the others?" Addy asked. She took his arm as they made their way to the conservatory. Addy knew nearly all the board members and their wives, having socialized with them and their children and grandchildren over the years, so she took Mr. Forsythe on a circuit of the glass-enclosed room, introducing him to everyone. A few minutes later, Mother and Mr. Barrow returned from what Addy assumed was a tour of the first floor, and Mother quickly won the attention and admiration of the other guests. At age forty-six, she was still as slender and beautiful as a young woman, with skin that glowed like fine porcelain, and fair hair that shone like gold. Addy noticed several board members' wives jealously steering their husbands away from her. Mr. Alberts, who Mimi Junie had called a curmudgeon and confirmed bachelor, seemed taken by Mother's allure as well. And Mr. Barrow, the widower Mother was meant to charm, couldn't seem to take his eyes off her.

When the dinner gong sounded, everyone made their way to the dining room. Mr. Forsythe held Addy's chair for her before taking his own beside her. She noticed him watching the others and, mirroring their manners, unfurling his napkin on his lap when he saw them doing it, watching to see which spoon everyone chose for the soup course from among the ten utensils surrounding his place setting. "Generally speaking," Addy whispered, "it's safe to start with the fork or spoon that's on the outside and work your way in."

"Thanks," he whispered back. "This is still very new to me, but I suppose I'll need to learn if I decide to be the next chairman of the Stanhope Foundation."

"So, you haven't given my grandmother your answer yet?"

"I'm still trying to decide whether or not to leave the law firm. It's a very big decision. Both options seem good."

"I would be happy to talk with you about your dilemma, if you think it would help."

"Thank you, maybe it would." He sat back for a moment, tugging on his too-short coat sleeves again to try to cover his shirt cuffs. "You see, I'm drawn to the foundation because of my family's past. I grew up in a parsonage, and although we weren't poor by any means, we were never wealthy either. Probably because my parents had a habit of giving everything away to the less fortunate," he said, chuckling.

"They sound just like my grandmother."

The servants removed their soup bowls and served oysters next. "Oyster fork," she whispered as she held up her own. He smiled in thanks and dug into the shells.

"My grandmother was a Scottish immigrant," he continued, "who became a widow when she was still very young. She raised my mother in a very special boardinghouse created for widows with small children to care for. It was run as a cooperative and was very much ahead of its time, supported by wealthy donors like the ones who support your foundation."

Addy grew still. The description of his grandmother's boardinghouse sounded very familiar. "What's your grandmother's name?" she asked.

"Meara Galloway."

Addy nearly choked on her oyster. Meara Galloway was Neal Galloway's sister-in-law. It couldn't be a coincidence, could it? She wanted to ask if his mother's name was Regan, and if his grandfather had gone off to the California gold fields and perished in a shipwreck, but she knew she would give away too much. Mimi Junie had chosen to keep Mr. Forsythe's identity a secret for a reason.

"Why do you ask, Miss Stanhope? Is this another of your interesting questions, like whether or not I slide down banisters?"

"Not at all. I thought I might have met her through one of my grandmother's charities." She looked at Mimi Junie at the head of the table, coaxing laughter from Mr. Alberts, and felt peeved with her for not telling her the truth about who Mr. Forsythe was. But she would have to wait to confront her until after their guests left. "Please continue your story, Mr. Forsythe. You were telling me about your family."

"My mother trained to be a nurse after the Civil War and met my father, a former army chaplain, when he visited veterans in the same hospital. My brothers and I grew up better off than my mother or grandmother, but we still led a modest life. Nothing at all like the extravagant life that your family or some of my law firm's other clients—" He halted, a look of horror on his face as if he feared he might have offended Addy. "I'm sorry. I didn't mean to sound disparaging. My mother and grandmother couldn't have survived without wealthy benefactors like your family. In fact, I find wealthy Christians to be very generous toward the less fortunate."

"I took no offense at all, Mr. Forsythe." The waiter removed their oyster plates and served the next course, trout almondine. "So, from everything you've told me, it seems that working for the foundation would be the logical choice for you."

"Yes. Except I also feel I have a debt to repay." He took a sip of water, then turned to her, speaking earnestly. "My education was paid for by a wealthy sponsor who later recommended me to my prestigious law firm. I have the opportunity to become a full partner one day, with an income that would allow me to support the same charities that helped my mother and grandmother."

"Do you know who your sponsor was?" she asked. She glanced at her grandmother again, guessing it was her.

"No. He wanted to remain anonymous. I always speculated that he must be someone who knew my father. Perhaps someone he'd helped during the war. This benefactor didn't want to be known so I wouldn't feel indebted. And yet I suppose I do feel indebted."

"I can see why that would be a difficult decision. Yet, either way you decide, it seems to me you will be able to repay a debt of gratitude, won't you?"

"Yes, I suppose that's true. But it will also be a disappointment to the other party. So what's your advice, Miss Stanhope?"

"Well, I have a feeling you will be successful no matter which path you chose."

"Thank you. You're kind to say that."

"I know my grandmother will be thrilled if you accept the position with the foundation. But my advice is for you to decide based on where your true interests and passions lead you, not because you feel pressured by an obligation to your family or—" She stopped, struck by the irony of her words.

"Miss Stanhope?"

"I'm sorry. It's just that . . . I'm offering you the same advice that my grandmother has been giving me for my own dilemma."

"Would it help to talk about it? You've been kind enough to listen to me go on and on."

"I would love to hear your advice, Mr. Forsythe, because I believe you are an honest and trustworthy man. But I can't share my own dilemma just yet." If she did, she would be forced to admit that she had courted an older man like Mr. Weaver because he was wealthy, and had flirted with a dozen young men at the ball for the same reason. It was also why rude yet wealthy Mr. Durand had been invited to dinner. Mr. Forsythe knew about their financial straits, but it was embarrassing to admit the part she was playing in trying to solve them. Addy quickly dug into her repertoire of suitable dinner topics and smoothly managed to change the subject. If Mr. Forsythe noticed, he was too polite to comment.

After the evening had ended and she had bid Mr. Forsythe goodbye, Addy had to admit that she had enjoyed her evening with him. He was easy to talk to and had a witty sense of humor that she found refreshing. Her conversations with most other young men, including Alfred Rhodes, seemed stiff and formal in comparison. But perhaps that was because Mr. Forsythe wasn't a marriage prospect to be wooed into courting her.

Mimi Junie gave a great sigh as the door closed behind her last guest. "Well! Thank you very much, my dears," she said to Mother and Addy. "The evening appeared to be a huge success, thanks to the two of you. And now, I'm off to bed."

"Mimi, wait!" Addy had been dying all evening to ask her about Mr. Forsythe's mother and grandmother. "There's something I need to ask you. Mr. Forsythe told me—"

"Can it wait until morning, Addy dear? I'm dreadfully tired." Mimi limped toward the stairs, leaning on her cane and looking up at them as if facing a steep mountain.

"But I want to know—"

"I'm unaccustomed to so much excitement, and I'm afraid I had a little too much wine in an effort to keep Mr. Alberts happy. Good night, all."

Mimi was still asleep when Addy and Mother left for church the following morning, which was very unusual for her. But she was waiting for them in the small dining room afterward to eat the cold buffet lunch the servants had left for them. She looked pale and tired, as if the few extra hours of sleep hadn't done any good, but she greeted them with a smile. "I hope you don't mind, Sylvia, but I told the cook not to prepare lunch for the three of us today. Nor for the servants to wait on us. They worked so hard last night on my special dinner, and Sunday is supposed to be their half day off."

"This is fine," Mother said.

"I want to thank you again for being such gracious hostesses last evening. I'm happy to say that I made headway with curmudgeonly Mr. Alberts, and he has agreed to join the board. How did you get along with Timothy Barrow, Sylvia? It appeared you were having an enjoyable evening with him."

"It turns out we've met before a few times when A.B. was still alive. I knew his wife from several of my clubs. He seems very eager to join the foundation's board of directors."

"Wonderful! That's great news. And thank you, Adelaide, for entertaining Mr. Forsythe and helping him feel comfortable. You seemed to be getting along well too."

"Mm. We had a very interesting and enlightening conversation. When he started telling me about himself, his stories sounded very familiar, Mimi Junie."

"Oh, really?" She seemed nonchalant as she cut into her cold beef.

"Yes. It seems his mother grew up in a boardinghouse for widows with her Scottish-immigrant mother—whose name happens to be Meara Galloway."

Mimi wore a playful smile. "I see."

"I could have asked him if his mother's name was Regan and if his grandfather had died in a shipwreck on the way to the California gold fields—but I didn't."

"Aha! I see you've been paying attention to my tales, and now you're putting all the pieces together. Good for you, dear."

"Why didn't you tell us who Mr. Forsythe was? And that his mother is Neal Galloway's niece, the little baby he once hid in the carriage house?"

"Because I didn't want him to know that I've been supporting his education all these years. I didn't want him to feel obligated to me or to our family in any way. Meara, Regan, and I decided a long time ago that it was the best course to take, back when Howard and his brothers were still boys."

"You could have told me."

"Did he tell you about his wonderful father? Or his two brothers? One of them attends Princeton Seminary and is going into the ministry like their father. His other brother is a civil engineer. I've been privileged to help all three boys in various ways, and it has been a joy to see them grow up to be such fine young men."

"So, you knew who he was when he was assigned to help with Father's will?"

"I specifically requested him."

"But you acted as if you'd never met him and—"

"Please don't tell him what you know, Addy. I would like Howard to feel free to decide for himself whether to continue with the law practice or to join my work with the foundation."

"You may have to tell him, Mimi, because right now he's torn between the two choices. He wants to work for the foundation, but he feels obligated to continue at the law firm out of loyalty to his mysterious sponsor. You need to tell him that it's you. And that you wouldn't be disappointed with either choice he made."

"Did you tell him it was me?"

"No. He asked for my advice, and I told him he should follow his heart and not feel pressured."

"That's wonderful advice. I hope you'll follow it yourself, when the time comes, and that you'll choose love over obligation."

Addy recalled how often Mr. Forsythe had been appearing in their lives lately, and a sudden thought occurred to her. "Were you playing matchmaker when you asked me to entertain Mr. Forsythe last night?"

"Me?" she asked with an innocent smile. "Your mother would never approve, would you, Sylvia? Howard has no money at all."

"But you were playing matchmaker with *me*, weren't you?" Mother said.

Mimi gave another seemingly innocent smile. "Mr. Barrow is a very fine gentleman who just happens to be a widower. He's very wealthy too. You know, Addy isn't the only one who could rescue your mansion by marrying well."

Mother seemed speechless. She didn't dare to criticize Mimi Junie's plan or techniques because they were the very same ones she'd been using. Adelaide was tempted to laugh, but didn't think Mother would find any humor in the situation.

"Let's not forget," Mimi continued, "that the important thing was to get Mr. Barrow on board with the foundation. And see? It turned out he was also captivated by you, Sylvia—as I knew he would be. You've always had that effect on men."

"You are a very devious woman, Junietta."

"I prefer the word *clever*," she said with a smile. She turned to Addy and said, "From the moment your mother made her New York debut, she could have had her pick of suitors. Every eligible young man in the city was in love with her—and more than a few married ones, as well."

"How did you choose Father?" Addy asked. She found herself hoping it was because they'd been in love.

"Yes, Sylvia. I would like to know why you chose him too," Mimi said. "After all, A.B. was my son."

Mother hesitated, running her finger around the rim of her teacup. "I'll tell you the story, but you aren't going to be happy with my reasons . . ."

# 24

### ~ Sylvia ~

I walked down the grand staircase in my summer ball gown as if entering
a dream. For a moment, it was as if my parents were alive again and welcoming guests to one of their parties at our mansion. The bright laughter, the tinkling glasses, the soft music—everything was as I remembered
it from my childhood before my father's bankruptcy. But this evening
was even more magical because now I was entering the festivities myself.

It was August, and my aunt Bess and I were guests at her sister-in-
law's summer home in Newport. At the close of every summer season,
Mr. and Mrs. West threw a sumptuous celebration that filled their mansion and spilled out onto their veranda and back lawn facing the sea. I
had become so socially backward after being raised in near isolation at
Ferncliff that it had taken me nearly a year to get ready for my debut.
Aunt Bess had enrolled me in a woman's finishing school for six months
to learn proper manners and etiquette and posture, and how to engage in

polite conversation. There were dance lessons, dress fittings, trips to the milliner for hats, and to the dry goods store for gloves and silk stockings. I had gone without shoes for so long that I had to get used to wearing them again, then learn how to walk gracefully. Aunt Bess introduced me to her social clubs and took me calling with her. My uncle, who'd been ten years older than Bess, had passed away by then. They'd been childless, so she launched into her task of presenting me to society with great fervor. I had attended a few smaller parties and dinners during the past few months and had done well at them. But this grand summer lawn party would be my biggest test yet. Every prominent family that summered in Newport would be there with their eligible sons. I was nineteen years old and very aware that a suitable marriage was the next step for me.

"You'll do wonderfully well," Aunt Bess had assured me as she'd helped me dress. "You're ready, darling girl, and I'm proud to present you on your father's behalf."

"How much should I tell people about myself? Should I explain where I've been all these years?"

"You don't owe anyone an explanation. Your father's financial collapse was fifteen years ago, and although some might remember it, most people won't. If they do, just tell them that he retired to his country house and preferred living there. And now that he has sadly passed away, you're living with me."

It would have been enough to simply enjoy the beauty of this magnificent fete, let alone participate in it. Fairy lanterns twinkled on the lush green lawn. Banks of flowers in shades of lavender, periwinkle, and white decorated the ballroom and spilled onto the adjoining veranda. Buffet tables with white damask cloths were laden with more flowers, fine wine, champagne, and every type of seafood imaginable. More than two hundred guests in summer finery laughed and mingled and waltzed to the music of a string orchestra. And always in the background, the sea added a soothing, shushing sound. I didn't ever want the evening to end.

I danced and flirted and danced some more, aware of the sensation I was causing as young gentlemen flocked to meet me. I would barely finish one glass of punch when someone would offer me another. Gentlemen cut in on each other for a chance to dance with me. I had just returned to the veranda after freshening up inside the mansion when an eager-looking gentleman with curly brown hair and dark eyes strode up to me and said, "I wonder if I may have this next dance with you, Miss Woodruff."

"You know my name? Have we been introduced?" I asked.

"Not formally. I know who you are because your beauty has made you the talk of New York and Newport. Allow me to introduce myself. I'm Arthur Stanhope."

I stared at him, unable to speak. *Arthur Stanhope.*

"My friends and family call me A.B."

*Arthur Stanhope.* The unscrupulous man who had ruined my father? The merciless man who had stolen Imperial Flour and Grain from us and caused my family's exile and misery?

"Miss Woodruff?"

I heard him speaking but couldn't reply. The Arthur Stanhope standing in front of me was too young to be the man my father had cursed nearly every day of his life, but he was surely related to him. I cleared my throat, but my voice came out in a near whisper. "Is—is your father also called Arthur Stanhope?"

"Yes, and my grandfather too."

The air suddenly seemed very warm. I couldn't catch my breath. I wanted to strike out at this man for all the grief and sorrow his family had caused mine, yet my strength had drained as if poured from a pitcher. I feared I might fall over. His smile turned to a look of concern. "Miss Woodruff? Are you all right? You look quite pale."

The veranda whirled. We had lost our beautiful home and had been forced to move to Ferncliff Manor because of Arthur Stanhope. Freddy and Harry had drowned in the Hudson River because of him. Mother would be alive and presiding over my debut instead of Aunt Bess if not for him. And Father, my handsome, gregarious father, wouldn't have drunk himself to an early grave from anger and grief and loss.

Young Mr. Stanhope wrapped his arm around my waist and led me toward a wrought-iron bench. I didn't want him touching me, but I surely would have fallen over without his support. He made me sit down and signaled a waiter to bring me a glass of water. "Are you all right, Miss Woodruff?" he asked again. "Forgive me for being forward, but I thought you might faint."

"I-I'm fine. I'll just sit for a moment." I wanted him to go away. No, truthfully, I wanted to tie rocks to his ankles and throw him into the sea to drown. I bristled when he sat down on the bench beside me, but he didn't seem to notice.

"It is a lot, isn't it?" he said. "The people, the noise, the excitement. You must be dizzy from all the waltzing you've done. I've been waiting, not very patiently, for my turn to dance with you, but perhaps it's better if we sit out this dance instead."

*Go away!* I wanted to say. *Go away before I scratch your eyes out!* But he kept on talking. "I don't know if you're aware, but we're neighbors. Our 'cottage,' as everyone calls these palatial homes, is right next door, on that side of you." He pointed to the east. His mansion was hard to miss, built like a Greek temple with rows of soaring white pillars. It was even larger than the Wests' house, which I had thought very grand. That knowledge made me hate him even more. His family had built that mansion with money they'd stolen from my family. My parents should be living in his luxurious summer home by the sea. My brothers should be attending this party tonight, dancing with pretty girls and bringing laughter wherever they went.

"Maybe you've met my mother, Junietta Stanhope?" he continued. "She's friends with your hostess, Mrs. West. But then, my mother makes friends with everyone she meets. My father says the only reason she comes to Newport is so she can corner all the wealthy wives at their lawn parties and get them to support her charitable foundation. If you meet her and she asks if you've heard of it, just nod and change the subject, or she'll talk your arm off."

His words were barely sinking in. He seemed so friendly and at ease, chatting with me as if we were old friends, unaware that I longed to spit in his face. I didn't think I could even speak his name without adding the flood of curse words my father always attached to it.

"Mind you, I may tease Mother," he went on, "but the Stanhope Foundation is very well respected. It's a charitable trust she created that supports orphans and immigrants and a host of other good causes. I used to go around to all those places with her when I was a boy, so I've seen the work she does. But once Grandfather decided I was old enough to learn the family business, I didn't get to spend much time with her anymore. My father complains that she gives his money away as fast as he earns it."

I was starting to recover from my shock. His grandfather or possibly his father must have been the Arthur Stanhope who'd ruined my family, because the garrulous man talking to me appeared to be not much older than I was. Even so, he had surely enjoyed a fine life at our expense. I managed to find my voice and ask, "Is your grandfather here at the party?" He gave me a funny look.

"No, he died about five years ago, not long after completing our house next door. Are you feeling better, Miss Woodruff?"

"A little." I took another sip of water as I calculated. His grandfather had lived for another ten years after bankrupting my father in 1857. He must have been the hated villain of our tragedy. I wanted to stand up on the bench and shout for everyone's attention, then expose Arthur Stanhope's descendant in front of all his wealthy friends, explaining just how unscrupulous his family was. How unmerciful they'd been in not granting my father more time to repay his debt. I would ruin this man's reputation the same way he had ruined ours. But of course, I would do no such thing.

"Say, I've been doing all the talking, haven't I? Why don't you tell me a little about yourself, Miss Woodruff? I understand you're staying with your aunt, but where do you call home?"

I didn't have a home, thanks to his family. The truth brought bitter tears to my eyes, which I quickly blinked away. The last thing I would allow him to do was to make me cry. Yet even as I silently mourned my homelessness, the seed of an idea began to grow. If the mansion next door rightfully belonged to me and my family, why not claim it? I could have it for my own, along with all the Stanhope wealth, if I tricked this talkative Stanhope heir into falling in love with me. I could reclaim everything that Father had lost. It was all mine by rights. If I became a Stanhope, my sons would own Imperial Flour and Grain once again. My children could have everything my brothers and I deserved to have.

The thought of revenge revived my spirits. I turned to him, smiling, and said, "You've been so patient with me. I apologize for being a bother when all you asked of me was one dance. I felt a little dizzy for a moment, but I'm much better now. Thank you." I tilted my head and gave him my most adoring look. He melted like candle wax. For the very first time, I experienced my power over a man, and I wanted to shout in triumph. I could do this. I could make the unsuspecting Arthur Stanhope fall in love with me and pour all his wealth—my father's wealth—at my feet.

"I'm glad to hear it," he said. "Is there anything I can get you?"

"No, but let me repay your kindness with the dance you asked for." I offered him my hand and he quickly took it to help me to my feet. I allowed him to continue holding it as he led me to the dance floor and took me into his arms. He studied my face as we whirled around, as if he couldn't take his eyes off me. I could feel his attraction to me like the pull of a powerful magnet.

"Tell me, Miss Woodruff. How have you been enjoying Newport?"

"I've had a wonderful visit. It's so beautiful here by the sea. I brought my watercolors along, and I've been trying to capture the changing colors of the sky and water. But of course, it's quite impossible."

"I'll bet your pictures are as beautiful as you are," he murmured. Then he suddenly halted in the middle of the dance floor as if surprised. "Did I just say that out loud? I've been thinking it all evening, but I'm usually not so forward. Please forgive me, Miss Woodruff, if I sounded like a cad."

I merely blushed and coyly looked away. I needed to play this game just right. I would act cool and uninterested, making him work hard to win my affections. He needed to feel like he'd won a great prize after

defeating all my other suitors. Yet if I acted too cool, he might lose interest in the chase.

The waltz ended. I thanked him for the dance and turned toward
the refreshment table, where two gentlemen I had danced with earlier
were watching me from a distance. Would he follow me or let me slip
away? "Miss Woodruff?" he said, trotting close behind. "How long are
you planning to stay in Newport?"

"Only for two more days."

"Have you had a chance to go sailing while you're here?"

"Sadly, no."

"Then you must come sailing with me on my family's yacht, the
*Merriweather*."

*A yacht.* My brothers had longed to sail but could afford only a crude
homemade raft.

"I know we've just met, and you don't know me well, Miss Woodruff,
but I would love to take you out on the sea. Perhaps tomorrow, since
your time is so short. Your aunt and the Wests are welcome to join us—
to keep everything proper."

"Thank you. I'll see what they have planned for tomorrow and let
you know." Then I purposely turned to the two gentlemen I'd met earlier.
"Isn't this the most wonderful evening? I've never seen so many stars!"
They crowded close to me, pointing to the night sky and gushing as if
they'd been the first to discover the moon. Mr. Stanhope was edged aside.

The only question that lingered in my mind as I thought about putting my plan into action was whether or not I could pretend to love my
enemy. Could I set aside my hatred and allow a Stanhope to kiss me, marry
me, take me to his bed? The idea repulsed me, but in the end, I realized
that I had nothing at all—no home, no money, no family aside from Aunt
Bess. I wasn't looking for love. I had fallen in love with Will Eastman and
knew I would never feel the same attraction to another man that I had
felt toward him. With Aunt Bess's help, I would probably marry a wealthy
man one day, and live well. But if I wanted to reclaim what rightfully
belonged to me, I would have to marry into the family I hated.

Tomorrow was August 31, the day I was supposed to meet Will at Ferncliff. I was hundreds of miles away from there, and his memory was beginning to fade like the last of the summer flowers. Part of me was curious to know if he really would return for me. Did he still want me to run away with him? I would never know. I had to think of my future, and it could never be with him.

The sun was about to dawn when the ball ended. Mr. Stanhope was among the last to leave. He had asked me to dance a few more times, taking his turn in between my other eager admirers. Before leaving, he came to me and pointed to the brightening sky above the sea. "Look at the colors in that sunrise, Miss Woodruff. It would make a stunning watercolor, wouldn't it?"

"I'm surprised you remembered that I painted."

"I remembered. You won't forget about my offer to take you sailing on the *Merriweather*, will you? It looks like it's going to be a beautiful day."

"I will see what our hosts have planned and let you know."

I couldn't let A.B. Stanhope win my affections that easily. I sent a servant to the Stanhopes' home that afternoon with a note, thanking him for the invitation to join him on his yacht, but politely declining. One of his servants quickly returned with Mr. Stanhope's note, saying how sorry he was. *"But I hope to see you again when we return to New York. May I call on you there?"* The servant had been told to await my reply. I smiled with satisfaction. "Kindly tell him yes, he may call on me."

A.B. pursued me in earnest that fall. At first, I accepted invitations from other gentlemen as well, but none was as persistent as he was. Conquering my enemy proved easier than I'd expected, because I found his company enjoyable. He loved to talk but never about superficial things like so many of my other suitors. A.B. had a keen mind, a curiosity about life, and a broad range of interests, everything from how a steam engine works to the construction of the suspension bridge being built across the East River to Brooklyn. He loved music and bought season tickets to hear the New York Philharmonic Orchestra perform. Sometimes, after viewing a play, I would become so fascinated as we talked about the characters and plot that I would almost forget he was my enemy, and that I was supposed to be seeking revenge. I accompanied him to private parties and balls and dinners where he was a lively and sought-after guest.

A.B. kissed me for the first time on our way home from a ball at the Vanderbilt mansion. I closed my eyes, pretending he was Will Eastman, but A.B.'s kiss was tender and gentle, with none of Will's possessiveness. I knew A.B. was in love with me, and I reveled in my victory. Society gossip already paired us as a couple. His next step was to invite me to dinner to meet his parents. I had taken a carriage ride past the Stanhope mansion on my own and seen the impressive exterior of the home I was plotting to possess, but I wanted to shout in triumph when I saw the magnificent interior for the first time. The foyer alone took my breath away. A.B. was waiting there with his parents, and he introduced me to them. His mother welcomed me warmly.

"I'm so glad to meet you, Miss Woodruff. A.B. has told us so much about you." I had feared meeting A.B.'s mother, imagining that her woman's intuition would unmask me as an imposter, but I saw no such reserve. It was easy to see who A.B. got his warm, unpretentious nature from. His father seemed aloof and distant. Together they had raised this very complex man whom I had tricked into falling in love with me.

"Let me show you our gallery before we eat," A.B. offered. He'd remembered how intrigued I'd been by the artwork when we'd visited the newly opened Metropolitan Museum of Art. I could have spent hours in the Stanhopes' private gallery, admiring the works of Italian and French masters, surrounded by beauty everywhere I looked. But it was the Thomas Cole painting, which hadn't been moved to the dining room yet, that halted me and brought tears to my eyes. The style, technique, and color palette were so much like Will's paintings. "I especially like that painting too," A.B. said when he saw me swipe a tear.

"It . . . it reminds me of my family's country home on the Hudson."

He reached to take my hand. "You must miss your family. And your home."

"Yes." The evening passed pleasantly, and I knew I had passed an important test. Soon, this magnificent mansion with its furnishings, sculptures, artwork, and servants would all belong to me.

Two days later, A.B. came to Aunt Bess's home in the evening and asked to speak with me. I was in my room, but I quickly checked my appearance in the mirror and hurried downstairs, thinking he might have come to propose. But the moment I saw the look of concern on his face, I feared that something terrible had happened. "A.B., what is it? What's wrong?"

"I need to talk with you about something." We went into the parlor, and he took my hand in both of his as we sat down on the settee. "You've won my heart, darling Sylvia, like no other woman ever has. I want to marry you and spend the rest of my life with you. I know most marriages in our social circle are arranged by our parents, but my mother has always encouraged me to ignore convention and follow my heart. My father feels otherwise, however, and so what I'm about to share with you has come directly from him."

My heart pounded with dread. Had he learned about my father's heavy drinking? My mother's suicide? I couldn't breathe, fearing I was about to lose everything I had worked for. "Tell me."

"You came out of nowhere, darling, and so my father hired someone to look into your background. I told him I didn't care about it, but he went behind my back. What he learned puts a dark shadow on my family's past. It seems you come from a very fine family, but my grandfather's ruthless business practices during the Panic of '57 forced your father into bankruptcy. Evidently, he was unable to recover financially." He paused, studying my face. His dark eyes were filled with such sadness that my guilt nearly overwhelmed me. A.B. was a good man. He wasn't responsible for his grandfather's actions. And I had deceived him. "I'm so sorry, Sylvia," he continued. "I wouldn't blame you if you wanted nothing to do with me after what my family did to yours. But I felt you deserved to know the truth before you decided whether or not you'll marry me."

I couldn't reply. I saw myself clearly, painfully in the light of A.B.'s honesty and sincerity. My obsession for revenge had changed me into a hateful, deceitful person. I didn't know what to do. Should I confess the truth about myself, tell him I had known the truth all along? How could I ever fix the mess I had created? A.B. mistook my silence for shock.

"You're stunned, I can tell. I'm heartsick about this too, Sylvia. I wish I knew how to make it right. I'll understand if you need some time to think about what I've told you. Maybe you'll want to discuss it with your aunt. You were too young to be aware of what my grandfather did to your family, but she might remember. I wouldn't blame you if you wanted nothing more to do with us." I met his gaze and my eyes filled with tears. I still couldn't speak. "I'll come back tomorrow," he said. He lifted my hand and kissed it, then let himself out. I ran upstairs to my room and sobbed into my pillow.

What had I done? I remembered a Bible verse I'd heard in church about gaining the world but losing your soul and knew I had done that very thing. Yes, I had avenged my family's losses, and I was about to win back their fortune. But I had done it at the cost of an innocent man's heart. And at the cost of my own soul, which overflowed with deceit.

I rose from the bed and paced the room, my tears still streaming. I shouldn't continue to deceive this man who loved me, but how could I extricate myself from my own trap? If I told A.B. I couldn't marry him because of what his grandfather had done, it would break his heart. If I confessed that I had known the truth all along and had intentionally trapped him, that would also break his heart. My confession might ease the terrible guilt I felt, but it would also reveal what a vile person I was. I wouldn't blame A.B. for telling everyone in New York the truth about me. No other suitor would want to marry me. I would be ruined, and this time it would be my own fault. I didn't see any way out of my dilemma.

Unless . . .

I had grown fond of A.B. in spite of myself. And I knew he was in love with me. What if I truly gave him my heart in payment for plotting to entrap him? Could I return his love and be the devoted wife he deserved? I would have to live with my guilt in silence, but what if I did everything in my power to make it up to him? I could put my past behind me and sincerely try to become a better person.

My family had never been religious, but I had been to church often enough to know that God offered forgiveness. He might even give me a brand-new start. Didn't the Bible also say to love our enemies?

A.B. returned the following evening. I saw the fear and longing in his eyes, and I immediately went into his arms to give him my answer. "The past doesn't matter, A.B. You may have my hand and my heart." He kissed me, then held me tightly. I knew it wouldn't be hard at all to fall in love with this dear man. We were married a few months later.

Of course, I knew that married life wouldn't be at all like the whirlwind of courtship. I never doubted that A.B. loved me, but he became much more involved with work the following year when another economic crisis struck the country. The depression of 1873 lasted several years, but A.B. repeatedly assured me that the Stanhopes were well situated to weather the storm. I gave birth to Cordelia in 1874 and then Ernestine in 1876, but if A.B. was disappointed that they weren't sons, he didn't reveal it.

At last, the economy started to improve in 1877, and we could begin hosting parties again. My mother-in-law had little interest in being the lady of the manor and was happy to turn over all the social responsibilities as the Stanhope family's hostess to me. But just when A.B. was able to spend fewer hours at work every day, his father, Arthur Stanhope II, collapsed with a stroke and was partially paralyzed. Junietta spent hours by his bedside. Her devotion to him was touching. She told me she had studied nursing during the war and insisted on caring for him herself. In spite of her best efforts, and that of the finest doctors, Art passed away.

The burden of responsibility at work fell entirely on A.B.'s shoulders. By the time Adelaide was born, the weight of the Stanhope fortune had crushed the curious, spontaneous, and seemingly carefree man I had finally learned to love.

# 25

MAY 1899

### ~ Sylvia ~

Everyone had finished eating lunch by the time Sylvia finished her story. Reliving the memories had deepened the ache she felt at A.B.'s loss. She wished she could remember if she'd told him how much she loved him before saying goodbye to him in Newport.

"I wish I had known Father before he took over the company and began to change," Addy said. "He was always a distant figure to me, a man who rarely smiled."

"He was so handsome when he smiled," Sylvia said. His face became more blurred in her memory with each passing day, obscured by the darkness of time and grief.

Junietta pulled out a linen handkerchief to wipe a tear. "I noticed A.B. drifting away from us too, and it was sad to watch. I missed the little boy he once was. It's easy to believe the lure of wealth won't change you, but it does. A.B. acquired the drive for more and more from his father and grandfather. And now the company he sacrificed his health and his family for is no longer ours."

Sylvia wished she could make Junietta understand. "Don't you see? That's why I'm so determined to keep this house and our place in society. It's for A.B.'s sake as much as for Adelaide's and mine. He worked so hard for all of this, and I can't bear to be the one to lose it. He loved this mansion. It's part of his legacy. My best memories of him are here." She stood to leave.

"Just a moment, Sylvia." Junietta blocked her path with her cane. "You've admitted feeling remorse for deceiving A.B. into proposing, yet aren't you expecting Adelaide to deceive her suitors too? Her motive isn't revenge, but it's still deceitful to charm a man into marriage for his money."

"Money is the motive behind all the marriages in our social class! No one invites paupers and immigrants to their parties to meet their daughters." She caught herself losing her temper and changed her tone. "We all want to see our daughters well taken care of. And Adelaide deserves to inherit the beautiful home that her ancestors built and worked for. If there's a moral to my story with A.B., it's that I believe love will follow in time, as it did for me. Besides, I've made it clear from the start that Adelaide does have a choice in the matter. She doesn't have to marry a man she dislikes."

Junietta gave a short laugh. "That's good news. Now all she has to do is find a wealthy suitor she's attracted to and who's equally attracted to her before we run out of money. That plan doesn't seem to be going very well, from what I can see. Meanwhile, this house becomes a bigger burden every day. Am I right?"

Sylvia didn't reply.

"What are your thoughts, Addy?" Junietta asked. "You're frowning."

Adelaide exhaled and tossed her napkin beside her plate. "Sometimes it's really hard being a woman. Men seem to have all the advantages."

Junietta laughed and thumped her cane. "Ha! You're starting to sound like a suffragette!"

### ⤙ *Junietta* ⤚

Junietta didn't want to miss any discussions with Sylvia and Addy about their future, but she became winded each time she traipsed the endless hallways in order to find them, or made her way up and down the stairs to her room, not to mention going all the way up to the third floor. She hoped she was getting through to Addy, but it was hard to tell. Sylvia could be very persuasive too.

Her dinner party for the foundation's board members had been a success, but it had exhausted Junietta more than she'd imagined it would. Now that it was over, she knew it was time to face her growing limitations. Her heart was giving out. The painful reality was that she couldn't continue to do the things she'd always done. She could no longer travel back and forth to work in the foundation offices. And it was time to move her bedroom down to the first floor to avoid the stairs. The room she chose was off the library, paneled in walnut with a lovely stone fireplace and plenty of windows. Arthur Stanhope had used it to smoke his cigars, and the aroma did linger a bit, even after all these years. Junietta tried not to make a fuss about the move, asking the servants to be as discreet about it as possible. But Addy noticed the commotion and came looking for Junietta.

"Is it true what the servants are saying? That you're moving down here? This is such a small room, Mimi!"

"All I need are my bed, my wardrobe, and my favorite chair. And see? They all fit perfectly. Nice and snug, don't you think?"

"But why?"

"Climbing those stairs is like climbing Mount Everest, and I just can't make the trek anymore."

Addy's skirts rustled as she knelt beside Junietta's chair. "I'm worried about you, Mimi. Are you seeing a doctor?"

"Yes, he's here all the time, making a nuisance of himself with his pills and tonics and medicines. But the stairs were the last straw. I'll be fine if I don't have to go up and down them anymore. And this is a very nice room, don't you think? Change is part of life, dear. We have to accept it."

"I don't want to lose you, Mimi."

"And I don't want to lose you either, dear girl. Your sisters are already lost, and that's a shame—"

"What do you mean?"

She took Addy's hands in hers. "To me, people are 'lost' if they live empty lives without meaning or purpose. Without ever discovering what God created them to be and do. Poor people can get 'lost' too, but things like wealth and outward beauty can become very effective distractions. So can the search for a rich husband." Junietta wished she didn't have to add to the pressure Addy already was under, but her granddaughter's life was too important for her to remain quiet.

"I can't let Mother down," Addy said. "She's working so hard—for all of us."

"I know. I know she is. But she's rediscovering forgotten skills in the process, along with learning a few new ones. God has a plan for her as well, if she seeks Him. I'm praying that He'll show us a solution that will work for everyone."

There was a soft knock on the door, and the maid poked her head inside. "Miss Dawson from the foundation is here to see you."

"Thank you, Jane. Escort her into the library, please, and bring us some coffee. Addy will help me get there, won't you dear?" Addy's forehead wrinkled in concern as she helped Junietta rise from the chair and limp into the library. Junietta hated her own weakness. Yet she knew God wasn't surprised by it. He must have a plan for that too. "Until a new chairman can take my place," she explained to Addy as they walked, "I've decided to do my work for the foundation from here. We've set up our work in the library—a beautiful room, even if it is absurdly huge."

Junietta's heart was fluttering like butterfly wings by the time she sat down at the library table with her assistant, Miss Dawson. But it began pounding like alarm drums when Miss Dawson mentioned Randall Stanhope. "He came to the office yesterday, looking for you. He said he was a relative of yours."

"My nephew, yes. Did he say what he wanted?"

"He said he heard we were inviting new members to join the board, and he wanted to speak with you about inviting his wife to be one of them."

Junietta leaned back against her chair for a moment as she tried to absorb this blow. She couldn't let Randall or his family get their hands on the foundation's money. "What did you tell him?"

"I told him you were working from home, and he should come here if he wanted to speak with you. Then he asked if you were retiring, and he said if you were, his wife should be the one to take over the foundation. He said your successor should be a Stanhope since the foundation bears the Stanhope name."

Junietta pressed her hand to her chest against the burning pain, struggling to take a deep breath, battling not to show it. She couldn't let Randall take a wrecking ball to the Stanhope Foundation. She simply couldn't.

"He also wanted to know when the next board meeting was."

"Thank you for telling me, Miss Dawson. When you see him, tell him I'll be expecting him to call on me here." Yet she doubted that Randall would. It was more his style to work behind the scenes to undermine her.

She got busy with the work Miss Dawson had brought but had difficulty concentrating on any of it. Junietta asked the maid to help her return to her bedroom after Miss Dawson left. "Jane, dear, the next time Mr. Forsythe comes to see Sylvia, would you please ask him to come and see me too?"

"Of course, ma'am. Can I bring you anything now? Cook baked some gingerbread this morning."

"Nothing, dear, but thank you." She was too sick at heart to eat. Howard Forsythe needed to take over for her as soon as possible. Once he did, she would warn him about Randall Stanhope's motives.

She and Addy were visiting in her bedroom a few days later, sitting beside the fire, when Mr. Forsythe knocked politely on the doorframe. "May I disturb you for just a moment?"

"Why, of course, Howard! How nice to see you. Please, sit down, and I'll ask Jane to bring you some tea or coffee."

"No, thank you. I have to get back to the office." He fidgeted a bit, his smile a bit forced. "I know you're waiting for an answer from me about taking over the foundation, but I don't have one yet."

Her stomach plummeted. "It's a big decision and I want you to take your time," she lied. In truth, she needed him to hurry.

"I hope you'll forgive me if what I've come to ask you is way out of line, but my father would like to invite the two of you to the parsonage for dinner next Sunday after church." He quickly held up his hands to stop a reply. "Before you answer either way, I feel I need to explain. You see, I asked my parents for their advice on whether I should continue at the law firm or accept the chairmanship of your foundation. I respect their wisdom a great deal. I also asked for their prayers, so I can know God's will in the matter. But now they want to meet you, Mrs. Stanhope. And they invited Miss Stanhope to come as well."

"We would be honored," Junietta replied. "Of course we'll come." Adelaide looked at her in surprise.

"It will be a simple meal," he continued. "Nothing at all like the dinners I've enjoyed here in your home."

"I'm sure we'll enjoy it very much. It's the fellowship around the table that makes a meal enjoyable, not how fancy it is. As the Good Book says, eating a dry morsel in peace is better than feasting with strife and conflict."

"I agree. And you'll also get to meet my wonderful grandmother, Meara Galloway. She'll be there as well."

"All the better. Leave the directions with my driver, Henry, and he'll get us there."

Adelaide confronted her after he was gone. "You accepted for both of us and didn't even give me a chance to decide."

"I couldn't imagine why you would refuse such a gracious invitation."

"Are you finally going to reveal that you're his mysterious sponsor?"

"I'm going to let Howard's family take the lead on that."

"So, you're just going to sit at their dinner table and pretend you don't know them? Why don't you just tell Mr. Forsythe the truth?"

"His parents are the ones who invited us. Let's wait and see what their plan is."

### ~ Adelaide ~

On Sunday morning, Mimi decided they should attend Reverend Forsythe's church service instead of their own before going to the parsonage for dinner. Addy hoped he would preach on the evil of lies and deceit—something her family seemed skilled at. But those words would also condemn her. Instead, the sermon was about putting faith into action by helping the poor. His text was, "Pure religion and undefiled before God and the Father is this, To visit the fatherless and widows in their affliction . . ."

Mimi leaned over to whisper to Adelaide, "That has always been one of my favorite Scriptures." Addy wondered if he had preached from that verse as a tribute to Mimi Junie or if it was his way of convincing his son to work for the foundation.

Mr. Forsythe—who insisted they call him by his given name, Howard—escorted them to the parsonage next door after the service. The modest home smelled wonderfully of roasting chicken. He hung their wraps on the coat-tree near the door, then grinned at Adelaide as he gestured to their staircase. "This is it, Miss Stanhope, our famous banister. Would you like to try it out?"

Addy laughed out loud in surprise. "Not today. But thank you for the kind offer."

The sitting room was small but comfortably furnished. They sat down to chat while they waited for the pastor to finish his morning duties and walk over from the church. Meara Galloway was already seated in a chair by the window, and she greeted them warmly. Addy wondered how long it had been since Meara, Regan, and Mimi Junie had seen each other. They acted as though they were strangers, but Addy was very aware of the loving looks they exchanged, even if Howard didn't seem to notice. Once Reverend Forsythe arrived, they gathered around the dining room table. Addy wondered if his family was playing matchmaker by seating her beside Howard. If so, they would be disappointed. Mother would never approve.

After Reverend Forsythe said the blessing over the meal, Howard gave Addy a little nudge with his elbow and pointed to his fork. "Only one, I'm afraid."

Addy smiled. "You must think us terribly wasteful and pretentious."

"Not at all. Every family has their own customs and rituals. It's only natural. Ours are different from yours, that's all."

The dining room table was small, ensuring that everyone could converse together while they ate. The simple meal of chicken, mashed potatoes, and apple pie was delicious, the conversation and laughter warm and genuine. Addy was surprised to find herself relaxing and having a good time. When they returned to the parlor after dessert, her curiosity got the better of her, and she drew Howard aside to ask, "Have you made up your mind which job to pursue?"

"I think so. And while my heart says to choose the foundation, I believe I should decline and continue with my law firm." She felt a stab of disappointment for Mimi's sake.

"May I ask why you aren't following your heart?"

He glanced at Mimi Junie. "Let's go for a walk and I'll explain." They excused themselves and he led Addy out the front door for a stroll around the block. "For one thing," he began as they passed the church, "after your grandmother's dinner the other night, I realized that I would never be able to preside over an event like that and entertain wealthy board members and donors the way she does. I know I'm out of my depth."

"I'm sure there would be board members' wives who would be happy to plan and host events for you."

"Perhaps. But my second reason is that I need to respect my anonymous sponsor. He made a huge investment in my education with private schools, college, and law school. Some of my duties as chairman of the foundation might involve legal work, but I think my sponsor would be disappointed in me if I abandoned law altogether. He could have been supporting someone else all these years, someone more appreciative of the opportunity he provided to work with such a fine law firm."

Adelaide didn't reply. She felt annoyed with Mimi for not being honest with Howard, and for putting him in this situation where he wasn't free to follow his heart. Then she saw the irony of her own decision to pursue a wealthy suitor instead of following her heart. No wonder Mimi was frustrated with her.

"I can only hope that your grandmother will understand my reasons," Howard said. "And that she'll be able to find a suitable chairman soon."

Addy sighed and stopped walking. She needed to tell him the truth. "I shouldn't be telling you this," she began, "but I know who your mysterious sponsor is. And I can say with complete confidence that they would want you to follow your heart and choose freely, not because you feel indebted." He looked down at her, his gaze intense. His eyes were really very blue. And he was tall, taller than her by a good six inches. She wondered what it would be like to be held in Howard's arms and dance with him. She shook her head, quickly dismissing the thought.

"Is it Mr. Wilson or someone else from my law firm?" Howard asked, breaking into her thoughts. "He has spent so much time and effort mentoring me and—"

"It isn't anyone from your law firm."

"If he's someone who my father helped during the war, I would hate to—"

"Nothing like that."

"Am I going to have to play twenty questions, Miss Stanhope, or will you just tell me?"

"I should have kept my mouth shut," she mumbled. She stared at the ground, shaking her head as she struggled to decide. She knew she was biased, but Howard had such a good heart and was so full of life and humor that she wanted him to work for the foundation, not for Mr. Wilson's stuffy law firm. She sighed again. "Do you know anything about your maternal grandfather, Gavin Galloway?"

He stared at her. "How did you know his name?"

Addy winced. "I'm no good at secrecy and subterfuge. Please, tell me what you know about him first. Then I'll explain."

"It's funny you should ask. His story always seemed like a cautionary tale that my parents made up to teach my brothers and me the evils of greed. I was never convinced that it was true. But we were told that he left my grandmother behind when my mother was very young to try to make his fortune on the California gold fields. His decrepit ship sank, however, and he never made it there."

He looked at her expectantly, but Addy hesitated, still unsure if she should give away her grandmother's secrets. He grabbed her hand and tugged on it to shake her from her indecision. "Come on, Adelaide, you can't leave me in suspense now. What does my grandfather's lust for gold have to do with my mysterious sponsor?"

Mimi Junie would be disappointed, but she had to tell him. "The gold rush tragedy isn't made up. Gavin Galloway had a brother named Neal Galloway. They went off to seek their fortune together, and they died together."

"Yes, so I've been told."

"My grandmother and Neal were in love with each other."

"What? *Mrs. Stanhope?*" He looked incredulous. She nodded as she gave him a moment to digest her words. She guessed he was having trouble picturing elegant Junietta Stanhope with a vagabond immigrant like his grandfather.

"Neal hoped to strike it rich so he could ask for my grandmother's hand in marriage. After he was lost at sea, Mimi Junie was pressured into marrying Art Stanhope. Her first charitable project was to buy a boardinghouse so she could help your mother and grandmother."

"So, she's my anonymous sponsor?" He sounded breathless.

Addy nodded. "Please don't tell her I told you. But do you see why she would want you to follow your heart? She won't be disappointed with either choice you make." He was still holding Addy's hand. He gave it a gentle squeeze before releasing it.

"Thanks for telling me. But I think it makes my decision even more difficult."

"Why? I hoped it would make it easier."

He turned and started walking back toward the parsonage. She kept pace beside him. "It won't be easy for anyone to follow in your grandmother's footsteps," he said. "The foundation oversees a great deal of money, more than I can even imagine. It's a huge responsibility. And Mrs. Stanhope seems to have more faith in me than I have in myself. I wondered why she chose me to lead the foundation, but if it's only out of loyalty to my grandfather and his brother, then that changes things."

Adelaide was furious with herself. She had tried to do the right thing, but her efforts had backfired. Howard was even less inclined to accept the chairmanship now. He was quiet for the rest of the way and seemed deep in thought. He halted again when they reached the front steps. "So, they all know each other in there?" he said, gesturing toward the house. "And they're pretending not to?"

"They've known each other for fifty years." Addy feared he might be angry, but instead, he burst out laughing.

"That's unbelievable! I don't know about you, but it makes me wonder what other secrets they're keeping from us."

"Listen, I sincerely hope you'll help me keep their secrets. And that you won't tell anyone what I shared with you."

"Don't worry," he said, patting her shoulder. "We can put on a good act too, can't we?"

"I suppose we have no choice now."

### Junietta

Sunday dinner at the Forsythes' home had been wonderful. Junietta felt tired, but she had loved seeing her old friends again. "Henry, I would like to take a little detour on the way home if you don't mind," she told her driver. "I would like to visit the family cemetery plot."

"Of course, Miss Junietta." He helped her and Addy down from the carriage when they arrived, and walked with her across the grass, halting beside the Stanhope obelisk. It seemed to cast an even larger shadow now that Junietta felt her own life drawing to a close. She stared at her son's tombstone, remembering the shock and numbness she'd felt nearly a year ago when she'd stood here at his funeral. She wished she had thought to bring flowers for his grave today. The grass had grown back, concealing the scarred earth and the body buried beneath it, but she didn't have enough time left in this world to heal the hole that A.B. had left in her heart.

"That was such a lovely dinner today, wasn't it?" she asked Addy.

"Yes, it was."

"It made me think of that Bible verse from Ecclesiastes. Something about how it's better to go to a house of mourning than to a house of feasting because death is everyone's destiny, and we need to take it to heart."

"I don't want to talk about dying, Mimi. And I don't want you to die."

"I know. But if we remember that death comes to all of us, we'll pay better attention to how we live."

Addy pointed to David Stanhope's grave at the end of the row. "I barely noticed his grave before, but now that I know about his suicide, his loss seems terribly tragic."

"It was. And so unnecessary." Junietta remembered her own part in David's death and whispered a silent prayer for forgiveness. When she spoke again, her voice was hoarse with emotion. "I've been talking about Art and A.B. so much lately that it has made me miss them terribly. They both left us so suddenly. We always think we'll have more time with our loved ones to let them know how much they're loved, yet often we don't."

Addy reached for her hand and squeezed it. "I do miss Father," she said softly, "even if I hardly ever saw him. I know he was disappointed in me because I wasn't a boy. Our family has lost everything because of that."

Her words surprised Junietta. "That's simply not true! That choice was in God's hands, not yours or anyone else's. Please don't hang on to your false guilt for another moment. Your father loved you, even if he wasn't able to show it. The Stanhope men all had trouble showing their families how much they cared."

"I don't remember ever telling Father that I loved him."

"Don't carry any regrets either. Just go forward from now on, remembering to tell people how you feel."

Addy looked up at her. "I love you, Mimi Junie."

Junietta pulled her into her arms. "And I love you, my darling girl. That's why I'm fighting so hard for you to be able to choose your own future."

After they released each other, Addy said, "At Father's funeral, you mentioned your other son. Did you mean Neal's son?"

"Yes, I suppose I was thinking of him. The shock of losing A.B. so suddenly brought back the memory of losing him so unexpectedly as well."

"Did you ever find Neal's son?"

Junietta shook her head. "I took Reverend Cooper's advice and stopped looking for him. But I've never forgotten him, even after all these years. I celebrate his birthday in my heart every year on the day he was born. July 15. And oh, it was so hot that day. A.B. was born a little more than a year later, and he helped fill the empty place my first baby son left behind. And I do have other sons, don't I? Matthew Murphy is one, and the three Forsythe brothers. I consider Henry my son as well." They had walked back to the carriage, and she smiled at Henry as she spoke those words. He returned hers with a grin. "Henry is as loyal as any son and won't leave my side, even though I've often encouraged him to. He owns his own stables and a thriving livery business now, which he'll pass on to his sons one day. Right, Henry?"

"You're my family too, Miss Junietta."

They were both quiet on the ride back to the mansion. As they pulled to a stop out front, Addy said, "I can't help thinking about how many, many people's lives you've touched with your love, Mimi. It seems like a much greater legacy to leave behind than houses and possessions and wealth."

Junietta's heart swelled with joy. Maybe Addy was finally getting it. "It's the only legacy worth leaving, darling girl."

# 26

JUNE 1899

*Adelaide*

Adelaide waited outside the study for Howard Forsythe to finish meeting with her mother. Ever since visiting the cemetery, an idea had been forming in Adelaide's mind of a way she could bless her grandmother and repay her love. But she knew she needed help. "If you have a moment, Mr. Forsythe," she said when he finally emerged, "I would like to speak to you about something."

"Certainly." He looked very competent and professional in his dark suit, wing-collared shirt, and silk necktie. And handsome. His blue-checked waistcoat made his eyes appear even brighter.

"Follow me, please. I don't want to be overheard." She led Mr. Forsythe to the drawing room, noticing how he gazed around at the vast room with awe, as if he would love to spend the rest of the day perusing all the artifacts and furnishings. They sat at a small table in the corner.

"I need to hire your services as a lawyer. Can you tell me what your hourly fees might be?"

"You don't need to worry about my fees, Miss Stanhope. I've been told that I'm to be at your family's service for anything you need, for as long as you need. Now that I know who my mysterious sponsor is, my assignment no longer comes as a surprise." His smile was warm and genuine. They had become friends these past months, going on Mimi's excursions, sitting together at Mimi's dinner, and visiting his parents' home. Why was she speaking so formally and keeping him at a distance? Could it be because she found everything about him attractive? She tried to soften her approach.

"You've been very patient in helping my mother, grandmother, and me, and we're all grateful. But now there's something that I would like to do for my grandmother. I regretted telling you her secret about how and why she'd become your sponsor, but now I think that knowing the truth will make it easier for you to understand my errand. I know you'll keep everything in confidence, even if I, apparently, am not very good at keeping confidences."

"You have my word. What can I do for you?" He folded his hands in front of him. She leaned toward him, lowering her voice.

"I need you to help me find someone. You already know that my grandmother was in love with your great-uncle, Neal Galloway. Well, she had his baby, a son he never knew about."

If Mr. Forsythe was shocked, he didn't reveal it. "Go on."

"Mimi's father sent her away to have the baby in secret, then took the child from her right after he was born and gave him away to be adopted. That was nearly fifty years ago, and she has grieved for him ever since. Mimi isn't well, and I would like you to help me find her son." She didn't say *before Mimi dies*, but it was what she was thinking. Mr. Forsythe leaned back in his chair with a look of surprise.

"I see. I've never had a request like that before."

"My grandmother has always done so much for other people and—"

"Oh, you don't need to convince me! I would do anything for her. Do you have time to get started on the search today?"

"Yes. But where, exactly, do we start?"

He opened the leather portfolio he carried and took out a fountain pen. "Tell me every scrap of information that you know about him."

Addy chewed her lip, straining to recall what she knew. "He was born in Tarrytown, at the home of a midwife who my grandmother boarded with. Her name was Elizabeth. I don't know her last name, but I gather this woman had sheltered other girls in need like my grandmother. Mimi's son was born on July 15, 1850. He was given away within a few hours, to a family that hadn't been able to have children. The wife had suffered several miscarriages, apparently. Elizabeth said they were a good family with a fine name." She watched him scribble down the information. When he finished, he looked up at her expectantly. "I'm sorry, but that's really all I know. Do you think it will be enough to go on?"

"I'm not sure. Like I said, I've never done anything like this before. But one idea that does come immediately to mind is to look at baptismal records. My father's church keeps records of all the infants who are baptized, and I believe those records also include the child's birth date. We can probably make a few assumptions—first, that the adoptive parents would want to have him baptized within a few months. And I think we can also assume that the adoptive parents lived fairly close to Tarrytown, since they were known to the midwife and the baby was taken to them when he was a newborn. Perhaps a local country doctor acted as a go-between with the parents."

"Those assumptions sound very plausible," Addy said. She shifted in her seat, her excitement growing. "And I think it's safe to assume the adoptive family were people of means, since poorer families rarely consider adopting more children."

"Good. That's likely true too. It might take time and patience to sift through hundreds of baptismal records in numerous churches—like searching for a needle in a haystack, really. But it's not an impossible task. I recommend we start with a map and a list of area churches. We could begin in Tarrytown and slowly work our way out within a larger and larger radius."

Addy's heart skipped faster. "You said 'we.' Does that mean we're doing this together?"

"I suppose we could hire a Pinkerton detective, but where's the fun in that?" His broad grin made her heart trip over itself. "Besides, I owe your grandmother a huge debt. Of course, I'm going to help you." Then his smile faded. "Unless you weren't planning on coming with me. I'm sorry. I shouldn't have assumed—"

"I think it's a marvelous plan. I can't wait to get started. My life is quite boring now that everyone has left town for the summer." In the past, Addy would be joining her friends for tennis and lawn parties, sailing on Narragansett Bay, attending balls on warm summer evenings, and dancing until sunrise. She sighed and tried to erase the picture of her cousin Cicely living in her beautiful home and spreading gossip about her and Mother. "I could use an adventure, Mr. Forsythe."

"Won't you please call me Howard?" he said wearily. "Especially if we're going to be spending time together, searching through a lot of dusty church records."

"Then you must call me Adelaide." He seemed hesitant. She knew Mother would never approve. "Please, I insist," she said.

"Very well . . . Adelaide."

"Thank you. Now, there is one other matter." She set the bag she had brought downstairs on the table and opened it, lifting out one of her mother's illustrated storybooks. She slid it across to him. Howard's expression revealed wonder and amazement as he leafed through the pages.

"These pictures are beautiful. The animals seem to breathe." He looked up at Addy. "Did you paint these?"

"No, my mother did, a long time ago. And there are more books just like that one. I was wondering . . . I mean, I would like to have them published for her. As a surprise. Even better if she was paid for her beautiful work. Would you know how to go about that sort of thing? That is, if you think they merit publication."

"They are definitely worthy of publication. I don't know much about the publishing business, but I'll be happy to look into it for you. May I keep this?"

"Yes, of course. When do you think we could start looking at baptismal records?"

"Is next week too soon? I'll need to finish up a few things first, then find a good map and a list of area churches."

"Next week will be perfect." She rose to go, but Howard stopped her before she reached the door.

"Miss Stanhope—Adelaide. I don't want to raise your hopes for an easy success. We might be embarking on a wild goose chase. But if we don't have any luck with baptismal records, I promise I'll come up with another plan."

She accompanied him to the door, then went in search of Mother to win her approval for Mr. Forsythe's plan. Mother was still in Father's study, seated behind his desk with a ledger book and piles of receipts in front of her.

"How long do you think it will take to find this missing son—if you ever do find him?" she asked after Addy explained her idea.

"I have no idea. But it's not like I have other obligations that I'll be shirking. All my friends and potential suitors are away for the summer."

Mother winced at the reminder. "I hate to think that we're missing out on some important introductions."

"I know. I'm feeling anxious about it too. Especially when I see how hard you're working to keep everything together. I wish I could do something to help you."

"Never mind. If your father's yacht sells this summer, it will be a big help to us." She sighed—something Mother rarely did. "It's sweet that you want to find Junietta's son, but I'm a little uncomfortable with the idea of you traveling the countryside with Mr. Forsythe unchaperoned."

"He'll be accompanying me as our lawyer. And it will mean so much to Mimi Junie if we do find him."

"Yes, I know. That's the only reason I would ever allow it. For her sake."

Henry drove Addy to Grand Central Station the following week, where she'd arranged to meet Howard. She was waiting inside for him when two nicely dressed young women carrying bundles of newspapers approached her in the busy passageway. "Would you like to read why we need better laws to protect women and children in the workplace?" one of them asked as she held a paper out to Addy. "You can read how you can help make a difference." Addy thought of the work Mimi did to protect women and children, and the idea of making a difference intrigued her. She took one of the papers. But before she had time to look it over, Howard arrived and she stuffed it into her bag.

"Ready?" he asked.

"I am." Howard purchased their tickets and they took the train twenty-five miles north to Tarrytown. The peaceful village was a welcome change from the noise and congestion of the city. Addy slowed her steps to admire flower gardens, shady front porches, and children playing as she walked from the station with Howard. They had decided to begin at the church that Mimi Junie had mentioned and were disappointed to learn that her friend, Reverend Cooper, was no longer the pastor there. Mr. Forsythe explained to the new pastor that he was a lawyer, that Adelaide was his client, and that they were searching for a lost relative.

"No one needs to know the details," Howard had told her on their way into the church. "Let people imagine that an inheritance is at stake." The pastor was very helpful and led them to the church's storage room to read through old baptismal records.

"By the way, Reverend," Addy said before he left them, "do you know of a midwife named Elizabeth who may have worked in this area fifty years ago?"

"I haven't lived here that long, I'm sorry."

The record books were fragile and dusty, causing Howard to sneeze repeatedly. They found the volume for 1850, which recorded births, deaths, and marriages along with baptisms, and began the slow task of perusing the old-fashioned script, searching for a boy born on July 15. They read all the entries for the following six months, just to be sure, but didn't find a record that fit. "I guess it was too much to hope that we'd have beginner's luck," Addy sighed.

"There are several more churches in Tarrytown. Shall we split up so it will go faster, or stay together?"

"Let's stay together." Addy found Howard's company pleasant and his competence reassuring. They walked from church to church, enjoying the warm day, and stopped at a small café for a quick lunch. Then they hired a carriage to visit the Old Dutch Reformed Church in nearby Sleepy Hollow, made famous by Washington Irving's story. The pastor of that church did remember an area midwife and recommended they talk to the retired local physician, Dr. Depew.

"Yes, indeed, I remember Elizabeth well," the doctor said when they visited his home in Tarrytown. "Elizabeth Duffield delivered half the population of this town. She's gone now, sad to say."

Addy took a chance and asked the next question. "Would you know about any babies that were given to adoptive homes? Maybe to parents who couldn't have children of their own? This would have been fifty years ago."

He thought for a moment, then sadly shook his head. "I'm sorry. My mind just isn't as sharp as it used to be. I have trouble remembering yesterday, much less half a century ago."

By the end of the afternoon, they had viewed hundreds of records in several churches without any luck. Adelaide's feet were beginning to ache. They'd found only two babies that had been born on July 15, but both had been girls.

"Shall we try again next week?" Howard asked as they took the train back to the city. "I'm free Tuesday, but if you're busy with other engagements—"

"I have plenty of free time to spare this summer," she replied. "We're usually at our home in Newport by now. But as you know, that home is no longer ours."

"I imagine that's been quite a loss for you. You must miss it."

Addy thought of the pressure she would be under if she were there, how every event would be tarnished by the need to find a wealthy suitor. She turned to Howard and smiled. "I'm surprised to find that I don't miss it nearly as much as I thought I would."

"Well in that case, I think we should visit the village of Dobbs Ferry, next." He pointed to the village on the map, and she was discouraged to see just how many little villages there were in the area.

"All right. Tuesday, then." She removed her shoes and massaged her aching feet as they sat together on the train, something she wouldn't have dared to do in front of her gentlemen suitors. "Remind me to wear comfortable shoes though," she said, laughing.

The following Tuesday, Addy saw the two women distributing their newspapers in the train station again. She had forgotten that she still had the first paper in her bag. "We need your help to make our city a better place," one of them told her. "Please join us to help improve education and sanitation in New York's poor, immigrant neighborhoods." The woman looked straight at Adelaide and offered her a newspaper. She took it but only had time to see that it was called the *Revolution* before Howard arrived.

They had no luck in any of the churches in Dobbs Ferry, then took a carriage to the nearby village of Elmsford. They were in the cramped storeroom of the Reformed Church, their jackets removed, shirtsleeves rolled up, struggling to decipher the faded ink and lacy penmanship when they both spotted the notation at the same time: *William Finch, born July 15, 1850. Son of Henry and Rachel Finch. Baptized August 5, 1850.* Addy was so excited she had the urge to give Howard a hug. "Could this really be him?" she asked. He seemed as excited as she was.

"I don't know. But he's our only candidate so far."

"How do we find out if it's really him?"

"That's a good question." He ran his fingers through his hair, leaving it rumpled. It softened his lawyerly appearance and made him look very endearing. "I suppose we start with this church's membership rolls to see if any of the Finches still attend this church." The pastor had been very help-ful when they'd told him of their quest, so they went to speak with him.

"Hmm, Bill Finch," he said, nodding. "Haven't seen him in church lately. Not since his wife took sick. He farms a patch of land north of town."

"Do you know anything about his parents, Henry and Rachel Finch?"

"Sorry, that was before my time. Bill must be . . . I'd say around fifty?"

They asked for directions, hired a local driver, and eventually found William Finch's farm at the end of a bumpy, dusty road. The smell of manure filled the air. Addy felt sweaty and thoroughly jostled when the carriage finally came to a halt. "I've never experienced such a bone-jarring ride!"

"You did say you were bored and wanted an adventure," Howard teased. They were greeted by a barking dog and a pair of honking geese, and decided to wait in the safety of the carriage for someone to come out of the stone farmhouse. A farmer in worn overalls eventually emerged from the barn and walked toward them. He looked to be the right age. Howard stepped down to meet him, braving the boisterous animals. "Hello, I'm Howard Forsythe," he said, offering his hand. "I'm looking for Mr. William Finch."

"That's me." He seemed suspicious of the strangers in city clothes.

"We're trying to locate a lost family member who was given up for adoption at birth. Do you know, by any chance, if you were adopted?"

He gave a rough laugh that was almost a grunt. "I was the fifth of nine children. My parents had too many of their own to feed and no reason at all to take on another one." Disappointment crushed Addy. All this time and effort, wasted.

"Well, thank you for your time, Mr. Finch. We won't bother you any further."

"I was so hoping we had found him," Addy said as the carriage rattled back down the road.

"I know. Me too. Shall we head back to the train station and call it a day?"

"Yes, I think we'd better."

They were both too tired to talk much on the journey home. But when they were almost to the station, Howard turned to her and said, "You don't have to go with me the next time if you don't want to. I can continue alone. I'm still not convinced my idea is going to help us find him." Addy could have accepted his offer. She was tired and hot and discouraged, and unaccustomed to spending her summer days this way. Yet when she thought about it, she found that she didn't want to stop searching with Howard. The challenge of solving this mystery was much more interesting than flirting with boring rich men at endless summer parties.

"I know this might sound odd," she said, "but I've been enjoying this quest. Up until this year, my life has been so uneventful and routine that I'm finding it educational to visit these small villages and quaint churches. It's easy for me to forget that there's a world full of people who don't live the way I do—and yet are quite happy."

"Good. I'm glad you feel that way, because I've really enjoyed doing this with you. Today, when I thought we'd found him, it made me happy to think that we would share the victory together."

Howard escorted her all the way home once they reached the city. "So, next week, then?" she asked him as he helped her down from the carriage.

"I'll look forward to it. We'll try a few villages north of Tarrytown next time."

Adelaide remembered the newspapers she'd stuffed into her bag once she was home. She sat beside the window in her bedroom after changing her clothes and took a few minutes to read through them. The well-written articles provided details of much-needed social reforms, such as clean drinking water in working-class neighborhoods, and improved conditions in poorhouses and mental asylums. The needs were enormous, but a group of very determined women were working hard to lobby for change. Their story inspired Addy. And she was very surprised to discover that the *Revolution* was published by the National American Woman Suffrage Association. The articles and the tone of the newspaper shattered many of her preconceptions about the group.

The women weren't in the train station when Addy arrived the following week, and she was sorry. She would have liked to hear more of what
they had to say. But then Howard arrived, and her excitement for their
adventure together quickly made her forget everything else.

They worked their way slowly north from Tarrytown, and when
Howard mentioned the village of Sing Sing, Adelaide knew they had to
visit it. "My mother grew up on an estate called Ferncliff Manor, just
outside the village. I would love to see it."

"We can easily do that."

"Mother has been telling me about her past for the first time that I
can ever recall, so I'm curious to see her childhood home. She moved
from there to the city after her father died, and the house was sold."

"We'll see if we can find it."

They began at the Presbyterian church in Sing Sing, which featured
such a tall spire it was used as a navigational aid for ship traffic on the
Hudson. The friendly pastor let them peruse his church records, then
gave them directions to Ferncliff Manor. "I understand the house was
quite run down before it changed hands, twenty-some years ago. I'm
told it was purchased by a wealthy New York tycoon who turned it into
some sort of Italian villa."

"Do you think he'd mind if we took a look?"

"I couldn't say. I doubt if anyone is there this time of year besides
the caretaker."

"Is the caretaker named Davies?"

"No, I knew Mr. and Mrs. Davies. Nice folk. They've been gone a
dozen years now."

Addy and Howard rode in the hired carriage as far as the gate and
the *No Trespassing* sign, then got out and walked down the long drive-
way. The house looked nothing at all like Mother had described, with a
stepped roof and climbing vines. Instead, it resembled pictures Addy had
seen of villas on Lake Como in Italy. No one rushed out to stop them as

they approached, so they continued around the corner of the house and were met by a breathtaking view. "Wow!" Howard said.

"I've seen this view in one of Mother's paintings, but the real thing is spectacular! And look—they've replanted the formal garden. It even has a fountain." They walked around the grounds for a few minutes, absorbing the beauty of the winding river below them and the distant mountains and forests. "I wonder if I would ever get used to this view if I lived here every day," Addy said. "I think I can understand why Mother was inspired to paint."

"Speaking of her paintings," Howard said. "I showed her book to one of the partners who has worked with publishers. He agreed to show it to a few people he knows."

"That's wonderful news!"

"Yes, but I caution you not to get your hopes up just yet."

"I'll try not to. But her watercolors mean so much more to me now that I've seen Ferncliff—or what remains of it."

There was an Episcopal church in Sing Sing they needed to visit, along with a few others, so they returned to the village. They had no luck with any of their baptismal records either and left for home feeling discouraged. Addy couldn't stop thinking about Ferncliff Manor and brought it up again on the train journey home. "I don't know if my mother shared any of her story with you when you were working with her, but she has suffered so many losses in her life. Her parents moved to Ferncliff after they lost their home and business in an economic crisis. Later, her two brothers drowned there, and her mother died of grief. She had to sell Ferncliff after her father died. All that tragedy, and now my father has suddenly passed away at such a young age. I think I can understand why Mother is so determined not to lose her home again."

"Mrs. Stanhope did share some of her tragic past with me when we were going over the finances. She asked if I thought she was being foolish for struggling so hard to keep your mansion."

"What did you tell her?"

"I told her it was a decision only she could make. And without even thinking, I told her she should pray about it."

"You did? What did she say?"

He gave a little shrug. "Nothing. She simply nodded and we went back to work. I didn't think before I spoke, and I worried afterward that the advice I had given her wasn't very lawyerly. I guess I sometimes forget that I grew up in a parsonage, and that not everyone thinks about faith the same way I do."

"I think prayer is always good advice," Addy said, then realized it was something she should do before deciding her own future path. "My mother and grandmother have been sharing their stories, and I've learned a lot of things I didn't know about my family. Before my father died, I took my wealth and privilege for granted. I just assumed my life would always be this way, and if it was an empty, shallow life, I was too immature to notice. Then my grandmother showed me the work she does, and now I don't think I could be completely happy if my life returned to the way it used to be. It scares me to think we could lose everything the way my mother's family once did. I'm ashamed to say that I wouldn't know how to live without servants. But it also scares me to think of living a wasted life. One without a greater purpose. Now that I've seen what true poverty and need look like, it's hard to simply turn away again."

"You don't need to apologize for the way you were brought up. That was out of your control."

"I know. But aside from praying, what other advice would you give me so I can try to help my mother?"

Howard took a moment to reply, gazing out the window at the dwindling farmland as they approached Manhattan Island. "My parents raised my brothers and me to believe that God has a purpose for everyone's life. We'll find the most satisfaction in life when we discover it and live it."

"That's what my grandmother keeps telling me."

"It's not a sin to be wealthy, Adelaide. And there's no spiritual advantage to being poor either. God may have a very good reason why you were born wealthy. Your grandmother's life and what she did with her wealth is a wonderful example of that."

"I admire her so much. So many, many people love her. Even our servants adore her and would do anything for her."

"Your wealthy childhood helped make you who you are, Adelaide. I think the key is to ask God what He wants you to do with the legacy you've been given. The answer may not even be something big, like the work your grandmother does. One of the reasons why I decided to stay with the law firm is because I believe God enabled me to become a lawyer for a reason. The important thing isn't what we do, but whether we're willing to obey God when we do it."

"I would like to be willing, but how do I figure out what God is saying?"

"Ah! That's a wrestling match sometimes. I never experienced that struggle until I faced this decision between the law firm and the foundation. But the process of asking and listening and waiting often draws us closer to God. And I think that's what He's really after."

"Waiting is the hardest part."

"I agree. But as you're waiting, perhaps you can think back on all the things you've learned, and the experiences you've had since losing your father. That's when your life was first turned upside down. If you reflect on all those lessons, perhaps you'll find that God has been speaking to you after all."

Adelaide saw the wisdom in his advice. She would take time to reflect on everything, from her embarrassing experiences with Mr. Durand, her trips to the poor areas of New York with her grandmother, her enjoyable evening at Mrs. Rhodes's ball, and now her travels with Howard to search for Mimi Junie's son. She would add to it everything her mother and grandmother had shared about the Stanhope family's past. It was a lot to think about.

As the train slowed and pulled into the station, Addy turned to Howard and asked, "Have you told my grandmother about your decision not to work for the foundation?"

"I did. I told her I thought the director should be someone who understands the inner workings of high society and has earned the respect of the millionaires they'll be asking for support."

"What did my grandmother say? That is, if you don't mind me asking."

"She said she understood. That I was right about finding someone from your social class. She said she has another candidate in mind."

"She does? Any idea who?"

"None whatsoever."

When she arrived home that afternoon, Adelaide was surprised to find two letters waiting for her. The first was from Alfred Rhodes, inviting her to the theater and to dinner next Friday night. The second was from George Weaver with an invitation to attend a party given by one of his associates on Saturday night. She was excited by the first, dismayed by the second. "Do you know where my mother is?" she asked the servant who had given her the letters.

"She and Hattie are upstairs in the attic."

Adelaide went in search of her mother, unable to imagine her in such a dusty, dreary place. Might their finances be sinking so low that the remnants of furniture in the attic would need to be plundered? Mother and the maid were just closing the attic door when Addy got there. "Did you find anything of value?" Addy asked.

"I'm not sure. I'll need to have an appraiser from the auction house look over my findings." She removed the kerchief she had tied over her hair, releasing a mist of dust. "I'm going to need a thorough bath before dinner. When did you get home, Adelaide?"

"A few minutes ago. I wanted to show you these two invitations that came in today's mail." Addy watched as Mother read them. She seemed very pleased when she finished.

"Well. I'm surprised these gentlemen are still in the city, but I'm glad they are. It looks like our efforts have begun to bear fruit. How do you feel about them, Adelaide?"

"I enjoyed Alfred Rhodes's company at the ball. Mr. Weaver is pleasant enough, but I worry that he's a bit too old for me. Should I decline his invitation?"

"That's up to you. But it wouldn't hurt to give Alfred Rhodes the impression that he has competition. Most gentlemen enjoy a little rivalry."

"Very well." She would do anything for Mother's sake. The memory of Ferncliff and all that her mother had lost was still fresh in her mind. She unbuttoned the jacket of her traveling suit as she and Mother made their way downstairs to their bedrooms.

"You look tired, Adelaide, and that's not an attractive look to a potential suitor. I think you've had quite enough of your travels for a while."

"It has been tiring, but it has also been very interesting to visit all those little towns and villages outside the city. And the countryside is so beautiful." She hesitated, wondering if she should tell Mother about visiting Sing Sing and Ferncliff, then decided not to.

"I also got mail today," Mother said. "A letter from Dorinda Rhodes inviting us to stay with her in Newport for two weeks after the Fourth of July. It seems your cousin Cicely is spreading gossip about us, and she needs to be stopped."

"How can we do that?"

"Well, she is much less likely to gossip if we're there to defend ourselves."

Cicely needed to be stopped, it was true. But then Addy thought of Mimi Junie, and how tired she'd seemed these last few weeks. Should they leave her here all alone? It would be horrible if she died alone like Father had last summer. But Mimi would never go to Newport with them, even if she wasn't ill.

"Adelaide?" Mother said when she hadn't replied.

"I'll go if you want to."

"I do. I'll write and tell Dorinda we're coming."

Adelaide felt dispirited as she returned to her room, and couldn't quite decide what was bothering her. Some of it had been the shock of seeing her elegant mother being forced to pick through discarded furniture in the attic to ensure their livelihood. Adelaide would need to do everything she could to help her, even if it meant flirting shamelessly with Alfred, or going out with Mr. Weaver again. Both of those prospects dismayed her, for some reason. So did the thought of returning to Newport and enduring Cicely's gossip. She would much rather stay home and continue her search for Mimi's son. It was much more fascinating. And she truly enjoyed Howard's company and—

Oh, no! That was it! Adelaide had put her finger on the root of her sadness. She wouldn't see Howard for a few weeks. She thought of his smile, the humor in his clear blue eyes, the thrill she felt in having him near her as they crowded into basement storage rooms or rode side by side in carriages or on the train. She had become very fond of Howard Forsythe—and Adelaide knew he could never be part of her life. The differences between them were just too great. Perhaps it was a good thing that she wouldn't be seeing him until later in the month. In fact, perhaps she should tell him to continue the search without her.

That thought caused the most sadness of all.

# 27

JULY 1899

*Adelaide*

Alfred Rhodes was clearly bored. He sat alongside Adelaide in the theater on Friday night and yawned repeatedly throughout the first act. He became so restless that he vaulted from his seat the moment the curtain fell at intermission. "I get the feeling you're not enjoying the play," Adelaide said as they mingled with the crowd in the lobby for drinks.

"I'm sorry it was so obvious," he said, looking sheepish. "It has nothing to do with you, believe me. It's just that this play isn't something I would have chosen myself."

"Then why are we here?"

"These are my mother's tickets. She's in Rhode Island."

Addy understood. Alfred's mother was playing the same game that her mother was. "Let's go someplace else. I don't mind." Addy didn't know what had prompted her to suggest leaving, except that she was tired of pretense and obligation, always doing what was proper and

307

expected of her. She wondered if Alfred was too. Besides, it would be nice to chat with Alfred and get to know him better instead of sitting silently beside him in the theater.

He pulled his watch from his pocket and checked the time. "Our dinner reservations aren't until after the theater, ninety minutes from now."

"There must be something we could do in the meantime—unless you really want to stay and see the end of the play."

"You're right. Let's get out of here." They swam against the tide of people returning to their seats and escaped the theater through an exit door. The humid summer night smelled of hot metal and too many horses. Alfred scanned the busy street for a hired carriage. "Where shall we go?"

"Where do you usually go on a Friday night when your parents don't give you their theater tickets?" she asked. He smiled.

"Brighton Beach Race Course. But it's too late to watch the horses tonight. I also enjoy a good baseball game at the Polo Grounds, especially if the Giants win. But I'm not sure there's a game there tonight."

"Both possibilities sound interesting. I haven't been to either place."

"I'm not surprised. They're hardly on the list of approved places for our social set, are they?"

"That's true." She envied Alfred's freedom. Addy thought of how Mimi Junie had explored the city when she was a young woman—and of her own recent excursions with Howard. A year ago, she never would have dared to contemplate breaking society's rules, but now the restrictions felt too confining. "Where else do you like to go?"

"How about Steeplechase Park at Coney Island? Have you ever been there? Critics call it 'Sodom by the Sea,' but I think it's great fun."

"I've heard of it, of course, but my suitors are much too proper to take me there."

"If you weren't dressed so beautifully—and me in this penguin suit— I would take you there tonight. We could ride on the Ferris wheel and eat hot dogs for dinner."

Addy couldn't even imagine it. "You seem to enjoy very different amusements than most gentlemen of our class."

"True. That's because middle-class amusements are much more amusing than ours." He finally succeeded in hailing a vehicle, and they settled inside.

"Where to?" the driver asked.

"I know the perfect place," Alfred said suddenly. "Have you seen Edison's new moving pictures?"

"No, but I've heard of them."

"Take us to Proctor's Pleasure Palace on Lexington Avenue and 58th Street," he told the driver. It sounded scandalous, but the Pleasure Palace turned out to be a vaudeville theater with Kinetoscope viewers featuring short black-and-white films for a nickel. Adelaide was aware of the many stares they received in their formal attire, but Alfred didn't seem to notice or care. He seemed comfortable rubbing shoulders with ordinary people. The neighborhood was several steps above Five Points and the other areas where Mimi Junie's foundation did their work, but still far from the upper-class streets where she and Alfred lived. Her dainty theater slippers were no match for all the walking they were doing, and she was dismayed to see that the hem of her gown was becoming hopelessly soiled. Yet Addy was enjoying herself.

The films they watched on the Kinetoscope viewers seemed almost magical, capturing scenes of New York City streets and ships sailing into New York Harbor. "You're looking at the future of entertainment," Alfred told her. "I tried to convince my father to invest in new ideas like this, but he's too stuffy and old-fashioned. Just like that stuffy, old-fashioned play we saw tonight."

"Change is very hard for some people," she said. It was a lesson she had only begun to learn since her father died, and one that Alfred probably hadn't experienced yet. Afterward, they sat on a bench and watched the people and the nightlife for a while before taking another carriage to the Waldorf-Astoria Hotel, where Alfred had made dinner reservations. Again, he made it clear that the restaurant choice was his mother's, not his.

"Tell me what you're doing with yourself these days," Addy said, after they'd ordered from the menu. "You must have finished college by now. I assume you're working for your father's company?"

Alfred made a face. "I've never been interested in joining the family business. My father and I had a huge argument about it, and in the end, he agreed to give me a year off. He's hoping I'll change my mind about working for him by then."

"And if you don't change your mind?"

"He'll disinherit me." He gave a casual shrug, but she saw the tension in his face.

Addy took a sip of wine to hide her shock. Yet she shouldn't be surprised after hearing about the Stanhope family's manipulations. Mimi Junie had begged her husband to try to escape his father's control, but the lure of wealth had been too strong. "What are your plans for your year of freedom?" she asked.

Alfred's face lit up the way it had at the Pleasure Palace. "I'm intrigued by wild America. I've done some hunting and fishing and camping out in the wild, and I've loved every minute of it. I'm headed out west with friends next week, and we're not coming back until we've bagged a buffalo, a grizzly bear, an elk, and a moose."

Addy laughed as she pictured him with a rifle, surrounded by piles of dead animals. "I can't imagine living in the wild."

"It'll be an adventure!"

She waited until after the waiter served the soup course and asked, "What would your dream job be if you didn't have to work for your father?"

Again, Alfred seemed lit from within. "I'm fascinated by all the new inventions, like the moving pictures we saw tonight. And automobiles! My father calls them horseless carriages and doesn't think they'll ever catch on. I think he's wrong."

"My father bought one. I never rode in it though. It's been sitting in our carriage house ever since he died. Mother will probably sell it."

"Tell her I'll buy it!"

"Okay, I will." If nothing else came of this evening, perhaps Alfred would add a little cash to their coffers. He continued to talk as they ate their meal, and while she enjoyed his company, it became clear that Alfred wasn't ready to find a wife and settle down to a responsible life. She would never be able to charm him into marrying her in time to save her home. But she'd learned something else tonight. It seemed that the young gentlemen in her social class were as bound by family duty, obligation, and tradition as the young ladies were. Neither had much control over their own choices—which was exactly what Mimi Junie had been trying to tell her. Mimi would applaud Alfred's decisions.

"May I ask you a question?" she said as they ate dessert. "And I want you to promise you'll give me an honest answer."

"Let's hear the question first."

She took a deep breath and plunged in. "You mentioned that the theater tickets belonged to your parents, and that this restaurant was your mother's choice—was it also her idea for you to invite me out tonight? Might your mother have been pressuring you just a bit?"

He gave a wry smile. "She has been very persistent in bringing up your name. But I liked the idea when she suggested it. I enjoyed dancing with you at the ball. And I'm enjoying your company tonight too. It's not every society girl who would leave the theater for a vaudeville palace."

"Thank you for your honesty. I suppose our parents feel it's their duty to try to control our future. They mean well. But I truly hope you'll be able to choose the kind of work you want to do, someday." She sounded like Mimi Junie.

"Thanks. Now, may I ask you a question?"

"That seems only fair."

"It's a very different question from yours, and feel free to tell me to mind my own business if you don't want to answer it."

"I will."

"There are rumors that your branch of the Stanhope family tree has gone bankrupt. That your uncle and cousins have inherited everything."

Addy's skin tingled with sudden heat. She hesitated as she decided how to reply honestly, without revealing her anger and embarrassment. "It's true that my great-uncle Roger and his son inherited full control of the Stanhope businesses. That's to be expected since Mother and I know nothing about business affairs. But it's not true that we're bankrupt. My father left my mother and me our mansion, along with an inheritance for each of us."

"I've heard rumors that you're desperate to marry a wealthy husband in order to keep your mansion and avoid poverty."

Her face and neck grew hotter still. "I've heard those rumors too. My cousin Cicely is responsible for most of them." In that moment, Addy longed for revenge. She wanted to hurt Cicely and her family as much as she had hurt Mother and her. Then she remembered Mother's and Mimi's stories of how the desire for revenge had led to even more misery. Besides, there was truth in Cicely's rumors. Addy was fishing for a wealthy husband in order to keep their home. She was ashamed to hear her motives spelled out so clearly by one of those potential suitors.

"Are the rumors true?" Alfred asked.

Addy searched for an honest reply and remembered what the lawyer had told them after reading Father's will. "Let me assure you that even if I never marry, Mother and I will still be well off." Provided they moved to a smaller, more affordable mansion.

"That's good to know. I would love to see you again when I get back from my travels. I'll take you to the racetrack and to a ball game, if you want to go. We'll ride the Ferris wheel at Coney Island too."

"I would enjoy that."

"You're not like a lot of other rich girls. I think we'd have a great time together."

"I'll look forward to it. You can tell me all about your travels and show me your hunting trophies." But it would never happen. Addy needed to find a husband before then.

She crept into the house without searching for her mother after Alfred brought her home. Mother would be disappointed by how the evening went. At breakfast, Addy decided not to tell her where they had gone after leaving the theater or what they had talked about, saying only that she had enjoyed her evening with him, which was true. And that he'd asked to see her again, which was also true. "But it won't be for a while, I'm afraid. Alfred plans to travel for the next year."

"I don't think his mother is aware of that."

"I like Alfred, but he isn't ready to settle down with a wife." Which left Addy no choice but to pin her hopes on Mr. Weaver Saturday night. She was determined to get to know him better, to look for his good qualities, and to let him get to know her too. As Mother said, there was always room for love to grow, in time.

Mr. Weaver's fine, gentlemanly manners did impress Adelaide. He was handsomely dressed, he arrived in a splendid carriage with a matched team of horses, and he was attentive and interesting as they engaged in conversation. The dinner party, in a beautifully appointed mansion, was in celebration of his business partner's twenty-fifth wedding anniversary. But Addy was the only guest under the age of forty, and she felt awkwardly out of place as she struggled to find areas of common interest with the others. These were Mr. Weaver's closest friends and business associates, people he socialized with on a regular basis, people she would be socializing with if she married him. A few of the couples had children her age. One woman talked about her grandchildren. Addy guessed that none of them had been to Coney Island to ride the Ferris wheel or to a vaudeville show at Proctor's Pleasure Palace. She felt young and naive and hopelessly adrift.

"You didn't enjoy the evening very much. I'm sorry," Mr. Weaver said on the way home.

"No, I apologize. I wasn't at my best tonight. Forgive me if I was a disappointment to you and your friends."

"You didn't disappoint me, Miss Stanhope," he said with a sigh. "I'm disappointed with myself. I've been lonely since Ada died, and I'm afraid my loneliness has made me a fool."

"You're not a fool. You're a kind man and a gentleman. I sincerely hope you find what you're looking for in a companion."

The mansion's grand foyer never seemed as huge and overwhelming as it did after Adelaide closed the door behind Mr. George Weaver for good. She had failed for a second night.

### ◦◦◦ Sylvia ◦◦◦

Addy shared the grim news with Sylvia about her evening with George Weaver at breakfast. It wasn't what Sylvia had hoped to hear, especially after the disappointing outing with Alfred Rhodes the night before.

"What do we do now?" Adelaide asked her.

"Nothing. I'm certain there are other potential suitors out there. We'll simply bide our time until you can be introduced to them. We still own your father's yacht, so I'm thinking of planning a sailing party when we're in Newport next week."

"Can we afford that?"

"You don't need to worry about that." Although Sylvia had no idea where the money would come from. She hated to keep spending her inheritance, so she would have to find another way.

"Cicely is still telling everyone we're bankrupt and that I'm desperate for a husband."

"The rumors will die down. In fact, Cicely may become the subject of rumors herself. I've learned that Junietta's predictions about the fate of the Stanhope Corporation are proving true, now that it's in Uncle Roger's hands. It seems the business world has no confidence in his leadership. Investors are leaving. Deals are falling apart." Sylvia had once wished for the downfall of the Stanhope empire, but now its collapse threatened to topple her world, as well. Adelaide looked so frightened by the news that Sylvia hurried to reassure her. "Listen, let's forget all about that for now. We're going to have a lovely time with Dorinda and Felicity in Newport next week."

In years past, Sylvia had enjoyed her time away from the city each summer. Being near the shore soothed her, and she'd always felt a lightness in the air along with the salty breezes. But not this year. The moment she stepped off the train, all the shock and grief from the summer before came rushing back, and she knew it had been a mistake to come. A.B.'s absence was everywhere, leaving a void that could never be filled. She decided not to plan a sailing party after all, unable to set foot on the boat he had so loved. But for her daughter's sake, Sylvia kept her grief and pain hidden, participating in social events with her usual cool detachment, hiding her tears in the darkness of night.

The Rhodeses' summer party was magnificent in every way—the sumptuous food, the finest wine, and a lively band that had guests shedding their shoes to dance on the soft grass beneath the fairy lights. Everyone important was there and seemingly having the time of their lives, including Adelaide. Sylvia had learned the names of a few more potential suitors for her, and Mrs. Rhodes had arranged the introductions. Sylvia watched her daughter dance with one partner after another and was happy for her.

Sometime after midnight, a nearly full moon rose above the water, its reflection shimmering on the gentle waves. Sylvia walked down to the shore alone and found herself imagining how she would paint the scene, which colors she would use, how she would capture the water's movement. She wondered how long it had been since she'd held a brush in her hand and faced the exquisite promise of a blank canvas. She turned around to look back at the party and was stunned to realize that the excitement of it no longer drew her. Something inside Sylvia had changed this past year. She had changed, and she no longer found enjoyment in the high-society life she had always led. It seemed phony to her, the glittering jewels gaudy, her friends not really friends in the deeply devoted way her brothers had been. Was it the memory of Junietta's words about finding purpose and meaning that suddenly made this life feel hollow?

Sylvia's life hadn't been meaningless as she'd supported her husband and raised their daughters all these years. Wealth and privilege had come with that purpose and had been the setting for it. Now her husband was gone, her daughters grown, and Junietta was right—Sylvia's life was changing. What would it look like to truly start all over again? And if Sylvia was just now seeing the emptiness in it all, why did she want this life for her daughter? Yet, what else was there for Adelaide? Or for her?

At the end of the week, Sylvia returned to the stifling city and to a pile of bills that needed to be paid. She felt the weight of them on her shoulders all over again. For the first time in her life, she felt lost in the enormity of her own mansion, burdened by it. Even if Adelaide married and filled it with children, it would still seem monstrous.

Faithful Mr. Forsythe returned to help Sylvia sort through the invoices. As he was leaving later that morning, he said, "Now that you're back, would you please let Miss Stanhope know that I'm willing to continue our search for Mrs. Stanhope's son? That is, if she still wants to."

The chances of finding one man among a million seemed hopeless to Sylvia. Yet it offered Adelaide an escape from her worries about the future, and gave her something to do until the summer season ended and the next season began. And it would mean a lot to Junietta if they found him. Sylvia pushed the bills aside and straightened her sagging shoulders. "Yes, of course. I think it's a lovely idea. I'll have one of the servants find Adelaide, and you can tell her yourself."

She walked with Mr. Forsythe to the front door, and when Adelaide joined them, Sylvia saw their excitement as they made plans. Afterward, she and Adelaide were having coffee in the morning room when a servant handed Sylvia an envelope. "This letter came for you, ma'am."

It was on heavy card stock, an invitation, not another bill, thankfully. She opened it and read it—and didn't know what to feel.

"Who's it from, Mother? Not bad news, I hope."

"Mr. Barrow has invited me to dinner."

"Oh!" Adelaide seemed as surprised as Sylvia was. "He seems like a nice man."

"He is. It's just that . . ." Her hands fell to her lap, still holding the letter. "Your father was larger than life. Handsome, confident, brilliant. He could command a room with his engaging presence. A.B. was a powerful man and he knew it, yet he didn't take advantage of it. He was never a tyrant. I suspect that was largely due to his mother's influence, and I've always loved Junietta for that."

"You and Father made a beautiful couple. I remember him best in his evening suit and white tie, standing in the foyer beside you in your gown and jewels. I always felt so proud that you were my parents."

"There will never be another A.B. Stanhope. I would hope Mr. Barrow could understand that. And yet—" She sighed and blinked back a tear. "And yet I enjoyed Mr. Barrow's company very much at your grandmother's dinner party." He understood Sylvia's grief and loneliness. It would be nice to have a friend and an arm to lean on.

"Are you going to accept?"

"I believe I will."

Adelaide rose from her seat and hugged her.

# 28

~~~

~~~ *Adelaide* ~~~

The train station was packed with people as Adelaide waited for Mr. Forsythe, but somehow the two women passing out newspapers stood out from all the others. She had been led to believe that suffragettes were strident and boorish, but these young women weren't. Addy walked closer to where a small crowd had gathered and listened to their speeches.

"Yes, women are different from men," one of them was saying. "We are softer and more caring, and we are concerned with the needs of our families and our homes. So, why aren't our opinions and experiences taken into account by lawmakers? Wouldn't they be wise to listen to our concerns as we work for a better society? All we're asking for is a voice in shaping our beloved country."

Adelaide took the offered newspaper, a different edition than the ones she'd read before, and went in search of Howard. She had no trouble spotting him as he waited for her beside the ticket counter. Most of the other men in the train station trudged forward grimly, wearing preoccupied expressions, but Howard seemed enthusiastic and hopeful, as if ready to embark on a grand adventure. She hurried toward him, her heart racing, feeling suddenly breathless as if she was sprinting, not walking. She willed her body to calm down as she greeted him. "Good morning, Howard. Where shall we begin?"

"I think we need to expand the radius of the search area again. I thought we could start further south in the village of Hastings-on-Hudson."

He purchased their tickets, then took her arm as they boarded the train together. Addy was ridiculously happy to be with him again as they sat side by side in the jostling, rattling railcar. He was a good and trusted friend, she told herself. Nothing more.

"Do you think we'll need to cross the river and search the west side of the Hudson?"

"Perhaps, but not yet. I don't know much about newborn babies, but I'm guessing they shouldn't travel very far in such a fragile state."

They made the rounds of churches in Hastings-on-Hudson as they had in the other villages, paging through fifty-year-old records stored in church closets and basements. Addy was better at reading the old-fashioned script than Howard, so he peered over her shoulder as she opened yet another record book in yet another church. She traced her finger down the column of entries for the year 1850, reading aloud: "'Andrew Matthew Browne, born July 15, 1850—'" She froze. It was the birthday they'd been searching for!

"Howard, look! It's a baby boy born on July 15! 'Baptized on July 30, 1850 by parents Charles and Gertrude Browne'! This could be him!"

He crowded closer, his hand on her shoulder. "I see it," he breathed, "but I can hardly believe it!" They both laughed, and as she turned to gaze up at him, her heart pounded wildly against her ribs. She had the urge to hug him. "I guess we shouldn't celebrate yet," he said. But he was grinning as if they had found a pot of gold.

"I'm feeling lucky today," Addy said. "Let's go talk to the pastor." He had invited them to come back to his study if they had any more questions, so they hurried upstairs from the basement.

"We've found an entry that seems promising," Howard told him. "Do you know a gentleman by the name of Andrew Matthew Browne, by any chance? Or his parents, Charles and Gertrude Browne?"

"Everyone in town knows the Brownes. Their family has owned the quarry since the late 1700s. They employ a lot of people in this area. Mr. Browne supports this church and is well known for his philanthropy."

Addy and Howard looked at each other. "That sounds like Mimi's son," she said with a smile.

"Can you tell us where we might find him?" Howard asked.

"This time of day, he's probably at work. Any local driver will know where the quarry office is."

Addy fidgeted with excitement as the driver took them there. Without thinking, she gripped Howard's hand tightly. "I'm afraid to get my hopes up, but I can't help it!"

"I know. I feel the same way." They halted beside a prosperous-looking quarry and stone-cutting business with offices in a stately stone building. Howard introduced himself to the clerk in the main office. "We would like to speak with Mr. Andrew Browne, if that's possible. We're searching for a lost relative and hoping he can help us." The clerk disappeared and returned a few minutes later to lead them down a corridor to a spacious office. A row of windows faced the river with loading docks visible in the distance. A jolly-looking man with his tie loosened and shirtsleeves rolled up came around from behind his desk to greet them.

"I'm Andrew Browne. How can I help you?" Addy's breath caught when she saw him. His thick hair was the color of mahogany, just as Mimi had described Neal's hair.

"I'm Howard Forsythe, and this is my client Miss Stanhope."

"Stanhope! Any relation to the millionaire Stanhopes?" he asked with a grin.

"Yes, in fact, I am."

"Really? I was just joking!" He laughed. "I had no idea—I didn't mean to—"

"That's all right. No harm done." Addy already liked this friendly, jovial man.

"Our company has done business with the Stanhopes. On construction projects, you see. But that's not why you've come to see me, is it? Please, sit down." Addy perched on the edge of her chair, too excited to sit comfortably. Howard seemed equally excited.

"Before we go into a long explanation that may prove to be a waste of your time," he said, "can we ask one rather personal question? If you'd rather not answer it, we'll be on our way."

"Fair enough. What's your question?"

"Do you know if you were adopted by your parents as an infant?" Addy held her breath, hoping.

"As a matter of fact, I was. My parents were unable to have children of their own, but they wanted a family, so they adopted me."

"Do you know where you were born, by any chance?" Howard asked.

"Odd you should ask. I was going through some papers and deeds after my parents died, and I found a legal document making me their rightful heir. The paper said I was born in Tarrytown to unknown parents."

Without thinking, Addy turned to Howard in the chair beside hers and hugged him tightly. Tears filled her eyes. "It's a miracle!" she murmured. Then she caught herself and pulled away.

Mr. Browne chuckled after they'd separated again. "Well! That was quite a reaction. I'm guessing you have a story to tell."

"We do," Howard said. He sounded breathless. "We believe we know who your birth parents were. We would be happy to share their story with you, if you're interested."

He looked taken aback. "Well, now. I would be very interested. To tell you the truth, I never thought much about my real parents. My mother and father were both over forty when they adopted me, and they doted on me so much that it was natural to think of them as my true parents. They're both gone now, I'm sorry to say, or they might be able to tell us more."

Addy could barely contain her excitement. "I understand. And I'm glad to hear you've had a happy life. But we believe you're the man we've been searching for. The woman who gave birth to you is my grandmother. She has thought about you every day of her life and still celebrates your birthday on July 15 every year."

"Fascinating!"

"She didn't want to give you away, but you were taken against her will. I hope you won't be too shocked or offended to hear this, but she was only eighteen years old and wasn't married to your father. He died tragically before you were born."

"Oh, my!"

"I'm also related to you, Mr. Browne," Howard said. "You and my mother are first cousins. Your father and her father were brothers—Neal and Gavin Galloway. They died in the same shipwreck off the tip of South America on the way to the California gold fields."

"What an intriguing story."

"My grandmother has had a good life, a very successful life, married to Arthur Stanhope the second," Addy said. "She doesn't know we've been searching for you, but I know it would mean the world to her to finally see you again. She would be thrilled to know that you've had a good life. That you've been happy."

"Indeed, I have. My wife Fiona and I have been married for nearly twenty-six years. We have two sons and two daughters. Maybe you noticed the sign out front, Browne and Sons? My grandfather started this business, and now my children will have the opportunity to work with me, if they choose."

"Would you like to meet your mother?" Addy asked.

"It would be a great honor to meet her."

They talked for another hour, and Addy couldn't help embracing her newfound uncle before leaving. They arranged for Mr. Browne to come to New York to meet Mimi Junie after they had a chance to tell her the news. Addy couldn't stop smiling all the way home. "We did it, Howard! We really, truly found Mimi's lost son!"

"To tell you the truth, I had begun to doubt that my crazy idea would work."

"It was a brilliant idea. And it worked splendidly." They laughed and talked all the way to the door of Addy's mansion. "Let's go inside right now and tell her and Mother. Come with me, Howard. Please!"

### ~ Junietta ~

Someone gently shook Junietta's shoulder, waking her from a nap in her chair. She opened her eyes, disoriented for a moment. "What is it, Hattie?"

"I'm sorry to disturb you, but Miss Adelaide, Mr. Forsythe, and Mrs. Stanhope are asking to see you."

"All of them? That's quite a delegation!" She yawned and lowered her swollen feet from the hassock.

"Shall I bring them in here?"

"Tell them I'll join them in the library." Junietta's bedroom was too small, and besides, she didn't want them to see that it had become a sickroom. She smoothed her hair, mussed from sleeping, and after Hattie helped her to her feet, she made her way to the library, leaning on her cane. The others were waiting for her, seated around a library table, looking lost in the vastness of the space. Junietta had always thought that this room, with its carved friezes of mythological figures and towering shelves full of books, belonged in a public building, not a private home.

"Goodness! What special occasion has called for this sudden and unexpected gathering?" she asked as she lowered herself into a chair at the table.

"Mimi Junie—" Adelaide started to tell her something, but then her throat clogged with emotion and her eyes filled with tears.

"What's wrong?" Junietta asked, her heart leaping. "Has something happened?"

Howard took her hand in his. "Something wonderful, Mrs. Stanhope. Adelaide and I have found your son. Neal Galloway's son."

The world suddenly seemed to stop, and her heart along with it. Her son. *Neal's son.* Could it really be true? She decided she must still be dreaming, yet Howard's strong hand, holding hers, felt very real. She tried to draw a deep breath but couldn't. "You . . . *what?* M-my son?"

"Yes. Howard and I found him, Mimi."

Her cane clattered to the floor as her body went weak all over. She might have fainted if she hadn't been seated. Sylvia ordered the maid to bring a glass of water, and Junietta took a sip. Hattie should have poured it over Junietta's head to help convince her she was truly awake.

"Is it really true?" she breathed. "You've really found my boy?"

"Yes, Mimi. It's true." Tears filled Junietta's eyes as Addy leaped up, then bent to hug her tightly, rocking her in her arms.

"It was Adelaide's—Miss Stanhope's—idea to search for him," Howard said. "As a surprise for you. We've been searching together these past few weeks, and today we found him."

"I certainly am surprised!" she said as Addy released her again. "I-I . . . I don't know what to say!" Addy picked up the cane and handed it to Junietta before settling in her chair again. Faces blurred and tears flowed silently down Junietta's face as she caressed the carved handle.

"His name is Andrew Browne, Mimi, and he's a wonderful man. He's looking forward to meeting you very soon."

"I'm finally going to see him again?" She remembered her tiny, red-faced son with hair the same color as Neal's, and shook her head in wonder.

"He wants to visit you when you're ready, but we thought we should prepare you first, rather than shock you."

"It is a shock—but a wonderful one! How on earth did you find him?"

"It was Howard's idea to search baptismal records in churches around Tarrytown, looking for a baby boy born on July 15, 1850. We combed through dozens of records in several villages, and it worked! We found him today in the village of Hastings-on-Hudson. Mr. Browne confirmed that he was born in Tarrytown and that his parents adopted him as an infant."

Junietta wiped her cheeks. She was beginning to believe it was really true, and joy filled every inch of her. She would see her son again. Hold him in her arms again. "Oh, my dears! How can I ever thank you? It's . . . it's a dream come true."

"We liked Mr. Browne right away, Mimi. He's such a nice man, so friendly and kind. His family has operated a quarry for several generations and are very well respected. His is a fine family name."

"And he's had a happy life?"

"Yes, Mimi. He'll tell you all about it when you meet him."

Addy and Howard took turns talking for several more minutes as they told Junietta their story, including something about a false alarm with a farmer and his honking geese. She couldn't concentrate on what they were saying, barely able to grasp the wonderful news that her lost son, Neal's son, had been found. She would be able to hold a little piece of Neal in her arms again.

"I should go," Howard finally said. He took Junietta's hand again and squeezed it. "It has been a joy to see you so happy, Mrs. Stanhope."

"You must come for dinner when I meet my son," Mimi said. "I'd like you to celebrate with us since you helped Addy find him."

"Thank you. It would be an honor."

He gazed around the room as if searching for the way out. Addy stood and said, "I'll help you find your way through the maze."

### ～ Adelaide ～

Addy's heart raced as she escorted Howard through the first-floor rooms to the front door. "'Thank you' hardly seems adequate," she told him as she said goodbye.

"There's no need to thank me. It has truly been a pleasure. In fact, it's been one of the most satisfying experiences of my life. Especially after everything your grandmother has done for me."

There was an awkward pause, and Addy recalled how she'd spontaneously embraced him in Mr. Browne's office. He had held her tightly in
return, his warm arms surrounding her, his spicy cologne tickling her
nose. She battled the urge to embrace him again, aware of how inappropriate it would be. She cleared her throat. "Well then, I guess I'll see
you again when Mr. Browne comes to visit."

"Do you think . . . ? I mean, will this be a formal affair? Should I
wear an evening suit and tie?"

"Heavens, no. That isn't my grandmother's style at all."

"Of course. Thanks." He started to leave, then turned back. "You
know, I've received quite an education in the ways of high society this
past year since I've been handling your family's legal affairs. I think
I can honestly say I've never envied the social elite—people like the
Vanderbilts and Astors and Carnegies. And Stanhopes. I never thought
much about money at all, or wished I had more of it, until—" He looked
down at the floor, shaking his head. "Never mind. Good day, Adelaide."

"Wait," she said, snagging his sleeve. "What made you change your
mind?"

"It's . . . nothing. I opened my mouth when I shouldn't have."

"Please tell me. Is it because you've seen all of this?" She spread her
arms to encompass the vast foyer.

"No. This isn't my idea of a home where I'd want to raise a family."

"Then why are you wishing for money all of a sudden?"

He had been gazing at the floor, but he finally looked up at her.
"Because if I had money, there might be a chance that we could become
more than friends." She was momentarily speechless. "I'm sorry. Now
I've embarrassed both of us. Goodbye, Adelaide."

She stared at the door after it closed behind him, tears unexpectedly
blurring her vision. "I wish there was a chance for us too," she murmured, then wished she had said those words aloud to him.

She gazed up at the marble staircase, and for a crazy moment, she
found herself wondering what it would be like to straddle the banister and fly down the curving rail. But no. She was a wealthy heiress,

wearing an expensive tailored skirt and imported lace petticoats. Young gentlemen like Alfred Rhodes might be able to defy convention, and hunt buffalo out west or ride the Ferris wheel at Coney Island, but young ladies like her certainly couldn't.

Howard's words echoed in her mind. *"If I had money, there might be a chance that we could become more than friends."* His declaration should have pleased her, but it made her ashamed. Ashamed that money and social status mattered to her and to her family more than character. Ashamed that she had held back her feelings for him all these weeks, forcing Howard from her mind because of money. If he had been wealthy and they had met at a society event, Addy knew she would be dreaming of him every night, longing for him to lead her out onto a balcony at someone's ball and kiss her beneath the stars.

But their relationship could never work. They came from different families and backgrounds. He was uncomfortable in her house, and she wasn't entirely at home in his. Addy had a duty to help Mother keep their mansion and way of life. She was a Stanhope. Howard Forsythe was her family's lawyer. He could never be anything more.

# 29

SEPTEMBER 1899

*Sylvia*

The charcoal felt good in Sylvia's hand as she added a few finishing touches to the new gown she'd designed. She held up the sketch pad, appraising it, and felt girlishly pleased with her work. The gown was simple yet elegant with pin tucks down the bodice, a wide, pleated sash, and a paneled skirt. It had just the right amount of lace trim on the circular sleeves, the bodice, and the hem to be stylish, yet not gaudy. Sylvia hadn't felt happy for a very long time, but today it was as if a heavy blanket had been yanked down from the windows to allow the sunshine inside again. She sent the maid to ask Adelaide to join her in her bedroom suite so she could show the design to her.

"I haven't shown this to my dressmaker yet," she said, handing Adelaide the sketch pad. "She's coming in a few minutes, but I would love your opinion."

"It's beautiful! If you decide not to have it made for yourself, can you make it for me?"

Sylvia smiled. "I debated whether it was worth the expense of a new gown for my evening with Mr. Barrow, but when I looked at my fall wardrobe, everything was either dreary black or out-of-date. I think it's time to shift out of mourning, but I don't want something too colorful or flamboyant. I've asked our dressmaker to bring some fabric samples in a deep berry color instead." Again, she felt girlishly pleased at the thought of spending a quiet evening with a kind, understanding man.

"You deserve something new for your first evening out. And this beautiful gown will convince the gossipmongers that we aren't bankrupt after all."

The dressmaker raved when Sylvia showed her the sketch. "Another ravishing gown! I don't know who your mysterious designer is, Mrs. Stanhope, but he could make a fortune in this city. I hung the sketches of his first two designs in my shop, and I've been offered bribes to reveal his identity. He would be in great demand and could fetch Paris prices— that is, unless you want to keep him a secret."

Sylvia hid a smile. "I'll give it some thought." Sketching the gown had provided her with a few hours of enjoyment and relief from worry. Even if she could afford a Paris designer again, she wasn't sure she'd want to give up designing her own gowns. "Now, let's see the samples you've brought," she told her dressmaker. They decided on a rich, wine-colored satin with matching lace, and the dressmaker left with the sketch.

"What a nice compliment she paid you," Adelaide said after she'd left. "Your fashion taste is the best in the city, so if designing gowns is something you enjoy, why not be compensated for it? You could always create them anonymously."

"I don't imagine it would remain a secret for very long, the way gossip spreads in this city."

"But you should be proud to be recognized. Did you notice that she assumed you were a man?"

"Yes, I did notice. I'll think about it." She gave a casual shrug. "Now, let's find your grandmother. There's something we all need to discuss."

Adelaide went to fetch Junietta, who had seemed stronger since hearing the news about her son. Sylvia was relieved that she was getting out of bed and joining her and Adelaide for meals again. Junietta had been a constant in Sylvia's life ever since she'd married into this family, a strong yet silent support like the sturdy beams beneath the elegant walls of this mansion. Junietta had never interfered in Sylvia's life when A.B. was alive, yet ever since he'd died, she had been making her opinions well known, especially to Adelaide. It frustrated Sylvia, yet she couldn't imagine her life without Junietta Stanhope.

They gathered in what had always been called the art gallery. The oversized, rectangular room had velvet-covered benches to sit and view the dozens of paintings lining the walls. Sylvia sometimes served hors d'oeuvres and cocktails here, but otherwise, her family had never spent time contemplating the artwork. The elegant gallery was beautiful but seemed to serve no practical purpose. It seemed like a metaphor for her life without A.B.

Junietta's cane thumped on the parquet floor as she limped into the room on Adelaide's arm. "I've always said that the paneling and cornices and painted ceiling in this gallery should have been much simpler," she said, gazing around. "They distract from the beauty of the artwork. I'm sure it was all Arthur Stanhope's idea. He liked things gaudy and ostentatious."

"I hardly ever come in here," Adelaide said. "It seems more like an art museum than a home."

"Well, it's the artwork that I want us to consider. I'm thinking of selling some of these paintings." Sylvia knew it had to be done, but it was painful to part with such magnificent pieces. "They belong to you and me, Junietta, and are part of Adelaide's inheritance, so the three of us should be in agreement before deciding to sell any of them. I asked an art appraiser to look them over last week, and I decided that these three will fetch enough money for us to live here for at least another year. It would buy us some time so Adelaide won't feel pressured to make any hasty decisions about her future."

"Wonderful!" Junietta whacked one of the velvet benches with her cane, raising a small puff of dust. "I vote to sell them all."

"I would be very grateful for a little more time, Mother. And you won't have to worry about finances all the time."

Junietta gave the bench another dusty thump. "Arthur Benton Stanhope controlled our lives when he was alive, and he's still doing it from his grave. He blackmailed me into marrying Art—although I will say that my own foolish mistakes made me vulnerable to his schemes. Then he took control of your future, Sylvia, by bankrupting your father and forcing your family to move to Ferncliff—but again, your parents made the choice to drink to excess and to withdraw from life. Arthur's cruelty and greed fueled your desire for revenge and your decision to marry A.B. And while I'm grateful for three beautiful granddaughters, I've often wondered what your life might have been like if you'd pursued your artistic talent instead."

Sylvia didn't dare to wonder about that.

"I was furious to learn," Junietta continued, "that Arthur Stanhope is still controlling the three of us through the terms of his will. He saddled us with his enormous house and left no provision to pay for it, meaning that he's controlling Adelaide's future and the choices she's forced to make." She whacked the bench a third time. "So! I'm glad we're all in agreement that it has to stop. Let's let the good Lord guide our futures from now on, not Arthur Stanhope."

"If that's decided," Sylvia said with a sigh, "I'll let the appraiser know he can take these three paintings to auction." She started to move toward the door, unwilling to dwell on the loss of such beautiful paintings, but Junietta's cane stopped her.

"Wait a moment. As long as the three of us are here, let's sit awhile and enjoy the paintings, one last time. I hardly ever come to this gallery." She limped over to a bench and sat down, patting the seat to invite Adelaide to sit beside her.

Sylvia hesitated, then joined them. "Oh, why not. Unless you're about to reveal more dark family secrets. I'm not sure I want to hear any more of those."

Junietta laughed. "No, you've heard all my secrets."

Sylvia hadn't planned to tell them what else she had decided, but why keep it a secret? "While we're on the subject, I'm also selling Willard Eastman's painting, and the Thomas Cole that's in the dining room."

"But you love the Thomas Cole," Addy protested. "And Mr. Eastman's painting—"

"Will bring a nice, tidy sum, according to the appraiser, that I can spend as I please. As for the Thomas Cole, the new Metropolitan Museum of Art would like to add it to their growing collection of American works. I'm pleased to think that it will be enjoyed by thousands of people."

"That's very generous of you, Sylvia. The paintings will start new lives, just like the three of us. I'll have my long-lost son again, Addy can enjoy the company of young gentlemen without feeling pressured, and you can stop counting pennies for a while."

"What gave you the idea to sell the paintings, Mother?"

Sylvia looked at the floor for a moment, remembering. "A few months ago, when I was going over the household expenses with Mr. Forsythe, I asked his advice for new sources of funds, and he suggested that I pray and ask God for advice. It sounded so . . . religious. And a bit ridiculous. That's when I realized I wasn't on very good speaking terms with the Almighty. I think I'm still angry with Him for taking my brothers at such a young age, and now my husband. But I did pray. I can't say that anything mysterious or miraculous happened, but the idea came to me late one night that I should sell some of our paintings."

"Excellent!" Mimi said. "Mr. Forsythe has a lot of wisdom for such a young man."

"He told me that he won't be accepting the directorship of your foundation," Sylvia said. "You must be disappointed. I hope you can find another candidate."

"I already have someone in mind."

"Oh? Who?" When Junietta didn't answer right away, Sylvia took her gaze from the paintings and turned to her. Junietta was beaming.

"*You*, Sylvia."

"Me?" she said with a little laugh.

"Yes, you. You're the perfect person to run the Stanhope Foundation."

"I don't know anything about running a charity."

"Neither did I when I founded it. But I've watched you handle the household finances this past year, so I know you can easily do that part of it. You can add your own personality to the foundation in the brand-new century and make it yours. You are a Stanhope, after all, so who better to lead it?"

Sylvia couldn't speak. Take over her mother-in-law's charity? The idea was absurd!

"I urge you to consider it, Sylvia. The position will allow you to keep your high social standing, even though A.B. is gone, and will raise you up as a leader among the other women. You can use your social connections and your considerable talents as a hostess for a very worthy cause, earning respect for who you are and what you do rather than for how much money you have. Yes, you are the perfect person for the position."

"I think Mimi's right, Mother."

Sylvia still couldn't speak. She still thought the idea was absurd, and yet . . . and yet. Her heart was whispering that it wasn't so absurd after all. The Stanhope will may have left Sylvia with nothing, but Junietta's lifework was a far more enduring legacy. And Sylvia was deeply moved that she would entrust it to her.

"Take some time to think it through, Sylvia, and make sure it's something you would love to do and have a passion for. Whatever you do, don't accept the position because you feel pressured to."

"I don't know what to say." She gave a little laugh. "This is the second job offer I've had today."

"What was the first?"

"Our seamstress thinks Mother can easily sell her dress designs. So do I."

334 | ALL MY SECRETS

"I don't doubt it. You have talent and style, Sylvia."

"Thank you. It seems the two of you have more confidence in me than I do in myself."

"The directorship is a salaried position, you know. You'll be well compensated for your time and efforts. So there you are, Sylvia. Plenty of new possibilities."

Sylvia gazed into the distance for a moment, the room shimmering through her tears. "I think A.B. would be pleased if I took over for you. He loved your foundation."

"He did."

"I'll give it some thought. It's . . . it's a lot to consider. And it would bring change—something I've never embraced very well."

"Well, it's time we all learned to embrace it."

<hr />

Sylvia was still considering Junietta's proposal a week later as the maid helped her into her new gown. The seamstresses had done a beautiful job, but Sylvia was already having second thoughts about her evening with Timothy Barrow. He would be arriving soon to take her to dinner, and she felt vaguely guilty each time she glanced at the photograph of A.B. on her dressing table or walked past the door to his adjoining bedroom. She told herself she was being foolish to feel that way. Her husband had been gone for more than a year. Timothy was a kind friend she had enjoyed talking with, nothing more. It helped that he was so different physically from A.B., tall and lean, where A.B. had been sturdy and robust; fair-haired with a trim goatee, where A.B. had been dark-haired and clean-shaven. Her husband had looked every inch the prosperous tycoon, while Timothy seemed more suited to quiet study in a library. Even so, if there had been a tactful way to bow out of the dinner, she would have taken it.

She made her way downstairs to wait for Timothy in the foyer and met Junietta's doctor, who was just leaving. The man seemed to come and go discreetly, and Sylvia had never taken the time to speak with him.

"Excuse me, Doctor, I'm Sylvia Stanhope, Junietta's daughter-in-law. Can you tell me how she's doing?"

"About the same as the last time I visited." He seemed reluctant to meet her gaze, and that worried her.

"Listen, whenever I ask Junietta how she is, she tells me she's fine, and she pretends that nothing is wrong, But I can see that she's growing weaker, and I hear her struggling to breathe at times. I'm worried about her—and I don't think you would be visiting her so regularly if everything was fine. Please, tell me the truth about her condition."

He gave a little nod and finally met Sylvia's gaze. "Her heart is failing. I've treated this condition before, and, sadly, there's not much that medical science can do except try to keep her comfortable."

"We can afford specialists."

"I know. And I have heard of a few experimental treatments being done, but she doesn't want to try any of them. She knows she's dying, Mrs. Stanhope. Yet I get the feeling she isn't afraid."

Junietta dying? Unthinkable. Tears burned in Sylvia's eyes. "What can I do?"

"She has made it very clear that she doesn't want everyone fussing over her."

"Thank you, Doctor."

Helpless. Once again, Sylvia was helpless. She was still battling tears a few minutes later when Timothy Barrow arrived, but she put on a smile as she greeted him and went out with him to his waiting carriage. She tried to make light conversation, but grief choked her throat.

"Is everything all right?" Timothy asked after a moment. "You're not regretting our evening out, I hope?"

"Not at all. I'm sorry, but I just received some upsetting news."

"Shall we go another time?"

Sylvia had spoken with him so freely at Junietta's dinner and decided she could use a friend. "I would still like to go. But may I speak with you about something in confidence?"

"Certainly."

"Junietta isn't well. In fact, she's dying." Tears filled Sylvia's eyes again.

"I'm so sorry to hear that."

"She is retiring as director of the foundation because of it, and she has asked me to take her place. I haven't given her my answer yet."

"Hers will be huge shoes to fill, but I hope you accept, Sylvia. You're the only woman I know who commands the same respect and admiration that she does. I think you would do an excellent job."

"I don't know anything about running a charitable foundation."

"I'll be happy to help any way I can. I'm on the board now, thanks to you."

"There have been so many changes in my life this past year, I'm not sure I'm ready for another one. Losing A.B. and now Junietta . . ." She couldn't finish.

Timothy knocked on the side of the carriage to get the driver's attention. "I think dinner can wait for a bit," he said as the vehicle slowed to a stop. "I'll tell the driver to take us the long way around, through the park. Do you mind?"

"Thank you for understanding." The dark coziness of the carriage was comforting. She would feel exposed, even in a dimly lit restaurant, until she could get her emotions under control. And Sylvia hated being out of control.

"I understand a little of what you're going through after losing your husband. And now with your mother-in-law's illness, you're facing another loss. I can share what I learned during my own journey of grief, if you'd like."

Sylvia nodded, still not trusting herself to speak.

"I've never been a very demonstrative person—men in our social class aren't allowed to be. I'm accustomed to power and being in control, and when Nancy became ill and died, I was powerless. For about a year, I silently raged at my helplessness and at all the upheaval in my life. Death brings the end of so many dreams that we have for ourselves and for our loved ones."

Sylvia thought of Adelaide, and of the dreams she'd had for her youngest daughter. They'd died along with A.B.

"I'll be honest, I took my wife for granted, thinking she would always be there, that nothing would ever change. But it did change. She was gone. And after my anger finally died away, I suffered guilt and sorrow and grief. But I had a business to run, two sons to pass the business to someday. I soon learned that the best way for me to deal with what I had lost, was to stop fighting against change and make the best possible decisions moving forward. I know it's a cliché, but life does go on." He paused for a moment, as if collecting himself. "Listen, Sylvia, Junietta Stanhope is a very wise and perceptive woman. If she believes you're the right person to run the foundation, then you can be certain that she's right."

"Change is never easy, is it?" she murmured.

"No. But it's the only certainty in life. And I think you may find that the challenge of doing something new will help you move forward."

They rode in comfortable silence for a while, as if Timothy was giving her time to think about everything he had said. Sylvia appreciated it. They eventually arrived at the restaurant, a small yet beautifully decorated place around the corner from the wildly popular Waldorf. They stopped to greet several people they knew as the maître d' escorted them to their table. "I suppose people are going to gossip now that they've seen us together," she said.

"I don't care, Sylvia. Do you?"

"No," she replied, and was surprised to discover that it was true.

They talked of many different things over dinner, comfortable with each other, as they had been at Junietta's dinner. Sylvia even found herself laughing with him. As the meal came to an end, Timothy reached across the table and covered her hand with his. "Another thing I've learned. We don't need to feel disloyal for being happy again. There will be many times when the wound we thought had healed opens up all over again, and we grieve. We honor the person we loved when we're sad, but we honor them just as much when we're happy."

Light spilled from only a few windows in Sylvia's mansion when they arrived, and the enormous building loomed in the darkness like a great black hole. The gaslights in the portico had been left unlit to save money. Sylvia shivered at the unwelcoming sight. "The house looks so huge and empty tonight," she said as Timothy escorted her to the door.

"It must be a lot to manage."

She wouldn't tell him—couldn't tell him—how much of a burden her mansion had become. "It holds so many memories."

"If I may, Sylvia—the memories don't live in the house. They're in your heart. You'll carry them with you no matter where you live."

They entered the foyer, and for the first time in her life, Sylvia understood Junietta's assessment of the ridiculous space with its hulking pillars and icy statues. Junietta had never liked this mansion and seemed content to spend her last days in a tiny former smoking room off the library rather than upstairs in a spacious, lushly decorated suite.

"This does seem too much for three people," Sylvia murmured. She didn't think Timothy heard her, but he had.

"If you decide to sell it, I know of a more manageable place—the Cyrus Monroe mansion. He died a year ago, and none of his heirs want it. They think it's too small. It's a very beautiful home, not too far from here."

Sylvia's maid left her alone in her bedroom after helping her into her dressing gown, brushing her hair, and hanging her dress in the wardrobe. The girl had turned down the covers, but Sylvia didn't climb into bed, knowing she wouldn't sleep. Timothy Barrow's words had left an ache inside her. *"Death brings the end of so many dreams that we have for ourselves and for our loved ones."*

It was her dream for Adelaide to have this mansion and the wealthy, privileged life that Sylvia herself had enjoyed. She wondered if it was Adelaide's dream. She'd been a dutiful daughter, following the script Sylvia had written for her as she'd entertained potential suitors. Yet during all these months, Sylvia had never seen Adelaide as vibrant and alive as she'd been the afternoon that she and Howard Forsythe had shared the news of finding Junietta's son. At the time, Sylvia had thought it was because they'd solved the mystery. But thinking back, she also remembered the way they had looked at each other, the warm intimacy they'd shared, and the almost magnetic power that pulsed between them. Junietta had been insisting that Adelaide should be free to marry for love. As Sylvia stood alone in the chilly room, she knew she was right.

She walked across the room to the door into A.B.'s room and turned the knob. It was cold in her hand. This time, she opened it and walked inside. Everything was pristine, the bed linens perfect, the surfaces dusted, the hearth bare and swept clean. But A.B. wasn't there. He was gone. And Timothy was right—her memories of him were in her heart, not in this grand but lonely space.

# 30

OCTOBER 1899

### ~ *Junietta* ~

Junietta couldn't ever remember being as nervous as she was while waiting in the foyer with Addy and Sylvia for Andrew Browne to arrive. Her heart had been tripping and skipping like a happy drunkard ever since hearing the news that he'd been found, and she prayed it wouldn't give out until she saw him again. "I hope he isn't overwhelmed by this marble monstrosity we call an entry hall," she fretted. "I always believed that a decent front closet or even a simple coat tree would be more useful than these ghastly statues."

Adelaide caressed her shoulder. "He's coming to meet you, Mimi. He'll hardly notice anything else."

"Well, let's make sure we hustle him right through here. Oh, my—is that him?" she asked as a carriage pulled up out front. Addy went to peer through the window.

"No, it's Howard Forsythe."

Junietta sank down on the nearest bench, her knees wobbling. Then a few minutes later, the door opened again, and there he stood! There was no mistaking Neal Galloway's son. He had his father's height and build and mahogany hair. And his smile as he greeted her was Neal's magnificent smile. She rose on shaking legs and looked up at him. "Oh, my dear boy! I see so much of your father in you! You have his smile and his hair—and yet you are you, a unique person in your own right."

"It's a joy and a privilege to meet you, Mrs. Stanhope. My wife Fiona and I have been looking forward to this evening."

"I know I'm a stranger to you, but may I hold you?" He opened his arms and they held each other tightly. What a gift God had given her! She had offered up her son years ago as Reverend Cooper had advised, and now God had brought him back to her. They both had tears in their eyes when they separated again. "It's been so long since I held you. So very, very long. Nearly fifty years. I lost all hope of ever seeing you again. Yet here you are!"

He laughed, and it wasn't a nervous laugh, but the contented chuckle of a contented man. "Imagine," he said, "we've lived within twenty-five miles or so of each other all these years and never knew it. We might have passed on the street."

"Amazing, isn't it? Listen, you're going to have to forgive me, but I know I won't be able to stop staring at you all evening."

"That's quite all right." They made introductions all around, and he asked her to call him Andrew. She took his arm as she led him to the family dining room. "Please don't look at this house and think it has anything to do with me," she said as they passed through the palatial drawing room. "It never has been mine and never will be. I just happen to have lived here for more than thirty years. You see, I've been blessed in spite of my many mistakes."

"The Lord has been very good to my family and me as well, Mrs. Stanhope. I'm very thankful for that."

She sat down at the table beside him and began peppering him with questions, barely touching the food that the servants put in front of her.

She felt like a girl again—her aging, aching body renewed as she listened with delight to her son. Neal's son. How very proud he would be of this wonderful man they had brought into the world.

### ~ Adelaide ~

Addy had convinced herself that her feelings for Howard were merely the result of the excitement and novelty of searching for Mimi's son. Their mutual attraction would surely fade now that they no longer had a reason to be together. But one look at Howard as he'd walked through her front door told her how wrong she was. It was more than his good looks—she had waltzed with gentlemen more handsome than him. It was his humor, his lack of pretense, and the way he made her feel when she was with him, as if he wasn't seeing a high-society heiress but a woman in her own right.

He had greeted Mother, then Mimi Junie, then Addy, and she had thought her heart might give out from beating so rapidly. His gaze hadn't lingered long on hers, but the spark that passed between them could have lit a hundred gaslights. Then he'd looked away as if embarrassed. He had declared his feelings for her the last time they'd been together, and she hadn't reciprocated.

Howard was seated beside her at the intimate table, close enough that she could smell his spicy cologne. An unusual tension seemed to stretch between them like a taut rope. She turned to him, hoping to break it, and said, "Look how happy my grandmother is! Thank you for helping me find him, Howard."

"You're welcome." He was buttering a roll and didn't look up. The invisible rope stretched tighter, until it seemed to carry an electrical current. If their shoulders or hands would happen to touch, Addy was certain that sparks would erupt like a Roman candle. She didn't understand what was causing this electrical force or why it was happening. She'd never experienced anything like it before, and it unnerved her. She quickly turned her attention back to Mimi Junie and Mr. Browne.

"They told me you had been adopted by a good family with a fine name," Mimi said.

"It's true. My grandfather founded the quarry and passed it on to my father, and now to me. My sons are welcome to join the business, if they decide to. Fiona and I want them to be free to follow their own dreams, not ours."

"That's very wise."

"My mother was forty-one when she adopted me, and she passed away when my children were small. They don't remember her. I think they would enjoy meeting you too."

"And I would love to meet them, Andrew. I'm overjoyed to hear how well God has provided for you after you were taken from my arms. The Lord knew I couldn't give you a respectable life. We would have been destitute, and you without a father or a name."

"I can't remember when it was, exactly, that my parents told me I had been adopted. But it made no difference in the way I felt toward them. They were my mother and father in every sense of the word, and I loved them dearly. I'm just sorry that you never got to meet them."

"Well, when we do meet in heaven, I'll thank them for loving my son and raising him when I couldn't. You know, beautiful houses filled with possessions mean nothing if a home lacks love."

"Indeed, and ours was never lacking in love. Now if you don't mind, I would like to hear a little bit about my father. What was he like?"

"Neal Galloway was a Scotsman. A wonderful, charming, stubborn Scotsman with hair the same color as yours, and warm, hazel-colored eyes. He was also a talented carpenter. We were together for such a short time, but I loved him with all my heart. And he loved me. Of course, my parents never would have consented to our marriage because Neal was an immigrant without a penny to his name. I didn't care. We could have figured out a way to get by. I told him that he mattered more to me than money but he wouldn't listen. He left for California with his brother Gavin to prospect for gold because he wanted to give me the life *he* wished for me. I never wished for any of this—I simply wanted

344  |  ALL MY SECRETS

to be with the man I loved. But Neal sailed away, and his ship was lost at sea, and all I had left of him was this cane—and you. Then you were taken from me too."

Mr. Browne reached for her hand. "That must have been heartbreaking."

"It was. But God had other plans for me, as well as for you. I married Art Stanhope and we had a son, A.B., who gave me three beautiful granddaughters, including my dear Adelaide. If Neal had lived, I never would have founded the Stanhope Charitable Foundation. It got its start because I wanted to help women like Gavin's widow and foolish girls like myself who find themselves in a family way with no means of supporting themselves."

"The foundation has done so many worthwhile things," Mother added. "It has changed the lives of so many people." She had been listening quietly until now, and Addy was surprised to hear her chime in. She must be thinking about the position Mimi had offered her.

"The Almighty has a way of bringing good things from our sorrows, if we let Him," Mimi said.

"Yes, He surely does." Andrew Browne turned to Howard next. "You mentioned that I'm your great-uncle. Tell me more about that."

"When Gavin Galloway sailed to California with your father, he left behind a wife and young daughter—my grandmother and mother. I never knew about their connection to Mrs. Stanhope until recently. It's one of the reasons why I was happy to help Adelaide search for you."

"Well, I'm very glad you did. To be honest, I've never been curious about the parents who gave me up for adoption. I've always felt that living the life I've been given, and being a good follower of Christ were more important than my origins. But meeting all of you has been a joy. And I look forward to seeing what's in store for all of us in the future."

After the dessert course was finished and they were about to leave the table, Mimi rapped the head of her cane on it to get everyone's attention. "I just want to thank all of you once again for this wonderful evening. You have made me a very happy woman." Addy turned to Howard as everyone applauded and was rewarded with a smile. As they were all rising from the table and moving toward the conservatory to see the "little touch of springtime" that Mimi promised, Mother pulled her aside.

"Adelaide, may I speak with you in private, please?"

"Yes, of course. What's wrong?"

"Let's go into the morning room so the servants can clear the table."

Addy followed Mother in the opposite direction that the others were taking, wondering what on earth she wanted to talk about with such urgency. Addy wished she had the words to tell Mother what a perfect choice she would be to lead the foundation, but she hesitated. Mother approached life with a cool detachment that Addy was just beginning to understand, like a thin layer of brittle ice that concealed deeper waters. They'd grown closer in the past months, and Addy didn't want to spoil their fragile friendship with her unsolicited opinions. They took seats beside each other, and Mother leaned close.

"As I listened to the conversation tonight, it made me think. I know your grandmother has been trying to get through to me about the choices I've been making, but I haven't seen it through her eyes until tonight. Neal Galloway made the foolish mistake of trying to give Junietta the life *he* wanted for her, not the life *she* wanted. My parents did the same. They became bitter and gave up living because they couldn't give my brothers and me the life *they* wanted for us—when all along we had a wonderful life at Ferncliff. Now I'm afraid I'm making the same mistake with you. I wanted you to have the things I wished for myself—this house, this lifestyle, a wealthy husband. Forgive me, Adelaide. I never asked if this is the life *you* wanted for yourself."

Her mother's words stunned her. She didn't know how to reply. "It's . . . it's the only life I've ever known."

"Yes, but Mr. Browne mentioned his children. They've grown up with the family wealth and business, yet he wants them to be free to follow their own dreams. I've never asked you about your dreams, Adelaide."

Addy fumbled for words. "I feel very shallow for saying this, but I've never imagined doing anything else. I always thought I would follow in yours and my sisters' footsteps and get married and live like this. It's only since Father died and Mimi Junie started telling all her stories that I began to look at my future differently."

"Good. And I want you to continue thinking about your future. I confess that I fell into a bit of a panic when your father died so suddenly and I learned about Arthur Stanhope's will. My life seemed to be crumbling, and I was so worried about both of our futures. But I'm starting to see that our steps can be guided by Someone with an even better plan than our own."

"Like when God placed Mr. Browne with a loving family?"

"Yes. Exactly. Listen, Adelaide. Your father left you an inheritance that is separate from mine. I was wrong to assume you would want to use it to keep this house and this way of life. You don't have to do that. You can use it to live your own life, marry the man you choose, or decide not to marry at all. I never asked you what you wanted to do with your inheritance, and I'm very sorry for that. But I'm asking now. What would you do if you were free from my expectations or anyone else's?"

Addy suddenly felt the whole world open beneath her feet—and it terrified her. She had never made a decision of this magnitude before, and nothing in her life had equipped her to make it now. It took her a moment to put her thoughts into words. "To tell you the truth, I don't know what I would choose. I'm still trying to figure that out. Howard Forsythe advised me to think about all the lessons I've learned and the experiences I've had since my life began to change after Father died. I've been trying to do that. I've wanted so badly to help you keep our home and this life, yet it seemed deceitful to marry someone for his money, even though everyone in our social circle does it. And after Mimi showed me the work her foundation does, it's been hard for me to return to a life that now seems very . . . shallow. I hope it doesn't hurt your feelings to hear me say that."

"Not at all. I'm starting to see a lot of things differently too. You don't need to give me an answer tonight, Adelaide. Selling the artwork has bought us some time to consider all the options we have. I simply wanted you to know how I feel. Junietta is right. You should be free to decide your own future." She pulled Addy into her arms for a quick hug. "Now come. We'd better catch up with the others."

Addy followed her mother through the mansion in a daze. She would need time to think about everything her mother had just said and the questions she'd raised. Addy's world had been upended once again and she wished she had a good friend to confide in. Her grandmother, certainly, but also someone her own age who hadn't been raised in the same shallow, privileged life and could analyze her situation honestly. Someone like . . . Howard.

They found Mimi Junie and the Brownes in the foyer as they were saying goodbye. Howard wasn't with them. "Where's Howard?" she asked her grandmother.

"He already left. He said to make sure I told you goodbye."

*Goodbye.* The word sounded so final.

They found Mimi Junie and the Brownes in the foyer as they were

Mimi Junie wasn't at breakfast the next morning. "Is she all right?" Addy asked one of the servants.

"She asked to eat breakfast in her room."

"Then please bring my breakfast there on a tray. I want to join her." Addy hurried through the hallways to Mimi's new bedroom and found her sitting up in bed with a tray of tea and toast on her lap. She still seemed to glow after meeting her son last night. Addy pulled up a chair beside her. "May I join you for breakfast?"

"I would love that. Last night was wonderful, but I'm afraid all the excitement wore me out." Her breath wheezed when she spoke.

"You deserve to rest, Mimi. But I wanted to tell you about the surprising conversation I had with Mother after dinner last night. She said you were right, and that I should be allowed to decide my own future. She doesn't want me to spend the inheritance Father left me in order to keep this mansion."

Mimi pressed her hand to her heart. "My dear child. You have no idea how happy that makes me!"

"She asked me what my dreams were—"

"*Sylvia* did?"

"Yes, and I didn't know what to say. I told her I would have to think about it, and I've been doing that all night."

Mother swept into the room just then with a cheery, "Good morning. I heard breakfast has been moved in here. Do you mind if I join you?"

"Please do," Mimi said.

Mother was followed by a servant bearing a breakfast tray, and another one with an extra chair. Mother sat down, smiling faintly as she looked at both of them, crowded together in the tiny room.

"I haven't had a chance to tell you, but when I had dinner with Timothy Barrow the other night, he convinced me to accept the director-ship of your foundation."

Mimi applauded, sloshing the tea on her tray. "Bravo! I'm so pleased! You'll raise millions for charity. I don't know a man in the city who could say no if Sylvia Stanhope asked for a donation." She sopped the spilled tea with her napkin. "And will you be seeing Mr. Barrow again?"

Addy saw the color rise in Mother's cheeks. "I made him promise to help me with the foundation until I get the hang of running things. So, yes, I will be seeing him again. We enjoy each other's company, and, at this point, neither of us is interested in anything more than that."

"Wonderful!" Mimi applauded again. Addy felt like cheering too, astounded by the change in her mother. "Adelaide was just telling me about some of your other recent decisions," Mimi continued. "I was very glad to hear we're no longer trolling for a wealthy codfish for Addy to marry."

Sylvia gave a little laugh. "True. And Mr. Barrow—Timothy—told me an interesting bit of news. Cyrus Monroe, the banker, has passed away—"

"That's old news, Sylvia. He died a year ago."

"Yes. But it seems his heirs aren't interested in his mansion. They think it's too small, and so they plan to sell it. It's not far from here, and Timothy thinks it might be just the right size for the three of us. He promised to make arrangements for us to look at it. What would you think about moving, Adelaide?"

The question was so unexpected, Addy had to take a moment to gather her thoughts. Leaving this mansion had been unimaginable a year ago. It was her home, the only one she'd ever known. But when she pictured all the lifeless rooms that sat unused, and the vast chilly spaces that kept the three of them at a distance from one another, it didn't feel like a true home anymore. Then there was the daily strain Mother was under to keep the mansion alive. "I would be in favor of moving."

Mother looked relieved. "Good. We'll find a time when the three of us can view the Monroe house together."

Mimi laughed heartily, sloshing her tea again. "I think I'm incapable of digesting any more good news! I can now die a happy woman. My son has been found, my life's work is in good hands, and Addy is free to fall in love."

*Free to fall in love?* The idea also had been unimaginable a year ago when Mimi first brought it up. But now? Did Addy even dare to dream of falling in love the way Mimi and Neal Galloway had? She had been awake most of the night with thoughts about her future but hadn't dared to dream about love. "There's something else I would like to talk about with both of you," Addy said. "I mean, as long as we're all here." *And we're all so happy,* she wanted to add. "Mother, you asked me last night what my dreams were, and I admitted I didn't really have any. But there is something I'd like to pursue, except I'm not sure how you both feel about it, and—"

"Just tell us, Adelaide."

She drew a deep breath. "Women's suffrage."

Mimi leaned back against the pillows and laughed so heartily Addy had to grab her tray before it fell off her lap. "Never in my wildest dreams!"

Mimi's reaction made Mother smile. "Tell us more, dear."

Addy set the tray on the nightstand, gathering her thoughts. "I picked up a few copies of the suffrage newspaper, the *Revolution*, at the train station, and I've been learning so much. What has bothered me the most about our situation after Father died, was how helpless we were because we're women, and dependent on Father for everything. It bothers me that control of the Stanhope empire had to go to a male heir—as if we didn't count. Granted, we know nothing about running the company, but that's only because we've never been given the opportunity to learn. Mother has been running our household successfully, and Mimi has been overseeing a million-dollar foundation for years. You both could have run the family business if you had been trained and groomed for it all your lives."

"My feelings exactly," Mimi said. "Please continue, dear. We're on your side."

"Meara Galloway and Ian Murphy's wife were left with small children to raise after their husbands died. Even if they'd been able to find work, they couldn't have earned a living wage because women are paid less for doing the same jobs as men. But if women could vote, we'd have the power to work toward social reforms like equal pay for equal work. Suffragettes don't want to replace men. They simply want justice and fairness for women. Do you know that if a woman is accused of a crime and goes on trial, she's not even allowed to have a jury of her peers? Only men can serve on juries!"

Addy stopped, surprised to find how impassioned she'd become. She looked at Mother, hoping she wasn't upset with her. *Suffrage* was a whispered word in their social world. She did appear stunned—and yet oddly pleased.

"It sounds like you've been learning a lot about it," Mother said. "I sense your passion."

Her words gave Addy the courage to continue. "I would like to attend some of the suffrage lectures in Steinway Hall, if that's all right, and find out what I can do to help. In fact, I would like to convince some of my friends to attend with me instead of wasting our time gossiping and looking for husbands."

"You'll be surprised to learn how many women in our social class already are avid supporters of women's suffrage," Mimi said. She was beaming with pride. "It's more popular than you'd think."

"I do want to get married and have a family," Addy said. "But I also want to work for worthwhile causes—like you did, Mimi Junie, and like Mother will be doing when she takes your place. I'm much more excited about that future than I ever was about marrying George Weaver or any of the other—what did you call them, Mimi?"

"Wealthy codfish!" She laughed again, and even Mother was smiling.

"So would you mind if I started attending meetings to learn more?"

"I'll go with you when I'm feeling stronger," Mimi said.

Mother hesitated and Addy watched several emotions play across her face. "You know how much I've wanted you to have the life I've always enjoyed," she finally replied. "With this mansion and a wealthy husband by your side to support you. It's hard to give up the dreams we have for the people we love." Tears shone in her eyes. "I do want you to follow your heart, Adelaide—to follow wherever it leads you, and yes, to dare to fall in love. But I also urge you to take your time. I've learned that with every choice we make, we're saying no to other paths."

The room was quiet for a moment. Then Mimi sighed. "Your wise words make me so happy, Sylvia dear. I can now die a happy woman."

"Please don't talk about dying, Mimi."

"Why not? We will enjoy this life more if we take time to contemplate the end of it."

Mother cleared her throat, and Addy saw her brush away tears. "Listen, I've just now decided what I'm going to do with the proceeds from Willard Eastman's painting. I'm going to throw a lavish ball in honor of your retirement, Junietta, with an orchestra and dancing and all the trimmings. Are you two ladies with me?"

"On one condition," Mimi said. "You must let me announce that you'll be replacing me."

"Agreed. Make a list of everyone you'd like to invite to celebrate with us."

"And if nothing else," Mimi added, "a spectacular ball will put an end to the rumors of the Stanhope women's downfall."

# 31

*~⁓ Adelaide ⁓~*

The afternoon tea in Addy's drawing room seemed to drag on forever. How had she ever thought that listening to giggling gossip and inane chatter was a good way to spend her time? Addy had grown increasingly impatient with the ritual and had decided that this afternoon, in her own home, she would speak up about her views on women's suffrage. She waited for a lull in the conversation and said, "I plan to attend a meeting at Steinway Hall Tuesday night, if any of you would care to join me. They'll be talking about a woman's right to vote." She hoped she sounded braver than she felt.

"Are you joking, Adelaide?" her friend Frances asked with a little laugh. The others chimed in.

"Why would you want to do that?"

"Don't tell me you became a radical suffragette while we were all away in Newport last summer."

Addy straightened her shoulders and lifted her chin like Mother would. "I'm not a radical, and neither are the other women at these meetings. They simply believe we should have a right to vote for the officials who represent us."

"But why? We've gotten along just fine all these years without voting."

Addy knew her subject and was ready for their questions. "Because women's voices need to be heard in order to make a better world. God created men and women to be different, and thankfully so. We each possess strengths and weaknesses that were meant to complement each other. Women are much more concerned about things like clean water, decent housing, better schools, and better sanitation in immigrant neighborhoods. But our viewpoint isn't being considered when men make new laws. We make up half the population, so why aren't we allowed to speak?" She glanced around at her friends and saw varied reactions. Some were shocked, others surprised, a few yawned in boredom. No one was nodding in agreement.

"Aren't you afraid you'll ruin your chances with a lot of eligible suitors?" Frances asked.

"I wouldn't want a suitor who didn't support a woman's right to vote."

Felicity frowned. "But that eliminates the majority of gentlemen in our social circle, including my brother Alfred."

The others seemed to agree with Felicity, but Addy didn't care. She knew she wasn't going to change their minds in one afternoon, but at least she had raised the topic and extended the invitation. She would do it again at the next afternoon tea. "If you change your minds, you're welcome to join me on Tuesday and hear more."

When it was time for her friends to leave, Adelaide opened the double mahogany doors leading from the drawing room to the foyer, and there, sitting on a marble bench near the front door with his leather portfolio on his lap, was Howard Forsythe. He leaped up when he saw her. "Adel—" Then he stopped when he saw the group of women following her. "Miss Stanhope. Good afternoon. I've been waiting to speak with you." His warm smile made Addy's heart gallop.

"You weren't waiting long, I hope."

"Only a few minutes."

Addy had the ridiculous urge to move into his arms, remembering how natural it had felt when she'd hugged him in Mr. Browne's office. What would it be like to kiss him? She cleared her throat. "Ladies, this is Mr. Forsythe, our family lawyer and friend." She took great delight in their frank appraisal of the handsome young lawyer as she introduced each one.

Felicity leaned close to Addy on her way out the door and whispered, "I thought all lawyers were old and dreary looking. He's charming."

If they only knew.

"What brings you here, Howard?" she asked when they were gone. He held up the portfolio.

"I have something to show you and your mother. Is she here?"

"I think she's in Mimi's bedroom, talking about the foundation. My grandmother hasn't been well this past week. I'll take you there." Her curiosity grew as she led him through the drawing room, down a corridor, past several other useless rooms. "Can you give me a tiny hint what your news is, Howard?" she asked when they were just outside Mimi's room.

"Remember the children's book your mother wrote?" he said in a low voice. "The one you gave me last June? Well, a publishing company would like to offer her a contract to publish it."

"Oh, no! I'd forgotten all about it."

"Why so worried? I think she'll be pleased, don't you?"

"I don't know. What if she isn't? I never asked her permission to show the book to anyone."

"Well, I guess we'll find out soon enough. But if it's any consolation, the publisher doesn't know who the real author is. We presented it to them under your mother's maiden name, Sylvia Grace Woodruff."

"That's a relief, I suppose." But Addy worried just the same as they joined Mother and Mimi Junie. The servants had helped Mimi make the tiny room a cozy place to work, and she and Mother were sitting together at a little table by the fireplace.

"What are you two up to?" Mimi asked as they entered. "I heard you whispering and conspiring outside my door."

"Howard has brought Mother some good news. But before he tells you what it is, I need to explain that it was all my idea. Please don't blame him, Mother."

"Let's hear it," she said.

"Well, you see, Mimi showed me a beautiful watercolor that you'd once painted, and she said you'd also created some children's books. I found them up in the attic, and they were just so lovely that I took one—"

"Adelaide—" Mother was no longer smiling. Addy hurried on, speaking faster now.

"I'm sorry I didn't ask you first, but I was afraid you would say no. I gave one of the books to Howard and asked him if he thought they could be published." She looked up at him, pleading silently for him to take over.

"Right," he said with a nod. Addy couldn't take her gaze off him while he explained. "One of the lawyers in our firm has experience with publishing contracts, so I asked him to take a look at it. The result is this contract." He pulled a sheaf of papers from his portfolio and handed it to Mother. "A very fine New York publishing company would like to negotiate with you for the printing rights."

Mother gave a little frown. "I don't know. I created those stories so long ago. I never imagined selling them."

"They used your maiden name, Mrs. Stanhope." Howard pointed to the page. "We haven't revealed your identity. You can remain anonymous, if you choose to."

Mimi tugged Mother's sleeve. "Don't you see, Sylvia? Your work was judged on its own merit, not because of the Stanhope name or any social connections you have. That should tell you the book's true value. And your value as an artist."

"This is unbelievable," she said, shaking her head.

"The publisher also understands that there are more books in the series, and he's interested in seeing those as well," Howard said.

"I assume Sylvia would be well paid for her creations?" Mimi asked.

"Yes, ma'am. You'll find the amount of the proposed advance for the first book on the third page. It isn't a great deal of money by your family's standards, but it shows their interest and their faith in the book. Future royalties could prove profitable if sales are as good as the publisher believes they will be."

"Well!" Mimi said. "You could always donate the proceeds to the Stanhope Foundation if you want to remain anonymous."

"I don't know what to say," Mother murmured.

"We don't need your decision today, Mrs. Stanhope. Take time to read over the contract. And please let me know if you have any questions. I'll be happy to stop by anytime."

Mimi laughed as she gave him a gentle poke. "I'm sure you would, young man."

Adelaide walked with Howard to the front door after they'd finished. "I'm so relieved that Mother wasn't angry with me," she said.

"She was surprised, I think, more than anything else."

"Maybe the anger will come later, once the surprise fades," she worried.

"No, I think she'll be pleased, Addy. And I like your grandmother's suggestion to donate the proceeds to charity if she isn't interested in fame and fortune for herself."

They reached the door, and once again Addy had the almost unbearable urge to hold him in her arms. She gave him a long look as they said goodbye, wondering if he could read her thoughts, wondering what he would think if he could. Her heart was sprinting so rapidly, she might have been running a footrace. She stood by the front window after the door closed, watching him climb into his carriage, and wondered what was wrong with her. None of the young gentlemen she'd talked to at parties or waltzed with at balls had made her feel such dizzy, breathless giddiness. Was she falling in love with Howard? Is this what love felt like—this magnetic attraction that drew her to him whenever they were together? Or this echoing hollowness he left behind whenever they parted? Was this why her grandmother had encouraged her to marry for love?

Addy trudged upstairs to change out of her afternoon dress, remembering the stories of Mother's and Mimi's first loves. Neither story had ended happily. Addy no longer needed to marry a wealthy suitor. She was free to follow her heart. Yet the only thing that Addy knew about love and courtship were the rituals she and her sisters and all the other high-society ladies followed. She had no idea how to go about the next step in a relationship with Howard, even if that's what they both wanted. She looked at her reflection in the mirror as if seeing a stranger. Would her first love also be doomed to end unhappily as Mother's and Mimi's had? She hurried downstairs again to Mimi's bedroom.

## Junietta

The good news that Howard brought had cheered Junietta. She hoped Sylvia would take advantage of the offer and sign the publishing contract. Yet it seemed as though the simplest gatherings, even joyful ones like today's, always drained Junietta's strength. Too often, she wouldn't awaken in the morning until well past noon. At times, she felt alarmingly weak, barely able to sit up in bed, let alone get out of it. She was trying to summon the strength to move from her chair when someone knocked on her door and Adelaide entered her room. Junie took one look at her granddaughter's troubled expression and said, "What's wrong, dear child? Has something happened?"

"No, but . . . Oh, Mimi . . . I think I'm falling in love with Howard Forsythe!"

Junie laughed. "That's wonderful, Addy! But I can't say I'm surprised. Anyone watching the two of you together can see your mutual attraction."

Addy smiled and a blush colored her cheeks. "I wish we could be together all the time."

"Falling in love is the most wonderful feeling in the world, isn't it? And Howard is such a fine young man. So why aren't you dancing around the room and twirling in circles?"

Addy's smile faded. "Do I dare fall in love with him? Is it going to end in disaster? We're from such different backgrounds, and what if things don't work out for us? I don't want to end up like—"

"Neal Galloway and me?"

Addy nodded. "Howard told me he wished he was rich so we could be more than friends."

Junietta smiled as she shook her head. "Just like Neal. Listen, the biggest obstacle in the way of our love was that we couldn't find a way to meet in the middle. Neal wanted to give me the privileged life I was born into. I told him it didn't matter to me, but truthfully, I never could have lived in a tenement and endured a life of poverty. But times have changed since then. There is more middle ground for compromise. Howard makes a good living, and you could have a very nice life together on his salary."

"I know I wouldn't need a huge mansion like this," she said, spreading her arms. "I've been discovering how ridiculous this life is, and I'm no longer content with it."

"I'm very glad to hear it. But you were born with great wealth and all the privileges it brings, and you've spent twenty years acquiring habits and attitudes that accompany such wealth. You take for granted things like clean clothes and meals that appear as if by magic. You can't expect to change your habits overnight, no matter how much you love Howard. And Howard won't be able to change overnight either. He would never be comfortable in a mansion like this, yet it may take a while before he stops feeling as though he's disappointing you by making you settle for anything less. Financial differences can cause a huge strain on a relationship."

"But I want to change. I want to be with Howard and make him happy."

"Then I'd advise you to look for ways to meet in the middle. Are you willing to let him support you and live more simply, even if it means doing without some of the finer things? Men have a great deal of pride, you know, so I caution you to resist coming to the rescue with the money you've inherited. Or spending more money than he earns."

"I have a lot to learn, don't I?" Addy said with a sigh.

"Yes, but plenty of time to learn it. You're still very young. Take your time, get to know each other. Enjoy being in love for a while. It's wonderful, isn't it?"

"It's amazing!" Her dazzling smile seemed to light up Junie's room.

"After your father died, I was so afraid you'd make a terrible mistake and spend the rest of your life with some rich dolt. Even worse, I was afraid you'd never discover the amazing person you were created to be. That's why I showed you some of the work that the foundation does, hoping you'd see how much more there is to life."

"I'm grateful for that, Mimi. You really opened my eyes."

"I see your growing passion for the suffrage cause, and I applaud you. But one lesson that I had to learn, and that I hope you'll see as well, is that we shouldn't do our work because we pity the poor, or because we feel guilty for being privileged, and certainly not because we want to feel good about ourselves when we go to sleep at night. We must do it because our heart overflows with love for God. And because He asks us to love our neighbors." She gave Addy a moment to digest her words, then said, "I know that I've reached the end of my life—"

"Don't say that!"

"It's something we'll all face one day, dear. But I can honestly say I'm at peace now. I've been so worried about the foundation and about your future this past year, but they're both in good hands. I've had the joy of meeting my lost son, thanks to you and Howard, something I never dreamed would happen. All the people who are dearest to me—Meara and Regan, Howard and his brothers, Matthew Murphy, you and your mother—every one of you is going to be just fine. I've carried you all like a heavy burden for so long, but I've come to see that God is perfectly capable of carrying you after I'm gone."

"Mimi—"

"No, listen. I know I'm dying. Isn't everyone? But me, probably sooner than most. I needed to accept it and prepare to face it, and I have."

"Are you frightened?"

"Yes, of course. But all my life I've wanted to serve the God who loves and forgives me, and if dying is what He's asking me to do next, then I want to be willing." And perhaps it was also her task to show her loved ones how to face the end with faith and hope. Addy bent over her chair and drew her into an embrace. Junietta hugged her tightly in return. "Stop crying now, child, and go out and live your life with joy and passion. Promise?"

"Yes, I promise. I love you, Mimi."

"And I love you, darling girl."

# 32

~ Sylvia ~

Sylvia knocked, then entered Junietta's bedroom, where the maids had just finished helping her get ready for the ball. "You look lovely, Junietta," Sylvia told her. Her black silk gown was simple and old-fashioned, but it suited her. She had never seemed to need jewelry in order to glow, as she carried herself like royalty.

"As do you, my dear," Junietta said. "Did you design your own gown?"

Sylvia nodded. "I've come to escort you to your 'throne'," she said, smiling. "We made a seat for you in the ballroom so you won't have to stand in the foyer with Adelaide and me, greeting everyone. Are you ready?"

"Not quite. I have something to give you, first. Jane, where are the things I asked you to wrap? Are they ready?"

"Right here, ma'am." The servant gestured to two unwieldy parcels leaning against the bed, wrapped in brown paper. Junietta wheezed as she sat down in her chair and pointed to the smaller one.

"Open that one first."

Sylvia could tell by the size and shape of it that it was a framed

361

picture. She carefully tore away the wrapping and was surprised to see that it was one of her own watercolors, painted years ago at Ferncliff, now mounted in a beautiful frame.

"There seem to be a few empty places on our gallery walls, so I thought your watercolor would fill one of them beautifully."

Sylvia gazed at the lush watercolor, the backdrop of her life at Ferncliff, and the memory of her brothers' laughter brought tears to her eyes. "Thank you," she whispered.

"Now open the other package."

It was larger and heavier than the painting, and Sylvia lifted it up, setting it on the bed. She removed the brown paper to find a cleverly crafted wooden box that resembled a briefcase. She opened the latches and found an array of oil paints, watercolors, and brushes inside. There was a sketch pad, canvases, and even a small folding easel. She couldn't speak or stop her tears.

"I know you will do a wonderful job with the foundation, Sylvia. But don't let it take up all your time. I hope you'll paint a few more pictures to help fill our empty walls."

Sylvia bent to hug her mother-in-law tightly. How could such a for-midable woman feel so frail? "Thank you," she murmured. "Thank you."

"You're very welcome. And now, let's get this ball started."

Sylvia helped her to her feet and made sure she had her cane as she made the long walk from her bedroom to the ballroom, leaning on Sylvia's arm. Junietta raved about the flowers and decorations. "If the events you organize for the foundation are as grand as this, the founda-tion's coffers will overflow. The mansion looks beautiful, Sylvia. You and Adelaide have done a magnificent job."

She led Junietta to the seat she'd prepared for her in the ballroom and stationed a servant by her side—Hattie, she believed the girl's name was. Yes, Hattie. "You may start the music," Sylvia told the orchestra leader. "Our guests will be arriving any minute." There had been a lot to do in just a few weeks, and Sylvia had thrown herself into the task with enthusiasm, planning menus, hiring caterers and musicians, and getting the mansion ready for their guests. The work had given her joy, and she felt happy now as she hurried to the foyer to greet her guests, remembering Timothy Barrow's words. *"We don't need to feel disloyal for being happy again."*

She spent the next half hour greeting their guests, some of whom Sylvia hadn't seen since A.B.'s funeral. Her daughter was by her side, directing everyone to the ballroom, where Junietta was the guest of honor. Suddenly, she heard Adelaide gasp. Sylvia followed her gaze and saw that Howard Forsythe was just arriving. "Did Mimi invite him?" Addy whispered.

"No, I did."

Adelaide stared at her in surprise. "You?"

"I was going through a mental list of dance partners I could invite for you, and I couldn't think of a finer young man than Howard." Sylvia gave her a brief hug, then pulled away again, brushing a wisp of hair from Addy's face. "I watched the two of you together the day you burst into the house to tell your grandmother you'd found her son, and your attraction to each other was so obvious. I thought it might fade once the search ended, but your feelings for each other were pretty clear the night we had dinner with Mr. Browne. You were trying so hard not to be in love with each other— and both failing miserably, by the way. The electricity between the two of you was still sparking like a live wire when Howard came with the book contract. So, go on now. Welcome him to our ball, Adelaide."

"Truly? You wouldn't mind if he and I . . . ?"

"Let's just say I've also grown very fond of Howard Forsythe. He's been an anchor for me these past few months." She gave Addy a little push in his direction. "Go on. I need to greet Mr. Barrow."

### Adelaide

Addy heard her pulse thumping in her ears as she walked toward Howard. The sight of him, tall and handsome, wearing a tailored tuxedo and crisp white shirt stole her breath.

"Good evening. Welcome to our celebration," she said, then wanted to kick herself for sounding so stiff.

"Thank you," Howard said with a little bow. He seemed ill at ease too, as he looked around at some of New York's famous millionaires milling in the foyer. He cleared his throat. "May I say how beautiful you look tonight?"

He caught her off guard. "Oh . . . well," she stammered.

"No, seriously, I really need to know if I'm allowed to say something like that. I've never been to a formal ball before, and I need someone to coach me through it. And if it turns out that I may say it, then you truly *do* look very beautiful, Miss Stanhope."

Addy couldn't help laughing. "Yes, you may say it. Thank you. But I think you've mistaken me for someone else. My name is Adelaide, not Miss Stanhope."

At last, his warm, disarming smile. "Yes, of course you are."

"The ball is this way," she said, taking his arm. "Have you ever seen our ballroom?"

"Only once, when you took me on a quick tour of the mansion."

"Well, the secret to finding it is to follow the music." It felt so natural to walk beside him, holding his arm. Had Mother felt this way when she'd walked beside Father? Or Mimi when she was with Neal? "You look very dapper tonight, Howard. Is that a new evening suit you're wearing?"

"It is. But that means you must have noticed how ill-fitting my old, borrowed one was."

"Well—"

"Don't worry. It seems you weren't the only one who'd noticed. I had no sooner accepted this invitation when a tailor arrived at the law firm with his measuring tape and proceeded to outfit me with a more presentable suit—supplied by an anonymous donor. So, here I am."

"I'm glad you came." They reached the packed ballroom and a waiter offered them champagne. Mimi sat on her throne, surrounded by a crowd of admirers. Mother entered the ballroom behind them, laughing with Mr. Barrow. "I can introduce you to some of the other guests, if you'd like. Is there anyone famous or scandalous you'd especially like to meet?"

"I'll let you decide," he said, laughing. They mingled for the next hour, eating hors d'oeuvres, and making introductions and small talk. Eventually, the music halted, and Mother stepped onto the orchestra platform, calling for everyone's attention.

"I have an announcement to make, and I've decided to do it early in the evening, so you'll understand the reason we're celebrating." A hush fell over the crowd. "As you all know, A.B.'s mother, Junietta Stanhope, founded the Stanhope Charitable Foundation many years ago, and has been the chairman and guiding force behind it ever since. The foundation has given away millions of dollars—much of it yours—to many worthwhile charities over the years. Junietta has recently announced to our family that she has decided to retire as chairman. This evening's celebration is in her honor, to thank her for her vision and her tireless leadership all these years." There was applause as Mimi Junie came forward and accepted a bouquet of roses from Mother. "Let's raise our glasses to toast one of the city's most outstanding women." There was more applause and cheers. Then Mimi Junie quieted everyone again.

"Thank you. And now is the perfect time for me to announce that dear Sylvia will be taking my place as head of the Stanhope Foundation. I can't think of a more capable and qualified person, can you?" Mimi's words were met with joyous applause and shouts of congratulations. Mother looked happy and serene and very, very beautiful.

"Thank you," she said. "I'm thrilled to become part of such a worthwhile organization. And I'm already planning the first annual fundraising ball, so you will be hearing from me again, very soon." She paused until the crowd's laughter died away. "As you can imagine, my work will keep me very busy in the future, and as much as I love this beautiful home, it has become much too large for three busy Stanhope women. I've decided that the cost of running such a spacious mansion can go to better use in supporting the foundation's very deserving charities. And so, this mansion will soon be for sale, if any of you are interested." More laughter and murmuring followed. "I'm in the process of purchasing the Cyrus Monroe house, and you can visit the three of us there in the near future.

It also has a spacious ballroom—for my future fundraising events, of course. Thank you so much for celebrating with us this evening. Please, have some more champagne. And thank you for your future support of the foundation."

Addy looked around at their guests and knew that Mother had scored a huge victory. There would be no more rumors of bankruptcy or murmurs of pity that they were losing their beautiful home. Mother's place in the society she loved would remain secure. Best of all, she would be admired and respected for her own accomplishments, not because she'd married a Stanhope.

"I think your grandmother made a very wise choice for her successor," Howard said as the music started up again. "I'm glad your mother accepted the position."

"I was surprised at first, when Mimi chose her. But the more I thought about it, the more I realized that Mother will be perfect for it."

"I'm happy for all three of you. But will you be sorry to move from your beautiful home?"

"Not at all. I toured the new mansion with Mother and we're very pleased with it. It won't require an army of servants to maintain, or a map to keep from getting lost."

"So, tell me more about tonight, Adelaide. Do I have another role to play for this occasion? When my invitation to this ball arrived, I wondered if it was a command appearance—the family lawyer is being summoned to attend. Are family lawyers usually outfitted with new suits and invited to attend these celebrations?"

Addy laughed. "I've never known Mother to invite her lawyers before. You may have noticed that Mr. Wilson and the other law partners aren't here."

"Yes, I did notice."

"My mother is the one who invited you, and I believe you're here for at least three reasons."

"Really? And what are they?"

"First, for my grandmother's sake. As Neal Galloway's great-nephew,

Mimi considers you and your family as part of her own, and we're cele-brating her tonight. Second, for Mother's sake. I know she wanted to show you her gratitude for all the help and wise advice you've given her this past year. And third, you've been invited for me."

"For you?"

"Yes. If you look around, you'll notice a startling lack of young gentlemen for me to waltz with. And a ball would be no fun at all without a dance partner. Waltzing is the reason people arrange balls in the first place."

"I see." His smile was warm, his expression filled with surprise and hope. "Then may I have this dance? Please don't say no. My mother made me take dancing lessons just for this occasion, and I would hate for them to go to waste." Howard opened his arms and Addy moved into them. Her hand felt natural in his, the warmth of his other hand on her waist sent shivers through her. She felt dizzy with happiness as they whirled around the floor.

"This is very nice," he said. "I can see why high-society people are fond of holding balls."

"No one would ever guess this is your first one. You waltz like an expert."

"I feel like I'm in a dream." He was gazing down at her as they waltzed, and Addy knew it was time to tell him how she felt.

"Howard, you once told me that you wished you had money so we could become more than friends. What I wish I had told you at the time, is that I would like to become more than friends too."

He stopped dancing. His eyes turned soft. "You would?"

"Yes. Remember your grandfather Gavin and his brother, Neal? They didn't need to leave home to find gold, because the women who loved them would've rather had them by their side than all the gold in California."

"What are you saying?"

"I'm saying you don't need to be wealthy in order to court me, because I have more than enough money for both of us. You're familiar with the terms of my father's will. You know how much I've inherited. One of the reasons Mother decided to sell this house is because she wants me to be free to spend my inheritance however I please. And I decided that I would rather spend it living a modest life with someone I love, than in a mansion with a wealthy stranger."

"How revolutionary." They started waltzing again.

"I'm also hoping that the man I fall in love with isn't opposed to the suffrage movement, because I've been spending a lot of time learning about it, and I'm almost ready to start carrying a banner."

"That's interesting. You didn't have a chance to talk with my mother very much when you met her, but she's a firm believer that women should be allowed to vote. She has been known to attend suffrage rallies when she isn't busy with her church duties. Mother believes God created Adam and Eve to be partners. And she raised her sons to believe the same thing."

"I'm very happy to hear that. And so . . . since I now have the gift of time to figure out my future, I'm hoping we can spend more of it together."

Howard closed his eyes for a moment, then he opened them again and met Addy's gaze. "Have you ever had a dream that's so wonderful you never want to wake up? I feel a bit like a male version of Cinderella tonight. Someone has waved a magic wand, giving me a brand-new suit and a chance to waltz at the ball with a beautiful princess. And unless the clock suddenly strikes midnight and I lose one of my shoes, I'm starting to believe that I might be able to live happily ever after."

Addy laughed, loving this wonderful man even more. She took his arm when the waltz ended, leading him off the floor. "Come with me. I want to show you a secret place I discovered when I was a little girl." She led him away from the others to a small alcove behind the stage. They had to snuggle close in order to fit inside. Addy's heart raced with anticipation as Howard's arms encircled her.

"I don't know what my great-grandfather had in mind when he added this little niche to the design of his ballroom," she said, "but now that we're here, will you do something for me, Howard? Something personal and not as our family lawyer?"

"Anything," he breathed.

"Will you please kiss me?"

He pulled her close and lowered his face toward hers. "With pleasure."

# A Note from the Author

When I decided to make the Gilded Age the setting for this novel, I looked forward to touring dozens of spectacular mansions from that era as part of my research. The opportunity to travel and the inspiration it brings are what make the research process fun and exciting for me. Then Covid struck, putting an end to travel and forcing me to rely on videos and photographs to recreate the splendor of the era. It just wasn't the same. If you enjoyed *All My Secrets* and happen to live near a historic mansion, I hope you'll treat yourself to the tour that I was unable to enjoy. It will help you step back in time and envision what life was like for Adelaide, Sylvia, and Junietta.

I wrote this novel from the viewpoints of three generations of women, hoping their stories would inspire readers of all ages. Younger readers like Adelaide often feel the burden of others' expectations, along with the pull of the culture, telling them what they should do and be. I want to encourage you to discover how remarkably different you are from everyone else, and to pursue God's purpose for your life.

For readers who are Sylvia's age and may be facing unwanted changes such as an empty nest, it's my prayer that you will look at your gifts and life experiences in new ways and see that God is always ready to use us if we're willing to embrace change. I had already celebrated my fortieth birthday when my first book was published, launching me into a new career. New beginnings can be exciting.

I'm now closest in age to Junietta, but I've discovered that God is still willing to use us if we say yes to Him. My grandchildren are as dear to me as Adelaide was to Junietta, and I believe it's important for grandparents to consider the legacy we would like to leave. How might our life stories inspire them? What might they learn from our mistakes? My two grandmothers were very different women, yet both were very important in my life, helping to shape me into the person I am today.

*All My Secrets* also explores the theme of God's forgiveness and shows the destructive consequences of bitterness and grudges. I pray that this story will convince you that God's forgiveness is available through Christ's sacrifice to anyone who realizes they have "missed the mark." And in turn, that you will be able to forgive others out of gratitude for God's amazing grace.

Blessings,
Lynn

# Acknowledgments

This novel proved harder to write than I had imagined. The manuscript I first turned in was quite different from this finished novel. In the first draft, I wrote exclusively from Adelaide's point of view. Then my editors, Stephanie Broene and Kathy Olson, along with my agent, Natasha Kern, gently pointed out that it would be a much better book if I also included Sylvia's and Junietta's viewpoints. They were right, and I think we're all very pleased with the result. A sincere thank you to them for encouraging me to make those changes. Thanks also to the rest of the Tyndale team, Andrea Martin, Andrea Garcia, and Katie Dodillet, for the hard work you do behind the scenes. Your expertise is invaluable.

I owe a huge debt of thanks to my faithful friends Paul and Jacki Kleinheksel and Ed and Cathy Pruim. I thank God for placing you in my life at the very moment I needed you. You keep me writing—and you also make great biking pals. I've lost track of how many miles we've biked together, but I know it's a lot.

And always I thank my husband, Ken, who has been my loving partner and cheerleader for nearly fifty-three years now. You believed in me long before I believed in myself and spent money we didn't have to buy my first computer. I'm so blessed to walk through this life with you.

# Discussion Questions

1. Addy's mother and grandmother both tell her their life stories to help her understand them better. How much do you know about your parents' and grandparents' stories? If you are a parent, aunt or uncle, or grandparent, what parts of your own story do you want to pass on to the younger generations?

2. Junietta and Sylvia have very different opinions about what to do next after losing most of their wealth. Is one of them right and the other wrong? How does learning each woman's background help you understand their perspectives?

3. Junietta tells the others, "I had learned from my brothers the futility of arguing with a man who was being stupidly contrary." Setting aside the gender generalities, have you ever encountered a situation where it's not worth arguing with someone? How can you tell whether someone genuinely wishes to understand a different point of view or is set in their ways?

4. Junietta feels shame and guilt for her past mistakes and for being associated with the Stanhopes, who have built their wealth on taking advantage of others. Her feelings lead her to establish a charitable foundation to help those in need and to break the family cycle of evil and cruelty. Have you or someone you know made a choice to consciously counteract the consequences of

past wrong actions? What are some ways this might play out in today's world?

5. Young Junietta first encounters God's forgiveness through reading the Gospel of John, especially verse 3:17, "God sent not his Son into the world to condemn the world; but that the world through him might be saved," and the story of the woman Jesus forgave in chapter 8. Do you or someone you know need to hear this message?

6. Reverend Cooper tells Junietta, "Sin is sin, and we all do it. Every one of us. Yours is just a bit more obvious than mine. No one can see me coveting the fine horses and carriages that fill the churchyard every Sunday morning, but even so, coveting, like adultery, is also a sin." Why is it so easy to judge others whose sins are more visible—or less culturally acceptable—than the ones we might struggle with ourselves?

7. Reverend Cooper also reminds Junietta that even though her sin is forgiven, she will still have to deal with painful consequences, perhaps for the rest of her life. He says, "If you do suffer for your mistake in the future, please don't ever let the enemy tell you it's because God hasn't forgiven you." How can we counteract the feelings of shame and guilt that often result when we are reminded of past mistakes, even though we've received forgiveness?

8. Sylvia has gifts and talents that she has hidden away for many years—her artistic ability and the organizational skills necessary for running the foundation. Why has she let these gifts lie dormant? Are there abilities or skills that you could be using to make a difference, either in your own life or in the larger world? What's holding you back?

9. Sylvia realizes that she's been promoting the kind of life for her daughter that she always wanted for herself. She also realizes that

her parents did the same thing to her and her brothers. Have you seen this at work in your own family? How can parents give their children a "good life" while also taking into account the children's own ideas about what a good life will look like?

10. Addy decides she wants a life with Howard, even though it will mean a change in the lifestyle she's grown up with. Her grandmother wisely counsels that they will need to figure out how to "meet in the middle" of their individual experiences and expectations. What are some other areas besides finances where married couples need to learn to meet in the middle? Why is this sometimes challenging?

# About the Author

Lynn Austin has sold more than one and a half million copies of her books worldwide. A former teacher who now writes and speaks full-time, she has won eight Christy Awards for her historical fiction and was one of the first inductees into the Christy Award Hall of Fame. One of her novels, *Hidden Places*, was made into a Hallmark Channel Original Movie. Lynn and her husband have three grown children and make their home in western Michigan. Visit her online at lynnaustin.org.

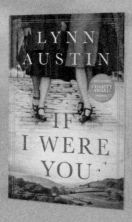
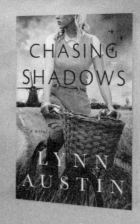

# CONNECT WITH LYNN ONLINE AT

## lynnaustin.org

## OR FOLLOW HER ON:

**f**  facebook.com/LynnAustinBooks

**y**  @LynnNAustin

**g**  Lynn Austin

CP1586

# TYNDALE HOUSE PUBLISHERS IS CRAZY4FICTION!

## Fiction that entertains and inspires

Get to know us! Become a member of the Crazy4Fiction community. Whether you read our blog, like us on Facebook, follow us on Twitter, or receive our e-newsletter, you're sure to get the latest news on the best in Christian fiction. You might even win something along the way!

## JOIN IN THE FUN TODAY.

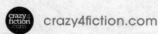 crazy4fiction.com

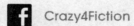 Crazy4Fiction

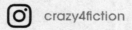 crazy4fiction

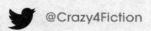 @Crazy4Fiction

CP0021